ACCLAIM FOR DOROTHY LOVE

"Dorothy Love writes with such rhythm and grace. Her attention to historical detail creates the perfect setting for characters we swiftly grow to love and cheer for. *The Bracelet* is a jewel of a story."

—TAMERA ALEXANDER, *USA TODAY* BESTSELLING AUTHOR OF *TO WHISPER HER NAME* AND *A LASTING IMPRESSION*

"*The Bracelet* by Dorothy Love was a fascinating and exciting antebellum novel that kept me flipping pages way into the night. I loved the insight into events that triggered the war, and Love's writing is beautiful and evocative. Highly recommended!"

—COLLEEN COBLE, AUTHOR OF *SEAGRASS PIER* AND THE HOPE BEACH SERIES

"*The Bracelet* is the perfect blend of mystery, history, and the quest for love and truth. A great read for not only lovers of period fiction, but for anyone who hungers for a well-told story."

—SUSAN MEISSNER, AUTHOR OF *A FALL OF MARIGOLDS*

"With a country on the brink of war and her own future uncertain, Celia Browning's faith will be tested and her very life put in jeopardy by the mystery of the bracelet. In a novel inspired by actual events, Dorothy Love artfully recreates the lavish world of power and prestige in 1850s Savannah with unforgettable characters and the attention to historical detail her readers have come to expect. Vivid and entrancing . . . I was swept away!"

—KRISTY CAMBRON, AUTHOR OF *THE BUTTERFLY AND THE VIOLIN* AND *A SPARROW IN TEREZIN*

"Subtle and suspenseful with exquisite descriptions of antebellum Savannah, Georgia, and a tender love story to boot, Dorothy Love's *The Bracelet* takes the reader on a chilling journey into the mysteries surrounding one of Savannah's most prominent families during the days before the Civil War. Love's careful research and poignant prose provide a story that will delight fans of historical fiction."

—ELIZABETH MUSSER, NOVELIST, THE
SWAN HOUSE, THE SWEETEST THING, THE
SECRETS OF THE CROSS TRILOGY

"Vivid and romantic . . . recommended for fans of *Gone With the Wind*."

—LIBRARY JOURNAL ON CAROLINA GOLD

"Beautifully portrays an independent Southern woman . . . Pitch perfect . . . A memorable book."

—HISTORICAL NOVELS REVIEW ON CAROLINA GOLD

"A beautifully written Southern historical that should appeal equally to Christian and secular readers alike."

—READING THE PAST ON CAROLINA GOLD

"*Every Perfect Gift* is certainly a gift to readers."

—PUBLISHERS WEEKLY

"Romance and a strong sense of place recommend Love's delightful Southern-flavored historical."

—LIBRARY JOURNAL ON EVERY PERFECT GIFT

"Romance, mystery, and intrigue . . . Love gives readers even more than they expect . . ."

—ROMANTIC TIMES REVIEWS ON EVERY PERFECT GIFT

"Love's amazing historical has all the elements readers expect . . . romance, mystery, and characters who want more out of their lives."

"With well-drawn characters and just enough suspense to keep the pages turning, this winning debut will be a hit . . ."

A Respectable Actress

OTHER BOOKS BY DOROTHY LOVE

A RESPECTABLE ACTRESS

DOROTHY LOVE

THOMAS NELSON
Since 1798

Published in Nashville, Tennessee, by Thomas Nelson. Thomas Nelson is a registered trademark of HarperCollins Christian Publishing, Inc.

Thomas Nelson titles may be purchased in bulk for educational, business, fund-raising, or sales promotional use. For information, please e-mail SpecialMarkets@ThomasNelson.com.

Library of Congress Cataloging-in-Publication Data

Love, Dorothy, 1949-
A respectable actress / Dorothy Love.
pages ; cm
ISBN 978-1-4016-8759-5 (softcover)
1. Actresses--Fiction. 2. Widowers--Fiction. 3. Murder--Investigation--Fiction. 4. Man-woman relationships--Fiction. I. Title.
PS3562.O8387R47 2015
813'.54--dc23
2015015160

Printed in the United States of America

15 16 17 18 19 20 RRD 6 5 4 3 2 1

for Natasha Kern

All the world's a stage and all the men and women merely players. They have their exits and their entrances and one man in his time plays many parts . . .
—WILLIAM SHAKESPEARE

CHAPTER 1

SAVANNAH, DECEMBER 20, 1870

GUNFIRE EXPLODED TO THE RIGHT OF THE STAGE, A burst of sound that temporarily deafened her. When the ringing in her ears subsided she was aware of screams, of shouts for policemen and for a doctor, of the ensuing chaos as officers arrived and began ushering patrons out of the packed theater. Two burly officers leapt onto the stage, seized her by both arms, and manhandled her into a police wagon parked in the alley, the officers with their weapons at the ready, the horses stamping impatiently in the cold.

Now it was midnight, and the city of Savannah slumbered beneath a veil of winter moonlight, the deep silence broken only by a rush of wind that rattled the palmettos and Pride of India trees lining the deserted streets.

Inside the Chatham County Jail, the walls rang with the shouts of drunken sailors and their painted escorts, the clang of metal bars, and snatches of lewd songs sung off-key. Jaded-looking policemen armed with nightsticks moved along the dimly lit corridors, checking the locks and admonishing the prisoners to quiet down.

"Step away from the door." An officer paused outside India's cell, one hand resting on his nightstick. As if a 110-pound woman posed any threat to his safety.

Weak with shock and terror, India retreated. Perched on the edge of a stained, musty-smelling mattress, she rested her head in her hands. What had she done to deserve such grave misfortune? She didn't belong here. And the last thing she needed was scandal. But this latest turn of events—as dramatic as it was tragic—would prove irresistible to the local newspapers. She imagined the typesetter over at the *Savannah Morning Herald*, rumpled and groggy from having been awakened so suddenly, his composing sticks clattering as he set a sensational new headline for the morning edition.

The officer checked the lock and moved on. She pressed her fingertips to her throbbing head and swallowed the tears building in her throat, wishing desperately for someone to guide and protect her. Someone to take charge of this awful misunderstanding and set her world to rights again.

In the cell next to hers, two women began a loud, drunken argument made all the more unbearable by the overwhelming stench of unwashed bodies, spirits, and stale coffee that hung like fog in the dank, chilly air.

The noise abated as the night wore on, and the singing and shouting gave way to snoring as prisoners succumbed to the effects of custody and too much alcohol. India barely moved from her mattress as the hours crawled toward morning. Eventually she rose and crossed her cell to the door. By pressing her cheek to the cold iron bars and craning her neck, she caught a glimpse of gray daylight.

Father had often reminded her that every situation seemed less daunting in the light of a new day, and now, as she watched a flock of sparrows winging past a high, dusty window glimmering with frost, she felt a surge of hope. All she had to do was explain to the magistrate or the judge or whoever was in charge of such matters exactly what had transpired during last night's performance at the Southern Palace Theater. Surely he would see that she was not to blame.

At the far end of the hallway, a door opened and a policeman came in on a blast of frigid air. India patted her curly hair into place and brushed at the dried blood still clinging to the ruffled skirt of her costume. The arresting officer had hustled her from the stage to this dank and sorry place without allowing her even five minutes to wipe away her stage makeup or to change into her own clothes. She felt grimy from head to toe. She could imagine the streaks on her face from where the greasepaint had run. Not exactly the image she wanted to present to the authorities.

The officer paused before her cell door and fumbled with a set of keys. Iron-gray hair peeked from beneath his cap. The brass buttons on his uniform gleamed dully in the lambent light.

"India Hartley?" His breath smelled of coffee and sleep.

"Yes." She rotated her shoulders, hoping to ease the throbbing at the back of her neck.

He swung open the door and immediately caught her wrist in a viselike grip strong as any manacle. "Come with me."

THE PREVIOUS EVENING

Her carriage rocked along the street, headed for the theater. India settled into the plush velvet seat and watched the crowds of Christmas shoppers coming and going from stores decorated with wreaths of greenery. At Madame Louis's hair salon, an elaborate poster invited ladies to come in for styles of the highest art. Flyers offering children's toys, European fashions, and grand action pianos fluttered from shop windows illuminated by gaslight.

At the corner of Drayton and Congress, the carriage paused for a man and a small girl crossing the street, their arms laden with packages from Thomas Bateson's store. At the sight of them, India felt a fresh sting of loneliness. For most of her life, she and Father had lived alone, traveling from London to Philadelphia and then Boston, where he managed various theater companies before finally organizing his own. He had recognized her talent and her instinctual understanding of how the theater worked, and groomed her for a life on the stage. But he had failed to teach her anything about how to survive in a harsh and indifferent world.

Father had not been the most skillful of managers. India supported him more often than the other way around. But she never doubted his love for her. He was the touchstone that kept her grounded, and when she lost him she lost the everyday contentment she had taken for granted.

Upon his untimely death, she discovered they were nearly broke and her interest in the Classic Theater Touring Company had been taken over by an unscrupulous manager she'd once trusted. After months of scraping by on next to nothing, she arranged a ten-week tour as a visiting actress to theaters in Savannah, Charleston, and New Orleans. What would become of her after the tour finished was something she did not let herself think about.

"Here we are, Miss Hartley." The young driver opened the carriage door and extended a gloved hand to assist her as she exited.

When she paused to straighten her hat, he fumbled in his pocket for a scrap of paper and a pencil.

"Would you mind?" He thrust the paper and pencil into her hands. "I mean, I know it's an awful imposition, but my little sister reveres you. It sure would be the best Christmas present ever for her to have your signature."

"Of course." India took the paper and pencil. "What plays of mine has she seen?"

"Oh, we can't afford the theater. But she reads about you in the ladies' magazines she gets from the circulating library. She tries to style her hair like yours. I reckon just about every girl in Savannah wants India Hartley curls." He watched as she fished a carte de visite from her reticule. "She tries to talk like she's from London, too, when she thinks nobody is listening. But I don't reckon the Queen's English mixes too well with our way of speaking."

India scribbled her signature on the back of the photograph—made at Mr. Sarony's New York studio—and pressed it into his hand. "Present this at the theater tonight. I'll have two tickets waiting for you and your sister."

He gaped at her. "You mean it? We're goin' to the Southern Palace?"

India smiled. "You are indeed. The curtain is at eight. Don't be late."

"Well, I sure . . . I won't. I mean, thank you, Miss Hartley. Thank you so much. Just wait till I tell Mary. She won't believe it."

He climbed up and flicked the reins. The carriage moved along the crowded street and disappeared around the corner.

Lifting her skirts to avoid the mud and horse droppings littering the street, India hurried to the stage door on the narrow alley and entered the deserted theater.

On the lower level, a long hallway ran the length of the building. Here were dressing rooms, the property room, and the manager's office. At the opposite end of the corridor, a spiral staircase led upward to the stage. At this early hour she was alone in the dimly lit space, but she didn't mind the solitude or the chill seeping through the walls. She and her father had made a habit of arriving at the theater early. She liked having plenty of time to get into costume and quiet her mind, focusing on the story she was about to tell.

A loud crash from above and a man's shouted curse sent her rushing up the staircase and into the theater wings. Riley Quinn, the young assistant to the stage manager, was sitting on the floor, an overturned ladder at his side. In his hands was a large mirror framed in black. He startled when he saw her, then scrambled to his feet.

"Mr. Quinn, are you all right?"

"Yes, ma'am, Miss Hartley. I didn't mean to disturb you. I was just puttin' up this mirror in that far corner, so as to cast more light downstage." He gestured to the corner where a flame torch sat next to a large block of lime. During the performance the lime would be heated to incandescence. Mirrors and gaslights installed along the sides of the stage would provide illumination far more powerful than the candles of old. "I reckon Mr. Sterling will have a harder time keepin' you in the shadows now."

India nodded. Apparently her leading man's ungenerous actions on opening night had not gone unnoticed by the stage crew.

"It wasn't fair, what he done," Quinn went on. "He may be Savannah born and bred, but he sure didn't act like a gentleman last night. Folks can see him in a play most all the time. But it ain't often we get someone of your stature around here. And I for one am mortified by his behavior." Quinn indicated the mirror. "This'll fix him, though, don't you worry."

India returned to the lower level of the theater and entered her dressing room. Larger than most, it had space for a comfortable chair, a dressing table and mirror, hooks for holding her costumes, and a wig stand. She removed her cloak and draped it over a chair, then picked up the script she'd left behind after opening night. *Suspicion* was the work of Jackson Morgan, a local playwright who had attended every rehearsal and was not shy about shouting stage directions to the actors charged with bringing his tale of mystery and betrayal to life. His behavior had not set well with the Southern Palace's actor-manager, Cornelius Philbrick, or with the leading man, beloved local thespian Arthur Sterling.

India flipped through the script, rereading the notes she'd penciled into the margins, and felt her old excitement returning. For all of its hardships—uncomfortable travel, fleabag hotels, shady managers, vicious critics—a life in the theater was the only one she could imagine for herself. Something magical happened when the curtain parted and she stepped into the circle of light, transformed into a wholly different person, able with her words to move an audience to laughter or tears. Father had often reminded her that fame was as insubstantial as smoke, blown this way and that. And she knew the day would come when audiences withdrew their affection for her and gave it to someone newer, younger, and she would become a footnote. But she had never been interested in being famous. All she wanted was to bring something of beauty into the world and to understand why people sometimes behaved in ways that seemed at odds with who they really were.

Footsteps sounded in the hallway. India rose and went to the door.

"Miss Hartley." Cornelius Philbrick removed his hat and blew on his hands to warm them. "Getting chilly outside."

"Is it? I hadn't really noticed."

He stepped into her dressing room without an invitation. "I'm glad you're here. I want to talk to you about a change in the script."

She frowned. "I don't think Mr. Morgan will approve."

"Any playwright worth his salt knows to expect changes. Morgan understands as well as anyone that words that seem fine on the page sometimes fail to work when spoken aloud."

"Of course. But I must confess I'm not comfortable with last-minute changes. I'd prefer to wait until we can at least rehearse them."

Philbrick's fleshy face went red. "There's no time to rehearse. This afternoon I learned that Richard Thayer will be here this evening," he said, naming the region's most important critic. "He is most fond of plays with an unexpected twist. I have nothing against Mr. Morgan, but you must admit for a play called *Suspicion*, it's rather tame."

"That depends upon how it's interpreted, don't you think?"

"Are you saying my performance last night was not up to par?"

"Not at all. I think you've done a remarkable job of making a small role seem large. I know from having watched my father juggle the roles of actor and manager that it isn't easy to do both jobs well. But I think you ought to have more confidence in my abilities. And in those of Mr. Sterling."

"I've got plenty of confidence in you. But around here the theatergoing public wants sensation. I aim to give them what they want." Mr. Philbrick pinned her with a stern look. "I'm quite aware of your loyal following. A person can't pick up a magazine without reading India Hartley this and India Hartley that. Even the Savannah Rose Society has named a rose after you. Did you know that?"

"No, but I'm flattered."

"None of that matters, though. I'm sure you know that in the world of the theater, the manager's word is law." He pulled a sheet of crumpled paper from his pocket and smoothed it out. "Now, at the end of the first act, when you are supposed to throw a vase at the head of Mr. Sterling, I want you to—well, here. I reckon you can read it for yourself."

She scanned the page and stared at him, incredulous. "You're suggesting that I pretend to shoot him? I'm afraid it's quite impossible without—"

He silenced her with a frown and jabbed a finger at the page. "And then at the beginning of act two, just here, Sterling's line will be changed to—"

"I'm sorry. I can't do it. Not this evening."

"You can and you will, or I will replace you with the understudy. Miss Bryson is chomping at the bit to make her mark. If you don't intend to cooperate, I can see to it that she gets that chance."

Though inside she trembled with indignation, India forced herself to appear calm. If her father were in the lead role, Mr. Philbrick would never dare suggest such a drastic change. Especially without a rehearsal. What if something went wrong? She handed the paper back to him. "I don't want to seem immodest, but the patrons of the Southern Palace have come to see me. Not an unknown understudy."

"The audience will be sympathetic when I announce that you've taken ill." The theater manager dropped the paper onto her dressing table. "When you come to your senses, the stage will be yours again."

"Has Mr. Sterling been informed of this change?"

Mr. Philbrick took a revolver from his pocket. "Here's your prop."

India studied the weapon, pressing a hand to her midsection to quell her nerves.

"It's quite harmless," Mr. Philbrick said, "as it has no firing pin. You needn't worry about anything apart from making the shot look real." He let out a short laugh. "After Sterling's attempts to steal the limelight last night, I should think you'd enjoy the chance to even the score. Metaphorically speaking, of course."

"But—"

"I'll see that the gun is delivered to the stage for you. And please do try to wipe the frown off that lovely face of yours."

He pocketed the prop and clumped along the hallway, his steps fading as he reached the spiral stair. India collapsed onto a chair, torn between anger and despair. The loss of her father's theater company had left her with few resources and an uncertain future. As maddening as this last-minute change was, she couldn't afford to give up even a single night's pay.

The door opened and India's dresser, Fabienne Ormond, rushed in, her cheeks pink with the cold. "*Cherie*, sorry I'm late," she said, her French accent thickening in her haste. "One of those rich ladies on Madison Square sent for me at the last minute, wanting me to do her hair. She is quite an admirer of yours, is Mrs. Sutton Mackay. Oh, what a fancy house. Silk carpets and black marble fireplaces everywhere. And her husband! *Never* have I met a more handsome man. They are coming to the theater tonight, so perhaps you will catch a glimpse of them. You will recognize Mrs. Mackay, because she will have the most beautiful hairstyle and the most dashing escort of all."

Despite her dark mood, India smiled at the young Frenchwoman's enthusiasm and confidence. Fabienne shrugged out of her dark green woolen cloak and began assembling the tools of her trade—hairbrushes, combs, pins, and pomades. "Mrs. Mackay told me—what's the matter, *mamselle*? You do not look one bit happy."

"Mr. Philbrick has taken it upon himself to rewrite Mr. Morgan's play. To make it more sensational and thus more pleasing to some critic."

Fabienne's dark eyes went wide. "Mr. Sterling will not be pleased. He likes to claim all of the attention for himself. But what can you do? Mr. Philbrick is the boss of the theater, *non*? Come, let me do your hair. You will be even more brilliant tonight than last, and all of Savannah will fall at your feet. Even the—"

"Miss Hartley." Arthur Sterling appeared in the open doorway. "I have just spoken to Mr. Philbrick about tonight's changes." His voice was a rich baritone, exquisitely trained.

She nodded, noting that he didn't seem any more pleased with the changes than she did. But then, he always seemed to be brooding about something. With his dark curls, black eyes, and high cheekbones, he reminded India of the poet Lord Byron.

"You don't approve," Mr. Sterling said.

"No, but as Mr. Philbrick has pointed out, I have no say in the matter. Nor does Mr. Morgan." India motioned to Fabienne to begin dressing her hair. "If you will excuse me, sir?"

"I saw that stagehand just now." Mr. Sterling leaned against the door frame and crossed one ankle over the other. Behind him, the other actors were arriving, hurrying for their dressing rooms, carrying costumes, wig stands, and makeup cases. "Mr. Quinn. Your not-so-secret admirer."

India studied Mr. Sterling in the mirror. It was a cliché to say so, but according to the local papers, the men of Savannah wanted to emulate him and the ladies wanted to marry him. Though India readily admitted that his extraordinary good looks and restless energy commanded attention on the stage, she couldn't fathom why any woman would find such an insufferable narcissist the least bit attractive.

"Mr. Quinn has repositioned the stage mirrors," he went on. "The better to keep you in the limelight. He thinks I upstaged you too much last night."

India opened her silver-topped makeup jar and leaned into her mirror to apply the greasepaint to her face.

"I wonder whatever gave Mr. Quinn that idea?" Mr. Sterling's rich tones turned brittle with barely contained anger. "I'd hate to think you complained to Mr. Philbrick about me."

India twisted around in her chair to face him. "Anyone who saw last night's performance knows it's true. You kept me in semidarkness for the last half of the first act. Not only was your behavior lacking in generosity and professionalism, it was also dangerous. I could have tripped on a prop or fallen onto a burning torch. You are so widely admired in this city I confess I expected better from you than that."

He laughed. "Then the change in tonight's performance ought to please you. Since you hold such a low opinion of me."

Just then, Victoria Bryson, the understudy, arrived. "Good evening, Miss Hartley."

"Miss Bryson." India motioned to Fabienne to continue dressing her hair.

"Are you feeling well this evening, Miss Hartley?" The understudy assumed an expression of concern, but she couldn't keep a note of hopefulness from her voice. "The opening-night party went on for so long, I thought the loud talk and the late hour might have done you in. After all, a woman of your age needs her sleep."

India couldn't suppress a good-natured laugh. "I'm so sorry to disappoint you, but I'm feeling just fine."

The young woman slipped her arm through Mr. Sterling's and smiled up at him. "I've just seen Mr. Philbrick. He's terribly excited about this evening. I cannot tell you how much I admire your ability to change what you do at the snap of a finger. It's brilliant, really."

Mr. Sterling preened at the compliment and patted her gloved hand. "All in a night's work, my dear."

The door opened and another woman came into the hallway on a blast of cold air. Wrapped in a purple hooded cloak that hid her hair and shadowed her face, she paced back and forth in the hallway, casting frequent glances at Mr. Sterling and the understudy. India felt a stab of sympathy for her. No doubt she was another of Mr. Sterling's admirers, desperate for a word with him, and now in his presence, too overcome with shyness to do more than glance longingly at the object of her affection.

India rose, stepped past Mr. Sterling and the understudy, and entered the hallway. The woman darted away, her steps slowing when she encountered a stack of hatboxes and props at the bottom of the stair.

"May I help you?" India asked gently. "If it's Mr. Sterling you've come to see, I'm happy to introduce—"

"No." The woman's startling blue eyes held an expression akin to panic. She shook her head and bolted from the theater.

India returned to her dressing room and resumed her seat at the dressing table.

"What was that all about?" Mr. Sterling asked.

"An admirer of yours, I'm sure. She seemed quite anxious to speak to you, but lost her nerve."

Miss Bryson laughed. "He does have that effect on people." She gazed up at Mr. Sterling and sighed. "It seems I'm doomed to spend another evening waiting in the wings. But I know you will be wonderful even though you and Miss Hartley haven't rehearsed tonight's change."

"We'll get through it," India said, picking up her jar of lip pomade. "So long as we both remember to respect the other's space."

Mr. Sterling's black eyes held a mixture of derision and amusement. "Actually this might be quite entertaining. So long as you don't take those new stage directions literally."

He waggled his fingers at her and headed for his dressing room.

India let out an exasperated breath. "Don't tempt me."

❧ CHAPTER 2 ❧

HALF AN HOUR LATER, DRESSED IN HER RUFFLED cream-and-violet costume, her makeup in place, India mounted the spiral stair to the wings. Behind the velvet curtain the atmosphere was one of barely controlled chaos as a small army of stagehands positioned the painted flats at the rear of the stage. The settee and the mahogany side table required for act one were placed to take advantage of the light cast by the mirrors and the gaslights flanking the stage.

Fabienne, carrying extra face powder and a brush and the costume India would wear for the second act asked, "All set?"

"I think so." India parted the curtain at the side of the stage and peered through the narrow opening. Though this was only her second night at the Southern Palace, it had already become a favorite. The owners had spared no expense in its construction and furnishings. The seats were upholstered in red plush and were tiered so that every patron had an unobstructed view of the stage. Above the proscenium were fanciful paintings of cherubs, angels, stars, and doves rendered in the softest shades of pink, blue, and apricot. Along each long wall were raised boxes with seating for six that could be enclosed with gold-tasseled curtains for privacy. An orchestra pit and a trapdoor that slid open on silent bearings were hidden from view by baskets of greenery.

Tonight every seat was taken. The theater buzzed with whispered conversations and the rustle of silks and satins as patrons settled in for the performance.

Butterflies danced inside India's midsection, but she welcomed them as a sign that she cared about this audience and wanted to please them. She wouldn't let her anger at Mr. Philbrick, or her anxiety about the substitution he'd made in tonight's performance, distract her.

Mr. Philbrick, in costume for his small role in act two, strolled past. "Five minutes, Miss Hartley."

She blew out a few quick breaths, took her position, and waited for the curtain to rise. Opposite her, in the other wing, Mr. Sterling stood, hands on hips, his head thrown back.

A ripple of applause built to a thunderous roar as the curtain rose. India stepped into the dazzling limelight. She took her position downstage and waited for silence before delivering her opening line.

"A lie is the truth in masquerade, written in dark misfortune's book."

On cue, Mr. Sterling made his entrance, the bright white light illuminating his black curls and chiseled features. India waited while the audience applauded his entrance. He delivered his opening lines, and they settled into the rhythm of the performance. As the end of the first act approached, India moved to her position downstage. Mr. Sterling followed, as he had done the previous evening, leaving her little choice but to step once more into the shadows. Her anger flared, but she had trained herself to set aside her personal animosity for the sake of the performance.

"Act well your part," Mr. Sterling recited. "For that is where the honor lies."

"And what do you know of honor?"

He laughed at her, as the script required.

That was India's cue to pick up the revolver that was to replace the vase she'd hurled at him the previous evening. She reached out a hand to a nearby table and delivered her next line. "You would mock me, sir?"

Oh mercy. Where was the blasted gun? She peered into the shadows and slid her fingers across the tabletop.

The silence lengthened. Someone in the audience coughed. In the wings there was the faint sound of shuffling feet.

Her heart hammered. Her worst fear was realized. The play, or at least this first act, was ruined. And Mr. Philbrick would accuse her of deliberately sabotaging it.

"Pray tell, has a cat stolen your tongue?" Mr. Sterling abandoned the script and was improvising his lines now, stalling for time.

No, but someone had stolen her prop. Quivering with humiliation and anger, India bent down to peer more closely at the table. And found the gun at last.

Just as she lifted it there was a deafening explosion and a quick flash of fire. An anguished scream.

Mr. Sterling crumpled onto the stage.

"This way, miss." The brawny policeman, his voice still thick with sleep, guided India out of the jail and into a waiting police wagon. "If you promise not to run, I won't put the cuffs on you." He dropped his gaze. "My wife is an admirer of yours. She won't speak to me if I embarrass you in front of the whole town."

"I won't run," India said. "I have nothing to hide. This is merely a grave misunderstanding."

He nodded but she suspected he didn't believe a word of it. She couldn't blame him. She supposed every person who was arrested, guilty or not, professed innocence. She glanced up at the imposing Gothic Revival jailhouse with its shuttered windows and enclosed yard and prayed she had seen the last of it.

The wagon rattled along the street, which was just coming alive in the morning light. In the alleys, draymen loaded wagons for deliveries. A couple of older women in faded dresses carried baskets of freshly laundered linens to the fine houses on the squares. A group of neatly dressed Negro children headed off to school, their arms laden with books and lunch pails.

The wagon halted before a large two-story building situated on a corner of Wright Square. White columns graced porticoes on two sides. Deep porches sheltered wide entry doors. In the yard stood a couple of handsome rigs pulled by sleek horses that stood patiently cropping grass.

"Here we are," the policeman said. "Chatham County Courthouse."

He escorted her across the yard and into a wood-paneled courtroom on the first floor. He motioned India to a chair, crossed the room, and knocked on a door. "Judge? I've got Miss Hartley out here."

India suddenly felt faint. She hadn't done anything wrong. But could she convince the judge? And would she be permitted to speak to a lawyer? She was sick with nerves, fatigue, and terror. She licked her lips. "May I have some water?"

"When His Honor gets in here. I can't leave you unattended."

"No, I suppose not." She clasped her hands in her lap. "Is there any word on Mr. Sterling?"

"I'm not allowed to say, miss."

The door opened and two men came in. The first, clad in a black robe, took his seat on the bench. He was thin and light haired and younger than India had expected. His pale eyes behind thick gold-rimmed spectacles blinked owlishly. "Miss Hartley."

"Yes." She studied the other man, who was everything the judge was not. Tall and broad shouldered, he was impeccably dressed in a gray woolen suit, white shirt, and dark blue cravat. Thick curly hair the color of molasses framed a perfectly proportioned face. His tawny eyes held hers.

"Miss Hartley," said the bespectacled man, "I'm Judge Russell. Now, I know you must be frightened and I want to assure you, we are here only to get to the bottom of the tragic events of last evening. We aim to determine whether a crime has been committed. If so, there will be a trial later on to determine by whom."

"I understand." She cast a pleading look at the policeman, who hurried from the room.

"The gentleman to my left is Mr. Sinclair," the judge continued. "He is a member of the Georgia Bar, and even though in my opinion it's too soon for you to need his services, he is here at the insistence of Mrs. Sutton Mackay to see to your interests. I believe you know the lady."

"I have never met her, but I know of her."

The officer returned with a glass of water. She drank half of it before setting it down.

"Very well." The judge signaled to the policeman, who opened the door and ushered in a half-dozen men, most of them bleary-eyed but well dressed and wearing expressions as somber as the judge's. The judge cleared his throat. "I've sworn these men as an inquest jury, Miss Hartley. Now." He opened a leather binder and took out a sheaf of papers. "From what I understand, Mr. Arthur Sterling suffered a gunshot wound last night during a performance at the Southern Palace. Is that correct?"

"Yes."

"All right. What happened?"

India took another sip of water and tried to marshal her wits. What if she said the wrong thing? She could not bear another moment inside the bedlam that was the Chatham County Jail. She had to make the judge see that what had happened was an accident not of her making. "The theater manager came to my dressing room before last evening's performance and told me he wanted to make a change in the play. I didn't want to do it because I knew the playwright, Mr. Morgan, would be upset, and I wanted at least one chance to rehearse it first. But Mr. Philbrick refused. He told me to do it his way or he would send the understudy onstage in my place."

Mr. Sinclair crossed the room and pulled up a chair next to India's. Something about his solid presence and his kind expression calmed her. He motioned for her to continue.

From his bench, Judge Russell peered down at her. "What kind of a change?"

"Well, the script calls for my character, Viola, to throw a vase at Mr. Sterling's character. But Mr. Philbrick thought it wasn't sensational enough. He told me I was to pretend to shoot Mr. Sterling instead, but of course I would miss. Otherwise there could be no second act."

The judge's thin lips formed a slight smile. "I suppose not. Go on."

"I told Mr. Philbrick I was uneasy about pretending to shoot a gun without a rehearsal, but he insisted."

"Surely you didn't intend to fire an actual gun in a crowded theater."

"No, sir. Mr. Philbrick showed me the prop. He said the firing pin was missing and it was perfectly safe. During the argument between Mr. Sterling's character and mine, I was to grab the gun and level it at Mr. Sterling. The prop man would simulate the sound of gunfire by clapping two pieces of wood together from behind the stage."

"Fascinating. So the play began. Then what?"

"We got to the scene near the end of the first act where I was to fire at Mr. Sterling. I was working in the semidarkness, because despite the addition of extra mirrors to reflect more light, Mr. Sterling had once again usurped my place on the stage."

"And you were angry at him for doing so."

Mr. Sinclair touched India's sleeve. "Don't answer that."

Judge Russell frowned. "So, Miss Hartley. You were standing in the dark?"

"Yes, sir. And I felt around for the gun Mr. Philbrick was supposed to have put there."

"And was it there?"

"At first I couldn't find it, and I was nervous because the timing of the scene depended on the sound of gunfire. When I finally located it, I picked it up, and the next thing I knew Mr. Sterling fell and—" India started to cry.

"We need a break, Judge." Mr. Sinclair handed India his handkerchief.

"Almost finished, Mr. Sinclair." Judge Russell paged through his report. "When did you realize the gun was not disabled after all?"

"When Mr. Sterling collapsed and the house lights came on." India shuddered at the recollection of what happened then: the audience in an uproar, police whistles blaring, two men carrying Mr. Sterling from the stage. The hem of her costume soaked in blood.

The courtroom door opened. Another policeman entered, crossed the room, and whispered to the judge.

"When the house lights came up, and you could see more clearly, Miss Hartley—then did you recognize the weapon?"

Dizzy with terror, she whispered, "Yes."

"So even though it obviously was not the gun Mr. Philbrick had supplied for the scene, you had seen it before?"

"Yes."

"And how is that?"

"The gun is mine."

✒ CHAPTER 3 ✒

MR. SINCLAIR BOLTED FROM HIS CHAIR. "YOUR HONOR, I insist on a break to consult with my client."

"You'll have plenty of time for that, sir."

The judge turned to the men seated in the jury box. "I have just been informed that Mr. Sterling has succumbed to his injury. Do you gentlemen wish to retire to consider an indictment?"

The men murmured among themselves. One of them rose, thumbs hooked into his suspenders. "No need, Judge Russell. We are in agreement that enough evidence exists to hold a trial."

India swayed in her chair and barely heard the judge's next words. "India Hartley, you are charged with the murder of Arthur Sterling and are hereby bound over for trial at a date to be determined."

She went numb. Yes, the gun was hers, but she had no idea how it had wound up on the stage. And hadn't she just explained that what happened was an accident? Surely she would not be condemned to the gallows because of an unfortunate mistake. The officers were already moving toward her, preparing to take her back to the stench and racket of the county jail. With Christmas coming, who knew how long she would languish there before a trial could be arranged?

"Your Honor." Mr. Sinclair approached the judge's bench. "I have not even been properly introduced to my client. I cannot possibly prepare her defense without time to uncover the facts and discuss them with her. You cannot remand her into custody."

The judge frowned. "Mr. Sinclair, I remand criminals into custody every day of the year. Other lawyers manage to mount a defense while their clients are behind bars. I don't see why this case ought to be any different."

"Let's speak privately and I'll tell you why."

The judge pulled out his watch. "I've got a case starting in fifteen minutes."

"I won't need that long."

India studied the lawyer's face. Could she trust him? She had never laid eyes on him before today, and now her future, perhaps her very life, rested in his hands.

The judge rose, and Mr. Sinclair followed him out of the courtroom. The two policemen flanked India, arms folded across their chests. The older of the two, the one who had brought her here from the jail, handed her the half-empty water glass. She drank the rest of it and then stood with her eyes cast down so they wouldn't see her tears. She fumbled in her pocket for the handkerchief Mr. Sinclair had given her. If only Father were alive. If only her touring company had not been stolen from her. If only Mr. Philbrick hadn't insisted on changing the script. How quickly a life could be destroyed.

She pressed the heels of her hands to her burning eyes.

Mr. Sterling was dead. How had her own gun found its way onto the stage?

The door opened, and Mr. Sinclair came out alone. He flashed a paper at the two policemen and offered India his arm. "Come with me."

She blotted her tears. "I don't want to go back to jail."

"You aren't going to jail. You're going to St. Simons. With me."

"St. Simons?"

"It's an island about a day's journey by steamer from here. I've a plantation there. Or I did have, before the war. It's mostly a ruin now."

She followed him out of the courthouse and into the bright December sunlight. He helped her into his rig and sent her a reassuring smile. "Indigo Point is slightly better than the Chatham County Jail. The house is still standing, and it's quiet there. We'll have time to prepare your defense away from the prying eyes of this city. I love Savannah, but I must admit folks here find it hard to ignore a juicy scandal."

He flicked the reins and turned the rig. "Did you leave anything at the jail?"

"They wouldn't let me bring anything. Not even a comb."

"We'll go by the theater and collect your things."

"Most of my clothes are at the hotel."

He nodded.

"Mr. Sinclair, I am beyond grateful for your help, but I confess I don't understand why you are going to such lengths to assist a total stranger. Especially since I haven't the means to pay you."

"As the judge said, Miss Hartley, you have an ardent patron.

Mrs. Sutton Mackay happened to be in the theater last night. She was quite incensed by the way you were hauled off to the jailhouse like some common thief. She has some experience in dealing with scandal and wanted to spare you the same unhappiness." He slowed the rig as they turned onto Bull Street. "She and her late father, Mr. Browning, were very protective of this city. She hasn't said so, but I suspect she offered to help you in part to save Savannah's face. It wouldn't do to have such a distinguished guest treated so poorly."

"I would like to call on her, to thank her for her generosity."

"There isn't time. Captain Mooreland's boat leaves for the island in an hour. We've barely time to collect your belongings and get to the wharf."

India hesitated as another thought hit her. Was she to be alone on this remote island with a strange gentleman? Was there a Mrs. Sinclair in residence?

He turned to her, and the look in his eyes told her that he understood her unspoken question. "My sister, Amelia, lives with me at the Point. As does our housekeeper, Mrs. Catchpole. Since the war, several of my former bondsmen have taken up sharecropping with me. And Fan Butler has just returned to St. Simon's to check on her father's holdings. My house is a big house. There's plenty of room. Plenty of people about. We'll be well chaperoned, if that's what's bothering you."

"I . . . I don't know how to thank you."

"Just tell me everything you can remember so we can win your case." He sent her a rueful smile. "Now that my plantation is falling into ruin, all I have is my law practice."

"And winning my case would cement your reputation."

Something flashed in his eyes. "Perhaps. But that isn't why I chose to defend you." He halted the rig at the hotel then helped her down. "Let's get your things."

"I need to speak to my dresser. And Mr. Philbrick," she said as they made their way into the hotel's spacious lobby.

"No time, I'm afraid. I'll go by the theater while you're packing. You can leave a note for your dresser. The hotel manager will see that it's delivered."

"But Fabienne is—"

"Miss Hartley, I do sympathize. But you do not want to be here when the news of Mr. Sterling's demise hits the streets. Please hurry and pack. I'll be back in half an hour."

He left her there. Aware of the curious stares of the hotel staff, India went up to her room and collapsed on her bed, dizzy with hunger and paralyzed with disbelief. Alone. Nearly broke. Accused of murder. How had her life come so unraveled?

The little French mantel clock chimed, reminding her of Mr. Sinclair's imminent return. She rose and began packing her things, folding petticoats and chemises, stockings and dressing gowns into one of her two large trunks. Day dresses and her one still-stylish evening dress went into the other, along with a fine woolen cloak, a pair of buff-colored half boots, and three pairs of kid gloves. She had brought along only three hats for this Southern theater tour, and now she carefully packed two of them into pink-and-white-striped hatboxes.

Opening her writing box, she took out paper and ink and sat at the small escritoire beneath the window to pen a note to Fabienne. She couldn't simply disappear without a word, though surely Fabienne would learn soon enough what had happened.

Pen in hand, India tried to express her affection and gratitude to her young dresser. But in the end all she could manage
were a couple of sentences and a fervent wish for a speedy trial
that would set everything to rights. Though she could hardly
afford to do so, India tucked a ten-dollar note inside the letter,
sealed the envelope, and addressed it to Fabienne in care of the
Southern Palace.

She poured water into the blue porcelain washbasin, bathed
her face and hands, and tidied her hair. She brushed the skirt of
her heavy costume clean, though traces of the blood were still
visible along the hem. She wanted nothing more than to burn
the dress, but travel by steamboat would be a long and dirty
affair, and she needed to save her best clothes for the day when
she must appear in court.

She made one last sweep of the room, then pulled the little
velvet cord beside the bed to summon the bellman. When he
appeared, she followed him silently down to the lobby, where
she avoided meeting the manager's eyes as she quickly settled
her bill.

Moments later, Mr. Sinclair returned and saw to the loading
of her trunks onto a hired carriage. He helped her enter, closed
the curtains, and called to the driver.

"Word has reached the street," he said when the carriage
turned toward the waterfront. "Crowds are forming outside the
theater and in front of Mr. Sterling's house. I thought it best to
travel unobserved. An event like this can whip normally sedate
folks into a frenzy."

India's face flamed. She lowered her head.

Mr. Sinclair reached out a gloved hand and tilted her chin

up. "The first rule of winning a case. Keep your head up. Don't look guilty."

"I'm *not* guilty! I told the judge what happened. He didn't believe me."

"I'm not so sure he didn't. But a man has died, accidentally or not, and—"

"So you, too, think I'm a murderer."

"I don't know what I think yet. We need to talk about it. That's the whole point of retiring to Indigo Point. Here in the city there will be too many sensational newspaper stories, too many gawkers, too many rumors." His eyes sought and held hers. "I'm inclined to believe your story, just as you told it to Judge Russell. But I won't deny we have a difficult case. People may naturally suspect an actor accustomed to hiding her true self on the stage."

India pressed a palm to her throbbing head. Perhaps he had a point, but she couldn't think about that just now.

"The better I know you and the more I can learn about your life and work, the better I can defend you," he said. "It will be easier to do that away from curiosity seekers and gossip mongers."

It had never been easy for her to share her innermost thoughts with others, not even with her own father. For one thing, Father's emotions were fragile as a girl's. Bad news upset him to such an extent that India tried to shelter him from anything that might prove distressing. For another, a life of travel from theater to theater, from city to city, didn't lend itself to forming the kind of deep and lasting friendships that made it easier to pour out her heart. And there were the inevitable disagreements and petty jealousies that often arose among cast members, making it hard to know who could be trusted and who was best avoided.

The carriage rocked to a stop.

"Here we are." Mr. Sinclair helped her out of the carriage and saw to the loading of her trunks.

Aboard the *Neptune*, he settled her into a cramped, dingy cabin then went to stand with the captain as the steamer left the pier and started down the Savannah River.

Buffeted by a gust of wind, the small craft rose on a swell that sent spray splashing over the rail. Shivering in the damp cold of the December morning, India watched from her window as Savannah grew smaller and smaller, wondering whether she would return to be declared a free woman or punished for a crime she didn't commit.

❧ CHAPTER 4 ❧

NIGHT WAS FALLING AS THE *Neptune* ROUNDED THE southern end of St. Simons and nudged a pier. India rose, stiff from hours of sitting alone in her cabin, and picked up her reticule.

Mr. Sinclair tapped on the door and called softly, "Miss Hartley?"

She opened the door and glanced past his shoulder to the two men who had come aboard to offload supplies.

Following her gaze, Mr. Sinclair said, "They'll bring your things on up to the house. Come. I want you to meet Amelia and Mrs. Catchpole. We're not exactly expected for dinner, but I'm sure Mrs. Catchpole will rise to the occasion."

He offered her his arm. Overcome with worry and exhaustion, she leaned heavily against him. Beneath a frail winter moon, they walked up the creaking gangway to the pier and then passed beneath a thick canopy of towering moss-bearded oaks that formed a long allée to the house.

"My grandmother planted these oaks more than seventy years ago, when she came to Indigo Point as a new bride." Mr. Sinclair raised his voice a bit to be heard above the gentle thunder of the sea. "I climbed them often when I was a boy."

Despite her fatigue, India smiled at the mental picture of him shinnying up the thick, knobby branches, the Spanish moss stirring ghostlike in his wake.

"Grandmother Sinclair was quite the gardener," he went on. "She planted all kinds of flowering plants. Back in those days, sailors rounding the point said they could smell the flowers before they spotted land. Of course, there isn't much left now. But one day I'll replant. I owe it to her memory. And to the next generation of Sinclairs."

In the growing dusk, India could see the abandoned gardens, dark and blossomless in the winter gloom. Beyond the gardens lay several outbuildings, and farther into the forest, half a dozen slave cabins, the windows aglow with lamplight. Smoke from the chimneys threaded into the black tree branches overhead.

"Here we are," Mr. Sinclair said. "Home at last. Such as it is."

The house was of the West Indies style, built above a tabby basement, with wide, covered verandas and tall windows framed by shutters. He led her up a flight of steps and across the veranda to the front door. Before he could open it, India saw a quick movement at one of the tall windows, and then the door opened.

"You're home!" A thin-faced woman with eyes the color of robins' eggs launched herself into Mr. Sinclair's arms, her unbound hair a brown shawl falling across her shoulders. "Mrs. Catchpole told me not to—oh!"

Noticing India at last, she stepped back.

"Amelia," Mr. Sinclair said. "This is Miss Hartley. She's going to be staying here while we sort out a legal matter."

Amelia blinked. "Hartley? India Hartley?"

India summoned a smile. "Hello. I'm so sorry to impose on

you with no warning. I hope my presence here won't be too much of an inconvenience."

"An inconvenience? Heavens, no. It's an honor, Miss Hartley. I've been reading all about your theater tour. And you can't imagine how dull life can be here. I'm grateful for the company. How long will be you be staying?"

"That's hard to say," Mr. Sinclair said. "But it's getting cold out here. Do you think we might come inside?"

"Of course. Heavenly days, where are my manners?" Amelia stood aside to let them in. "I didn't hear your rig on the road."

"I asked Captain Mooreland to drop us off here instead of going all the way up to the bluff." Mr. Sinclair removed his hat and coat and hung them on the hall tree beside the door.

"I don't imagine he has begun dining service on the *Neptune*," Amelia said.

"Not yet."

Amelia led them into a spacious parlor furnished with a jumble of couches, chairs, and tables that had all seen better days. A piano sat in one corner. Dark rectangles on the faded wallpaper spoke of paintings lately removed, and a large pot in the corner hinted at a leaky roof. Heavy curtains were drawn against the evening chill. A fire crackled and popped in the grate.

Amelia went in search of the housekeeper. India threw off her cloak and sank into a wingback chair near the fire, realizing how close she was to total collapse. Hunger gnawed at her insides, but all she wanted was a bed and the sweet oblivion of sleep.

The men arrived with her trunks. Mr. Sinclair went outside to speak to them and returned just as Amelia came in with an older woman, whom India supposed was Mrs. Catchpole.

"You see?" Amelia said to the older woman, setting down a tray laden with soup bowls, a basket of bread, and a teapot. "It's Miss Hartley. In the flesh."

Ignoring India, the housekeeper nodded to Mr. Sinclair. "I didn't expect you until Friday."

"Change of plans," he said, taking the chair next to India's. "Mrs. Catchpole, I have the honor of presenting Miss India Hartley."

Arms akimbo, the housekeeper studied India through narrowed eyes. "Amelia tells me you're an actress."

"Yes."

Mr. Sinclair poured tea and handed India the cup. To his housekeeper he said, "Many critics say she's the new Fanny Kemble."

"If that's so, then it was a mistake bringin' her here, seein' as how that woman hated Butler's Island and made no bones about sayin' so."

"That was a long time ago," Mr. Sinclair said, pouring himself a cup of tea. "Indigo Point is not the same as Butler's. And I'm no Pierce Butler."

"Saints be praised." The housekeeper stared at India so intently that India wondered whether she had soot on her nose.

The older woman's disapproval came off her in waves. To cover her discomfort, India spooned sugar into her tea. She was grateful to Mr. Sinclair for offering her sanctuary, but she was all too familiar with feelings of not being acceptable to polite society. Maybe she ought to have stayed in Savannah. Scorn was scorn regardless of where one encountered it.

Mrs. Catchpole waved one hand. "Is there anything else you need, sir?"

"I don't think so. And if we do, I know my way to the kitchen."

The housekeeper's lips formed a thin straight line, as if she were struggling to hold back her words. "I'll make up a room for Miss Hartley before I turn in. Come, Amelia. I need your help."

She spun on her heel and stomped up the stairs, Amelia trailing behind her. Soon India heard footsteps overhead, the creak of wooden floors, the opening and closing of doors.

Mr. Sinclair gestured with his spoon. "Eat your supper before it gets cold."

Obediently, India dug in. The soup was rich with bits of ham and potatoes, carrots and turnips, and the bread was yeasty and soft.

"You mustn't take offense at Mrs. Catchpole's behavior," Mr. Sinclair said. "She's from the older generation that still thinks of theater performers as belonging to a lower class."

His careful attention to her feelings warmed her more than the soup. "It isn't anything I haven't encountered before. It hasn't been that long since anyone in my line of work was considered less than respectable. Thankfully things are changing."

"Just be patient with old Starch and Vinegar. She'll come around." Mr. Sinclair finished his tea and poured himself another cup. "Tomorrow, I'll show you around the Point, and then we'll get to work on your case."

India nodded. Now that she was warm and her hunger satisfied, she was half asleep and too tired to think of anything.

Amelia ran lightly down the stairs. "Miss Hartley? Your room is all ready. I can show you, if you'll come up."

"I am tired." India rose.

"Go on," Mr. Sinclair said. "I'll bring your trunks up in a moment."

He went out to the porch, and Amelia led India up the stairs, their footsteps echoing on the bare planks.

"I'm very glad for your unexpected company," Amelia said as they started down the hall. "I've never been outside Georgia. I've always thought it would be exciting to travel to so many great cities. I know you'll be busy working on your legal matters, but I do hope you'll have time to talk to me. Even though more families have settled here this year, I'm afraid we don't entertain very much. Mrs. Catchpole hasn't been quite herself since my brother . . . well, in a very long time. Here we are."

Amelia opened the door to a room overlooking the back of the house. Like the parlor, it was furnished with a jumble of old and mismatched pieces—a single wingback chair with a rip in the upholstery, a tester bed, and a battered chest atop which sat a chipped wash basin and matching water pitcher, a stack of towels, and a sliver of soap. A single oil lamp gave off a faint wavering light. A small fire flickered in the fireplace grate.

"I apologize for the shabby accommodations," Amelia said. "Since the war we've had to make do with the odds and ends the Yankees left behind. They stole everything of value. Except our piano and our resolve."

India felt an instant kinship with the younger woman. Amelia's kindness and open, guileless expression was a balm for India's troubled spirit. She set down her reticule and unpinned her hat. "No need to apologize. I've stayed in many a hotel that was not nearly so well appointed. Nor so welcoming."

Amelia smiled. "I made some room in the clothespress for your things. The chamber pot is under the bed."

Footsteps sounded on the stairs, followed by a knock at the door. "Miss Hartley?"

"Come in."

Mr. Sinclair stepped into the room and set down her trunk. "I'll be right back with the other one."

Moments later he returned with the second trunk and her two pink-striped hatboxes. He glanced around the room. "Is there anything else you need?"

"I can't think of a thing. Thank you."

He nodded. "Sleep as late as you need to. Mrs. Catchpole will give you breakfast whenever you appear. I'm going up to Gascoigne Bluff in the morning to meet with Mr. Dodge at the lumber mill. I'll be back by noon."

"All right." India eyed the fluffy bed with longing.

"Well," Amelia said, "Good night."

"Good night. Thank you both."

They left. India shucked off her clothes and rummaged through her trunk for her nightdress. She gave her hair a few licks with the brush, washed her hands and face, and slid beneath sheets that smelled faintly of mildew and lavender.

A clatter below startled India awake. She sat up, blinking in momentary confusion, then remembered everything. The inquest, the journey aboard the *Neptune*. Mr. Sinclair. How kind and handsome he was. How cultured and well spoken. She let her thoughts linger on him much longer than was prudent. Even though they had arrived too late for her to see very much of the plantation, she understood how much it meant to him. The land and the sea surrounding it were in his blood.

She admired his courage and his kindness. True, he was counting on winning her case to bolster his own career, but she didn't fault him for fighting to keep what was his. Last night in the glow of the lamplight, he had looked even more attractive than he had in Judge Russell's courtroom.

The fire had gone out. India threw back the covers and padded barefoot across the floor. She tended to hygiene and pulled her oldest day dress from the trunk and dressed, her fingers stiff at the buttons. How she missed Fabienne's skill in hairstyling, and her nimble fingers, which made short work of corset stays and buttons. India arranged her hair as best she could and went downstairs.

Following the tantalizing smells of bacon and coffee, she crossed the empty parlor and stood hesitantly at the door to the dining room. Amelia was seated alone at the head of a plain pine table, a writing desk and a cup of coffee before her.

"Miss Hartley." Amelia set down her pen. "Did you sleep well?"

"Very well, thank you."

Amelia picked up a silver bell and rang it. Soon a young Negro woman in a bright green dress came in.

"Binah," Amelia said. "Please fix a plate for our guest, and bring the coffeepot back with you."

"Yes, miss." Binah eyed India, her expression a mix of curiosity and disapproval.

India folded her hands and sighed inwardly. Perhaps Mrs. Catchpole had already prejudiced the servants against her too.

Binah left and came back moments later with an empty cup and saucer and a plate of bacon, eggs, and biscuits, which she set in front of India before filling both the women's cups. She stood to Amelia's right, hands on her hips. "Is there anything else you be needing, miss?"

"I don't think so, Binah. But you might remind your mother that we've a guest. Miss Hartley's room needs making up."

"That isn't necessary," India said. "I don't want to be a burden."

"Oh, you're no burden," Amelia said. "These days, Binah and Almarene are paid to look after us." She waved a hand to dismiss Binah and said to India, "Eat your eggs before they get cold."

Binah retreated. India buttered a biscuit and took a bite of the eggs, which were lukewarm and too salty for her taste, but she managed to finish them, thanks to two cups of excellent coffee doctored with cream.

"Philip has left for the bluff," Amelia said. "He and Mr. Dodge are cooking up another scheme to bring prosperity back to the island. Heaven knows we need something." She poured more cream into her coffee. "The lumber mill is a start, but it will take much more, I'm afraid, to make up for everything we lost during the war."

Until this moment India hadn't known Mr. Sinclair's given name. She liked it. Philip Sinclair was a strong name. A confident name that would command respect in the courtroom. She was counting on that. "Yes, he told me last night he intended to see Mr. Dodge this morning."

Amelia cocked her head and regarded India over the top of her cup. "I've been a lawyer's sister long enough to know I'm not supposed to ask questions about his clients. But I do hope your difficulties, whatever they are, will soon be sorted out."

"Thank you. I hope so too." Soon enough, the Savannah papers would arrive on the island, and her troubles would be laid bare. Until then, India saw no point in discussing them. The room seemed to be closing in. She got to her feet. "I'm feeling the need for some fresh air. Would you mind if I took a walk around the grounds?"

"Of course not. I'd go with you, except I promised to finish writing these letters in time to send them back with the *Neptune* this afternoon. My cousins in Charleston are thoroughly convinced that I'm wasting away out here with so few people for company. They worry if they don't hear from me each and every week."

India hurried upstairs to get her hat and coat, and when she returned to the parlor, Amelia opened the front door. "Just turn right past the old rose garden and follow the footpath. It winds through most of the property and comes out on the other side of the house, by where the slave hospital used to be. Stay on the path and you won't lose your way."

India set off. The morning had dawned sunny and clear, with a stiff wind blowing in from the Atlantic. She passed the abandoned rose garden and found the footpath, a narrow track bordered on both sides by overgrown hedges, blighted orange trees, and the remains of several outbuildings. Here was what appeared to be a chicken coop on brick pillars, the front still covered with rusting wire; ahead stood the remains of a large carriage house. The doors had been torn away, revealing an old leather-topped conveyance missing one wheel. Everything spoke of loss and ruin. The very air seemed tinged with sadness.

She paused to pick a small yellow bloom pushing through a patch of dead grass, then continued on her way. The path led deeper into the thick woods and across a narrow stream choked with weeds and blackened tree limbs. Mockingbirds called from a thicket draped in wild jasmine and carpeted with red and green mosses. The pale winter sun filtered through the trees, dappling the water. She crossed a crumbling causeway that led across a salt marsh and stopped to watch tall brown grasses that moved in the wind like a living sea.

A smooth red pebble at the bottom of the stream caught her eye. As India bent to retrieve it, she was grabbed roughly from behind and yanked off her feet.

A scream escaped her lips and echoed through the deserted woods.

CHAPTER 5

INDIA WRENCHED FREE AND SPUN AROUND, HER HEART thudding against her ribs. "Mr. Sinclair! You frightened me."

"I'm sorry. But you were in danger." He picked up a stick lying beside the footpath and stirred the water. A long black snake thicker than a man's wrist roiled and twisted in the water before slithering away.

India's knees buckled, and his arms came around her. "I thought it was a rotted limb," she said, her cheek against the rough wool of his coat.

"It's a cottonmouth. Some folks call them water moccasins. It's highly poisonous by any name."

She drew back and looked up at him. "Why . . . why didn't you kill it?"

"These waters are rife with them. One snake more or less won't make any difference. You must be careful of them, and the alligators, when you're out here."

He released her and studied her with such an intense and odd expression in his eyes that India felt an unaccustomed shyness. "Is something wrong? Do I have dirt on my nose?"

He laughed. "Nothing of the sort. I'm afraid I've set your hat askew. Your hat pin is coming out."

India reached for it at the same moment he did, and her fingers brushed his, sending an unexpected wave of longing rushing through her.

"Here," he said. "Let me." He secured her hat pin and retied the satin bow under her chin. "Good as new."

The look in his eyes, a mixture of wonder and surprise, mirrored her own emotions.

She strove to school her voice. "Thank you."

He offered his arm as they continued along the footpath. "I wonder. Is it too soon to ask if I may call you India?"

She shook her head, inordinately pleased with his request and with the sound of her name on his lips.

"Good. And you ought to call me Philip."

"All right." She was still trembling, still shaken by the intensity of his unintended embrace. To cover her confusion she plucked another wild bloom. "How did you know I was here?"

"I got back from the bluff earlier than expected, and Amelia told me you'd gone for a walk. I thought I'd better find you." She nodded, her attention drawn to the remnants of a burned-out building barely visible through the stands of oaks. Only the foundation, a portion of one wall, and the chimney remained. Mounds of shattered glass, hardened ash, and blackened rubble protruded spire-like into the bright December sky.

Mr. Sinclair—Philip—pressed her arm more closely to his and hurried her along the path. "That was our chapel," he said. "My grandfather built it in 1800. It survived the war virtually intact, only to burn down four years ago."

She glanced over her shoulder as they moved into the sunlight again. "It looks dangerous. As if it might collapse at any moment."

"I've been meaning to have it torn down. Maybe I'll get to it after Christmas. In the meantime, I don't want you anywhere near it."

They emerged into a clearing where a few slave cabins—also made of tabby—still stood. Chickens pecked at the dirt, scattering at the approach of a small black dog. A Negro girl pegging clothes to the line raised her eyes to them as they passed. From inside her cabin came the thin, reedy wail of an infant.

They crested a small rise that afforded a view of the old slave hospital, and beyond it, the marshes and the line of cobalt blue marking the beginnings of the sea. Despite the ruin around her, India was drawn to the island's rugged beauty. Light shimmered on the blue water. Winter had turned the wind-stirred marsh grasses to a deep amber. An osprey circled lazily above the water before disappearing into the twisted limb of an old oak draped with Spanish moss. She could imagine how beautiful Indigo Point must have looked before the war destroyed everything.

She followed Philip along a narrow strip of sandy beach, listening to the whisper of the incoming tide and the sharp cries of gulls wheeling overhead. Remembering a long-ago walk on a beach with her father, India took a deep breath, willing herself to let go of the persistent emptiness of bereavement. Philip walked beside her in companionable silence, as if he understood how vast and inhospitable the world seemed to her now.

"This was my favorite spot when I was a boy," he said after a time. "When my grandmother came to take care of the servants in the hospital, I'd bring my books out here and read for hours, waiting for the steamboats to pass. Usually she'd find me fast asleep by the time she was ready to start home."

"You spoke of her last evening," India said. "You must have loved her a great deal."

"Grandmama Timmons was the only mother I really knew. She looked after me from the time I was ten. She was everything to me."

"You were lucky to have her. After my mother died, it was mostly just Father and me," India said. "He did his best, but sometimes I felt more like his parent than the other way around."

"How did your mother die?" He took her hand to help her over a patch of nettles in the path.

"Childbed fever. When I was three days old."

India wondered what had happened to his mother, but he became quiet and withdrawn and she didn't want to pry. To lighten the mood she asked more questions about his boyhood. He seemed grateful for the change of subject and regaled her with elaborate tales of fishing expeditions, failed pirating adventures, and the broken arm he'd suffered in a rough-and-tumble fight with his cousins. "It still pains me some when the weather turns."

He told a silly joke, and the sound of her own laughter startled her. It made no sense that she should feel so lighthearted when her freedom was at stake, but perhaps it was sometimes necessary to surrender to happiness, no matter how fleeting.

"What about you, India?" he asked. "What did you do for fun when you were a child?"

"I don't remember many times when I felt like a child. I was usually rehearsing for a play or traveling with Father to a performance. Once we went to an outdoor circus, and a magician tried to teach me a trick. But I never could master it. In Boston I went to tea parties at my aunt's."

"Tea parties?" He grinned and arched his brows. "Sounds deadly."

"Oh no. My aunt was an eccentric and prone to inviting all sorts of people to the house. I never knew who might turn up from one week to the next. She was just as apt to invite a band of gypsies as the mayor. She played the mandolin and kept canaries and several cats and had a library filled with books."

"Anybody who collects books can't be all bad."

India smiled. "Life became much more ordinary after her death. I don't remember much more than that, but I do miss her sometimes, even now."

A few minutes' walk brought them into the yard again. On the porch, an ancient black woman wearing a faded blue dress wielded a broom.

Philip and India mounted the steps to the front door.

"Morning, Almarene," he said. "How's your rheumatism today?"

"Not too bad, Mr. Philip. Not too bad." Almarene finished sweeping the porch and leaned on her broom handle. "'Course these cooler mornings been makin' it act up some, but I don't reckon we can do nothing 'bout the weathah."

"I suppose not." Philip inclined his head toward India. "This is our houseguest, Miss Hartley."

"Uh-huh." Almarene eyed India. "I made up your room. Made you a fire." The woman sent India a pointed look. "Took some doin' but I cleaned up that mess off the bottom of that fancy purple skirt."

India's stomach clenched. She was grateful to the woman for removing the bloodstains and saving her costume from the rag bin. But people talked. No doubt every person on St. Simons would know about those stains before the sun set on this day.

"Thank you," India said. "But I don't expect you to—"

"Long as you sleep under this roof, you fam'bly, and that means you bear lookin' after. That's how Miss Amelia runs things at Indigo Point." Almarene cocked her head. "Now, Mr. Philip, I 'spect you got important work to do."

"Yes, ma'am, I surely do."

"Then why're you standin' here jawin'? I got work to do my own self."

His eyes lit with amusement, but he bowed gravely. "You are absolutely right. Come, Miss Hartley."

They went inside. Philip helped India with her hat and coat and showed her into a study off the main hallway. Here, the desk, chairs, and tables were newer and finer. India surmised that he had furnished this room recently. A fire danced in the grate, casting a warm glow over the polished wood and the silver tea service that waited on a mahogany side table.

He directed her to a chair by a window that overlooked another of the gardens, then took his seat behind his desk. India noticed his hands as he rummaged in the desk drawer for a pad and pencil. His were the long slender fingers that might belong to a musician or a sculptor. She touched her face where his thumb had brushed her skin, and heat suffused her cheeks.

He poured tea and offered her a cup before picking up his pad and pencil.

"Now," he said. "I think you ought to tell me about that gun."

CHAPTER 6

INDIGO POINT, CHRISTMAS DAY

PHILIP INVITED THE LUMBER MILL OWNER—MR. Dodge—and a few of the other islanders to a small reception on Christmas afternoon. India had tried to avoid making an appearance, but Philip insisted it was better to show up and act as if she had nothing to hide. She dreaded it, but his careful questioning as they worked on her case had convinced her of his sound judgment. If he thought it best to mingle with the locals, then she would gather up her resolve and do it.

She chose the deep-green velvet dress she'd bought in New York last winter and draped it across her bed while she attended to her hair.

Binah knocked and came into the room, her arms laden with wood. "Mr. Philip said to bring you some firewood." She dumped it onto the hearth and brushed off her hands. "There it be."

"Thank you. I am a bit chilly."

Binah sidled closer to the dressing table. "What's that?"

"This?" India picked up a small silver box. "It's rice powder. It keeps my nose from getting shiny."

50

"Huh."

India picked up her hairbrush and attempted to arrange her famous curls, but the pins kept slipping out.

"You ain't doin' it right," Binah said.

India turned in her chair. "Is that so? Do you know how to dress hair?"

The girl shrugged. "A little, I guess. Used to do Hannah June's hair 'fore she run off. Been some time back since she up and went. Didn't say a word to nobody."

"Oh? Who was she?"

"My sister. I used to do other folks' hair at Indigo Point, too, but that was a long time ago."

"I see. Would you be willing to give mine a try?"

Another shrug.

"I'll pay you, Binah. I must go downstairs in a little while to meet a group of strangers, and I want to look my best."

"All right." The girl took up the hairbrush and pins. "I heard Mrs. Catchpole tell Mama you a theater lady."

"That's right."

"She says Mr. Philip ought not to of brought you here. She says theater folks ain't respectable."

India had long since learned not to let such opinions rankle. "I don't expect to be here for very long."

The girl began pinning India's hair. When she was finished, it was not the perfect coif Fabienne could have achieved, but it was superior to India's own efforts.

Binah leaned forward, and India caught a glimpse of a necklace half hidden inside the girl's worn blouse. It was made of fine gold wires twisted together to form a loose collar that winked in the gray light coming through the window. It was so distinctive India couldn't resist remarking on it.

Binah tucked the necklace back into her blouse. Her expression softened. "My sister had one too. They was gifts from a gentleman who fancied her."

"I see. Well, it's quite striking. Perhaps you ought to put it away and save it for special occasions."

"Special occasions?" Binah laughed. "I ain't going nowhere. Hannah June, she used to say if you got something that makes you happy, you best enjoy it while you can."

"She has a point." India took out her powder brush and leaned into the mirror.

"Mrs. Catchpole says theater women goin' to the devil 'cause they paint up they faces."

"I don't know about that. I hope it isn't true." India dipped her finger into her jar of lip pomade and smoothed some on.

Binah watched, apparently fascinated. "How come they paint up they faces?"

"So we can change the way we look. We can make our skin darker or lighter, make our cheekbones look sharper and our eyes more deeply set." India smiled into the mirror. "You wouldn't recognize me at all if you saw me in my greasepaint."

Binah frowned. "What's greasepaint?"

India took her makeup case from the wardrobe. She opened it and showed the girl the row of small jars within. "Greasepaint is made from lard and pigments."

"Lard and pigs?"

"Pigments. Different colors made from things like crushed rose petals and charcoal."

"Oh."

"Would you like to try some on?"

Binah backed away. "No, ma'am! I ain't goin' to the devil when I die."

Stung, India snapped the case shut. "I wouldn't believe everything Mrs. Catchpole tells you."

"I got to go."

India took a coin from her reticule and pressed it into Binah's palm. The girl pocketed it and left the room. India slipped into her green velvet dress and went downstairs.

Amelia came forward to greet her, her eyes warm with welcome. "What a pretty dress. And so appropriate for Christmas. Though it doesn't feel much like Christmas, does it?"

India shook her head. "It's my first one since my father died. He loved Christmas and always made a fuss about it."

"Oh, so did my papa. He always went with Philip and me to decorate the church at Fredericka for Christmas services." Amelia's eyes clouded. "But of course that's a ruin now, too, thanks to the Yankees."

She looped her arm through India's. "Philip and Mr. Dodge have gone out with the gentlemen, but you must come and meet the ladies."

India followed Amelia into the parlor, where a Christmas tree decorated with bits of ribbon and strings of popcorn had been set up in front of the window. On the dining table were platters of sandwiches and assorted sweets. A dozen or so women stood in groups of twos and threes chatting quietly. When they saw India, all conversation stopped.

"Everyone, this is Miss India Hartley." Amelia drew India

into the center of the room. "She's staying with us for a while. I'll let you introduce yourselves."

India accepted the cup of tea Amelia offered and smiled at the women. "Hello."

A tall woman in a plain blue dress and a faded velvet hat cocked her head, her arms folded across her chest. "I heard about you just yesterday. My husband come back here from Savannah with the newspaper. It says you killed a man and Mr. Sinclair is trying to get you off."

Amelia blanched but quickly recovered and said smoothly, "The newspapers always exaggerate everything. If indeed there was a story about Miss Hartley, I'm certain the facts are wrong."

"The papers don't lie."

"That's right." Another woman bobbed her head. "They aren't allowed to print lies."

"You'd be surprised," Philip said from behind India.

She turned away, her face flaming, tears welling in her eyes. Philip shouldn't have made her come. These people hated her on sight. A white-hot fury seized her. But beneath her anger was a sorrow so deep it stole her breath.

Philip moved to India's side. "Ladies. You were invited to Indigo Point to celebrate the holiday, and I'm delighted to welcome you. Heaven knows there are far too few causes for celebration in these parts of late. But if you insist upon insulting my guest, then I must ask you to take your leave."

A pall of surprise and suspicion fell across the room. India struggled to maintain her composure. Nobody in this house— except for Amelia—trusted her. At times during her meetings with Philip she wondered whether even he completely believed her version of events.

"Begging your pardon, Mr. Sinclair." The woman who had spoken first gave India a grudging nod. "How do? I'm Mrs. Garrison. My husband was an overseer here back before the war."

All India could manage was a stiff smile. She wanted to march back upstairs and wait until they had gone. But Philip was looking at her, encouraging her, so she stood where she was, her back to the fragrant Christmas tree, as the other women introduced themselves.

Yesterday at breakfast Philip had mentioned that many families had been reduced to scratching out a living on worn-out land, forced into sharecropping with their former slaves. Others had found work at Mr. Dodge's lumber mill. India could understand their bitterness at finding themselves in such reduced circumstances. Even so, she chafed at the unfairness of their judgmental expressions. They didn't realize that her own future—even if Philip won her case—was just as uncertain and as fraught with potential hardship as their own.

The sound of footsteps on the wooden porch announced the return of several of the men who had seized the holiday as a chance to go hunting. They left their guns on the porch along with the few rabbits they'd shot, then came inside.

Philip made quick introductions. Mrs. Catchpole, her round, pasty face a mask of harried disapproval, came in with more food, and the reception went on. Four of the women formed an impromptu quartet around the piano, and soon the sound of carols filled the parlor.

Philip filled two plates and motioned India into the hallway. "It seems the chairs are all taken. Do you mind sitting on the stairs?"

"Not at all." She recognized this as his way of protecting her from further embarrassment, and her heart expanded with gratitude. Oh, what a man was this Philip Sinclair! She couldn't remember the last time she had felt so sheltered. So safe. She took her seat beside him on the uncarpeted stair, watched him polish off a frosted petit four and wondered, not for the first time, why such an attractive and accomplished gentleman had not taken a wife.

He chose a sandwich from his plate and eyed it. "What do you suppose is in there?"

"Ham, perhaps? Or sausage and cheese?"

He sniffed and returned it to his plate. "Sausage. Too far removed from the roast turkey we enjoyed at Christmases of old." He sighed. "A turkey dinner with all the trimmings is one of the things I miss the most. Do you know that Mr. Couper's chef up at Cannon's Point could debone a turkey with such skill that it retained its shape?"

She grinned. "That must have been quite something."

"It was the talk of the island. I miss coconut cake, too, and a good pot of low-country rice and . . . tell me, India, what do you miss? What would you eat today, if you could?"

India didn't have to think twice. "Plum pudding. I haven't had one since Father and I left England. I think he looked forward to it as much as I did. Once, when we were in—"

"There you are, Sinclair." A thin, pale-eyed gentleman in a full beard and a hunting jacket that had seen better days strode into the hallway and peered down at them. He nodded to India before turning his attention to Philip. "Please forgive me for injecting a business discussion into the middle of a Yule celebration, but I wonder if I might have a quick word with you."

"All right." Philip got to his feet as the quartet launched into an enthusiastic rendition of "God Rest Ye Merry, Gentlemen."

"Miss Hartley? May I return you to the ladies?"

"Everyone seems to be enjoying the concert. I don't want to interrupt. Would you mind if I retired to the study?"

"Not at all." He enveloped her hand in his and drew her to her feet.

India took her cup and escaped to the study, where a fire had been laid and the curtains drawn against the afternoon chill. She took the worn wingback chair closest to the fire and watched a flock of small birds flitting in and out of the bushes beneath the window.

"I hate crowds too."

India jumped at the sound of a man's voice.

He emerged from the far corner, his green cravat askew. He gestured with a glass of amber-colored spirits. "Welcome to Indigo Point. What's left of it."

"You startled me." She set her cup on the scarred wooden side table.

"I'm sorry." He held his glass aloft. "Want one?"

"No thank you, Mr.—?"

"Cuyler Lockwood. I was the last overseer here before the war. Replaced Garrison when he went 'round the bend."

"I see."

Mr. Lockwood leaned against the fireplace. "Do you? Growin' sea island cotton isn't a task for the faint of heart. Some

people couldn't take the heat, the snakes and gators, or the mos-
quitoes. To say nothing of dealin' with the Negroes day in and
day out. Garrison was one of 'em. He was a mean son of a—that
is, he was too hard on the slaves, and they revolted in '61. Nearly
killed him. He never was the same after that."

"I suppose not."

Mr. Lockwood scratched at his arm, and India noticed
that his fingernails were long and ragged and caked with dirt.
He regarded her through half-closed eyes. "You're the famous
India Hartley."

"Yes."

"I saw you in a play once, in Philadelphia. The Walnut Street
Theater."

She nodded, surprised that a man like him would appreciate
theater. "My father managed it for a while. He died last spring."

"I'm sorry to hear that." Mr. Lockwood finished his drink
and with a less than steady hand poured another from a crystal
decanter sitting on the side table. "It's Christmas. You're sure
you don't want something stronger than tea?"

"I'm sure."

"Suit yourself." He took another long sip and studied her
over the rim of his glass. "Word has it that Sinclair is defending
you on a murder charge."

India rose. "Excuse me."

"Certainly." He paused. "You want some advice?"

She waited, hands clasped at her waist.

"Cottonmouths and alligators are not necessarily the most
dangerous creatures you'll run across in these parts." He drained
his glass. "Be careful who you trust."

CHAPTER 7

DECEMBER 28

PHILIP BENT TO LIGHT THE LOGS ALMARENE HAD LAID in the fireplace. The kindling flickered and caught, sending orange sparks flying up the chimney. The faint smell of wood smoke perfumed the study as the logs caught fire and the flames chased the morning chill from the room. Outside, a bitter wind soughed in the trees, and a steady rain lashed the windows.

As Philip collected his pad and pencil and took his chair opposite India, she poured tea and settled into her chair, both hands wrapped around the delicate china cup. In the three days since the unpleasant Christmas Day encounter with his neighbors, she had seen little of him. Now she noticed faint worry lines creasing his forehead and the slightly rumpled shirt he wore beneath his woolen jacket. She couldn't help noticing everything about him: his strong jawline still slightly pink from the morning's shave; the clean, masculine scent of bay rum on his skin; the expression in his extraordinary amber-colored eyes that revealed sympathy and concern. And something else. An old sadness perhaps. An unspoken grief. His imposing physical presence and his determination and confidence made him all the more appealing. India understood his worries for the future of Indigo Point and for the entire island. It pained her to know that her situation only added to his burdens.

"Is anything wrong?"

He tapped his pencil against the paper. "I had a letter from Judge Russell yesterday. We have a trial date."

Her insides roiled. For a time, despite the island gossip, she had been able to pretend that her troubles weren't real, that she was onstage in full costume and makeup, merely an actor in a play that soon would reach its final curtain. She licked her lips. "When?"

"Last week of January. We'll need to make a trip to Savannah ahead of the trial date. I'll need to meet with the prosecutor. And I want you to walk me through that night in the theater. Moment by moment. Can you manage that, India?"

She closed her eyes as images rose in her mind—bright white limelight reflecting from the mirrors onto the shadowed stage. Arthur Sterling's look of astonishment as the unintended bullet found its mark. His blood spreading in a deep purple stain across the wooden stage floor. She nodded, her voice barely a whisper in the room. "Yes."

"All right. Tell me more about your childhood."

When she hesitated, he offered a quiet prompt. "You've said your mother died when you were born."

"Yes."

"And your father brought you up by himself?"

"For the most part. Father and I spent several years in London, working in various theaters. He had a sister in Boston—my aunt Anna. I told you about her."

"Yes. The eccentric mandolin-playing tea-party hostess. Go on."

"I've already told you what I remember about her. She died when I was ten."

"When it was announced that you were coming to Savannah to appear at the Southern Palace, the newspapers printed a story that said you began performing at age twelve. Is that true?"

"Yes. I debuted at the Theater Royal in Drury Lane. I performed at the Adelphi. Occasionally at the Queens Theater Longacre. Shakespeare mostly. Though my father and I once played opposite each other in *The Soldier's Daughter*."

"He was an actor too?"

"Many actors manage theaters and give acting lessons and lectures. Anything to earn money between engagements." She sipped the tea, grateful for its warmth and its steadying effect upon her nerves. "A life in the theater is fraught with uncertainty."

"Especially a woman's life."

She nodded, deeply pleased that he understood. "And it isn't only a matter of financial difficulties. Society thinks women are fragile and expects them to be dependent upon men, but the theater requires a different sort of woman entirely."

Philip made a few notes. "According to the papers from Philadelphia, your father was in dire straits when he died."

"Yes. But he was trying to earn more money. He was experimenting with formulations for greasepaint, hoping to standardize the various shades and sell them commercially. And he formed his own theater company in an effort to better our circumstances."

"How so?"

"Until a few years ago, so much of theater was bawdy. The plays were mostly farces that were inappropriate for families and for those with more refined sensibilities. We hoped to elevate the theater arts and broaden the audience by performing plays of beauty and substance. Plays easier to understand than Shakespeare's works. Plays that speak more closely to modern lives."

"I see. And?"

India leaned forward in her chair, her old enthusiasm returning despite her circumstances. "We were quite encouraged, because last year Mrs. Keen remodeled the Chestnut Theater to great success. She installed better seats and viewing boxes, complete with decorative hangings and baskets of flowers everywhere. Father noticed that the quality of the audience improved right alongside the quality of the venue. The Chestnut was just the sort of place where an acting company such as ours could thrive. But he had a long patch of bad luck."

"During which time he was dependent upon you for his support."

Her face went hot. Though she had often resented her grueling schedule, giving eight performances a week to support her father, living in cheap, flea-infested hotels, eating bad food, and fending off the unwanted attentions of men of ill repute, and even though she silently railed at having to be the parent instead of the child, she loved her father desperately. It hurt to admit to anyone that he had so often failed her, and himself. "He did his best."

Philip consulted his notes. "But he sold his theater company to a rival."

"He knew he was dying, and he thought he was protecting my interests. After he died I discovered he had been cheated, and the promises made to him regarding my welfare were broken."

"You were left destitute. And—"

"Enough!" Her cup rattled in her saucer. She set it aside, then rose and walked to the rain-streaked window. "Must we dwell on this? I don't see that my father's troubles have any bearing on what happened to Mr. Sterling."

"India." He came to stand beside her at the window. "I don't want to cause you any unhappiness. But you must realize that a trial, especially one of this nature, is its own kind of theater. Lawyers, witnesses, judge, and jury all have a part to play. The outcome often hinges upon who tells the most compelling story. My job is to paint as complete a picture of your life as I can. To let the jury get to know you as an individual. Not simply as the accused."

India watched rivulets of rain sliding down the window pane.

"The other side will try to paint you as a spoiled, impulsive, self-centered woman who was willing to commit murder for her own selfish purposes."

"What selfish purposes? I didn't like Mr. Sterling. I thought him vain and arrogant, but I didn't intend him any harm."

"We must prove that to the gentlemen of the jury," Philip said gently.

She looked into his eyes. They were kind eyes, the color of warm honey. "I want to testify. Please, Philip. I'm not afraid to tell the truth in court."

"That won't be possible. The interested-party rule expressly prohibits criminal defendants from testifying. It will be up to me, and to whomever we can find as witnesses, to prove that you had no motivation to murder a man you hardly knew."

"Several people knew he had upstaged me on opening night and that we quarreled over it. Suppose they think I killed him for that reason?"

"Did you?"

She gaped at him. "If that's what you think, then you have no business defending me."

"It's my job to ask. Even if you did intend harm, there are mitigating circumstances a jury might consider. Heat of passion, momentary loss of reason, mistaken—"

"I've told you what happened. Someone must have substituted my gun for the prop. I picked it up and aimed it, as Mr. Philbrick had commanded me to do, under threat of losing my job, and it went off."

He sighed and consulted his pocket watch. "All right. Enough for today. I'm due at the lumber mill at ten. Mr. Dodge has some preliminary drawings of our proposed resort to show me."

She let out a long breath, grateful for the change of subject. "Is it worth going out in this rain?"

He relaxed then. "It's nearly stopped, and it isn't far to the bluff."

"Amelia says the lumber operation is off to a good start."

"I hope so, for the sake of everyone on the island." He started for the door. "I'm taking the steamer to Savannah this afternoon to consult with another of my clients. I'll be back late tomorrow. In the meantime, I'll need a list of anyone you can think of who might make a good witness for your defense."

"I'm at a disadvantage," she said. "I don't know anyone in Savannah, except Fabienne and Mr. Philbrick. And I'm not so sure he thinks I'm innocent."

"What about others in the cast? The stage crew?"

"I'm afraid I don't know any of them very well. People think that being famous assures one of countless friends. But I have found the opposite to be true. Whether because of envy or shyness or some other reason, people like me are often given a wide berth. And I'd been in town for only a couple of weeks for rehearsals. There wasn't time to form strong bonds with anyone."

"What about those outside Savannah? Is there anyone from your days in Philadelphia or Boston?"

India shook her head. "When Father sold our theater company, many of the actors left."

"Did they say why?"

"The new owners intend to organize a tour of the West, and most of the company think it has little chance of success. Mr. Forrest, an actor of some repute, toured California a few years ago and lost quite a bit of money. Naturally, people are hesitant to embark upon so arduous a journey with so little prospect of reward."

"I see."

"And some of those in our old company blamed me for my father's string of failures." India shrugged. "Even if we could find them, I'm not certain I could count on their support."

"But surely for a lady so beloved as you, someone would rise to your defense."

"The manager of the hotel where Father and I lived for a time, Mr. Page, thought quite highly of my father. They often played chess in the evenings when the theater was dark. He enjoyed hearing me sing." She paused, considering. "In New York I knew Napoleon Sarony. He owns a photography studio on Broadway that caters to the theater trade. I posed in his studio for a couple of carte de visites. Father and I often dined with him when we were in town."

"Give me their addresses, and I'll write to them." Philip stepped into the hallway and turned toward her, one hand on the doorknob. "While I'm away, try to remember anyone else who might vouch for you. And please try not to worry."

The door closed behind him. His footsteps faded into the silence. India sat for another half hour in the quiet of the study, watching as the rainstorm weakened to a slow drizzle that dripped from the eaves and soaked the brown winter grass. Through the murky window she caught a glimpse of wood smoke rising from the chimneys of the former slave cabins, and in the distance, the gray, wind-tossed sea.

How could she not worry? After all, she was the one holding her own weapon when Mr. Sterling fell, though the actual event was a blur in her mind. She remembered her panic when she couldn't find the weapon, then the weight of the gun in her hand, the sound of gunfire. But she could not remember crossing to stand next to the wounded actor, though the blood on her costume meant that surely she had.

When the burned logs in the fireplace collapsed with a soft sigh, she left the study and went upstairs to her room to make her list of potential character witnesses. Finding no paper or pencil, she opened her door and peered into the dimly lit hallway. A series of doors opened off the gallery. Outside a door at the far end of the hall stood a pair of men's riding boots. Clearly, that room was Philip's. Which room was Amelia's? Philip's sister was rarely without pen and paper, endlessly composing long missives to her far-flung relatives. Perhaps Amelia would lend her a pen and ink and a few sheets of paper.

India stopped before a closed door on the back side of the gallery and knocked softly. "Amelia?"

Hearing no reply, she turned the knob. The door swung open. India sucked in a breath.

A tester bed made up with a pale blue coverlet and six lacy pillows sat beneath one long window. Across the coverlet was draped a cranberry-red ball gown several years out of fashion. A pair of white kid shoes sat at the foot of the bed as if waiting for their owner to step into them. On the dressing table was a forest of cut-glass perfume bottles and a black lacquered jewel case coated with a fine film of dust.

India stepped into the room and closed the door. The dull winter light illuminated a massive portrait of a young woman mounted above a black marble fireplace that had been laid with logs and kindling. The air around her seemed to thicken, stealing her breath.

India felt cold, as if she'd stumbled upon a grave.

Footsteps sounded in the hallway. India whirled around just as the doorknob turned. Too late to make her escape, she darted behind the curtains framing the window and held her breath. Fabric rustled as someone moved about the room. In the next moment, India heard the striking of a match. The room filled with the smell of sulfur and something else. Beeswax?

With her every muscle tensed, India remained frozen in

place, taking shallow breaths through her mouth. Minutes passed before footsteps sounded on the bare plank floor. India waited, not daring to breathe until she heard the solid click of the latch as the door closed.

Her heart hammering, she stepped from her hiding place. In the light cast by a brace of flickering candles, she saw what her eyes had missed before: a table covered with half a dozen smaller candles, each in its own red glass vase. And on the table, a Bible and a silver reliquary necklace. Clearly this room was a shrine to the woman in the portrait.

Who was she? And who was the keeper of the flame?

CHAPTER 8

THE FOLLOWING MORNING INDIA WOKE TO THE SOUND of voices raised in song. She threw back the quilt and padded to the window. Drawing aside the curtain, she peered out. Sunshine had supplanted yesterday's wind and rain, and now the sky was a perfect bowl of blue. Binah and Almarene were singing as they pegged the wash. Bed linens, tablecloths, and half a dozen petticoats fluttered in the breeze.

India hurried through her morning ablutions and went downstairs.

"There you are." Amelia looked up from her letter writing. "Mrs. Catchpole told me to wake you an hour ago, but I thought you needed your sleep."

"Oh?"

Amelia poured coffee into India's cup. "You seem to have had a restless night."

India frowned. It had taken her a long while to fall asleep last night. But at last she had slept soundly. Or so she thought.

"I heard you prowling the upstairs gallery after midnight,"

Amelia said. "I'm sorry you were unable to sleep. Is there anything I can do to help?"

India shivered at the memory of the candlelit room she'd discovered yesterday. She didn't believe in ghosts or evil spirits. She hadn't been the one walking the halls in the darkness. And she had not heard anything unusual in the night. But something had disturbed Amelia's sleep.

"Thank you, but I'm all right."

India wanted to know about the woman in the portrait and why the room was kept as if awaiting the return of its occupant. But she had been at Indigo Point for only a week. As accommodating as Amelia had been, Philip's sister might not take kindly to such inquiries. India sipped her coffee and cast about for a safe topic of conversation. "The weather seems fine this morning."

"Yes. Quite mild for this time of year. Almarene and Binah are doing the wash. Mrs. Catchpole is in the kitchen house, figuring out what to make for supper this evening. I'll ask her to bring you some breakfast."

"Please don't disturb her preparations. I'm not really very hungry." India smiled. "When I'm working, I rarely eat anything before eleven in the morning."

Amelia pushed aside her paper and pen. "If you want to talk about why you are here, I'm ready to listen. I know you are in terrible trouble."

"Your brother says it's a circumstantial case, but he has made no secret of the difficulties we face in proving my innocence."

Amelia nodded. "I saw the newspapers Mrs. Garrison mentioned. But you don't seem like the kind of person who would take a life. Not unless your own was threatened."

India finished her coffee. "You're very kind. But I don't think I can bear to speak of it today."

"Then we shan't," Amelia said with a determined lift of her chin. "Fan Butler invited me over to Butler's Island this afternoon. Why don't you come too? Her mother is *the* Fanny Kemble of London stage fame. I'm sure you have much in common."

"I know of Mrs. Kemble's work. Some critics have compared us one to the other. And you're kind to offer, but I'm afraid I wouldn't be very good company."

"All the more reason you ought to come. You are in need of a diversion, and word has it that Fan has agreed to become engaged to Reverend Leigh. She says he calls her 'a fair princess who entertains with royal grace.'" Amelia smiled. "I would not have expected such romantic words from a man of the cloth. But by all accounts they are equally smitten. I'm sure today's conversation will consist of even more romantic details. It could be quite exciting."

Amelia paused to help herself to more coffee. "I met the good reverend when he visited Butler's Island last winter. He preached to Fan's Negro workers, and they seemed quite taken with him too." She stirred in some sugar. "It's too bad he has returned to England. From what Fan says, the man she left in charge on Butler's has made a mess of the accounts, and now she needs to find someone to straighten it all out."

India could feel her hairpins slipping, and she impatiently shoved them back into place. She would never be good at dressing her hair, even if she lived to be 110. "An engagement is always an occasion for happy conversation. And I am grateful for your invitation. But I promised your brother I would compose a list of witnesses who might speak on my behalf when the time comes. If you can provide paper and pen."

"Of course." Amelia slid the items across the table. "I suppose that is more important than making a social call. I won't be back until suppertime, but you can ask Mrs. Catchpole for something whenever you get hungry."

Almarene came inside with her empty laundry basket and acknowledged India with a slight nod. "You need something to eat, miss?"

"Thank you. That would be nice."

The older woman bobbed her head again and tightened her knobby hands around her basket before hobbling toward the kitchen house. Half an hour later, Amelia set off for Butler's Island in her rig, the feathers on her velvet hat quivering in the breeze.

India ate the food Almarene brought, finished a second cup of coffee, and returned to her room. Last night she had been too unnerved to think clearly, but now she sat at the rickety escritoire in the corner of her room and wrote out more of the names she remembered, praying these witnesses would be persuasive enough to win her case.

When the sound of hoofbeats drew her to the window sometime later, India was surprised to see that the morning had flown. She looked down and saw Philip riding into the yard. She blew on the pages to dry the ink and went downstairs just as he entered the foyer carrying a small white box tied with a gold ribbon.

His face lit up when he saw her. "Ah, Miss Hartley. Just the one I was hoping to see." He handed her the beribboned box. "For you. A few days late for Christmas, but better late than never." He pulled off his riding gloves and tossed them onto a chair. "Go on. Open it."

India untied the ribbon and lifted the lid, releasing the tantalizing scent of raisins and spices. "A plum pudding!"

He laughed. "Probably not the kind you're accustomed to, but Mrs. Hammond at the bakery in Savannah did her best on short notice."

"I . . . I don't know what to say."

"How about, 'Where's a spoon?'"

She grinned. "Only if you join me. I've just realized that I haven't eaten since this morning."

"No argument there. I'm famished too."

Together they entered the dining room. Philip motioned her to a chair. "Wait here. I'll get plates and spoons." He eyed the silver coffeepot sitting on the sideboard. "And more coffee?"

"Yes, please."

India plopped into the chair, overcome with gratitude. She could not remember the last time anyone had brought her a present. She brushed her fingers over the box lid and thought again of the day he had rescued her from the water snake. What she wouldn't give to have a man like Philip Sinclair by her side. But he seemed not to remember their shared embrace or the way their eyes had connected as he calmed her fright.

In a moment he returned with Mrs. Catchpole. The housekeeper eyed India, one brow raised. "Ruining your stomach for my supper, are you?"

India was too delighted with her unexpected gift to let the housekeeper's disapproval upset her. "I'll still be plenty hungry by the time Amelia returns from Butler's Island."

Philip poured the coffee. "She's gone over to see Miss Butler?"

"Yes. She invited me, but I wanted to finish the list I promised you."

"You probably got the best of that bargain," he said. "Miss Butler is toying with the notion of importing Chinese workers to farm her land, and aside from her approaching marriage, it's her only topic of conversation these days."

Mrs. Catchpole set down plates, forks, a serving spoon, and linen napkins, rattling the china more than India thought necessary. "Will that be all, Mr. Sinclair?"

"Yes, thank you, Mrs. Catchpole," he said without looking up. He picked up the serving spoon and dug into the pudding. "This smells good."

"Well, if you need me, sir, you just call."

"I will." Philip took a bite of the pudding and closed his eyes, and India noticed for the first time how long and thick his lashes were. Unfair, really, when her own were so much less luxuriant.

Mrs. Catchpole clumped out to the kitchen. India took a bite of the pudding. Of course it hadn't been aged in the traditional way, but the flavors of dried fruits and spices were perfectly balanced, and the buttery concoction practically melted on her tongue. She sighed. Pure ecstasy.

"Well?" Philip smiled and lifted his cup.

"Perfection. I don't know how to thank you."

"Seeing you enjoy it is thanks enough. Heaven knows you've had little happiness in your life lately." He sipped his coffee. "Last evening I went by the theater to see Mr. Philbrick. While

I was waiting for him, I discovered the theater has a trap room beneath the stage."

"Yes. Though it wasn't needed for *Suspicion*." India scooped another bit of pudding onto her plate. "I was down there once or twice. There wasn't room at my hotel for all Father's things. Mr. Philbrick allowed me to store my trunk there."

Philip nodded. "When I asked you to tell me about the gun, you said it must have been stolen just before the curtain rose that night."

"Yes. I'm not overly fond of firearms, but Father insisted that I know how to use one. Some theaters attract unsavory types. But I felt safe at the Southern Palace, and I left the gun in the trunk."

"You're positive."

"Yes. The reticule I carried that night was scarcely large enough for my calling cards and a handkerchief."

"Who else knew where you kept the gun?" Philip took another bite of pudding.

"Fabienne knew. Mr. Philbrick, perhaps. I can't be certain. It was never a subject of conversation."

"I noticed there is no lock on the door to the trap room."

"According to Mr. Philbrick, there once was a lock. But my understudy, Miss Bryson, was terrified of being trapped in a small space and asked that it be removed."

"Even though she would have no cause to be in the room during this particular play? That's curious."

"As I said, the trapdoor was not needed."

He smiled. "I like it."

"Pardon?"

"This gives us the chance to present the jury with a different scenario. Your weapon was stored in a trunk in an unlocked room. Anyone could have taken it—either by mistake, thinking it was a prop, or on purpose—and placed it on the stage, where you picked it up, as you were directed to do, and it went off."

"Do you think they'll believe it?"

"It's always a mistake to try to guess what a jury will do. But if they like you, if they want to believe in your innocence, then all they need is another plausible explanation for what happened. A pathway to reasonable doubt."

India felt lighter than she had since the whole episode began. Perhaps there was reason to hope.

He finished his coffee and sat back in his chair. "That was delicious."

"Yes. Thank you."

"We'll have another one when the trial is over and you are declared innocent." He got to his feet. "I was thinking of riding over to King's Retreat tomorrow. Or to what used to be King's Retreat, anyway. Mr. Dodge thinks it might make a good location for our tourist resort. I'd love you to come along, if you don't mind braving the outdoors again."

"I don't mind." In fact, it sounded perfectly lovely.

❧

The following afternoon Amelia returned to Miss Butler's, having hatched a plan with her friend to reestablish the island boat races in the new year. It was a fine day, and India joined Philip at the stables. Because Amelia had taken the rig, India mounted his fine chestnut mare, arranging her skirts over the saddle. Philip swung up behind her. His arms encircled her as he adjusted the reins. He spoke to the horse, and they set off down the long oak-lined allée, winter sunlight falling across their shoulders.

He gave her a running commentary as they turned toward King's Retreat, describing Mrs. King's efforts to keep her expansive gardens—and her ten children—thriving during her husband's long absences. India struggled to concentrate on the story. With Philip so close, keeping her mind on the late Mrs. King and her troubles was difficult.

"After the war, the Freedmen's Bureau took it over," Philip said. "Mrs. King had passed on by then, and her children decamped to Ware County. A sad thing if you ask me."

They passed the ruins of a lighthouse. "More of the Yankees' work?" India turned her head to look at him and found the close proximity more than a little unnerving. She forced her gaze elsewhere.

"Actually our side destroyed it to keep the Yanks from using it to signal their ships." Philip shifted in the saddle. "Mr. Dodge thinks the wreckage is an affront to the eye and wants to finish the job, but I'd like to see it restored. It's a part of our island's history that our Yankee visitors ought to appreciate."

They rode past the former cotton fields, the remnants of out-buildings, and the skeleton of a rowboat rotting in the marshes. Brown marsh grasses had grown up between the cracks in the weathered gray planks, partially obscuring a coil of frayed rope near the bow. India frowned. The boat seemed out of place so far from the beach. But perhaps years of tidal flow had changed the contours of the marshes. The constant movement of wind and tides here altered everything in due time.

Moments later Philip reined in. They dismounted and walked the fields while he pointed out possible sites for a resort hotel, complete with a boathouse and riding stables. "That is, if we can get the Kings to sell."

"It sounds like an enormous undertaking," India said.

"It is. But the land is too worn out to continue cultivation of large crops, even if we had the labor to work them. We must find some other means of support if the island is to remain habitable."

India fell into step beside him. "St. Simons means a great deal to you. More, perhaps, than the practice of law."

"Practicing law is a means to an end. This island is my life. Or where I hoped my life would be, anyway." His face clouded, and once again India caught a fleeting glimpse of something haunted behind his eyes. "But hopes and dreams can be dashed in the blink of an eye."

"I suppose the only thing anyone can do is find a new dream to hold onto." India paused to pluck a burr from her sleeve. "I've pondered that a great deal these past few days. Even if we win my case, I won't be able to resume my stage career."

"Why not? You'll be even more famous for having survived the ordeal."

"Yes. And the last thing I want is to be famous because of my misfortune. But that's all people will see when I step onto the stage. They won't be able to imagine me as Juliet, or Portia, or any other character. Oh, they might flock to the theaters, but for all the wrong reasons. And all they will see is India Hartley, accused of murder."

"People will be curious. But perhaps after some time has passed, you can work again. Would it help if you went abroad until the furor subsides? Perhaps I could arrange for you to visit Mrs. Kemble in England. Miss Butler's mother might welcome a visit from someone like you."

"I wouldn't want to—"

"Philip!" A man on horseback tore along the deserted road, his black coat flapping in the wind. When he reined in next to them, India recognized the man she'd met in the parlor at Christmas.

"Miss Butler is asking for you," Cuyler Lockwood said. "Amelia has taken ill. Miss Butler said everything was fine one minute and the next your sister was burning up with fever."

"I'll get her. Can you see Miss Hartley back to Indigo Point?"

"Of course."

Philip turned to India. "Miss Hartley, this is Mr. Lockwood."

"We've met," the man said, with a slight nod to India.

"Mr. Lockwood was kind enough to keep me company for a while during the Christmas reception," India said.

Philip nodded. "When you get to Indigo Point, please apprise Mrs. Catchpole of the situation. I'll be back from Butler's as soon as I can."

He strode across the fallow field, swung into his saddle, and wheeled the horse.

"Well, shall I give you a boost into the saddle, ma'am?" Cuyler Lockwood appraised her a bit too closely. She wondered whether he'd been drinking again.

Though riding with Philip had been very pleasant indeed, India had no desire to be in such close contact with this roughened character. "I don't mind walking."

He grasped the reins and fell into step beside her. "Suit yourself."

CHAPTER 9

WITH MR. LOCKWOOD, INDIA RETRACED THE ROUTE she had taken with Philip. A breeze gusted off the water, stirring the dust in the barren cotton fields and bringing with it the fecund smells of pluff mud and salt.

"Appreciate that you didn't spill the beans to Sinclair about my condition during Christmas," Mr. Lockwood said after a time.

"I've seen worse, Mr. Lockwood."

"I bet you have." He raked a hand over his chin. "That's one thing I never figured out. Why a fine lady such as yourself wound up in a business known for its undesirables."

"Not everyone in the theater is an undesirable."

"No, ma'am, I reckon not. No offense meant."

She slowed her steps to secure her hat, which had blown askew in the wind. "To answer your question, I was born into the theater. It's all I know."

When they reached the turnoff to Indigo Point, Mr. Lockwood swung into the saddle. "I ought to get back to Miss Butler's. Got me a new job there looking after her accounts. I was just getting started when word came that Miss Amelia is ill."

"I see."

"I wish Miss Butler hadn't left the Negroes in charge of managin' things though." He spat onto the ground and wiped his chin on the sleeve of his coat. "She's got some fool idea that if she puts them in charge, they'll rise to the occasion."

"Perhaps she's right."

"Not hardly. Not based on what I've seen the last thirty years. But it's her land. She can do as she sees fit." He turned his horse and spoke to India over his shoulder. "I sure hope Miss Amelia gets along all right. She's a fine woman, is Miss Amelia."

India hurried along the allée to the house and ran inside. "Mrs. Catchpole?"

No answer.

India checked the backyard and the kitchen house. Also deserted. She went upstairs.

The doors along the corridor were closed, but a faint seam of light shone beneath the door of the shrine room. India knocked and called for the housekeeper. But the only reply was a sharp *click* as the key turned in the lock.

India sped down the stairs and out to the kitchen. What medicines were available for Amelia? The application of cool compresses was the only remedy that had soothed her father when he was ill. Perhaps Mrs. Catchpole had more efficacious treatments at her disposal. India pumped water into the basin and rummaged in the cupboard for clean towels. She took them up to Amelia's room and nearly collided with Binah.

"Mercy, you startled me!" India entered Amelia's room and set down the basin and towels. "Where is Mrs. Catchpole?"

The girl shrugged. "Out to the henhouse, gathering up eggs."

India frowned. So Binah was the one who had locked her out of the room just now? India fluffed the pillows on Amelia's bed and turned back the coverlet. "Miss Amelia has taken ill, and Mr. Sinclair has gone to bring her back from Miss Butler's. Please find Mrs. Catchpole. She'll be needed when they arrive."

Binah cocked her hip and regarded India with sharp and spiteful eyes. "I don't got to take orders from you."

India spoke through clenched teeth. "Think of it not as an order but as a request. For Miss Amelia's sake. Not for mine. We need whatever medicines are available to help fight a fever."

Binah didn't move. "Won't do no good. Miss Amelia might die anyway."

"She won't die. She can't be all that sick. She was fine this morning."

Another shrug. "Me and Mama heard the hooty owl last night right outside this window. Hooty owl screech like that, means somebody goin' to die. Unless somebody takes the spell off. But sometimes, the spell is too strong."

"That's just a superstition, Binah. Owls don't cast spells on people."

"That's all you know. Hooty owl screeched outside my grand-mama's window last spring, and she was dead 'fore sundown."

"It was a sad coincidence, that's all." India parted the curtain and looked out. She didn't believe in Binah's nonsense, and yet the girl's talk of owls and death and spells was making her nervous.

"'Course, Miss Amelia might have a chance," Binah went on, "if I put the pokers in the fires." Binah indicated the fireplace.

"Pokers make the owl stop screechin', and then Death don't know where to look for you."

"Well, that's a comfort," India muttered.

Downstairs the door opened, and Mrs. Catchpole called "Almarene!"

Binah raced from the room and sprinted down the stairs. India followed.

"Mama is feelin' real poorly today," Binah told the house-keeper. "She's too stove up to move."

"Well, somebody's got to finish turning Mr. Sinclair's collars. And there are socks to be mended too." Mrs. Catchpole handed Binah the egg basket and glared at India. "I thought you'd gone off with Mr. Sinclair."

India briefly explained the situation. "Mr. Sinclair is bringing Amelia home from Miss Butler's."

"Well, why didn't you say so? Why are you just standing there?"

"I have taken water and towels up to her room and prepared her bed. I asked Binah about medications, but she seems disinclined to help me."

"You'll find a medicine chest in the storeroom out back. Get it while I put some water on for tea."

India went out the back door and down the steps to the storage room. Inside were barrels of flour and sugar, two sacks of coffee, a hogshead of rice. On a shelf were boxes of candles, assorted vats, and blackened pots. India found a wooden chest and opened it. Inside were paper packets labeled valerian, chamomile, ginger, milk thistle, feverfew, huckleberries.

She returned to the house just as Philip arrived in the rig, his bay mare trotting behind. Amelia slumped in the seat, her head on her brother's shoulder.

He reined in, exited the rig, and turned to lift Amelia.

"Her room is ready." India peered into Amelia's pale face. "How is she?"

"Burning up. Miss Butler was already treating her with cold compresses when I got there, but we must try to get her fever down."

He lifted his sister and carried her up the front steps, then up the staircase to her room. Mrs. Catchpole followed, huffing and puffing beneath the weight of the laden tray in her hands.

Philip laid Amelia on her bed and removed her shoes.

"I've made some huckleberry and molasses tea for when she comes to." Mrs. Catchpole set down the tray and drew a chair close to the bed. She motioned for the basin and towels. "I'll sit with her a while, Mr. Sinclair. You look plumb done in."

"Thank you. I could use something to drink."

"I left you a pot of tea in the dining room." Mrs. Catchpole caught India's eye. "I'm sure Miss Hartley will be happy to pour and to keep you company."

The housekeeper's words were meant to sting, but India refused to take offense. Nothing was as important as Amelia's recovery.

India followed Philip down to the dining room and poured their tea.

"Will Amelia be all right?" She took a chair that afforded a view of the yard and the beach in the distance. The lowering sun cast rectangles of gossamer light on the brown grasses. A solitary osprey winged over the glittering sea.

Philip rubbed at his eyes. "I hope so. She's a strong woman. But fevers are unpredictable."

"Perhaps Mrs. Catchpole's huckleberry tea will do the trick."

"We must pray so." He sipped his tea. "My father refused all manner of herbal remedies until the day he died. He was of the opinion that more people die of their medicines than of their diseases."

"I don't know much about medicines, I'm afraid," India said. "My father often brewed a tea of valerian and whiskey to help him sleep. But I can't be sure the spirits wouldn't have worked just as well on their own."

He managed a tired smile. "Whiskey is often the medicine of choice around here. And too many use it to excess."

"Of course, Binah tells me that putting the poker in the fire wards off death." India refilled her cup. Despite her concern for Amelia's condition, she felt a certain peace come over her as she sat with Philip in the pleasant room, watching the winter twilight descend.

"Yes, Binah and her mother hold onto the old beliefs."

"I could like Binah if she gave me half a chance," India said. "She isn't stupid by any measure. She simply lacks an education."

"She's not alone on that score. I tried to establish a school here last year, but the whites refused to sit alongside the Negroes. Fights broke out every other day, and finally the teacher gave up and left." He stared out the window. "The day my father died and Indigo Point came to me, I manumitted every slave on the place. Some of them went with the Yankees, but most of them wanted to remain here. St. Simons is the only home they know. But right now there isn't much of a future here for any of us."

"Well, I wish I could do something for Binah and the rest too. But I have a feeling she wouldn't take any help from me."

"So many of these people are held back by superstitions that date back to the time this island was first settled."

"Binah was quite offended when I suggested that her pokers wouldn't work." India toyed with her cup, overcome with curiosity about the room upstairs. "When I got back here this afternoon from our visit to King's Retreat, I couldn't find anyone." Her eyes sought his. "May I ask you about something?"

He nodded.

"There is a room upstairs that—"

He rose abruptly from his chair, his expression unreadable. "Excuse me. I've just remembered I haven't yet taken care of the horses."

Chapter 10

INDIA KNOCKED ON AMELIA'S DOOR AND PEEKED inside. "Are you awake?"

"I am." Amelia waved India into the room. "Binah told me you took turns with Mrs. Catchpole, tending me until my fever broke."

"I was glad to do it. I'm relieved you're feeling better." India set down the tea tray and opened the curtains. Sunlight streamed into the room. "Mrs. Catchpole has sent more huckleberry tea."

Amelia wrinkled her nose. "She means well, but honestly, I cannot bear the thought of drinking another drop. What I need is a plate of biscuits and gravy. And some decent bacon."

"The doctor says to—"

"Oh, I know. But he's accustomed to looking after old folks with weaker constitutions than mine." Amelia threw back her covers and got unsteadily to her feet. She reached for her dressing gown, which hung on a peg near the fireplace. "See? I'm good as cured."

"I hope so. You wouldn't want to miss the boat races."

Amelia laughed. "With so few amusements available around

here these days, any diversion is welcome." She sat at her dressing table and picked up her hairbrush. "Before the war, we held boat races every year. Everyone brought their fiddles and banjos and food to share, and we made a day of it."

India perched on the edge of the unmade bed. "It sounds like fun, but I can't imagine boat races in the dead of winter."

"Oh, it rarely gets too cold down here. And besides, we make a big bonfire to keep everyone warm." Amelia finished pinning her hair. "I'm already looking forward to the seventeenth."

India's stomach clenched. By then her trial would be just two weeks away. How could she enjoy any outing when her future was hanging by the thinnest of threads?

"I suggested that day to Fan so I'd have time to remodel my winter dress." Amelia's eyes sought India's in the mirror. "Can you keep a secret?"

India nodded. Apparently the ability to keep secrets was a requirement at Indigo Point.

"I'm hoping Mr. Lockwood will ask me to attend the races with him."

India struggled to hide her surprise. Cuyler Lockwood was entirely unsuitable for someone like Amelia Sinclair. For all kinds of reasons.

Amelia swung around in her chair. "You don't approve."

"I am surprised. But of course you hardly need my approval."

Amelia's eyes filled. "Oh, I know he takes a nip of spirits now and then. He isn't well educated. He isn't half the man Thomas was, but since the war, there are so few gentlemen from which to choose, and I don't want to live alone for the rest of my life."

India didn't know what to say. She expected to be alone for the rest of her life, too, even if she avoided the hangman's noose. But she wouldn't settle for someone like Cuyler Lockwood.

"After Thomas died, I never expected to feel anything for anyone ever again. But Mr. Lockwood—"

"I didn't realize you'd lost a husband."

"We were betrothed. I wanted to marry before Thomas left for the war, but he wanted to wait. He died at Gettysburg." Amelia opened the drawer of her dressing table and took out a small tintype. "This is the only likeness I have of him."

India studied the image. "He was very handsome."

"He was. And he was kind, and he made me laugh. Just as Mr. Lockwood does." Amelia let out a long sigh. "I'm sick to death of being sad. I don't think I can take another minute of mourning."

India thought of the mysterious room down the hall. It seemed that everyone in this house was secretly mourning someone.

Almarene came in without knocking and plopped a stack of clean linen onto the bed. "Got you some bath water heated up, Miss Amelia. Best get in the tub 'fore it gets cold."

"I will."

"I'll be there directly to help you dry off. Don't want you gettin' sick again. Makin' more work for ever'body."

Amelia winked at India. "I'm so sorry to have caused you extra work, Almarene. I promise never to get a fever again."

"Huh. Words don't cook rice."

"Where's Binah this morning?" Amelia opened her clothespress and took out a clean petticoat.

Almarene shrugged. "Off in the woods runnin' around with them girls from Miz Garrison's place, I reckon. And that bunch from plumb up at Darien too. I told her I'll switch her good if she comes back too late to help me fix supper." Arms akimbo, Almarene frowned at India. "You thin as a reed. I 'spect you need some breakfast. Put some meat on those bones."

"Not if it's inconvenient for you."

Amelia gathered her things and headed for the door. "Give her some of your hot biscuits and butter, Almarene. That'll fatten her up."

The older woman's expression softened, and she bobbed her gray head. "Come on then, miss. I got coffee on the stove. I 'spect Miz Catchpole got the eggs gathered by now, and the grits is about done."

"Save some for me." Amelia disappeared down the hallway.

India followed Almarene to the dining room. Apparently Philip had already eaten his breakfast. A plate and half-empty cup sat at the head of the table. Almarene went to the kitchen house and soon returned with India's breakfast on a tray.

"It looks delicious. Thank you, Mrs.—?"

"Just Almarene will do."

"All right. Almarene." India buttered a biscuit. "It seems Mr. Sinclair has gone out early this morning."

"Yes'm. He left more'n a hour ago to post some letters for Miss Amelia. Said he had some important business with the steamboat captain."

"Oh? Did he say what kind of business?"

Almarene huffed out a noisy breath. "Now do I look like the kind of a person Mr. Philip gonna tell his personal business to?"

India bit back a smile. "I suppose you're right. Mr. Sinclair seems to keep most things to himself."

"Yes'm, I reckon that's true enough." Almarene's dark eyes bore into India's. "And folks who know what's good for 'em don't go diggin' into things that don't concern 'em." She wiped her hands on the front of her apron. "Anything else you need?"

"Just some time to enjoy this lovely meal."

"Huh. Biscuits and grits ain't lovely, if you ask me. Ham and collard greens, sweet potatoes and peach cobbler, now that's lovely." Almarene headed for the hall. "I got to tend to Miss Amelia. That fever took the stuffin' right out o' her. She ain't as strong as she thinks she is."

"Almarene? Would you tell Miss Amelia I'm going for a walk?"

"I'll tell her."

India finished her breakfast and lingered over a second cup of coffee. Through the window she watched the play of morning sunlight in the ancient moss-bearded trees and a flock of sparrows settling into a hawthorn bush. Despite the run-down condition of the house—the water-stained ceilings and the broken railings, the faded wallpaper and mismatched furnishings, and the unsettling, melancholy secrets that lingered in every room—Indigo Point gave her a sense of safety akin to a mother's embrace. Or what she imagined a mother's embrace to be.

India retrieved her cloak and hat from the hall tree and set off along the footpath toward the beach. The tide was out, exposing the mudflats, which gave off the odor of rotting fish. Beyond the flats lay the unbroken expanse of sun-brightened sea. A fishing boat bobbed like a cork in the waves breaking beyond the remains of a jetty. She skirted the beach and turned toward the slave hospital, the leaves above her rustling like a silk petticoat. Something about Indigo Point conjured the past. She imagined Philip's grandmother, a woman no longer young, tending to the slaves lying sick and injured within the hospital's tabby walls. She imagined the slaves, too, watching the ebb and flow of the sea, reaching toward freedom and compelled to remain forever in the same hopeless place. No wonder Philip had set them free.

Reaching the skeleton of the old hospital, India heard a chorus of young voices followed by peals of laughter. She stood in the open doorway and peered inside.

Binah and half a dozen other girls, some white, some black, were seated in a circle on the bare floor, passing a bird's feather from one to the other. A thin girl with freckles and an upturned nose took the feather from the Negro girl seated next to her. Closing her eyes, she waved the feather above her head and chanted, "Blue bird, blue bird, flyin' out to sea, who is the one to marry me?"

She released the feather, and each girl called out a name as it floated to the floor.

"Tommy!"

"Paul!"

"Custis!"

As one, the girls leaned forward to peer at the feather.

"Awww, it be Custis!" the Negro girl said.

"No!" the freckled girl yelled. "I can't stand him. Let me do it again."

"You don't get a second turn," Binah said, reaching for the feather. "The feather already said the truth."

"Well, this is a stupid game." The girl pushed to her feet. "I'm going home."

The girls looked toward the door and saw India. Everyone froze.

Binah jumped up. "Miss, what you doing down here?"

"I was just out for a walk." India stepped inside. "I heard your voices and wondered what you were doing."

Another of the white girls, the best dressed of the group in a pink satin frock, folded her hands in her lap. "It's only a silly way to pass the time."

"Because it's so dreadfully boring here," said another, a girl wearing a small plumed hat. "I hate this place. I wish I could run away."

One of the other Negro girls, an angular girl with coffee-and-cream skin laughed. "Oh? And where you gonna run to, Miss High and Mighty?"

"I don't care. Anywhere but here."

"Well, maybe when Tommy Dawson marry you, he'll carry you clear to Atlanta. Won't never see Indigo Point no more."

"Fine by me."

India smiled. "My friends and I played a similar game when we were your age. We peeled an apple and let the peel fall, and it was supposed to form the letter of the first name of our one true love."

Binah's eyes widened. "Did it work?"

"I don't think so. It was just for fun."

The girl in the velvet hat frowned. "Are you the one staying at Indigo Point with the Sinclairs?"

"Yes."

"Binah says you're a real theater actress."

"Yes."

"Miss Hartley got fancy costumes and greasepaint and ever'thing," Binah said. "I seen it for myself. I do up her hair sometimes."

"Oh, you do not," said the freckled girl. "Anybody knows a theater lady got her own servants. My mama said so. And I reckon she ought to know. She's been to Savannah at least three times. Once she stayed at the Pulaski Hotel. Had a bed all to herself."

India took a seat beside Binah. "I once had someone to tend to my clothes and hair, but she couldn't come with me here. Binah has been a great help to me."

Binah beamed, and the other girl stuck out her tongue.

The girl in the pink dress scooted closer. "What's it like, being on the stage?"

"It's hard work. One has to remember all of the lines in the play and remember just where to stand on the stage. Sometimes the theaters are drafty and the walls are so thin we have to speak very loudly to be heard. But it's also a lot of fun to pretend to be someone else and to tell a story that makes an audience feel happy. Or sad."

The freckled girl nodded. "I was in a play once. Before the teacher up and left. I was Pocahontas."

"If I was in a play, I'd want to be Jo March from *Little Women*," Pink Dress said.

"I want to be in the play too," said the older, lighter-skinned of the Negro girls.

"You can't be in *Little Women*," Pink Dress said. "There are no Negroes in *Little Women*."

India watched the girl's expression cloud, and her heart turned over. "Do you know the most wonderful thing about being in a play? With greasepaint, it doesn't matter whether your skin is light or dark. You can be anyone you want to be. Once, in England, I was in a play with Sir Robert Atwood. His skin was as white as fresh-washed laundry. But he put on the greasepaint to play a black man named Othello. And at the end of the play, the entire audience was surprised to learn he was not a black man at all." She reached past Binah to place a hand on the other girl's arm. "What's your name?"

"Flora."

"Well, Flora, if you wanted to be in *Little Women*, you certainly could be. You're so tall and regal looking, I think I would give you the part of Jo."

"What's regal?"

"It means you look like royalty. Like a princess."

"Oh." Flora beamed.

The girl in the velvet hat cocked her head. "I'm Elizabeth. Who would I be?"

India considered. "Amy perhaps. Because you have such a kind face."

Pink Dress got to her feet. "This is silly. Because there is no theater and we haven't any costumes and we haven't any greasepaint and we can't be actresses and that's that."

India was stunned to see how quickly and completely the

idea had taken hold in their hearts. How deeply disappointed they were to realize the girl in pink was right.

"I have an idea," India said. "The boat races are coming up in two weeks. I understand there will be a bonfire and a picnic. Suppose we meet here every day and practice some lines from *Little Women*. Then you could give a reading during the festivities. It won't be the same as being in a real theater, but it might be fun."

India watched seven pairs of eyes light up as if she had magically turned back the calendar and Christmas had come again. And then they were all talking at once.

"Who gets to be Beth?"

"I don't want to be the one who dies."

"Somebody dies?"

"Yes, silly. You haven't read the story?"

"Don't know how to read. I want to wear the geese paint."

"It's 'greasepaint,' Flora. Not 'geese paint.' My stars! Don't you know anything?"

"I know as much as you do."

"Where we gon' get any costumes?"

"Girls!" India clapped her hands and they quieted. "Since there are only four little women and seven of you, we will take turns saying some of the lines. Everyone will have a costume, and everyone who wants to can try on the greasepaint. But not until the day of the performance, because I don't have much of it left and we can't afford to waste it. Now tell me your names, and one at a time please."

"I'm Susan," said the skinny, freckled girl. She pointed to the girl in the velvet hat. "That's Elizabeth, my sister."

"I already said my name," Elizabeth said.

India smiled. "So you did. Hello, Elizabeth."

"I'm Margaret." The quietest of the group also seemed to be the youngest. No more than ten or eleven, India guessed. And from a family barely scraping by, judging from her patched calico dress and scuffed shoes.

"My name is Claire," said Pink Dress. "My papa manages the lumber mill for Mr. Dodge."

Binah pushed forward a darker-skinned girl with mesmerizing honey-colored eyes and the most beatific smile India had ever seen. "This Myrtilda. My cousin."

"Hello, Myrtilda," India said. "What a beautiful name. How old are you?"

The girl shrugged. "Dunno."

"Yes, you do," Binah prompted. "You be eleven come June."

"Miss Hartley?" Claire said. "I have the whole first half of *Little Women* in my room at home. I got it for Christmas last year. I can bring it tomorrow if you wish."

"That would certainly save time," India said. "Otherwise I'd have to send to Savannah and hope to find a copy in the bookstore there."

Claire twirled around, belling her pink skirt. "I'm so excited I could just spit!"

"Well don't spit on me." Flora headed for the open doorway. "I got to go."

"Me too," Binah said. "Mama will switch me good if I stay away too long."

Elizabeth drew a small notebook from her pocket. "What time do we come tomorrow, miss? I must write it in my calendar."

"Oh, of course!" her sister said. "Because you have so many things to do you can't possibly remember them all."

"You're only jealous because Papa gave me the calendar for Christmas and not you."

"Jealous of a silly old notebook?"

India placed a hand on each girl's shoulder. "No quarreling. That's my first rule. Break the rules and you won't be allowed to try on the greasepaint. Understood?"

"Yes, miss," Elizabeth said. "But what time?"

"Can you all be here at ten?"

The girls nodded.

"All right. I'll see you tomorrow. Shall we keep this a secret, so we can surprise everyone at the boat races?"

Margaret, the quiet one in the patched calico, beamed at India and whispered, "I love secrets."

"Me too," India whispered back.

India watched as they hurried from the old hospital and disappeared along the footpath. She set off in the opposite direction, skirting the old slave cemetery and the sharecroppers' cabins. She reached the wooden footbridge spanning the shallow river and hurried across, one eye out for snakes and alligators. Today the water ran fast and so clear that she could see the rocky bottom and patches of brown fern undulating in the current.

The path grew more narrow, the trees more dense and overgrown as she approached the charred remains of the chapel that Philip's grandfather had built. Though it was not yet noon, a deepening gloom blotted out the sky. Beneath her feet the dead leaves and brittle vines seemed to whisper a warning. Gazing at the blackened bricks and crooked chimney, India shivered. She couldn't give it a name, but she could feel something dark and foreboding gathering there, waiting in the shifting shadows.

CHAPTER 11

THE ENTIRE HOUSEHOLD WAS UP EARLY, PREPARING FOR
the boat races. Even before first light, India heard the faint squeak
of the kitchen door as Mrs. Catchpole went to gather eggs, then
the voices of Almarene and Binah as they arrived for their morning chores. Soon Philip's footsteps sounded below, followed by
Amelia's. The smells of bacon and coffee wafted up the stairs.

India rose, washed her face in the frigid water, and managed
to fashion her hair into an approximation of her famous coiffure.
Into the large drawstring bag she often carried to theaters, she
put her hand mirror and her precious stores of greasepaint and
lip pomade, and added a few things for embellishing the girls'
Little Women costumes—a ruffled shirtwaist, a prim lace collar,
a set of jet hair combs.

She was almost as excited as her young charges, who had
spent the past two weeks arguing over lines, worrying about
their costumes, and finally, settling down to memorize passages
from Louisa May Alcott's beloved book. In the end, Flora had
proved too shy to actually take part, but she had come every day
to the old hospital to listen to her friends learn their lines.

The girls had blossomed under India's direction, growing more confident each day. During one practice, Claire had declared her desire to become a stage actress. Elizabeth, who wore her velvet plumed hat every day, wanted to live in Savannah and own a hat shop. Binah's cousin Myrtilda wanted to raise horses.

India finished packing her bag and released a contented sigh. Even if none of their dreams came true, for this one day, the girls would experience a small taste of adventure and possibility. For India, being able to provide a glimpse of a different kind of life was the highest calling of her art. Whatever happened when her trial opened in two weeks' time—if she was to be denied her freedom, perhaps even her life—at least she would have the satisfaction of knowing that she had had some small, positive influence on these young girls.

With a final glance into the cheval mirror, she picked up her bag and cloak and went downstairs.

"There you are." Amelia met India at the bottom of the stairs, as if she had been awaiting her arrival. "Just leave your things in the hallway, and Philip will pack them into the rig. If he can find room."

Amelia laughed, and India smiled, too, relieved to see her friend looking more like her old self, the last vestiges of the fever finally gone.

"I hope you won't be afraid of my driving," Amelia said, motioning India toward the table where breakfast waited. "You'll be with me and Mrs. Catchpole in the rig. Philip will take his horse."

They took their places at the table. Binah appeared and

poured coffee. India winked at her, and the girl ducked her head and smiled. India hadn't really expected the girls to be able to keep a secret for two solid weeks, but if anyone had broken the code of silence, India had no inkling of it. Binah looked as if she would burst if she had to keep quiet much longer.

Philip arrived, having seen to the horses. "Good morning, India. Amelia."

His smile made her heart turn over. This morning, in brown woolen trousers and a matching jacket, his dark hair curling over his collar, he looked boyish and excited about the day ahead. She searched his face, longing for the closeness of that moment by the river, but he seemed bent on keeping her at a polite, professional distance.

He plopped into the chair opposite hers and motioned to Binah. "Some of that excellent coffee, if you please, Binah."

"Yessir."

"Where's your mother this morning?" Philip buttered a biscuit.

"Back at the house, gettin' ready for the boat races. Packing up our dinner." Binah filled his cup and set the coffeepot down.

"You be sure and remind your mama to bring along her warmest coat, Binah. It's chilly this morning. The cold isn't good for her rheumatism."

"Yessir, I know it. Mama walked over here this mornin' to help Miz Catchpole fix your dinner."

He grinned. "Is that so? Care to tell me what we're having? I hope it's fatback and cornpone."

Binah giggled. "I ain't tellin', Mister Philip. You just got to come on and be surprised."

Mrs. Catchpole loomed in the doorway. "Binah, if you have so much time on your hands that you can stand there laughing like a complete lunatic, come on out to the kitchen and help me pack up the beef stew and biscuits."

"Uh-oh," Philip said to the girl, "Binah, your secret is out."

"That's all you know!" With a saucy grin, Binah turned and followed the housekeeper out to the kitchen house.

Philip regarded India with a raised brow. "What has put that child in such an agreeable mood?"

"She's excited about the boat races and the picnic." India polished off a bite of biscuit slathered with butter and blackberry jam. "And I've been working with her and a few of the island girls on a special event for today. It's to be a surprise."

"Ah. I see."

Amelia nibbled on a slice of bacon. "I thought you were up to something, India. I've hardly seen you at all these past couple of weeks. I was beginning to think you had tired of Indigo Point and of my scintillating company."

"Not at all. The whole thing was spontaneous, but I won't deny it has given me a sense of purpose, and it has taken my mind off the trial."

Philip regarded her from across the table, his expression thoughtful. "I've had letters from your friends in Philadelphia and New York. They vouch for your character absolutely and are distressed by your troubles. The photographer in particular is outraged that such an accusation should be lodged against you."

"Mr. Sarony was very kind to both my father and me. He always told me I was a pleasure to photograph. And I enjoyed posing for him. Somehow, he was able to help me relax before the camera. The pictures are better for it, I think."

"But not as beautiful as India in person," Amelia said.

"I couldn't agree more." Philip smiled at India as he lifted his cup.

His words sent a frisson of pleasure through her. She smiled and refilled her own cup.

Philip finished his eggs and got to his feet. "Please excuse me. I should see if Mrs. Catchpole is ready for me to pack the rig."

As if on cue, the mantel clock in the parlor chimed. Amelia reached across the table and patted India's hand. "We ought to get going too. We don't want to be late for your surprise."

Half an hour later, they set off along the road, Amelia at the reins of the smart little rig, India and Mrs. Catchpole wedged in beside her. At their feet were blankets, dinner baskets, and India's drawstring bag. The morning wind was sharp off the ocean. India burrowed into her cloak, her eyes on the thick forest lining the road. Now and then through the trees she glimpsed patches of blue sky and brown river, abandoned slave cabins, stands of amber-colored marsh grasses, and fallow fields.

As they neared Butler's Island, others joined them on the road. Philip, riding ahead on a chestnut mount, called out greetings to the lumber mill workers, sharecroppers both Negro and white. It seemed to India that he knew everyone on the island, and they knew him.

They reached a large clearing, and Amelia pulled up next to a line of wagons, rigs, and carts. Women in cloaks and warm hats gathered near the place where logs had been placed for the bonfire. Children raced among the trees, their voices rising on the wind. Men in heavy coats and gloves tended to half a dozen boats bobbing in the wide Altahama River. Good-natured teasing filled the air. Philip dismounted and went to join the men.

A couple of young men brought out a fiddle and a banjo, and the music began. A group of young boys found a stick, drew a circle in the dirt, and began a game of marbles.

Claire and Elizabeth raced over to India. "Miss Hartley?" Claire's blue eyes fairly danced with excitement. "When can we have our play? Can we be first, before the races? Because I don't think I can keep our secret for another minute!"

"Where are Susan and Margaret?" India asked. "And has anyone seen Myrtilda? We can't start without her." India glanced around the clearing. She recognized Mrs. Garrison, Mrs. Taylor, and several of the others who had attended the Christmas reception at Indigo Point. The women seemed as disapproving and distant as ever. But there was nothing India could do about it. "I don't think Binah is here yet either."

"Don't worry. We'll find them," Elizabeth said. "Come on, Claire."

The girls moved off as Amelia arrived to spread a heavy blanket on the cold ground near the newly ignited bonfire. Logs sizzled and popped as the flame caught and rose into the chilly air.

Amelia let out a long sigh. "Mr. Lockwood isn't here."

"Maybe he'll be along later." India indicated the group of men standing at the river's edge near the tethered boats. "He's probably seeing to the last-minute details."

"Maybe." Amelia patted her hair. "I'd hate to think I went to the trouble of doing up my hair just to impress old Mr. Hornbuckle." She indicated a wizened man in tattered denim pants and a flannel work shirt who stood warming his backside before the fire. "He had the temerity to wink at me when I walked by just now."

India smiled. "You have an ardent admirer then."

"Oh, you can laugh," Amelia said. "You have thousands of admirers. For us mere mortals, attracting the attention of a suitable gentleman is much more difficult."

India stared into the fire. "Admirers, yes, but in the same way one might admire a painting or a piece of sculpture. No one wants to claim me for his own."

Amelia patted India's gloved hand. "Don't worry. When we are as old as Almarene, we'll live together in a falling-down house with a passel of cats. Children will tell fanciful tales of our haunted house. On Halloween we'll be the most popular ladies in town."

"I can hardly wait."

Amelia grinned. "That's the spirit."

India looked up to see her young actresses coming across the clearing, Claire and Susan in the lead, Binah and Myrtilda bringing up the rear.

"Miss Hartley," Susan said, "we're all here now. And we can't keep the secret one minute longer." The girl punched her sister's shoulder. "Elizabeth nearly spilled the beans to Mr. Sinclair just now. And that would have spoiled everything!"

"All right. Let me get my things, and we'll meet behind that row of wagons over there."

"So nobody can see us putting on the greasepaint," Margaret said.

India followed the girls across the clearing, which had grown crowded as more of the island residents gathered for the boat races. She retrieved her drawstring bag from the Sinclairs' rig and began helping the girls with their makeup.

Claire, who was already blond and fair, needed only a bit of rose-colored greasepaint on her cheeks to transform her into pretty and ladylike Amy March. Tall, thin, and brown Myrtilda became the tomboy Jo. Elizabeth and Binah, who had decided greasepaint was not so bad after all, were to take turns as Meg, while Susan and Margaret shared the role of Beth. India completed their transformations and let them take turns looking at the results in her hand mirror.

"I look just like myself, only prettier," Claire said. "I wonder where I can get some greasepaint of my own."

Myrtilda frowned at her image. "I don't look like myself at all."

"That's the point, when one is in a play," India said. "I think you make a spectacular Jo. Do you remember your first line?"

"'Christmas won't be Christmas without any presents,'" Myrtilda quoted.

India studied her little group and felt her heart expanding. They were so full of excitement and high hopes. So innocent of the many ways life could cut them down. She looked away before they could see her sudden tears, then said a silent prayer for their protection.

"Very good. Now you all wait here while I introduce our play. I'll wave to you when it's time to make your grand entrance."

India returned to the clearing and spoke to the two young musicians, who nodded and launched into a version of a fanfare that ended with a piercing squeak of the fiddle. She looked around for Philip, wanting him to share in the surprise. But he and most of the other men were still downriver, discussing the boat race.

"Ladies and gentlemen," India said. "Introducing the Indigo Point Theater Company in their debut performance of readings from Miss Alcott's popular children's novel, *Little Women.*"

She motioned to the girls, who raced across the clearing and took their places.

"Christmas won't be Christmas without any presents." Myrtilda heaved a long, Jo-like sigh.

"It's so dreadful to be poor." Binah recited Meg March's line, and with a dramatic sweep of her arm indicated her worn dress.

Claire stepped forward. "I don't think it's fair that—"

"Stop! Stop this instant!" A woman in a worn woolen cloak and an old bonnet pushed her way through the crowd and grabbed Claire by the arm. India froze. It was Mrs. Garrison. "What in the name of heaven are you doing?"

Claire looked stunned. "We're giving a play, Mama. Just like Miss Hartley."

Mrs. Garrison strode over to where India had stationed herself, close enough to prompt the girls if they forgot a line but not so close as to impinge upon their space. "What is the meaning of this? Painting up these children to look like hussies. Encouraging immoral behavior. Have you no sense of propriety?"

India opened her mouth to reply, but old Mr. Hornbuckle spoke up. "Oh, pipe down, why dontcha? Ain't no harm in what they're doing. Let them girls go on with their play actin'." He

spat a stream of tobacco juice into the fire. "I'm kind of enjoyin'
it myself."

Mrs. Garrison glared at him. "I'm not in the least surprised,
Jonas Hornbuckle. You are just the sort of man who would frequent theaters if we had them here. Which thankfully we do
not." She fished a handkerchief from her pocket and handed it
to Claire, who was near tears. "Wipe off your face and wait in
the wagon. I will deal with you later."

"Please don't punish Claire," India said. "The play was
my idea."

"Yes, I'm sure it was." Mrs. Garrison drew herself up and
looked at India with utter contempt. "It's bad enough that our
children are mixing with the Negroes, picking up their superstitions and fanciful stories about death and people who sprout
wings and fly to Africa. Just the other day I had to punish Claire
for walking around with a basket on her head. Because she had
seen the Negroes doing it." She waved a hand. "But this theater
nonsense is even worse. We may have lost our fortunes, but we
have not lost our sense of decency, or our hopes that our children
may somehow make respectable lives for themselves. The last
thing we need is the corrupting influence of a . . . murderer."

"Now wait a minute, Lizzie." Mrs. Taylor stood up. "When
your husband was arrested for fighting with Mr. Soules last year,
you were incensed anytime anybody even hinted that he might
be guilty of provoking the whole thing. Don't you think you owe
Miss Hartley the same benefit of the doubt?"

India wanted to weep, but she squared her shoulders. "I have
offended the very community I only wanted to help, and for that
I apologize. But I'm not sorry for showing these young ladies

their own potential to grow and learn. For encouraging them to dream."

India walked out of the clearing and down to the riverbank. Amelia found her there and threw both arms around India's neck. "Oh, my dear, I am so sorry! And yet so proud of you. Myrtilda's mother just told me she has never seen the girl so happy and excited."

"Well, Myrtilda will probably get her legs switched until they bleed, and it's my fault."

"I don't think so. But poor Claire is probably in for a good switching. Mrs. Garrison is the meanest woman on this entire island. I swan to gracious! I have never met anyone as bitter and fearful as she is. The way she acts, you'd think hers was the only family that has suffered."

A gunshot echoed through the trees. India jumped.

"That's the signal for the races to begin," Amelia said.

"You go ahead."

"Absolutely not. If you hide out down here by yourself, Mrs. Garrison wins. Mrs. Taylor and Mr. Hornbuckle came to your defense, and I am sure others felt the same way, even if they were too timid to say so."

"I hate to face the girls. It's humiliating."

"I'll be with you every second, and even Mrs. Garrison won't risk offending us Sinclairs. Her husband still owes Philip a boatload of money for defending him against that assault charge." Amelia narrowed her eyes. "If that woman dares to say one more word, I will remind her of it in the most public way." She held out her hand to India. "Come on, now. We don't want to miss the races."

India released a heavy sigh and forced herself to think of more pleasant topics than the contretemps that threatened to spoil the entire day. But Amelia was still stewing. "Honestly, India, I don't know why Mrs. Garrison has been so mean to you just because of your profession. She was certainly not so disapproving of Mr. Sterling."

India stopped walking. "I don't understand. Arthur Sterling was here? On St. Simons?"

"It was years ago. He visited us at Indigo Point a few times. Usually with a party of other people from Savannah." They continued along the overgrown path that paralleled the river. "I thought surely Philip would have told you."

"He never mentioned it." India jammed her fists into her pockets. "I'm surprised he is willing to defend me in the death of his friend."

"Oh, they weren't friends. At least I don't think so. Of course I could be wrong. My brother keeps his own counsel when it comes to his personal feelings."

"Yes, I have noticed that."

"Mr. Sterling certainly charmed everyone around here. Even Mrs. Garrison." Amelia's skirt snagged on a thorny bush and she stopped to pull it free. "She certainly didn't think he was unworthy of respect. But that's the problem with being a member of the fairer sex. We are judged so much more harshly than men. They can get away with anything."

They reached the landing where the boat racers had assembled. One of the men read out the rules, another gunshot was fired, and the race began.

Three boats from Butler's Island competed with three from

other properties on St. Simons. Amelia gave India a running commentary about the lost plantations—Couper's, Hamilton, King's Retreat—and how the men once had competed for prizes for growing the best sea island cotton, the best rice. "Now the boat race is the only thing left."

As the boats neared the buoy that had been placed downriver to mark the turning point in the race, India lost herself in the excitement of the crowd, whooping along with the rest as the boats made the turn and headed back. When one of the boats from Butler's Island was the first to scrape bottom and pull onto the narrow strip of beach, the crowd cheered. Another blast from a gun signaled the end of the competition.

All of the boaters, their clothes damp, their hats askew, clambered onto the bank and joined the others in the clearing. Old Mr. Hornbuckle shuffled over to the winning team and pounded their backs. "Good show there, boys. A mighty good show. Just like in the old days, eh?"

A familiar laugh caused India to turn. She saw that one of the winning boaters was none other than Mr. Lockwood. He seemed in fine form today. His eyes were clear, his cheeks red from the cold.

Amelia saw him, too, and hurried over to greet him.

Mr. Lockwood removed his hat and offered a courtly bow. "Miss Amelia. You're looking well. No more trouble with that fever, I trust."

"None at all, Mr. Lockwood, I'm happy to say. That was quite a performance out there today. You ought to be proud of your racing team."

"They're a good bunch of boys. I'm out of practice when it

comes to rowing, but since I'm managing Miss Butler's accounts now, I thought I should get to know the workers." He blew on his hands to warm them. "It's too bad Miss Butler wasn't feeling up to coming out for the day."

"Oh, I do hope it's nothing serious."

"Just a cough is all, but she thought it was safer not to spend the day out of doors."

Amelia drew India forward. "You remember Miss Hartley, of course."

"Yes." Mr. Lockwood touched the brim of his hat.

"Mr. Lockwood, have you seen my brother?" Amelia looked around the milling crowd. It was nearly noon, and families were headed to their wagons and rigs for the food they'd brought.

"He's helping John Taylor with his boat. He'll be along directly."

"Would you consider joining us for dinner? We've plenty of food."

"Thank you. I'd be obliged. I was so busy this morning I didn't pack a thing."

"Oh, here comes Philip." Amelia waved him over. "I'm glad you're here. I'm about to starve."

"Go find us a place by the fire, and I'll get our basket."

Philip headed off. Mr. Lockwood offered his arms to India and Amelia, and they returned to the clearing where Amelia had left their blanket. Someone had replenished the fire. The flames danced in the cold January air. They settled themselves and waited for Philip. India surveyed the crowd. Binah and Almarene were talking with a group of their friends gathered near the wagons. Susan and Elizabeth, their cheeks reddened and eyes downcast, were seated with their parents at the edge of the clearing. Mrs. Garrison and her daughter were nowhere in sight. Soon, India saw Philip returning, Mrs. Catchpole striding along beside him.

"Here we are," Philip said, setting down the basket. "I hope the stew is still warm."

He opened the basket and took out bowls and spoons, plates and knives. Linen napkins. A dish of butter. Mrs. Catchpole opened the glass jars of stew and set out platters of bread and a jar of jam, avoiding India's eyes all the while.

Finally the housekeeper got to her feet. "If you're all set, Mr. Sinclair, I think I'll go on home. The Garrisons are leaving. I can ride with them."

He frowned. "So soon? You're welcome to stay."

"I'm too cold. And I have things to do."

Philip smiled. "Suit yourself, but today is supposed to be a holiday of sorts. I'm sure your chores can wait."

"This one can't." Mrs. Catchpole caught India's eye then.

India tried and failed to read the meaning in the woman's expression. Pity? Malice? Condemnation?

"All right," Philip said. "We'll be home in a while."

The four of them ate with gusto. The stew was still warm, the biscuits light and fluffy.

Philip polished off three biscuits and two bowls of stew before peering into the basket in search of dessert. Which apparently had been forgotten.

He sighed. "I was looking forward to one of Mrs. Catchpole's pies. She makes the best chess pie in the state of Georgia."

"I like it too," India said. "It's the one thing I learned to make when Father and I stayed at a boardinghouse in New Orleans. The trick is to use just the right amount of cornmeal to form a crust over the custard."

Mr. Lockwood leaned back on his arms and sighed. "That was delicious. Nobody makes a stew as good as Mrs. Catchpole's."

Amelia nodded. "I'm stuffed as a Christmas goose. Anyone care to join me for a walk?"

India started to respond before realizing this was Amelia's way of being alone with Mr. Lockwood. And though she still wasn't completely convinced of the man's suitability for her new friend, it was hardly her place to thwart Amelia's plan. "I think I'll sit here a while and enjoy the fire."

"Me too," Philip said. "I'm still thawing out."

"I'd be honored to walk with you, Miss Amelia," Mr. Lockwood said. "On the way here this morning, I spotted an osprey's nest. Largest one I've seen in a while. It isn't far, if you'd like to see it."

He helped Amelia to her feet, and they set off.

Philip wiped his hands on his napkin and began loading the empty plates into the basket. "I heard about your play."

"Bad news travels fast, as they say."

"I appreciate your motives, India, but trying to turn these island girls into actresses was a mistake."

"Yes, I see that now. I wasn't trying to recruit them into a life of sordidness and infamy. It was only a pastime, something to break the monotony of the days."

"For you or for them?"

"I can't think about the trial all of the time. I'll go crazy if I do. Working with the girls gave me something else to think about. I feel terrible that I've upset Mrs. Garrison. Not that I care one whit for what she thinks, but I fear she will take out her anger on Claire, and it wasn't the child's fault."

"What's done is done. But for the next two weeks, perhaps you should—"

She stopped him with an upraised hand. "I'll live like a cloistered nun."

He sighed. "I'm sorry this is so difficult for you. Maybe it was a mistake bringing you here. But I couldn't bear to think of you sitting in the Chatham County Jail for weeks and weeks."

"I'm the one who should be sorry for embarrassing you. I am grateful you brought me here. Especially as my days of such freedom may be at a permanent end."

"You mustn't allow yourself to think that way. Assuming Judge Russell hears our case, we have a good chance of acquittal."

"Oh, I pray so."

"So do I." He closed the basket lid. "What will you do, once you go free?"

"I haven't let myself think about it. I would like to finish my tour. I need the money. I should have opened this week in New Orleans. But it hardly matters. I doubt the theater managers will want me to continue. So many of them have worked hard to bring respectability to their establishments. Having someone like me will only be seen as a setback."

She was aware that he was watching her closely. Her face warmed beneath his penetrating gaze.

"You love the theater."

"Yes. Of course there are difficulties and discouragements. But in that moment before the curtain rises, as I'm waiting for my entrance, the expectant silence in the theater is exhilarating. Every night I have a chance to walk out of the shadows into the light and change someone's life. To bring something of culture and beauty and promise to the audience." She paused, remembering. "The applause, the newspaper stories, the flowers at my feet are lovely, but that isn't why I do it. I only want to make people happy. That's all I was trying to do with these young girls. But I made a mess of it."

The crowd had begun to thin. People were packing up the remains of their meals, gathering blankets and baskets and children. India looked up to see Amelia and Mr. Lockwood returning from their walk.

"Are you ready to go?" Philip reached for her hand. His clasp was warm, confident, reassuring.

He picked up their basket. She folded the blanket, and they headed for the rig. He packed away their things and assisted her and Amelia inside.

Amelia picked up the reins and called out "Good-bye, Mr. Lockwood!"

"Miss Amelia. Miss Hartley." The overseer tipped his hat and headed for his own mount.

Philip swung into the saddle and turned his horse. "Let's go home before Mrs. Catchpole sends out a search party."

India's stomach clenched. No doubt she faced even more condemnation from the housekeeper.

✦ CHAPTER 12 ✦

"TELL ME MORE ABOUT YOUR LIFE IN THE THEATER." Philip tossed another log onto the fire before resuming his chair behind his desk and taking up paper and pen.

"I don't know what else there is to tell," India said. "Like any profession, it has its routines and irritations. And its pleasures."

"Let's start with the pleasures."

"Well, as I've already said, there is great satisfaction in a story well told, whether on the page or in the theater. There is nothing more enjoyable than hearing the collective breath of an audience that is surprised or delighted by a performance." She paused to sip her tea. "Seeing the expressions on their faces when I take the final curtain call somehow compensates for the difficulties."

He laughed and scribbled on his paper. "What about friendships?"

She sighed. "There is a certain camaraderie, of course, among the players. But there are also jealousies and petty disagreements, and hurt feelings when one actor gets a better notice than another. We are human after all."

"Exactly. That's what I must convey to your jury. Those men are bankers and shipping merchants and the like. To them the theater is an exotic and not altogether respectable world. I must show them that you are just like them, a professional with a job to do, and with the same kinds of concerns."

India chewed her bottom lip. "Will they believe you?"

"I don't think it's immodest to mention that I have had many successes in the courtroom. But we can't take the jury for granted." He opened a thick folder lying atop his desk and paged through it. "I've collected letters from your photographer friend, Mr. Sarony, your theater manager in Philadelphia, and the lady who ran the boardinghouse where you lived for a time. Those will be read into the record. In Savannah, we have your dresser Fabienne."

Philip studied her from across his desk. "It wouldn't hurt to find additional local witnesses. People who will vouch for your character, or people who saw you at the theater that night and can attest as to your mood and movements." He sat back in his chair. "Is there anyone you haven't already mentioned?"

India closed her eyes and recalled the details of that evening. Arriving at the theater in the carriage, giving her card to the young driver, speaking to the stagehand Mr. Quinn, then the return to her dressing room. The confrontation with Mr. Philbrick regarding the fateful script change. Fabienne's arrival, followed by that of Mr. Sterling and India's understudy. The young actress had latched onto Mr. Sterling's arm and whispered in his ear just before they left.

"My understudy, Victoria Bryson, was there. She and Mr. Sterling were quite enamored with one another."

Philip made a note. "Good. We'll talk to her."

India remembered the strange woman who had lingered outside her dressing room door before disappearing like an apparition into the darkened hallway.

"There was someone else."

Philip sat up, instantly alert. "Someone else backstage?"

"Yes. In the hallway outside my dressing room. She was watching Mr. Sterling. But I didn't think anything of it. I've never worked in a theater in which admirers didn't try to sneak inside to get a glimpse of the actors. I assumed she was waiting to speak to him."

"And did she speak to him?"

"Not in my presence. Miss Bryson was with him. They left my dressing room together."

"Can you describe this woman?"

India frowned. "Not really. She was wearing a dark-colored cloak with a hood that hid her hair. The hallway is not well lit, so I couldn't see her face clearly. I got the impression she was rather brown-skinned."

"A Negro woman then? Or a mulatto?"

"I can't be sure. I remember only her piercing eyes. She seemed nervous, and very intent upon Mr. Sterling, but if she was an admirer of his, I would expect nothing else."

"And you didn't see her after that?"

"No. Fabienne finished helping me dress, and I went upstairs to the wings and waited for my cue."

He sighed. "Well, it's a slim lead, but worth pursuing. When we get to Savannah, I'll see what I can find out. In the meantime, I'm going back to King's Retreat this afternoon to take some measurements of the old gardens for Mr. Dodge. I'd love some company."

"I'd love that too."

He put away his files, his papers and pen. "I'll be back at noon. That should give us plenty of time before the light goes."

"All right." She rose and together they went to the door of the study.

He collected his hat, cloak, and gloves, and a few minutes later India heard the pounding of his horse's hooves on the dirt road. She wandered out to the dining room, hoping to find Amelia still at breakfast, but the room was deserted, the table bare. The smell of baking bread filled the air, and she followed the scent to the kitchen house.

Mrs. Catchpole was just taking a loaf from the oven. She banged the pan onto the wooden table and frowned at India. "Something you wanted?"

"The bread smelled so good, it made me hungry. Is there any chance I can have some?"

Wordlessly, the housekeeper took down a plate, sliced the steaming loaf, and fetched butter from the pantry. "I suppose you want some jam too."

Not if you are going to begrudge me every bite. India shook her head. "This will be just fine."

She buttered a piece and took a bite. "This is very good, Mrs. Catchpole. Mr. Sinclair tells me you are the best cook on the island. I have to say I agree."

"Mr. Sinclair is a peach of man. He gives me more credit than I deserve." The older woman wiped the knife clean and returned it to the drawer. "I owe him a great deal. I never forget it."

India looked up, surprised that the woman had managed to string together four sentences, and none of them accusatory. Surely a record since India's arrival. She took another bite of the warm bread and looked around the kitchen. Everything was spotless. Everything was in its proper place. Pots and pans hung from hooks above a deep sink. To the side was a shiny red-handled water pump. Wood waited in a basket beside the stove. Jars of spices covered the top of a pie safe in the corner. A wooden mixing bowl and a rolling pin still covered in flour sat on the counter.

"Mrs. Catchpole? Would you mind if I borrowed your kitchen for a while?"

"What? Whatever for?"

"At the boat races on Tuesday, Mr. Sinclair mentioned that he is fond of chess pie. I haven't had the chance to master many dishes, but I do know how to make a chess pie, and I'd like to bake one for him. As a kind of thank-you gift."

"I'm sure he knows you're grateful, the way you stick to him like a cocklebur every chance you get."

India frowned. Was this woman jealous? Of Philip? She was old enough to be his mother. Maybe that was how she saw herself. As his protector. "I wasn't aware that I was clinging to him. But I'd still love to make that pie."

"He may have mentioned chess pie, but vinegar pie is his favorite. He likes the meringue on top."

India frowned. "I'm afraid I wouldn't know where to begin."

"The filling is easy enough. Sugar, egg yolks, butter, and a dash of vinegar, of course. It's the meringue that's tricky."

India rolled up her sleeves. "I'm willing to try. Would you

teach me? My father always said one should never pass up an opportunity to learn something new."

The housekeeper shrugged. "I suppose I could show you how. You'll need some eggs from the springhouse."

"I know where it is. Amelia showed me."

"Flour and lard are in the bin. Don't let the fire get too hot. It'll burn the crust."

India went out the back door to the springhouse, gathered the eggs and butter, and returned to the kitchen. She measured out flour and lard for the pie crust and rolled it out. Following Mrs. Catchpole's directions, she broke the eggs into a mixing bowl, separating the yolks from the whites before adding sugar, butter, and vinegar.

India poured the filling into the pie crust. Mrs. Catchpole opened the oven door and stood aside while India slid the pan onto the rack.

"Half an hour oughta do it," the housekeeper said. "There's coffee if you want some."

She filled a couple of cups and handed one to India.

India sat at the table and took in the particular sights and smells of the kitchen—rectangles of winter sunlight falling across wide cypress planks permeated with years of wood smoke and coffee, the freshly baked bread still cooling on the wooden table. The mellow scent of custard as the pie began to bake.

Mrs. Catchpole sipped her coffee, her pale gray eyes watchful as a cat's. "I heard you and Miss Amelia talking an' carrying on last night. Something sure seemed to amuse the two o' you."

"I was telling her about the time I was in *King Lear* in London opposite Thomas Abbott. In the middle of a very serious scene, his wig came unglued, and every time he turned his head, his wig would spin around and cover up his eyes. Finally he reached up and tore it off his head and stomped it as if it were a rat. The theater manager was outraged, but the audience loved it."

Mrs. Catchpole reared back and let go a belly laugh so unexpected that India jumped. "I ain't much of a theatergoer, but I woulda paid money to see that."

For the first time since arriving at Indigo Point, India found herself relaxing in the woman's presence. "It was funny. I had to bite my lip to keep from laughing along with the audience. And then a few weeks later, Father and I were acting in a comedy. At the end of the first act, he was supposed to exit through a door at the rear of the stage. He delivered his line, which was very dramatic: 'I'm leaving, and nobody can stop me!' Then he went to the door to make his exit. And it was locked."

Mrs. Catchpole listened, spellbound. "Mercy. What did he do?"

India laughed at the memory. "I was struck with panic, but Father whirled around, came back downstage, and said, 'But before I go, there's one more thing!'"

"That was clever." Mrs. Catchpole chuckled and poured more coffee.

"It was very clever. Since the play was a comedy, the audience assumed the locked door was part of the act. But of course Father complained mightily to the stage manager, who was most apologetic. After he stopped laughing."

The housekeeper shook her head. "I reckon it must be a strange kind o' life, bein' in the theater, travelin' around from pillar to post. Must feel kinda like a boat tossing around in the sea without any moorings."

"It doesn't seem strange to me, but I can see how it might seem so to others." India finished her coffee. "In the old days Father and I traveled with the Morettis, an acting troupe from Italy. They fought and teased one another and played jokes, but there was never any doubt of their love for each other. For a while, they shared that love with Father and me. They were the only family we knew. I miss them still. I miss having a family around me. I miss not having friends."

"Huh. What will happen when you get old?" Mrs. Catchpole crossed her arms. "Who will look after you then?"

India looked away. Even before Father died she'd worried about the day when some new young actress would supplant her in the public's affections. When her beauty faded and the applause stopped. But she couldn't worry about that. She was too consumed by the very real possibility that she might not have a future at all.

"I should check on the pie." India opened the oven door, releasing the rich smells of custard and warm crust. She grabbed a thick towel to protect her hand while she gave the pan a gentle shake. She turned to the housekeeper. "I think it's done."

"Let me take it out. You don't want to burn yourself." Armed with two towels, Mrs. Catchpole lifted the pie and set it on the window sill. "There now. We'll let it cool just a bit before we make the meringue. By the time suppertime gets here, it ought to be just right." She smiled at India. "The perfect surprise for Mr. Sinclair. Just like you wanted."

"I hope he will enjoy it." India headed for the door. "Could you possibly make the meringue? I didn't realize it was so late. I must get ready. We're riding over to King's Retreat this afternoon."

"Huh. Just the two o' you?"

"Yes. I believe so." India rolled her sleeves down and buttoned her cuffs. "He invited me this morning as we were going over my case."

"You might be kind enough to ask Miss Amelia to go with you. She—"

"Oh, there you are." Amelia swept into the kitchen house carrying her cloak and hat. She dropped them onto a chair and helped herself to bread and butter. "Ask me what?"

"Your brother and I are going out to take some measurements of the gardens at King's Retreat for Mr. Dodge," India said. "Mrs. Catchpole thought you might like to come along."

Amelia arched her brow. "And be a third wheel? I wouldn't dream of crashing your outing. Besides, I promised to return some books I borrowed from Mrs. Wheeler." Ignoring the housekeeper's dour expression, Amelia smiled at India. "It's going to be a beautiful afternoon. You two ought to get out and enjoy it."

A short time later, India sat next to Philip as the rig rolled along toward King's Retreat. Amelia's weather prediction had come true; a cool breeze gusted off the water, which today reflected the clear blue sky. A flock of blackbirds rustled in the sedges beside the road, and in the tangled undergrowth there appeared an occasional patch of violets. On such days it was hard to remember it was still January. Back in Philadelphia people picked their way along snowy streets to homes warmed by roaring fires, where they sat thawing their hands and feet, waiting for the first days of spring.

Philip seemed content with the warmth and the silence and did not speak until they arrived at the old plantation. He halted the rig, helped her out, then turned to get his paper and pencil. For half an hour they walked the old gardens while he made notes regarding the size and placement of olive and orange groves, rose gardens, and vegetable patches.

In the middle of a concentric brick rose bed, India noticed a faint patch of green and knelt to examine it.

"What is it?" Philip wandered over to stand beside her.

"I think this rose bush is trying to come back. After all this time."

He knelt beside her, so close their shoulders touched. So close she caught a faint whiff of soap and bay rum that sent her senses—and her imagination—reeling. What must it be like to belong—body and soul—to someone as fine as Philip Sinclair?

The sun pressed onto her head like a benediction. Something about being with Philip felt right. She watched him from the corner of her eye. Was this what falling in love was like? This strange, weightless sensation, this heightened awareness of his every movement? Or were these feelings the result of her need for protection and reassurance?

He took off his glove and gently probed the tender plant. "This must have been one of the first roses Mrs. King ever planted. I remember her telling my grandmother about some new specimens she planned for her paved garden."

"If it does come back, perhaps Mr. Dodge will give it a place of honor in the new gardens. A tribute to Mrs. King."

"What a lovely thought." He held out his hand and drew her to her feet.

India's breath caught, and a tremble went through her. Yes, she was definitely falling. She just hoped for a soft landing.

Philip inclined his head. "I want to walk back to the rear of the property to check on the old dependencies. Some were made of cypress, and the wood may still be useable."

"Is it far?"

"Too far for you in those shoes, I'm afraid."

He had noticed her shoes?

"Will you be all right here for a little while?" he asked. "I won't be gone more than half an hour. Then we'll start for home."

She was disappointed at being apart from him even for a moment, but of course she couldn't say so. "I'll be fine. Maybe I'll find some more roses."

She watched him stride through the tangled vines and brambles until he was lost from view. For a few minutes she wandered among the overgrown garden plots, but nothing else was alive. King's Retreat seemed a place of lost dreams, and the thought depressed her. Father often said that misfortune subdued small minds, while great minds rose above it. But some misfortunes were beyond overcoming.

The horse whinnied, and she retraced her steps, skirting patches of brambles until she reached the road. Shading her eyes, she searched for Philip, but he was nowhere in sight. She patted the horse and was rewarded with a warm snuffle that made her laugh. "Oh, you are a dear. Too bad I don't have an apple for you."

Minutes passed. Bees buzzed in the undergrowth. An osprey wheeled overhead. India sighed, wishing Philip would hurry. A few minutes more and she set off along the narrow path they had ridden on their first visit. If she remembered correctly, it led to the rear of the house, then past the remains of the outbuildings before angling toward the tidal creek. She would wait for him there.

The path curved and soon was nearly obscured by tall stands of marsh grass. Here the ground turned damp and spongy, and India realized too late that her shoes were probably ruined.

A patch of gray in the marsh grasses caught her eye. Moving closer she saw that it was the abandoned rowboat she had seen on their earlier trip. The oarlocks were rusted and broken. A coil of rotted rope lay in the stern. She was about to turn away when a gleam of metal beneath the coil of rope caught her eye. She lifted her hem and stepped into the boat. The rotted wood gave beneath her weight, and she felt the scrape of the jagged edge on her ankle and the trickle of blood in her stocking. She lifted the rope. A rusty metal box was wedged into the stern next to what seemed to be the remains of a woolen garment. She pried open the box. Inside, wrapped in an oilcloth, was a small leather book.

"India?" Philip's voice came to her on a gust of wind.

Startled, she tucked the book into her pocket and returned to the path in time to see him just rounding the house.

She hurried to meet him, the raw scrape on her ankle pulsing painfully with every step.

"I looked for you in the garden," he said.

"I'm sorry. There wasn't much else to see, so I took a walk."

"We ought to get back. I want to organize these notes for Mr. Dodge before supper."

She almost told him then about the book she'd just found, but he seemed intent on his work. And it probably wasn't a very interesting book anyway. Otherwise whoever owned the boat wouldn't have left it behind. She looked up to see that Philip had stilled and was watching her intently. Everything seemed magnified—the determined song of a cardinal in the trees, the play of sunlight across his shoulders, the faint jingle of the horse's harness. The void in her soul waiting to be filled.

She turned toward the rig. He stopped her with a hand on her shoulder and a single word. "India."

He took her face in his hands and kissed her, a warm, slow meeting of lips that stole her breath. When they drew apart he regarded her with an expression she couldn't quite fathom. Was he sorry for her? Embarrassed that he had let the moment overwhelm them both?

"Philip?"

He made a small noise in his throat. "I shouldn't have done that."

Regret then. She bit her lip.

He smiled. "But I can't say I'm sorry. Are you?"

"No." She slipped her hand into his, and they returned to the rig. "Though I never can tell just what you are thinking."

He grinned as he handed her into the rig. "I was thinking about how pretty you look in that hat."

"Thank you."

"And about something my father used to say: 'Where there is ruin, there's hope for treasure.'" He settled himself beside her and picked up the reins.

She glanced at him. "Are you referring to me, or to Indigo Point?"

"You're far from a ruin." He flicked the reins.

Unsure of how to respond, she changed the subject. "King's

Retreat is still beautiful. Did you find what you were looking for?"

"A few old buildings that might yield a bit of useable material." He turned to smile down at her. "How about you? Any more roses?"

"I'm afraid not." She sighed. "I hope the one we found today survives."

"We'll keep an eye on it and hope a freeze doesn't get to it before spring." He guided the rig around a deep rut in the road. "In the meantime, I need a good meal. I wonder what Mrs. Catchpole has made for dinner."

✑ CHAPTER 13 ✑

PHILIP LEANED BACK IN HIS CHAIR AND DABBED HIS lips with his napkin. "That stew was good."

Amelia chewed and swallowed the last of her biscuit. "Nobody makes a better stew than Mrs. Catchpole. Don't you agree, India?"

"I do. It's particularly comforting on a chilly evening."

Throughout the meal India had watched Philip from beneath lowered lashes, hoping he would send her a look, a gesture, some private sign that he remembered their kiss. That they were beginning to belong to each other. But he hadn't.

She turned her eyes to the fading light glimmering through the trees, casting a golden glow across the beach, the end of as perfect a day as she had known since arriving here. There wasn't much that excited her these days, so fraught as they were with worry, but as they waited for Mrs. Catchpole to bring in the vinegar pie, India felt her anticipation rising. She could do so little to repay Philip for everything he was doing for her. To see him enjoying food that she had made for him—well, all but the meringue—would bring her a rare sense of pleasure and well-being.

The door to the dining room swung open and Mrs. Catchpole came in, Binah walking behind her. Binah set down a stack of plates before lighting the lamp and turning up the wick.

Mrs. Catchpole glanced at India before serving wedges of the pie. "Here's dessert, Mr. Sinclair."

"It looks good. You've outdone yourself, Mrs. Catchpole."

"Oh, I can't take credit. It was Miss Hartley made the pie, just for you." Mrs. Catchpole motioned to Binah, and they left the dining room.

Philip's smile warmed India like a thousand suns. "How thoughtful of you."

"I had help with the meringue." India picked up her fork, anxious for Philip's first taste of her creation.

He took a huge forkful. Chewed and swallowed. A look of disbelief came over his face. "This is vinegar pie."

"Yes. Is something wrong?" India's heart beat hard. She was aware of Amelia's intent gaze. "Too much vinegar? It's my first attempt so perhaps I—"

"No. It's all right. I'm just surprised."

"I hope you like it. I wanted to make chess, but Mrs. Catchpole said vinegar was your favorite."

Amelia pushed back her chair and got to her feet. "I'm sorry. I'm suddenly not feeling very well. Will you excuse me?"

Philip rose from his chair as his sister fled the room.

India frowned, bewildered. Clearly she had made a mistake. She had let her guard down with the housekeeper. In the warm intimacy of the kitchen she had felt safe. *Be careful who you trust.*

Why had Mrs. Catchpole deliberately steered her wrong? She looked up at Philip. "I'm sorry. I've upset you, and I don't even know why. I thought the housekeeper said vinegar pie was your favorite. Obviously I misunderstood."

He rang the small silver bell beside his plate, summoning Binah, who arrived, eyes wide, to clear the table.

"I'm going to read for a while in the parlor," he said when Binah had gone. "Care to join me?"

But her happy anticipation had given way to confusion and embarrassment. "Thank you, but I'm tired. And perhaps I ought to check on Amelia."

He caught her hand as she started for the stairs. "India. Please don't be embarrassed. It isn't your fault. Vinegar pie was my favorite . . . a long time ago."

"Then why did Mrs. Catchpole say—"

"She's getting older. Her memory is fading. And she's like a lot of people around here, wishing things were the way they used to be."

It was like him to defend the older woman. To give her the benefit of the doubt. But India had no doubt Mrs. Catchpole knew full well what she was doing. Trying to turn Philip against her.

Philip squeezed her hand. "I enjoyed our outing this afternoon."

"So did I."

"Perhaps we'll go back again before we leave for Savannah. See how our rose is getting on."

"I'd like that. Good night."

India went upstairs, arriving just in time to see Amelia hurrying from the unoccupied room near the end of the hall. What a strange household this was.

India pulled off her ruined stocking and bathed the deep scrape on her ankle, pressing the cool compress to her bloodied skin. When the stinging eased, she readied herself for bed. Binah knocked and entered with an armload of firewood.

"Mr. Philip says it's gone be cold tonight. Said you might want a fire."

The girl knelt before the fireplace, added a couple of logs, touched a match to the kindling. The room glowed with a soft light that picked up the metallic shine of her necklace. She rose and dusted off her hands. "That'll keep you warm till mornin', I reckon."

"Yes, thank you, Binah."

"Can I ask you somethin'?"

"Of course."

"How come you don't like Miz Catchpole?"

"What makes you think that?"

"'Cause you was frownin' at her when we served supper tonight."

"Was I? I suppose I was thinking about something else."

Binah cocked one hip and grinned. "Like Mr. Philip?"

"Maybe a little bit. I have a lot to think about these days."

The girl nodded. "Miz Garrison told Mama they might hang you for murderin' that man in Savannah. But Mr. Lockwood told her she crazy. He said Georgia ain't sent a woman to the gallows in more than a hundred years. And anyway, they usually hang black folks, not people like you. Then he said if anybody can get you off, it's Mr. Philip. He said Philip Sinclair is the best lawyer in the whole state of Georgia. He said it must cost a fortune to hire somebody like him."

"I suppose it does."

"How much?"

"I don't know, Binah."

"More than a hundred dollars?"

"I would guess so, yes." India watched the fire dancing in the grate. "Why so many questions? Are you in some kind of trouble?"

"Who, me? No, miss." Binah touched the golden necklace at her throat. "Next week is Hannah June's birthday. I always miss her extra bad ever' time that day roll around. If I had me a lawyer maybe he could find her for me. Convince her to come on back home. What happened wasn't her fault."

"I thought you said she merely decided to run away."

"No, miss. She wasn't merry at all. But she—"

"Binah!" Mrs. Catchpole loomed in the doorway. "What in the name of heaven is taking you so long?"

The girl fled. Without a word, the housekeeper followed, her steps heavy on the wooden stair.

India lit the lamp, retrieved the small book she'd found in the abandoned boat, and retreated to her warm bed. Perhaps a few minutes spent engrossed in a story would calm her thoughts. She opened the book and saw that it wasn't a novel at all, but rather a series of notes written in two distinct hands and with two colors of ink. One a faded red, the other black and smudged here and there.

BLACK INK: You cannot know how often I have thought
  of you since our parting.

RED INK: And you cannot know what happiness your

presence has brought to this dreary place. Can you come again? Send your answer and leave it. You know the place. Be careful.

BLACK INK: What happiness is unleashed in my humble heart to know that you wish for my company. Thursday next? You must tell me where to get some red ink.

RED INK: Thursday cannot come soon enough. As for the red ink, I learned to make it myself from necessity. It comes from the sap of gall-oak nuts.

BLACK INK: You amaze me with your—HERE, INDIA PAUSED AS AN INK BLOT OBSCURED AN ENTIRE LINE. THEN—Wicked purpose and malignant mischief. What could not be achieved by valor was achieved by privation. But let us speak no more of it.

India flipped to the next page, which was torn and splotched with ink.

BLACK INK: In the lemon grove?

RED INK: Such wild declarations! They touch me much more profoundly than is good for me. Surely you know how strong is my admiration, and how wrong it is of you to exact such a promise in the face of my circumstances. And why I must not see you again.

BLACK INK: I will not apologize for my intemperate declarations, for they come from a place of tender and holy affection which I cannot live without.

RED INK: Oh, it is all so hopeless! I am thinking of
oleander leaves. Castor beans and foxglove leaves.
Any one of them in a large enough dose ought to do
the trick.

The logs in the fireplace dropped and settled. India blinked.
Were these two nameless lovers willing to face death, like Romeo
and Juliet, rather than be apart? Or was one of them planning
murder?

BLACK INK: Or else a bottle of benzene and a match.
Simple enough. Tell me when the deed is done.

Another ink blot obscured the next line, leaving only two
letters, *AS*, visible. India turned to the final entry.

RED INK: Fire is bright. Let temple burn, or flax; an
equal light leaps in the flame from cedar plank or
weed. And love is fire. PS: I think he knows.

Let temple burn. India reread the lines she recognized
as one of Mrs. Browning's famous sonnets. She stared at the
scrawled initials, her heart pounding. *AS*. Was Amelia Sinclair
the author of the entries in black? Did she have something to do
with the fire in the chapel? And who was the "he" mentioned in
the postscript?

Be careful who you trust. India got up to add a log to the
fire. She had thought Mrs. Catchpole was the one to guard

against. But perhaps Amelia's sweet smile and unfailing charm covered dark secrets. India hid the letter book in the bottom of her trunk until she could decide what to do about it.

≈

January 24

India rode with Philip to the bluff to meet the steamer and collect the mail. Last night's torrential rains had turned the road into muddy puddles that splashed onto the rig with every turn of the wheels. The sky remained overcast, the sea a muted gray broken only by the dark silhouette of a northbound steamer and a lone fishing boat lying at anchor closer to shore.

Only four days remained until their return to Savannah. With the start of the trial set for January 30, every moment spent out of doors was precious to her, no matter the weather. India took a deep draught of cold air. St. Simons was a place of great beauty, but it demanded much of those who had chosen to remain. Living here among the ruins of war required tenacity, ingenuity, and a stubborn optimism when there was no reason to suppose things would improve. She stole a glance at Philip and was rewarded with a smile.

"Warm enough?" He reached across to reposition the blanket that had fallen from her lap.

"Not really, but we must be almost there. I can hear the saws at the mill buzzing."

He gestured with one gloved hand. "Just around the next bend."

Moments later they came within sight of the mill. Wagons

were lined up outside a long shed. A fire burned in a barrel around which three or four men stood, warming their hands and smoking cheroots. Another group of men, faces and hands covered in fine sawdust, were stacking lumber on the new wharf in anticipation of the steamer's arrival.

Two men in woolen capes and hats emerged from a small building and headed for the wharf as the steamer rounded a bend and emerged from the gray mist. One of the men lifted a hand in greeting as they passed, and Philip called out, "Morning, boys. Cold enough for you?"

The older of the two paused and peered into the rig. "I've seen worse. Oh, pardon me, I didn't know you had a passenger with you. Morning, ma'am."

"Good morning."

"Miss Hartley," Philip said, "this is Mr. Hamilton."

The man tipped his hat. "I saw you at the boat races last week. I was sorry your playacting with the girls got interrupted. It was entertaining, what there was of it."

India nodded, wishing he would take his leave.

"Well," Philip said, "We're just here to collect the mail. I'll walk down to the wharf with you."

He got out of the rig before turning back to her. "I won't be a minute."

India drew the blanket about her shoulders and watched the constant swarm of men and wagons and machines, listening to the whine of the saws and the occasional swear word as the men came and went.

Another rig drew up beside hers and a woman stepped out. She was tall and . . . substantial, India decided, with a proud bearing and a sharp gaze that seemed to miss nothing. India struggled to remember whether she had met this woman at the Christmas reception at Indigo Point or at the boat races, but if she had, she couldn't recall.

The woman bent to take a parcel from her rig and smiled at India as she straightened.

"Well, I swan to gracious!" she said. "Isn't that Mr. Sinclair's rig?"

"It is."

The woman bobbed her head. "Ruth Wheeler. My husband worked for Mr. Sinclair back in the day. I don't believe we've met."

"India Hartley."

If the woman recognized the name she didn't show it. "How do? Where is that precious man, anyway? I haven't seen him in a coon's age."

"He's just over there. Waiting for the mail."

"That's why I'm here. I promised to return some books to my sister in Charleston." Mrs. Wheeler indicated her parcel. "She left 'em here at Christmas and has been after me ever since to send 'em back. I never have known a person who sets such store by books."

"I'm sure she'll be happy to have them back."

The woman continued to stare, her expression open and curious. "I always wondered when Mr. Sinclair would take himself another wife. 'Course I understand how tragic it was, losing her the way he did, but my gracious, that was years ago, and it's time he should be happy again."

Mrs. Wheeler went on talking, but India's mind had not moved past the woman's erroneous assumptions and the stunning revelation that Philip had been married. Why had he never mentioned it?

"I'm afraid you are mistaken, Mrs. Wheeler. I'm only his . . ." India's voice trailed away at the sight of Philip striding across the yard, his expression grim.

"Goodness, I must go," Mrs. Wheeler said. "I don't want to miss getting this parcel aboard the boat. I hope we meet again soon."

She waved to Philip as they passed each other, then hurried toward the wharf.

Philip got into the rig and tossed a stack of mail at her feet. He slapped the reins and spoke more sharply to the horse than she thought necessary.

As they drove toward home, India chewed her lip, deep in thought. In her most unguarded moments she had allowed herself to dream of a future with him. Of a life they would build together. She had thought she knew his temperament and his passions. She had trusted him with her life's story. But now he seemed like someone else. Someone she didn't know at all. During the long sessions at Indigo Point when he had prepared for her trial, she had told him every detail about her life. And he had kept his secret. And now he was angry about something.

She shivered and wrapped herself more tightly into the blanket. "Is there something wrong?"

He indicated the stack of mail. "That thick packet on top is from the court in Savannah. Judge Bartlett will hear your case."

"What happened to Judge Russell?"

"He's taken ill."

"What's wrong with the other judge? Bartlett?"

"Bartlett is a tyrant in the courtroom." Philip glanced at her. "Our job just became much more difficult, India."

She struggled not to lose her breakfast. This news on top of Mrs. Wheeler's startling revelation was almost more than she could bear. They rode the rest of the way in silence. When Philip drove into the yard, she got out without waiting for his assistance and hurried to her room.

Morning became afternoon. Dimly she heard Binah and Almarene going about their chores, and the muted chime of the dinner bell, but she was too sick at heart to eat a bite. As the afternoon waned she grew restless and went out again, walking along the footpath that paralleled the beach, and then, drawn by some nameless impulse, she cut across the stubbled grasses to the burned-out chapel.

The thick forest enveloped her, blocking out the thin winter light. As she neared the old ruin, the air grew heavy and still. India breathed in the scent of damp earth and the river—and a foul, dark odor like a breath from an old grave. The wind chilled her skin and soughed, ghostlike, in the trees.

She shivered. Hands in her pockets, she moved among the piles of rubble, looking for—what? She didn't know. Something that would help her make sense of the mysterious lovers, the devastating fire, Philip's hidden past, the disappearance of Binah's sister Hannah June. The unoccupied room upstairs that seemed to be waiting for someone's return. Perhaps it was her vivid imagination, her flair for theater, or plain old woman's intuition, but she couldn't shake the feeling that something more than mere sentiment for a long-lost woman accounted for the locked door.

The ground gave slightly beneath her weight. With the toe of her boot, she dug into the damp, gray soil and unearthed a rusted door hinge, a broken iron cross, shards of colored glass. She knelt to examine delicate bits of amethyst, emerald, and crimson—remnants, no doubt, of the chapel's stained-glass windows.

Voices sounded through the trees. Almarene and Binah came down the path. India crouched in the narrow space between the foundation and the chimney, holding her breath as they passed by, close enough that she could have touched them. When their voices faded, she got to her feet and spotted a faint gleam between two blackened bricks. India removed her glove and chipped at the metal until it came free. She brushed away a layer of dirt and ash and felt her breath catch. This was the remains of a necklace woven from fine strands of gold. A perfect match to the one Binah wore every day next to her heart.

Her mind racing, all senses on alert, India pocketed it and returned to the house as dusk was falling.

"India. There you are." Philip stood in the doorway to the parlor as she entered the house. "I wondered where you'd gone. I apologize. I shouldn't have upset you with my talk of Judge Bartlett."

"It was unsettling." But no more so than her discoveries of the past few days.

"We'll be fine. I've tried cases in his courtroom before."

"Did you win?" She removed her hat and gloves and slipped the necklace into her skirt pocket as she hung up her cloak.

He smiled. "Most of the time. I was just going over my

notes, but Mrs. Catchpole has announced supper, and I don't dare keep her waiting. It's stew again, I'm afraid."

"That's all right. I'm not very hungry." She looked around. "Where is Amelia?"

"Finishing up a letter. My sister is an inveterate correspondent. I have trouble writing a proper note of condolence, but she can write pages and pages on almost any topic you care to name."

He offered his arm, and they went into the dining room. Amelia ran lightly down the stairs and plopped into her chair. "Sorry I'm late."

"You aren't late quite yet," Philip said as Mrs. Catchpole came in with the soup tureen. "But almost."

Amelia grinned. "Where is Binah this evening?"

Mrs. Catchpole heaved a sigh. "Almarene was dragging around here like she was half dead and not doing a thing but gettin' in my way, so I sent them both home. They ought to be grateful they have a way to earn money at all these days."

Philip studied the housekeeper, one brow raised. "People in glass houses ought not to throw stones."

The older woman spun on her heel. "I'll be back with corn pone and butter."

"Philip," Amelia said when Mrs. Catchpole was out of earshot. "That was not a nice thing to say."

"Perhaps not. But sometimes her attitude rubs me the wrong way."

"Philip rescued her from a dire situation," Amelia told India. "Her husband was a ferryman at Darien before the war. But he drank too much, and one night he went after her with a kitchen knife." Amelia helped herself to a bowl of stew. "Philip heard about it and offered her a position here. She——"

Philip loudly cleared his throat just as the housekeeper reappeared with the rest of their simple meal. She banged a platter of cornbread and butter onto the table, followed by half of the buttermilk pie she had made for last evening's meal. "Coffee's not done yet. I'll bring it in directly."

"Thank you, Mrs. Catchpole," he said.

While they ate, he described the plans for the resort, Mr. Dodge's desire to expand the mill at Gascoigne Bluff, and the latest newspaper reports of progress on construction of the Brooklyn Bridge in New York.

He stopped midsentence as the coffee arrived, then set down his spoon and cocked his head at his sister. "Amelia. What's the matter? You haven't heard a word I've said."

"Yes, I did. The lumber mill needs to expand to keep up with demand now that Mr. Rockefeller has organized his big oil company. Because Mr. Rockefeller wants to not only drill the oil, but control the transportation of it, which will demand the building of many railroad cars." Amelia's voice broke, and she looked away.

"All right," her brother said. "You were listening after all. But something's bothering you. Out with it."

"It really has nothing to do with me. I'm just surprised, that's all." Amelia toyed with her spoon. "Mr. Lockwood rode over this afternoon from Butler's Island and announced he's leaving come spring."

"Leaving Fan Butler's employ? He only just started."

"He's leaving the island. Leaving Georgia. He's going to Texas to work as a ranch hand."

Philip laughed. "Surely he's joking. Cuyler Lockwood, wrangling cattle?"

"He wants to join a cattle drive. Texas to Abilene, Kansas. He says it'll be a grand adventure."

"Perhaps it will be, at that," Philip said. "Well, I wish him good luck." He glanced at India. "You have been very quiet this evening."

During the meal India had struggled to pay attention to the conversation. All she wanted was to escape upstairs to examine the fragment of the necklace she had uncovered, then decide what to do about it. "I'm sorry. Too much on my mind."

At last, the pie and coffee finished, Philip retired to his study. Amelia and India went upstairs together.

At the door to her room, India paused. "For your sake, I am sorry to hear about Mr. Lockwood's leaving. But that doesn't mean he won't return someday."

"Oh, I don't think he will," Amelia said. "And I can't blame him. There's no future on this island for any of us."

"Philip seems to think there's reason for optimism."

"Perhaps in the distant future, but not in my lifetime." Amelia shrugged. "I'm stuck here. I have the worst luck in the world when it comes to love. I always fall for the wrong man."

India thought again of the anonymous love notes. Had Amelia written them?

Amelia sighed. "Please excuse me. I'm suddenly very tired."

"Of course." India went into her room and lit the lamp. She poured water into the washbasin and gently scrubbed away the dirt and ash from the necklace. It lay in the palm of her hand, glittering in the lamplight, a tantalizing piece of the strange puzzle that was Indigo Point.

India waited an hour after she heard Mrs. Catchpole's step on the stair before opening her door and peering into the dim hallway. No light showed beneath the housekeeper's door, nor beneath Amelia's. Tiptoeing to the opposite end of the gallery, India peered over the stair railing. The door to the study was slightly ajar. Philip was still at his desk, his head bent to his work.

In her stocking feet, India crept to the shrine room and turned the knob. The door was locked. She returned to her room for her largest hat pin, then went to work on the lock, a trick she had learned while living at the boarding house in New Orleans.

"What are you doing?"

India whirled around, her heart hammering. "Amelia! You scared the daylights out of me."

"Apparently so." Amelia, in her white linen night dress, her hair unbound, feet bare, stood in the hallway, ethereal as a ghost.

"I . . . I was looking for my hat pin." India spoke calmly and felt her heartbeat slowing. She was an actress. After all, her ability to control every inflection, every gesture, was her stock in trade. She held up her hat pin. "It was a gift from my father, and I was worried I'd lost it when I went out this afternoon. But here it is, and I'm so sorry I disturbed your sleep." India moved toward her room. "Now that it's found, I can sleep. Good night."

She closed the door and leaned against it, waiting for her legs to stop shaking. Another hour passed. Philip came up to bed. India heard him moving about his room, the opening and closing of wardrobe doors, the thud of his boots hitting the wooden plank floor, and finally the creak of the bed frame as he settled for the night.

After her close call with Amelia, India was on edge, every muscle tensed, her ears attuned to the slightest sound. She waited in the darkness until the wee hours of the morning. Satisfied that all were asleep at last, she took up her hat pin and returned to the locked door. It took only moments before she felt the lock move with a soft click. She turned the knob, and the door swung open.

The room was just as it was the first time she was here. Candles guttered in their red glass globes. The ball gown waited on the neatly made bed, the white kid shoes on the floor. The reliquary necklace rested atop the Bible.

Outside, the January wind rose, rattling the tree branches that scraped against the window. A deep silence descended. India felt as if she had entered some unholy place. Taking up the tallest of the candles, she stepped closer to the portrait hanging above the fireplace. The woman had been painted wearing the opulent gown now lying on the bed. Her delicate white hands were folded gracefully on her lap, her full lips curved upward in a slight smile. Her only jewelry, a silver reliquary on a black ribbon, rested in the hollow of her throat. Her hair was arranged into a perfect cascade of pale gold curls. Blue eyes gazed uncertainly into the middle distance, as if the woman feared giving too much away.

She was undeniably lovely, but something about her expression filled India with deep unease. It was possible, of course, that time had darkened the portrait and the artist hadn't intended his subject to look so forbidding.

India moved even closer to the portrait, trying to remember where she had seen those eyes.

CHAPTER 14

THE DOOR BEHIND HER BURST OPEN. INDIA WHIRLED around, the candlestick still in her hand.

"Harlot! Get out! Get out!" The housekeeper advanced on India, a kitchen knife in one hand. The blade gleamed in the candlelight. "You have no right to sully this room."

India's heart kicked against her ribs, but she spoke calmly and took a step back. "Mrs. Catchpole. Please put that knife down. I mean no harm."

The older woman released a harsh laugh. "All you've done since you got here is harm. It ends now."

"What harm have I done?" India glanced over the house-keeper's shoulder, praying that Amelia or Philip had heard the noise and would come to investigate.

"Oh, you know well enough. Tryin' to make Mr. Sinclair fall in love with you." Mrs. Catchpole's pale eyes went to the portrait on the wall. "Tryin' to take her place."

"I'm not trying to take anyone's place. Mr. Sinclair is my lawyer. It was completely his idea to bring me here. I'm grateful to him but I—"

"Liar! Shut up. Just shut up!" The housekeeper lunged,

brandishing the knife like a sword. Instinctively, India raised one hand to defend herself and felt the blade slice through the underside of her forearm. She cried out as blood gushed from the wound and dripped off her elbow and onto her skirt.

The woman raised the knife again. India ducked and the candlestick fell from her hand. Caught off balance, Mrs. Catchpole tumbled onto the little forest of candles burning on the table before the fireplace. Her nightclothes went up in a whoosh of flame. She screamed.

"Fire!" India ran down the hallway and grabbed the water pitcher from her own room.

Philip and Amelia rushed into the hallway with buckets of sand.

"What's happened?" Philip asked.

India ran back to the room where the housekeeper had managed to roll onto the floor, smothering the flames. But her nightgown had burned away, leaving a mass of crimson blisters on her back. She was half conscious and moaning.

Philip lifted Mrs. Catchpole and carried her to her room at the far end of the gallery, then headed to the kitchen for medical supplies. Amelia ran back to her room for more water and linens. Together she and India gently peeled away the burned fabric and applied cold compresses to the older woman's burned flesh.

India wasn't squeamish, but she felt suddenly boneless and lightheaded. She swayed on her feet.

"Dear Lord!" Amelia helped India to a chair. "You're bleeding. What on earth happened in there?"

Philip returned with salve and bandages. Amelia took them

from his hands and said, "I'll finish with Mrs. Catchpole. Look after India."

India had begun to tremble and couldn't seem to stop. She was only dimly aware of being led to her room and of Philip's gentle fingers as he knelt before her and cleaned the wound. He went to Mrs. Catchpole's room and soon returned with salve, bandages, and a glass of amber liquid.

"Here. Drink this." He held a glass of brandy to her lips, and she swallowed a sip. The alcohol burned all the way down, but it soon quelled the worst of her trembling.

He brushed her tangle of curls off her face. "Feeling better?"

"A little."

Amelia came in, drying her hands on a towel. "I've given Mrs. Catchpole a dose of laudanum. There's nothing more to be done. She should sleep until morning."

Philip lifted the curtain and peered out. "It'll be light soon. I'll ride over to the bluff and get the doctor."

"I'll put some coffee on." Amelia returned to her room for a dressing gown and went downstairs.

"Let's go down to the parlor," Philip said.

India followed him down the stairs. Was it her imagination or was he holding his anger in check? Not that she could blame him. The fire could easily have gotten out of hand. And she had picked the lock to gain entry to the room. Of course she had been aware of the housekeeper's disapproval from the very first, but she never imagined the woman would behave so violently.

Philip lit the parlor lamp, motioned her to a chair, and turned to coax the dying coals in the grate back to life. The flames caught a fresh log that popped and hissed as it heated.

Taking the chair opposite hers, he leaned forward, palms on his knees. "What happened?"

Briefly India described picking the lock to gain entry to the room, Mrs. Catchpole's finding her there, and the altercation that had led to their injuries.

"Dear God," he muttered. "She might have killed you."

In the glow of the firelight his eyes were tawny as a lion's. And as fierce.

"It was wrong of me to break into the room. But I had a good reason for doing so."

"Apart from satisfying your curiosity."

"I won't deny I have wondered about it. Why no one wants to speak of the woman in the portrait."

"My bringing you here didn't give you the right to pry into my affairs."

"I know it. I have no excuse. Except"—she reached into her pocket and took out the fragment of the necklace—"have you ever seen this before?"

He studied it. "I don't think so."

"Binah has one just like it. I noticed it because it was so unusual. She told me an admirer of Hannah June had given them both a necklace. And that Hannah June wore hers all the time. As does Binah."

"And the point is?"

"Binah told me Hannah June disappeared four years ago. She wants to hire a lawyer to find out where her sister went."

"Many former slaves went off with the Yankees. I assume Hannah June was one of them. As she was perfectly free to do. I'm afraid there's no telling where the girl went."

"But Philip, she disappeared around the time the chapel burned. I suspect Binah thinks her sister ran away because she feared being blamed for the fire." She paused. "I found that bit of necklace in the chapel today."

"I told you not to go near there. It's falling in."

"I know, but don't you see? I don't think Hannah ran away. I think she perished in the blaze."

"Or she could have lost the necklace before she disappeared."

"I suppose that's true. But there's more."

"Go on."

"The last time we rode to King's Retreat, I found a letter book hidden in an old boat near the back of the property. It seems to be a series of love notes passed back and forth between two people. At first I thought it might belong to Amelia. That she was exchanging messages with an admirer. But the last entry mentions a temple burning." She paused. "It's a line from a sonnet by Elizabeth Browning."

He stared into the flames. "May I see the book?"

"It's upstairs. I won't be a minute."

India went upstairs to retrieve it. On her way back to the parlor, she crossed the gallery to peek into the housekeeper's room. Apparently the laudanum was working. Mrs. Catchpole lay facedown on the bed, the sound of her breath loud in the stillness.

India returned to the parlor and handed Philip the letter book. She sat down and waited while he read it.

Amelia came in with a tray and poured the coffee, her blue eyes troubled. "How is your arm?"

Blood had seeped through the bandage, and the wound

burned like fire. But India was more concerned with figuring out the connection between the love notes, the fire, and her growing conviction about the woman in the portrait. "I'll be all right."

"I'm so sorry, India. I never dreamed Mrs. Catchpole could do something like this." Amelia massaged her temples. "I should get dressed and check on her."

When she had gone, Philip leaned forward in his chair, the book in his hands. "Why didn't you tell me this sooner?"

"You've been busy. And I wasn't sure it meant anything until I found the necklace."

"It still might mean nothing."

India sipped the strong black coffee. "You probably noticed only one set of notes are initialed."

He nodded. "AS."

"As I said, I first thought they stood for your sister's name. But now I believe they might belong to Arthur Sterling."

"Go on."

She took another fortifying sip. "Mrs. Wheeler told me you lost your wife to a tragedy."

He blanched and looked away, but not before India saw the grief and hurt in his eyes. He picked up his cup. "I see."

"It isn't very pleasant to think about, but suppose your wife developed romantic feelings for him."

"For Arthur Sterling? Impossible."

"Is it? According to Amelia, everyone on this whole island was taken with him. Suppose they began a correspondence. You can tell from the notes that the gentleman had declared his love, and the lady at first resisted. She writes that she can't see him again, as any respectable married woman would. But the attraction proves so strong, and the situation so impossible, that she considers taking her own life."

"Oleander and castor beans."

"Benzene and a match."

He set down his cup and stared into the fire once more.

"I'm sorry. I'm probably wrong about the whole thing. And I certainly don't want to cause you any more grief. But she would not have been the first to fall under Mr. Sterling's spell."

"Preposterous. Laura had her problems, but she wasn't unfaithful."

Laura. So that was her name. "Remember the woman I told you about? The one who was at the theater that night, waiting around for Mr. Sterling?"

"What about her?"

"When I saw the portrait in the room upstairs, I realized she might be the woman I saw that night. I remember her eyes."

"Wait a minute. First you're suggesting she killed herself for love like some modern-day Juliet, and now you're suggesting she's still alive. Listen. I understand you're desperate to prove your innocence. I don't blame you for that. But you're grasping at straws here. None of this makes the least bit of sense." He released a long breath. "Besides, you told me the woman you saw at the theater was dark-skinned."

"Yes, but if she was Mr. Sterling's . . . companion, she would have had access to his dressing room. To his greasepaint. She could have darkened her skin easily enough."

"For what purpose?"

"Everyone knew Mr. Sterling was seeing Miss Bryson. They

were together constantly. Suppose Laura wanted to confirm their liaison without being recognized." She shrugged. "Hell hath no fury like a woman scorned."

The fire snapped in the grate. A sliver of gray daylight filtered through the curtains.

Amelia appeared in the doorway. "Philip? The laudanum is wearing off more quickly than I thought, and we don't have any more."

"All right. I'll clean up and be on my way. With any luck I can catch the doctor while he's at the mill." He rose and started for the stairs without so much as a glance at India.

She could see every muscle tense, could feel him holding in his anger. She set down her cup and trailed after him. "Forgive me. For going uninvited into that room. For Mrs. Catchpole's injuries. And most of all for making you doubt your wife's affections. I'm sure you're right and there is an innocent explanation for everything. Please forget the whole thing."

Amelia looked from one to the other, clearly confused. "Forget what? What's happened?"

"India knows about Laura," Philip said. "But not how I lost her." His tawny eyes sought India's. "My wife perished in the chapel fire that night."

He took the stairs two at a time, as if he couldn't remove himself from her company fast enough.

Chapter 15

"Here, miss. Let me help." Binah opened India's trunk and began folding petticoats and dressing gowns.

India didn't protest. Yesterday the doctor had arrived with salves and more laudanum for Mrs. Catchpole. India and Amelia took turns bathing the housekeeper's burns with cold water and applying the salve to prevent the skin from contracting too quickly. The doctor treated India's knife wound with carbolic acid to prevent sepsis and instructed her to repeat the process each day for the next few days. He bandaged her arm and gave her a tincture of laudanum as well. Still, her wound had burned and throbbed all night. But it wasn't only the pain from the knife wound that stole her sleep. She couldn't stop thinking about Laura Sinclair's fiery death and the look of utter desolation on Philip's face as he related the story. Clearly he was still grieving his loss. India felt ashamed that she had advanced so unflattering a theory about his lost love. But something about the whole thing still nagged at her.

"Mama said you and Mr. Philip goin' to Savannah in the morning," Binah said.

"Yes. We'll leave early."

"I wish I was goin' to Savannah. Ain't nothin' to do around here 'cause old Miz Garrison won't let Claire and them come here no more. Miz Garrison is still mad about *Little Women*."

India folded her stockings and placed them in the trunk. Her impromptu production had ended badly, but it had satisfied a hunger in her, and in the girls, to do something that mattered. People could say whatever they wished about her, but the theater was a respectable art, and she felt lucky to have shared it with the young women.

She retrieved her slippers from beneath the bed and set them in the trunk. Philip had asked her to have her things ready to transport to the bluff this evening for loading aboard the *Neptune*. Captain Mooreland planned to depart for the city at daybreak.

Binah peeked into one of India's pink-and-white-striped hatboxes. "When I go to Savannah, I mean to get me a hat like that. Won't I be a fancy-lookin' lady then?"

India smiled. She had grown fond of Binah, even more so now that she suspected Hannah June's fate. India and Philip had not spoken further about her theory, and she had to admit it did seem far-fetched. And yet, the longer she considered it, the more plausible it became to her. She removed the hat, a small toque festooned with tulle and a silver flower, from the box.

"Try it on."

Binah gaped at her. "Me?"

"Why not?"

India set the hat on the girl's head and adjusted the angle just so. Taking her by the shoulders, India turned her toward the mirror. "Voilà!"

Binah preened before the mirror, one hand on her cocked hip. "Don't I look mighty fine, Miss India?"

"You do. So fine in fact that I think you ought to have this hat for your very own."

Binah frowned. "You givin' me this hat?"

"I am."

"For nothin'?"

"Yes. It's yours."

"How come?"

"Well, you have been a great help to me since I've been here. Pinning up my hair. Looking after my room and helping your mother to prepare meals, and making the fires and such."

"But I got you in trouble with old Miz Garrison and the other ladies at the boat races."

"That wasn't your fault, Binah. Staging *Little Women* was my idea. I didn't stop to think how it would be received."

Binah studied her reflection in the mirror. "Reckon they will ever be a black girl on the stage?"

"I won't be surprised. When I was a girl, my father told me about a play called *The Escape*, written by a Negro playwright named William Brown. It's only a matter of time before a black woman becomes a famous actress." India smiled into the mirror. "Maybe it will be you."

Binah grinned, showing a set of perfect teeth. She ran her fingers over the hatbox. "Reckon where is a safe place to keep my hat?"

"Perhaps you ought to take the hatbox too."

"Perhaps I should."

Almarene plodded up the stairs and poked her head into the room.

"Look, Mama," Binah said. "Miss India give me a hat. But you can borry it if you—"

"You done helping Miss India yet?" Almarene frowned. "I need you in the kitchen house."

"I can spare her," India said. "She's been a big help."

Almarene bobbed her head. "They's a gentleman waitin' for you in the parlor."

"A gentleman?" India patted her hair into place and went downstairs.

In the parlor stood Cuyler Lockwood. He had gone to some effort with his appearance. His clothes were brushed, his black boots polished to a high shine. His pale gold hair still bore comb marks.

"Mr. Lockwood?" India paused at the foot of the stairs. Almarene and Binah followed her down and headed for the kitchen house. "We weren't expecting you."

"Sinclair's tied up with some men from the mill. He sent me to fetch your trunks to the boat landing." He jerked his thumb. "Brought my dray."

"I'm almost packed."

"I don't mind waiting."

"You're welcome to sit in the parlor. I'm afraid I can't offer you any refreshments at the moment. Mrs. Catchpole is—"

"I heard about the accident. Is she all right?"

"She's badly burned, but the doctor says she'll recover. Amelia is with her now, giving her some broth."

He leaned against the door frame. "How is she? Miss Amelia, I mean?"

"She's all right. Tired, as we all are. Concerned about Mrs. Catchpole's recovery. I'm sorry I must leave at a time when Amelia needs help."

"Sinclair told me your trial starts on Monday."

"Yes."

"I guess you heard, I'm leaving these parts myself. Soon as I can make some financial arrangements."

"Amelia says you're going to Texas."

"I am. Much as it pains me to leave the place I was born and raised, the truth is, I don't see much of a future here, Miss Hartley. But now that the transcontinental railroad is open to traffic, the future for men like me is in the West. I aim to learn cattle ranching and then head to Montana Territory maybe, or Wyoming. Get me a little spread of my own. Make something of myself."

"A noble goal, Mr. Lockwood."

"I hope Miss Amelia will wait for me."

"Have you asked her?"

"No, ma'am. Not yet."

"I wouldn't wait too long. Amelia is quite attractive. You never know when some other suitor might catch her fancy."

"She has other suitors?" He looked genuinely stricken. "Do you think she considers me a serious contender, Miss Hartley?"

"I can't presume to speak for her. All I'm saying is that one should never postpone the pursuit of happiness. One never knows whether tomorrow will dawn fair or foul."

"I reckon that's true enough." His blue eyes held hers. "I sure am sorry that a fine lady like yourself has to go on trial. I wish there was something I could do."

"Thank you." India motioned toward the parlor. "If you'd like to sit down, I'll finish packing. I don't want to detain you."

"I'm in no hurry."

India returned to her room and made short work of her packing, keeping out only the things she would need for tomorrow's journey to Savannah. She tiptoed down the hall to the housekeeper's room and peeked in. Amelia had fallen asleep in her chair. Mrs. Catchpole lay facedown, her burned back covered in compresses. India felt another stab of regret. What if her suspicions were wrong after all?

"I'm sorry," she whispered, then closed the door.

❧

JANUARY 28

The *Neptune,* loaded with mail, lumber, and a few passengers, eased away from the landing. Ensconced in her small cabin, India stared out through the winter fog pressing against the window. A cold rain dimpled the dark river. Whitecaps were brewing on the wind-ruffled surface.

She and Philip had left Indigo Point in the predawn darkness. Amelia accompanied them to drive the rig home. India had intended to tell Amelia about her conversation with Mr. Lockwood, but there hadn't been time. And she didn't want to broach the subject in front of Philip. She wasn't certain he had forgiven her for her suspicions regarding his late wife. She didn't dare annoy him further by encouraging a romance she wasn't certain he'd approve. Amid the flurry of last-minute preparations and a hasty breakfast of biscuits and coffee, there had been little time to reflect upon her situation. But now, as the long journey stretched in front of her, she felt dread seeping into her bones. Would she ever again be free to soak up the first rays of spring sunshine or wade in the river's rushing waters? Would she be able to walk a forgotten footpath, taking in the scents of jasmine and magnolia, or would she spend her life shut away forever in some dank cell?

The steamer emitted a shrill whistle as it rounded a sharp bend in the river. In the next cabin, two men were arguing in loud, rapid-fire French. India thought of the six months she and Father had spent at Mrs. Boudreaux's New Orleans boardinghouse. On nights when her father worked late at the theater, eight-year-old India often spent time in the kitchen with the woman the boarders called Mrs. B. A dark-eyed, dark-haired woman of uncertain age, Mrs. B had dispensed hot chocolate and wisdom in equal measure, the latter delivered in a thick French accent that the young India struggled to understand.

Once, passing an above-ground cemetery late at night, India had shivered in fear. And once, preparing for a role in one of Father's productions, India confided to Mrs. B she felt unprepared and terrified of forgetting her lines. On both occasions, Mrs. B had fixed India with her black eyes and told her to cast out fear. "One drop of it will spread through your soul like black ink in your milk glass, *cherie*. No matter what, *never* give in to fear."

Easier said than done.

"India?" Philip knocked and opened her door. "Would you like some tea?"

"Yes. Thank you."

She turned from the window, relieved that Philip no longer seemed angry with her. On the drive to the landing this morning he had been polite, if reserved. She longed to recapture the closeness that had sprung up between them during their visits to King's Retreat, but perhaps he had moved now into his professional role as her attorney. He came in with two steaming mugs and handed her one.

"How are you holding up?"

"All right, I guess."

They took the two chairs flanking the cabin's single window.

"Captain Mooreland says we'll arrive a bit early into Savannah this evening," he said. "If the Mackays' carriage is not there when we dock, you'll stay aboard until it arrives. I don't want the papers getting wind of our return before Monday."

"All right." India's benefactor, Mrs. Mackay, had offered India a room in her home until the trial opened, but Philip had explained that at the end of the day on Monday, India, like any other defendant, would be returned to the Chatham County Jail until testimony resumed the next morning.

In the meantime, he had arranged with Mr. Philbrick to visit the theater on Sunday afternoon. An armed policeman would accompany them in case, India assumed, she tried to make an escape.

India sipped her tea. "How long do you think the trial will take?"

"It depends on how many witnesses the prosecutor wants to call. We're sure to hear from the policemen involved. The doctors who treated Mr. Sterling. The coroner." He turned his tea mug around and around in his slender fingers. "It sounds like a lot, but in cases such as this, where so few facts are in dispute, things tend to go quickly. I'd say a day or two for the prosecution, and perhaps the same for our side."

"So it might be over in a week's time?"

"Barring any delays."

"And after that?"

His eyes held hers. He knew what she was asking.

"A sentence is usually carried out within a month or two. But India, you mustn't think about that. Truth is on our side."

"But will it be enough? I'm the outsider, accused of murdering one of their own. And you said yourself the judge is not—"

"Listen. Even if we lose the first round, I will find some reason to file an appeal."

"Which will only prolong the dread."

"It will also give us more time to find out what really happened that night. Since the authorities seem disinclined to continue the investigation."

She wrapped her hands around her teacup. "They have no intention of continuing an investigation. They have already decided I'm guilty."

Philip didn't deny it. "The prosecutor will be brutal. He will say the worst things he can say to denigrate you, to convince the jury of your guilt. He will give them half-truths wrapped in speculation. To which I will object at every opportunity. But you must not show any reaction, no matter what the prosecutor says. No anger, no outbursts. Nothing that could reinforce the perception that you are an angry woman capable of violence."

India realized she was crying. She fumbled for her handkerchief.

He patted her hand. "You're a strong woman. And you're an actress, accustomed to controlling your expressions, your voice, your gestures. Consider this the role of a lifetime, and we'll be all right."

He glanced out the window. "Looks like the weather is improving. Want to go out on the deck for a while?"

He proffered his arm, and they went onto the narrow deck. The two Frenchmen had brought their argument outside. They continued speaking in low, urgent voices that mingled with the noise of the engine, the churning of the water, and the cries of geese winging overhead.

"You're awfully quiet," he said at last.

"I can't stop thinking about Mrs. Catchpole. She wasn't the most welcoming woman I've ever met, but I am concerned about her. I can't forget the wild look in her eyes when she found me in that room. And the time she deliberately steered me wrong when I wanted to bake your chess pie. It's as if she wanted me to fail. To make you unhappy."

"She was never the same after Laura died." Philip braced both hands on the rail and stared out at the water. "She got it into her head that Laura would somehow come back if only she believed hard enough. If she kept Laura's room just as it was. Even though she was the one who found Laura's reliquary necklace in the ashes." He shrugged. "Perhaps Amelia and I were wrong to indulge such fantasies, but we are her only family."

India drew her shawl around her shoulders. Something inside hurt her every time Philip spoke Laura's name. She had no right to feel betrayed that he had kept this part of himself from her for so long. But the abiding affection she'd felt for him almost from the beginning had only deepened since their kiss. In the deepest recesses of her heart there burned a spark of hope that he might return her feelings. But he was still in love with Laura, and there was no competing with the dead, who, because of their absence, were often crowned with virtues they lacked in life.

Philip was studying her intently. She looked past his shoulder to the noisy Frenchmen, afraid that he would read her feelings in her eyes.

"I was wrong not to have told you about Laura sooner," he said. "I thought about it more than once, but somehow the time never seemed right."

"You're like me. A private person."

"Sometimes too private. But I wish—"

"Mr. Sinclair?" Captain Mooreland appeared on deck. "You asked me to let you know when we got close to Savannah. We'll be arriving soon."

"Thank you." Philip returned India to her cabin. "Try to relax until I come for you."

He left her there. Too anxious to sit still, she paced the small space and tried to calm her thoughts. Darkness was falling, and the gaslights along the waterfront were just coming on as the

Neptune nosed into her berth. India waited until Philip returned to her.

"The other passengers have gone," he said. "And the Mackays' carriage has arrived."

Taking his arm, India stepped off of the steamer and into her uncertain future.

CHAPTER 16

FROM THE CARRIAGE WINDOW, INDIA WATCHED AS THE winter twilight deepened the shadows and softened the hard angles of the handsome homes on Madison Square, the outlines of graceful columns and elaborate iron gates blurring in the glow of the gas lamps lighting her way. Though the gardens were dormant now in the middle of winter, the shutters fastened against the winter winds, and the shops closed for the evening, Savannah beguiled her with its quiet elegance.

Even General Sherman, upon capturing Savannah near the end of the war, had been so arrested by her beauty that he'd made an exception to his murderous scorched-earth policy that had laid waste to most of Georgia, and spared Savannah from destruction. It wasn't hard to see why Celia Browning Mackay loved it so. Why she had extended such extraordinary generosity to India in an effort to protect her native city's good name.

The harness jangled as the carriage rocked to a stop at the entrance to the Mackay home on Bull Street. Philip hustled India from the carriage to the front door and rang the bell.

A woman in a maid's apron and cap motioned them inside.

"Miss Celia's waitin' for you all in the parlor," she said. "Just go on in."

"This way." With one hand at the small of her back, Philip guided India across a wide entry foyer. It was dominated by a magnificent staircase leading to a long second-floor gallery lined with portraits. A marmalade-colored cat, busily engaged in licking his paws, lay stretched out on the bottom stair. He blinked solemnly as they passed.

At the open door to the parlor, Philip paused. "Mrs. Mackay?"

"Philip! You're here at last." The voice was rich and warm as honey. The woman to whom it belonged appeared at the doorway. Petite and curvaceous in a fitted dress of apricot silk that set off her dark hair and violet eyes, Celia Mackay took both of India's hands and drew her into the room. "My dear. I'm pleased to meet you at last, but sorrier than words can tell for the circumstances."

"Thank you. I'm grateful for your help. I don't know what I'd have done without Mr. Sinclair's assistance."

"He's the best lawyer in Savannah," Mrs. Mackay said, motioning them to chairs before the fire. "It's the least Sutton and I could do for so celebrated a visitor. I hope you won't judge all of Savannah in light of this grievous misunderstanding."

India took in her surroundings—the black marble fireplace, the graceful chairs upholstered in fine leather, a glass-fronted bookcase filled with volumes bound in red leather. The room radiated comfort, serenity, safety. It felt like home.

"Are the two of you hungry?" Mrs. Mackay directed her

question to Philip, who sat nearest the fire, hands clasped loosely between his knees.

"I am." He smiled at India. "It's been a long time since breakfast at the Point."

Footsteps sounded in the hallway, and the white-haired carriage driver poked his head into the room. "Beggin' your pardon, Miss Celia. I brought in your comp'ny's trunks. Where you want 'em?"

"I'll show you!" A little girl of about ten years of age appeared at his side. "Mama told me where Miss India is 'sposed to sleep."

"Frannie, please don't stand there and shout," Mrs. Mackay said. "Come in and say hello to our visitors."

The girl danced into the room, her blue skirt belling about her ankles. She was Mrs. Mackay in miniature, down to her small frame, her cloud of dark hair and extraordinary eyes. She made a little curtsy. "Hello."

Despite her worry and fatigue, India was charmed. "Hello yourself. What a pretty dress."

"Do you think so?" Frannie spun around. "I wanted a green one with a satin sash, but Mama said this one was better."

"It's very charming."

"That's what Miss Arnoult said. She's my music teacher."

"Miss Arnoult has very good taste."

Frannie peered into India's eyes. "My papa says you were framed. I thought he meant like a picture, but you look like a regular person."

India laughed.

Philip said, "Come and give me a hug, Little Bit. I haven't seen you in a coon's age."

"How many years is that?"

"I have no idea."

Frannie skipped across the room and leapt into his arms. "Guess what, Uncle Philip. Papa said if I do well on my studies this spring, I can go with him and Mama to Europe this summer."

"That sounds like a fine trip to me," Philip said with such gravity that India's heart turned over. What a wonderful father he would make.

Mrs. Mackay said, "Frannie, please do show Micah where to leave Miss Hartley's things. And then you may retire to your room. I'll be up later to hear your prayers."

"Yes, Mama." Frannie slid off Philip's lap. "Papa promised to read another chapter of *Mary West, Prairie Girl* when he gets home. It's very exciting."

She planted a swift kiss on her mother's cheek and raced to the hallway.

India watched her go. "What a beautiful child, Mrs. Mackay."

"We lost our first child, a boy, to a bout of fever. Francesca seems like a special gift. It's difficult not to spoil her silly." Mrs. Mackay smiled. "Not that my husband tries all that hard."

The maid came in and announced dinner. Mrs. Mackay rose. "I'm sorry Sutton isn't here. He had to go to Charleston to see about the repairs on one of our ships. I've asked Lucinda to prepare a buffet. I hope that's all right."

"That's kind of you." Philip offered one arm to their hostess and the other to India.

In the spacious dining room, they filled plates with ham and beaten biscuits, savories, and small apple tarts glistening with sugar. While they ate, Mrs. Mackay entertained them with news of the city. The new library for men that had opened last September to divert men from drinking and brawling seemed to be working, and now the Sons of Temperance were leading the movement to form a statewide organization.

"Of course the men aren't the only ones who have trouble with strong drink," Mrs. Mackay said, setting down her crystal water glass. "Poor Mary Murphy can't seem to break the habit no matter how she is punished."

Philip nodded. "I was in the Exchange one day last fall for some business in the municipal offices, and there was Mary Murphy, scrubbing out the place in lieu of another thirty days in jail, but I heard later she was arrested yet again."

Mrs. Mackay sighed. "People like her need help. Not only for their sakes, but my goodness, the reputation of our city is at stake too. Tourists certainly don't want to have to step over drunkards on the streets in order to go shopping or take in a play."

"We can't expect much improvement until we solve the employment problem," Philip said, helping himself to another biscuit. "Until we overcome the idleness forced upon men, black and white, by the seasonal nature of our economy, we can expect such difficulties to remain."

India finished her apple tart and relaxed into her chair, content to listen to the conversation.

"At least the river port is thriving again," Philip continued. "From what I hear, this year ought to be the best ever."

"Sutton is counting on it," Mrs. Mackay said. "It's no secret we nearly lost everything during the war." She studied Philip over the rim of her coffee cup. "The legal profession ought to do well, too, now that so many of our black citizens are filing claims for property they lost to the Union army."

"The Southern Claims Commission is handling most of that," Philip said. "And most of the claims are for only a few hundred dollars. But now that more citizens have legal status, more will seek justice for all kinds of things through the courts. And that will benefit all of us who practice law."

Lucinda, the maid, arrived to serve coffee. When she withdrew, Mrs. Mackay passed sugar and cream. "Are you all right, Miss Hartley? You're awfully quiet."

"I'm all right. A bit tired."

"Your room is ready whenever you wish to retire." Mrs. Mackay placed a hand on India's arm. "I can only imagine how terrifying this whole thing is for you. If there is anything else at all that we can do for you, promise you'll let me know."

"Thank you. I will."

Philip stood. "I should go and let India rest. We're going to the theater tomorrow to have a look around."

"I thought you did that the last time you were in the city." Mrs. Mackay rang the little silver bell beside her plate, summoning the maid.

"I did, but India wasn't with me. It will help to have her take me through the events of the evening in question." Philip caught India's eye. "I'll come for you once the police escort arrives."

India looked up, alarmed. She had forgotten this detail.

"Don't let his presence rattle you. I want you to take your time and walk me through your movements that evening, just as we discussed."

"All right."

Philip clasped both of Mrs. Mackay's hands. "Thank you for a lovely dinner, Celia."

"My pleasure. Our house is always open to you."

On his way to the front door, he stopped and placed a hand on India's shoulder. "Try to get some rest."

When he had gone, India thanked her hostess, and Lucinda arrived to show India to her room on the second floor. A fire had been laid in the black marble fireplace. The room glowed with golden light.

It was well appointed, with a view to the back gardens and to an old carriage house that seemed long abandoned, barely visible in the glow of gaslights lining the street. But India was too exhausted to take much notice of the fine linens, the elegant dressing table, and the matching escritoire. She could think only of sleep.

She changed into her nightdress, washed her face and hands, and brushed her hair.

"Miss Hartley?" Mrs. Mackay tapped softly on the bedroom door. "Are you still up?"

In her bare feet, India padded across the room and opened the door.

"You left your reticule in the parlor," Mrs. Mackay said, handing it over. "I thought you might want it."

"Thank you. I hadn't even missed it."

Mrs. Mackay's violet eyes swept the room. "Is there anything else you need?"

"I can't think of a single thing. It's been a long time since I slept in such a lovely place."

"Sleep as long as you want to in the morning. Frannie and

I will be up early to attend morning prayers, but Lucinda will give you breakfast whenever you want it." Mrs. Mackay paused. "How are you getting on with Mr. Sinclair?"

"He has been most kind. And I have the greatest confidence in his abilities." Even if he hadn't taken seriously her theory about the burned chapel.

"He seems quite taken with you," Mrs. Mackay said. "I noticed at supper tonight he hardly took his eyes off you. That's quite unusual for Philip." Mrs. Mackay leaned against the door frame, seemingly in no hurry to leave. "He has been widowed for some time, but I think he is afraid that loving someone else would somehow diminish the affection he felt for Laura."

India was tempted to ask Mrs. Mackay about Laura Sinclair. Had she been a woman capable of deceit? But somehow, even thinking of such a question felt disloyal to Philip.

"Of course this is not the time to think of romantic possibilities," Mrs. Mackay went on. "But I do wish that dear man would fall in love again." She smiled. "Maybe you are just the woman to dismantle the fortress he has built around that big heart of his. Once this dreadful court business is behind you."

"Mama?" Frannie Mackay appeared in the hallway, her dark curls falling into her eyes, a doll tucked under her arm. "You were 'sposed to read to me tonight 'cause Papa isn't home."

"I'll be right there, darling." Mrs. Mackay clasped her daughter's hand. "Good night, Miss Hartley. Sleep well."

CHAPTER 17

BULL STREET WAS CROWDED WITH PEOPLE TAKING advantage of the mild Sunday afternoon weather. On the corner a mother bent to speak to the little boy holding onto her skirts. A group of men dressed in their Sunday best stood beneath the ancient trees, smoking pipes and chatting. In the square, a young couple sat on a bench while a small black dog romped at their feet.

Philip offered India an encouraging smile as they headed down the sandy street, but a familiar and persistent shadow of unease had entered the carriage with them. India feared that she would never again enjoy the luxury of an ordinary life.

They drew up at the back entrance to the Southern Palace, where a red-bearded policeman in uniform waited. He wrenched open the door. "Better get her inside, Mr. Sinclair. I just chased off a reporter from the *Georgia Enterprise* who wanted to know why I was standin' here when the theater's been closed ever since—"

"Thank you." Philip got out and helped India down.

The policeman unlocked the door and ushered them inside. India stood motionless in the dim hallway that led to her dressing room, and beyond to the spiral staircase and the stage. She was overcome with sadness and fear, and yet strangely peaceful too. The hours spent on the stage were a refuge from her grief over her father's passing. Disappearing into her stage role, pretending to be someone else, had allowed a respite, however brief. She led them to her dressing room and pointed out where she had been sitting when Mr. Sterling had stopped at her open doorway to discuss the night's performance. Where his new companion, Miss Bryson, had stood. Where the mysterious woman in the dark cloak had waited none too patiently.

"So this is where you stopped first, when you arrived that night?" Philip turned away from the policeman and spoke in low tones.

"No. I had just come in when I heard a noise on the stage, and I went up there to see what had happened. That was when I saw Mr. Quinn. He had fallen off a ladder, but luckily he wasn't hurt."

"Show me."

India led him and the policeman up the staircase to the stage and pointed out the corner where she had seen the young stagehand.

"How long were you up here?"

"I don't know. Five minutes? Maybe ten. Mr. Quinn told me he'd noticed that Mr. Sterling had upstaged me on opening night. He was hoping to remedy the situation by installing an additional mirror that would cast more of the limelight onto the stage."

Philip moved about the stage, his golden eyes taking in every detail. "Did you talk to anyone else while you were up here?"

"No. I returned to my dressing room and waited for Fabienne to arrive."

He paced the perimeter of the stage, his footfalls echoing in the cavernous space. Reaching the slightly raised area near the footlights, he knelt and ran his fingers along the wooden floor. "This is the trapdoor?"

"Yes. The room directly below is where Mr. Philbrick allowed me to keep my father's things."

"Where the gun was kept."

"Yes."

He got to his feet. "Where were you standing when the gun discharged?"

She walked him through the stage set, pointing out the settee that was positioned upstage, facing the audience, and the small table downstage where she expected to find the prop weapon.

"And when Mr. Sterling fell?"

"I dropped the weapon then, and I ran to Mr. Sterling. Everything afterward is muddled. But last night, when I couldn't sleep, I kept going over it in my mind, and I remembered thinking at the time that I might have heard a second shot."

He put a hand on her arm. "Wait a minute. A second shot? Are you sure?"

"I think so. Just after the gun went off. But it was most likely the delayed sound effect. Perhaps an echo. Or the sound of something being dropped backstage."

"This could be important." Impatience tinged his words. "Why didn't you tell me this before?"

"Everything was in chaos. People were screaming, running every direction, shouting. The police arrived almost at once. I was shocked and scared. It's hard to remember everything that happened, and when. But—"

"You about done here, Mr. Sinclair?" The red-bearded policeman jangled the set of keys on a chain at his waist. "I'm missin' my Sunday dinner."

"Just a minute, Officer." Philip turned back to India, one brow raised in question.

She glanced at the darkened circle where Mr. Sterling's blood had seeped onto the stage. "I think I must have screamed. Someone turned the lights up. You know the rest."

Philip stood in her place on the stage and raised one arm, as if sighting a weapon. He dropped onto the floor in the same spot where Mr. Sterling had fallen, then rose to run his fingers over the boards and along the wall at the back of the stage, like a physician palpating a patient's skin. He paused. "Officer."

The policeman hurried over and heaved an exasperated sigh. "Yes, Mr. Sinclair."

Philip handed the officer a small round ball. "I want this marked as evidence."

India's heart sped up. "What is it?"

"It looks like a lead ball from a revolver."

"But how could—"

Philip stopped her with a quick shake of his head. "I think we're finished here. Let's lock up, officer, and you can go home to your Sunday dinner."

On the way out of the theater, Philip paused for another quick sweep of India's dressing room, then peered into the empty trap room and slid open the trapdoor. "I've always wondered how those things work."

"Trapdoors can be tricky," India said.

They reached the door that opened onto the street.

"Once, during a performance of *Macbeth* in Baltimore, I stepped backward and nearly fell into the trap room below. One of the stagehands literally shoved me back onto my feet." India pulled on her gloves. "He was eating an apple at the time, and it flew out of his hand and landed beside the witches' cauldron. Everyone had to step around it for the remainder of the first act."

Philip laughed, and she joined in. India heard a muted oath as a newspaper reporter lurking at the end of the alley regarded her through narrowed eyes.

※

JANUARY 30

"All rise."

Philip took India's hand and drew her to her feet as the judge entered the packed courtroom. Noise from the courthouse filtered in—footsteps on the stairs, the closing of doors, the buzz of conversations punctuated by bursts of laughter. Shards of sunlight poured through the windows, stabbing her eyes. The trees lining the street still dripped water from last night's rain.

Dimly, India heard the recitation of the charges against her and the judge's quick greeting to the men seated in the jury box. Behind her, spectators jostled for seating on the polished wooden benches, their excited whispers mingling with the rustling of fabrics as they settled in.

In the front row, newspaper reporters juggled bulky cameras, notebooks, and their winter coats, some of them clearly taking an unseemly delight in her misfortune. The morning's edition of the *Savannah Morning Herald* had featured a drawing of her and Philip laughing as they exited the theater under a headline that read "Murder No Laughing Matter."

Philip told her not to worry about it, but her mind filled with the heavy, relentless beat of doubt: she was an outsider. The gun was hers. Everyone knew Arthur Sterling had upstaged her the night before and that she had upbraided him for it.

Though Philip was feeling even more confident after finding the ammunition lodged in the wall, perhaps it would prove to be unrelated to her case. She pressed her hands to her midsection and tried to breathe.

Judge Bartlett, a brittle old man with a head of cotton-fluff hair, paged through a stack of documents and cleared his throat. "Mr. McLendon, are you ready to proceed?"

The prosecutor, whose appearance and demeanor oozed Southern charm, stood. "We are, Your Honor."

"Mr. Sinclair?"

Philip nodded.

"Very well, Mr. McLendon, call your first witness."

India heard Philip draw in a long breath. She reminded herself to remain calm and impassive, even as her character was impugned in open court. Before her on the table sat a pad and pencil. A glass of water. At her feet, the small travel satchel packed with the few things she would be allowed to have in her jail cell: her comb, clean stockings, a small bottle of rosewater Mrs. Mackay had pressed into her hands at the last moment.

"Your Honor," the prosecutor said, his voice rich and melodic, "the people call Dr. Wakefield Adams."

The doctor, a rotund man with the ruddy complexion and bulbous nose of a habitual imbiber, made his way to the front of the room and was sworn in.

"Now, Dr. Adams," Mr. McLendon began. "Were you called to the Southern Palace Theater on the evening of December 20 of last year?"

"No, sir. I wasn't called there. I was already there. To see Miss Hartley's play."

"Oh?" The prosecutor turned to look at the jury. "So you were an eyewitness to the shooting?"

India shifted in her chair. Clearly, Mr. McLendon knew what he was doing. Even she knew that a lawyer never asked a question unless he already knew the answer.

"Yes, sir, I was in the third row when the shot was fired."

"And did you see who fired that shot?"

"It was Miss Hartley."

"And what did you do then?"

"Well, sir, I saw that Mr. Sterling had been shot, so I left my seat and ran onto the stage to see if I could help him."

"And what did you see, Doctor?"

"He'd been hit once in the left femoral artery. He was bleeding bad."

"And did you render aid?"

The doctor nodded. "I applied a tourniquet and stayed with him until he was taken to the hospital."

"And did you have occasion to examine Mr. Sterling after that?"

"I went by the hospital the next morning."

"And how was your patient faring by then?"

"He was dead."

The prosecutor paused to let the murmurs die down, and to let the weight of the doctor's words sink in. "No further questions." He turned to Philip. "Your witness, Mr. Sinclair."

Philip got to his feet. "Doctor, I wonder if you could stand and show the jury the location of the femoral artery."

The witness glanced up at Judge Bartlett, who nodded. "Go ahead, Dr. Adams."

The doctor stood. "The femoral artery runs through the thigh and is the main artery that supplies blood to the lower limb."

"And can you identify for the jury the approximate location of Mr. Sterling's wound?"

The doctor pointed to a spot on his own thigh, just below the hip.

"Thank you, Doctor. Be seated." Philip paused. "Now, when you were tending Mr. Sterling, did you observe the nature of the wound?"

"Certainly. There was just one. A small, rather neat hole, typical when a cartridge penetrates flesh at fairly close range."

"A cartridge?"

"Metal cartridges tend to make a smaller hole than a lead ball."

Philip paused to look at the jury. "I see. Any other visible wounds to Mr. Sterling?"

"No, sir. Not that I recall."

"Did you notice whether the cartridge had lodged in the patient, or whether it had exited Mr. Sterling's body?"

"No, I did not. I was just trying to keep the poor man from bleeding out."

"Did you notice an exit wound later on?"

"No, sir."

"In your report, did you make a determination as to the type of bullet that injured Mr. Sterling?"

The doctor shrugged. "I've seen enough such cases in my time to know I was most likely looking at a wound from a metal bullet. But it made no difference by then."

"So it's likely the bullet remained in the body of the deceased and was buried with him."

"Sure. I guess so."

"This is a murder trial, Doctor. A woman's life is at stake. Let's not guess, if we can be more precise." Philip paced for a moment, his head down, his hands clasped behind his back. "How long have you practiced medicine, Dr. Adams?"

"Forty-seven years."

"Forty-seven years. Did you know that Mr. Sterling suffered from dropsy?"

The prosecutor shot to his feet. "Your Honor. Point of relevance. Mr. Sterling's medical history has no bearing on these proceedings."

Judge Bartlett peered down at Philip. "Where are you going with this line of questioning, Counselor?"

"Your Honor, if you will allow me just a few more questions, I think you will see that the victim's condition has a vital bearing on this case."

"Proceed." The judge waved a mottled hand at the doctor. "You may answer the question."

"Mr. Sterling was not a regular patient of mine," the doctor said. "I just happened to be there when he was shot."

"So you didn't know he had a severe heart problem?"

"Not firsthand. My wife keeps up with all the talk in Savannah. She heard that Mr. Sterling was not a well man."

"Doctor, in your expert medical opinion, can a damaged heart suddenly cease to function?"

"Of course."

"So it's possible that Mr. Sterling died not of the gunshot wound but because the shock caused his heart to give out?"

India felt a sudden surge of hope. Philip had just given the jury a pathway to reasonable doubt.

"Sure, it's possible. But I reckon we'll never know for sure."

"Exactly." Philip faced the jury and, in turn, looked each of the men in the eye. "We'll never know for sure."

He turned back to the doctor. "That's all."

The judge consulted his gold pocket watch and cleared his throat. "Mr. McLendon?"

"No further questions, Your Honor."

"Call your next witness."

The door behind India opened. She turned, and her stomach dropped. She grabbed her pencil, scrawled one word, and pushed it across the table to Philip.

✒ CHAPTER 18 ✒

FABIENNE?

Philip glanced at India's notepad and raised a brow. They had expected the Frenchwoman to testify for the defense. Clearly he was as surprised by this development as she.

India watched as her young dresser walked slowly down the aisle to the witness stand. The girl seemed entirely undone. Her hair was in a half braid, her eyes swollen and red rimmed. She wouldn't look at India. She was sworn in. She promised to tell the truth.

Mr. McLendon rose. "Now, Miss Ormond. Would you tell the jury the nature of your relationship with the defendant?"

"I was her dresser."

"And what does that mean?"

"I helped Miss Hartley at the theater. I dressed her hair and helped her change her costumes during the play."

"And were you serving in that capacity on the evening in question?"

"Yes, sir." Fabienne's voice was a hoarse whisper.

"Were you there when Mr. Sterling stopped at Miss Hartley's dressing room to discuss the evening's performance?"

"Yes."

"Would you say that Miss Hartley was angry with him?"

Philip shot to his feet. "Objection. Calls for a conclusion on the part of the witness."

"Sustained."

The prosecutor cleared his throat. "Do you remember what they discussed?"

"Just that Mr. Philbrick wanted them to do something more spectacular, because a critic was coming."

"All right." He consulted his notes. "Another witness who cannot be present for these proceedings has signed a sworn statement that as Mr. Sterling was leaving Miss Hartley's dressing room that evening, he cautioned her not to take the new stage directions literally. Do you remember his saying that?"

At last Fabienne lifted her head and looked at India, sorrow and fear mingling in her eyes. "I was busy. I cannot remember exactly. But Miss Hartley wouldn't—"

"Just answer the question, please. To the best of your recollection."

"Yes, sir."

"And did Miss Hartley make a reply?"

"Yes, sir."

"Which was?"

"Don't tempt me."

Every person in the gallery gasped. The reporters scribbled in their notebooks.

Mr. McLendon's eyes shone with triumph as he passed their table. "Your witness, Mr. Sinclair."

Philip took his time. He paused for a sip of water, then paged through his notes.

At last he approached the witness.

"Miss Ormond. How long have you known Miss Hartley?"

"Since last November, when she put a notice in the paper for a dresser."

"And were you hired right away?"

"*Oui.* The first day. When I answered the advertisement."

"How often did you see her, would you say?"

"Almost every day when she was rehearsing the play. I dressed her hair, and we practiced changing her from one costume to another. There are but a few moments between scenes and all of those buttons"—Fabienne rolled her eyes—"they take a very long time unless you have practiced."

"I imagine so." Philip smiled at the ladies in the gallery. "Now, you have testified that Miss Hartley said to Mr. Sterling at the theater that evening, 'Don't tempt me.' Is that correct?"

"Yes, sir."

"Because she was exasperated."

"Ex—?"

"Annoyed. Irritated."

"Mr. Sterling was a most annoying man."

"Objection." Mr. McLendon rose. "The victim is not on trial here, Judge."

"Sustained."

Philip paused. "Miss Ormond, have you ever been annoyed with someone?"

"*Oui.* Of course."

"And said something you didn't mean? Made an idle threat you had no intention of carrying out? Exaggerated your words for effect?"

"A million times."

Philip smiled. "Me too."

He glanced at the jury then turned back to Fabienne. "So when Miss Hartley said, 'Don't tempt me,' she might have been expressing her annoyance, but certainly not intending to act upon it. Is—"

"Objection, Your Honor." The prosecutor was on his feet again. "Is Mr. Sinclair asking a question, or giving his summation to the jury? Frankly I can't tell which it is."

Judge Bartlett peered down at Philip. "Counselor?"

"No further questions."

With another sorrowful glance at India, Fabienne hurried from the courtroom.

The judge consulted the large clock mounted on the rear wall. "Court is in recess until one o'clock."

He banged the gavel, stood, and disappeared into his chambers.

A policeman escorted India and Philip to a room down the hallway then took up his post outside the door.

Weak with nerves and hunger, India collapsed into a chair and massaged her temples.

Philip drew up a chair and sat beside her. "Are you all right?"

"I didn't expect Fabienne to speak against me."

"It's obvious she didn't want to. But I think I mitigated the damage with the jury." He sounded tired too. "We have a right to recall her if we think it's necessary, when it's our turn to present evidence."

The door opened and the policeman came in carrying a wicker hamper that clearly had been searched. The napkins were unfolded and lay in a heap atop a loaf of bread protruding from one corner. "Mrs. Mackay has sent you some dinner."

Philip took the basket. "Thanks."

The policemen shifted his weight. "If your client needs the . . . um . . . necessary room, I'll arrange it."

"We'll let you know."

The policeman withdrew. Philip opened the basket and took out wedges of cheese, a dried fruit tart, the bread, and a jar of soup. Everything smelled good, but India felt as if she'd swallowed a brick. She shook her head as Philip set the meal on a small table before her.

"India," he said, his voice filled with concern. "I realize food is the last thing on your mind, but you must eat something. It's apt to be a trying afternoon, and this food is much better than what you'll have in the jail tonight."

India forced down a few bites of bread and cheese and picked at the tart, but it might as well have been made of paste.

Philip ate, but without any sign of enjoyment, then paged once more through his notes.

At ten minutes to one, the door opened once more, and the policeman came in again with a piece of paper and a small paper bag. "Sergeant Trueblood said to give you this."

Philip glanced into the bag and read the paper, and India saw some of the tension leave his shoulders. He nodded to the policeman. "Thank you."

The door closed again. India looked up at him, wanting to hope but afraid of disappointment. "What is it?"

He smiled at last. "We may have caught a break." He took out his watch. "It's nearly one. Do you need the—"

"I'm all right."

He packed up the basket and left it to be returned to Mrs. Mackay. "Let's go."

India had hoped that after the initial excitement, some of the spectators would return to their own pursuits. But upon entering the courtroom, she saw that the crowd had swelled well past the room's capacity. The gallery was filled, and people stood three deep along the walls, each vying for a view of the proceedings.

The jury filed into the jury box, the judge came in and gaveled the proceedings to order, and Mr. McLendon rose from his chair. "Your Honor, the people call Miss Victoria Bryson."

India pressed her fingers to her temples as the young understudy sashayed down the aisle, the deep ruffles on her pink skirt whispering on the wooden floor.

Miss Bryson took her oath and made a production of arranging her skirts just so before turning to smile at the men in the jury box.

"Now, Miss Bryson," the prosecutor said. "Will you tell these gentlemen what you were doing at the Southern Palace the evening Mr. Sterling was shot?"

"I most certainly will." The understudy glared at India. "I was understudying Miss Hartley's role in case she was sick or something and couldn't perform. Mr. Philbrick required me to be at every performance. So I was there, and he told me about the change he wanted to make in the performance that night, and he said Miss Hartley was angry about it and if she didn't want to cooperate I could go on in her place."

"All right. What happened then?"

"I went to find Arth—Mr. Sterling, and he was talking

to Miss Hartley about it." The understudy sent India another withering look. "She hated him because she thought he was upstaging her all the time."

India glanced at Philip. Surely he would object to that last statement. But he kept his seat, his tawny gaze focused on the witness.

Mr. McLendon nodded. "Then what?"

"Mr. Sterling and I left for his dressing room, and"—her voice cracked—"the play began. I was watching from the wings when she shot him and—"

Now Philip rose. "Objection, Your Honor. It has not—"

"Sustained."

Judge Bartlett motioned to the prosecutor. "Mr. McLendon?"

"I don't have any more questions for this witness."

Philip lost no time in approaching the witness box. "Miss Bryson. I wonder if you can tell the jury how long you knew Mr. Sterling."

"Almost a year."

"And what was the nature of your relationship?"

Victoria Bryson blushed and fussed with her skirt. "I'm not sure I know what you mean."

"I think you do, but I'll be more direct. Were your dealings with Arthur Sterling strictly professional, or were the two of you romantically involved?"

Mr. McLendon rose. "Point of relevance, Your Honor?"

"I'll allow it. Go ahead, Counselor."

Philip waited while the understudy fidgeted in her chair. "Well, I admired him greatly, and he was trying to help me with my acting, and . . . and he was the kindest and most gentle man

I've ever known." She fumbled for a handkerchief and blotted her eyes. "And this . . . this stranger who thinks she is better than anyone comes to our town, and all she does is complain about him. She wanted him out of the way, and she killed him, and if you men can't hang her for murder just because she is beautiful and famous, you are all traitors to Savannah and a bunch of cowards besides. You are all as guilty as if you yourselves fired that gun."

She collapsed and began to sob.

"No further questions," Philip said.

Mr. McLendon motioned to a young man, who escorted Miss Bryson from the room.

Philip resumed his seat and murmured to India, "Quite a performance."

Judge Bartlett waited until the door closed behind her. "Are you ready with your next witness, Mr. McLendon?"

The prosecutor shuffled his papers and called a policeman to the stand.

"Now, Officer Avery," he began. "You were the first on the scene at the theater that night, were you not?"

"Yes, sir."

"And after Mr. Sterling was taken away, what did you do?"

"What we always do. I made a search of the premises to gather evidence."

"Did you find anything of significance?"

"A pool of blood on the floor of the stage. The weapon itself, of course. The defendant dropped it after she shot the actor."

"Objection." Philip rose from his chair. "The officer is stating a conclusion that has not been proven."

"Sustained." Judge Bartlett leaned forward and frowned at the policeman. "You know better than that, Officer."

Mr. McLendon cleared his throat. "Aside from the weapon, did you find anything else of significance?"

"No, sir. After Mr. Sterling was taken away, we cleared the theater and closed it."

The prosecutor nodded. "Thank you, Officer. That's all."

Philip approached the witness with a barely suppressed urgency that lifted India's spirits. She poured herself a glass of water and took a long sip.

"Now, Officer," Philip began. "Would you tell the jury how long you have served as a policeman here in Savannah?"

"Eleven years come next summer."

"And in that time, how many cases would you say you have investigated?"

"I don't keep count."

"Well, give us an estimate. Dozens, would you say? Hundreds?"

"Hundreds, I guess, but not all of them for murder, of course."

"Hundreds. So you have some experience in collecting evidence."

"I reckon so."

"Would you consider yourself a thorough investigator?"

The officer frowned. "Just what are you getting at? Because I—"

"I'm asking you how carefully you search for evidence."

"I know how to do my job."

"So when you finished your sweep of the Southern Palace Theater you were confident you'd found everything pertinent to this case."

The officer let out a gusty breath. "I had the weapon. I had a bloodied victim and a suspect who fired in front of hundreds of witnesses. Of course, I looked around, but I didn't see the point of wasting time looking for anything else."

"I see." Returning to the table, Philip picked up the paper bag and the note from the police sergeant. "Officer Avery. I wonder if you'd be good enough to read this note aloud to the jury."

"Objection, Your Honor," said the prosecutor.

"Overruled."

Philip nodded to the judge. "Now, Mr. Avery?"

The officer took the paper. "'The lead ball enclosed herewith was taken from the Southern Palace Theater on the afternoon of Sunday last, in the presence of Mr. Sinclair, Miss Hartley, and Officer McGee.'" He looked up at Philip. "What are you trying to prove?"

"That this ball was overlooked in your initial search of the theater."

"So? That don't prove it had anything to do with this case. It coulda been there for ages."

"Or it could have been fired that very evening and been overlooked. Isn't that possible?"

The officer thrust the paper at Philip. "You can say whatever you want, but I did my job, and we got the right person on trial here. Just 'cause she's pretty and more famous than God Himself don't mean she ain't guilty as sin."

\mathscr{R} CHAPTER 19 \mathscr{R}

JANUARY 31

THE NIGHT SEEMED ENDLESS. INDIA LAY ON HER LUMPY cot in her cell, alternating between wakefulness and dark, terrifying dreams. She woke, stiff and gritty-eyed, to a sliver of sunlight creeping across the floor and the hollow clanking of metal in the corridor. She lay quietly for a moment, waiting for her thoughts to clear. Yesterday, after Officer Avery read the note from the sergeant into the record, she had allowed herself to hope the judge might dismiss the charges against her. But it hadn't happened. Instead, Mr. McLendon had abruptly rested his case. Today, Philip would present his witnesses, and then her fate would be in the hands of the jury.

An officer unlocked her door and hurried her, along with three other women, through their morning ablutions. India splashed water on her face and hands and combed out her hair, grateful for the gift of the rosewater. Amazing how such small niceties mattered, when one was deprived of almost everything.

"Come along," the officer muttered when the last of the

women had taken her turn at the washbasin. "We don't want your ladyships' breakfasts to get cold."

The morning meal consisted of lukewarm grits and a hard biscuit washed down with weak coffee. India managed a few bites before her stomach rebelled. She set aside the tray and paced her cell, six steps up, turn, six steps back.

The woman in the cell across from her watched with an air of amusement. Cupping her hands around her tin coffee cup, she offered India a gap-toothed grin. "First time in, sweet pea?"

"I'm not a criminal."

A burst of laughter and then: "Of course you aren't. Ever'body in here is innocent."

India ignored the woman and tried to estimate the time. Court would convene at eight. Surely it was now past seven, and someone would come for her at any moment. She dreaded what was to come today, but if she didn't get out of here soon, if she couldn't see the sky and feel the sun and wind on her face, she would die.

"Say," the woman went on. "I know you. I heard the officers talkin' about your case last night. They say you'll hang for shooting the beloved Mr. Sterling." She slurped her coffee and tossed the cup aside. "Not that he didn't deserve it. From what I hear anyway."

India balled her fists and concentrated on taking one breath, then the next.

"You got a good lawyer?"

India was spared further conversation when the officer who had escorted her yesterday morning returned. "Ready, Miss Hartley?"

He unlocked the door and took out his shackles. "I'm sorry about this, but there's a passel of reporters outside, and rules is rules."

Wordlessly she held out her hands, and the manacles closed around her wrists. Outside, the officer halted while the police wagon was brought around. The reporters surged toward her, calling out questions. A photographer stepped behind the camera he had set up near the entrance. India was not about to stand stock still while a photo was processing. She turned abruptly. The officer boosted her into the police wagon, and they returned to the packed courthouse.

Philip was already in his chair at the table. He rose and clasped both her hands as the manacles were removed. "India. How are you? Did you sleep at all?"

"A little." She rubbed her wrists and surveyed the crowd. She recognized several faces from yesterday. But Mrs. Mackay was not among them. "It wasn't the most restful night I've ever had."

"Did they give you any breakfast?"

"Grits and biscuits. I wasn't very hungry."

"When was the last time you ate an actual meal?"

She shrugged. If the woman at the jail was right, and she was to die, what difference did it make?

His amber eyes searched her face. He looked tired too. And worried. "You can't starve yourself to a not-guilty verdict."

"I'm too frightened to eat."

He offered a gentle smile. "Today it's our turn. And we have a good chance. A very good chance."

"All rise," the court clerk intoned, and everyone stood.

Judge Bartlett swooped in, his black robe billowing like bats' wings. "Court is in session. Are you ready, Mr. Sinclair?"

"I am, Your Honor."

"Mr. McLendon?"

The prosecutor bowed. "All set, Your Honor."

Judge Bartlett sipped from a glass of water. "Very well. Mr. Sinclair. You may proceed."

Philip began by describing for the jury India's childhood in the theater, the death of her mother immediately following India's birth, and then the loss of her aunt when India was ten. In the absence of live witnesses, he read a few of her theater notices praising her talent and the letters he'd solicited from her friends in Philadelphia and New York. He stressed that she had never before been charged with any crime. One by one, he handed the letters to the clerk, who then passed them to the judge.

Judge Bartlett flipped through them and set them aside. "These seem to be in order. Duly witnessed and so forth." He looked down at Philip. "Have you any live witnesses, Counselor?"

Philip nodded. "The defense calls Colonel Joshua Culpepper."

India turned with everyone else to watch as a tall, bearded man, shoulders squared, his back ramrod straight, walked down the aisle. The clerk swore him in.

"Colonel Culpepper," Philip began. "You served in the Confederate army, I believe."

"I did indeed, sir. With the Chatham Artillery."

"Artillery. So you're an expert in weaponry."

"Some say so, yes."

Philip walked over to the table where the evidence lay in

view of the jury and picked up India's gun. "I wonder if you can identify this weapon for the jury."

The colonel barely glanced at it. "That, sir, is a .44 Colt revolver."

"You're familiar with it, then."

"Of course. It was one of the most popular revolvers made during the war. There are thousands of them still in use, I expect."

"Can you explain for the jury how this weapon works?"

"It uses black powder as a propellant. You need a percussion cap to provide ignition for the ball."

"By the ball, you mean the round lead ball that is propelled from the barrel when the weapon is fired."

"That's right."

"Is this a weapon that's quick and easy to load?"

The colonel shook his head. "Anybody who uses one can tell you it takes time, a steady hand, and considerable strength to do so. And it's cumbersome to reload. Heaven knows we paid a price for that on the battlefield."

"I see. Does the Colt .44 use any other type of ammunition?"

"Not to my knowledge. Colt tried converting to metal cartridges a couple of years ago, but the results were quite disappointing. And in any case, a metal cartridge wouldn't fit a .44 manufactured ten years ago."

Philip returned to the table, picked up the bag containing the ammunition he'd found at the theater. "Colonel Culpepper, this ball was taken from the theater two days ago. In your opinion, could it have been fired from Miss Hartley's Colt .44?"

The colonel studied the bullet. "Yes, of course."

"Thank you." Philip strolled to the table and poured himself a glass of water. He sipped it and took his time returning to the witness stand. "Dr. Adams has testified that in his expert medical opinion, Mr. Sterling's wound was likely caused by a metal cartridge. But you are quite sure Miss Hartley's weapon could not have fired such a bullet. Is that correct?"

"That's what I'm saying, Mr. Sinclair. These days, metal bullets most likely come from a Remington .44."

"Could you explain to the jury why this is so?"

"Metal cartridges come from more recent weapons, such as an 1868 breech loader. Remington has converted almost exclusively to metal cartridges."

"Why is that?"

"They can be loaded faster than lead balls. They are less likely to misfire and are considerably more accurate." The colonel shrugged. "It's too bad we didn't have these during the war. Things might have turned out differently."

Judge Bartlett banged his gavel. "Just stick to the facts, Colonel. This is not the time or place to debate the outcome of the war."

Philip clasped his hands and paced for a moment, his head down. Returning to the witness, he said, "Let me be sure I understand your testimony. You have testified that the lead ball found lodged in the wall at the theater and entered into evidence could have come from Miss Hartley's weapon."

"Yes. Or one exactly like it."

"And you have just told us that Colt .44s are less accurate and more likely to misfire than a Remington using a metal cartridge."

"Yes, sir."

"As an expert in weapons and ammunition, Colonel, would

you say it's possible that Miss Hartley's gun discharged a wild shot that missed Mr. Sterling altogether and lodged instead in the wall, where it was overlooked by the investigating officers?"

"Objection!" Mr. McLendon rose from his chair. "There is absolutely no evidence that anyone except the defendant fired a weapon that night. Mr. Sinclair is engaging in wild speculation that can only confuse the jury."

"On the contrary," Philip shot back. "I'm trying to show that there is more than reasonable doubt that—"

"Gentlemen!" Judge Bartlett banged his gavel, silencing them both.

"All right." The judge sat back in his chair. "Now, do you have any more questions for this witness?"

"No further questions."

Judge Bartlett raised his brow at the prosecutor. "Mr. McLendon?"

The prosecutor strolled over to the witness stand, his hands in the pockets of his smoke-colored trousers. "About this lead ball that was so conveniently discovered at the theater on Sunday afternoon. Can you tell how long it might have been lodged in the wall where Mr. Sinclair just happened to find it?"

Colonel Culpepper blinked. "Well, of course there's no way to tell for sure, but—"

"Thank you, Colonel. Now. Would you say that a person who owns a gun generally is acquainted with the feel and heft of the weapon?"

"I suppose so."

"So in the case of the defendant, even in the dark, she would reasonably be expected to recognize that the weapon in her hand was her own." The prosecutor looked over at the jury, a smug expression on his face.

"Not necessarily."

India watched in hopeful disbelief as the prosecutor paled at the unexpected answer.

"Not necessarily, Colonel?"

"That's what I'm saying."

"Very well. That's all."

"Judge?" Philip approached the bench. "Since Mr. McLendon has opened up this subject, I'd like to ask the colonel here another question."

"Go ahead."

Philip approached the witness box. "Colonel, I wonder if you would explain the answer you just gave the prosecutor. If I understand you correctly you have testified that my client could have picked up the weapon in question thinking it was the prop the theater manager had provided, and not recognized it as her own. Is that correct?"

"Yes, sir."

"Why is that?"

"Except for the kind of ammunition they use, the Colt and the Remington are nearly identical. They each weigh just under three pounds. They each have an overall length of approximately fourteen inches. And they each have an eight-inch barrel." The colonel leaned back in his chair. "Good gravy, Mr. Sinclair. In the dark like that, I doubt if even I could have told the two apart."

"Objection to that last observation, Judge," said the prosecutor.

"Sustained."

"I have no further questions, Your Honor," Philip said. "But

I'd like to request a meeting with you and Mr. McLendon in chambers."

"You mean now?"

"If it please the court."

"Very well. We'll be in recess for half an hour."

Philip glanced at India as he and the prosecutor left the courtroom. She couldn't read his expression, but she couldn't help feeling the colonel's testimony surely would sway the jury.

An officer appeared at her side, arms crossed, as if he needed to remind her not to flee. "You need anything, miss?"

"Some more water?"

He signaled to another officer, who hurried away and returned momentarily with a pitcher of fresh water. The minutes crawled by. India drank her water and ventured a look at the jury. Some looked anxious, some weary. Others looked annoyed at the delay.

At last the door to the judge's chambers opened, and the three men came in. One look at Philip's face and India knew that whatever legal ploy he'd tried had failed.

The judge resumed his seat and tapped the gavel again. India flinched. "Gentlemen," the judge began. "Mr. Sinclair has requested an immediate acquittal based upon reasonable doubt arising from the testimony of Colonel Culpepper. And while I see his point, I'm inclined to let the jury do its duty and decide the merits of this case. Mr. Sinclair, have you any other witnesses?"

"No, Your Honor."

"Then make your case, and let's get on with this."

Philip studied his notes. Took a long sip of water. He gave

India's shoulder a quick squeeze before crossing the courtroom to face the men who would decide her fate.

"Gentlemen. You have heard, in absentia, from many people acquainted with Miss Hartley's life and work. You have heard that she is a beloved mistress of her craft and a woman who brings delight to audiences all over the world. You have heard that she came here to Savannah to begin a tour of the finest theaters across the South. Theaters willing to pay her a great deal of money."

Someone in the gallery coughed. Skirts rustled. A door opened and closed.

"Murder is the result of fear," Philip went on. "Fear of losing money or love or position, fear of not getting what you want. Fear of losing what has been hard won. Miss Hartley has none of that fear. She enjoys the abiding affection of her public, the loyalty of her friends. In short, contrary to the emotional testimony of Mr. Sterling's . . . companion, India Hartley had no reason to kill a man she'd just met."

He paused, and India saw that he was assessing the effect of his words on the jury. The two men nearest her sat with heads down, but the others stared at Philip, their faces impassive. The room had gone still. The judge, the reporters, the spectators in the gallery sat rapt. Perhaps if her very life were not hanging in the balance, she, too, would have found his summation as fascinating as any play.

Philip went on. "Now, a beloved citizen of Savannah has been taken from our midst, and society demands that someone must pay. But that someone should not be India Hartley. You have heard testimony that Mr. Sterling may have had a heart condition that contributed to his demise. You have heard from Dr. Adams that in his opinion, Mr. Sterling's wound was caused by a metal cartridge. A cartridge that could not possibly have been fired from Miss Hartley's gun. A gun that uses only lead bullets identical to the one found in the theater. A gun that the police assures us is in fact the murder weapon, because they quit looking for evidence too soon.

"Gentlemen, I have no idea who shot Mr. Sterling, or why. But in all my years of practicing law I have never encountered a stronger case for reasonable doubt.

"You must search your consciences on this matter and determine whether there is enough doubt about Miss Hartley's guilt to set her free. The law does not ask you to provide a solution to what really happened at the Southern Palace that night. It asks only that you determine whether there is any other plausible explanation."

India poured herself another glass of water, her hands shaking.

"I believe the only fair verdict is a verdict of not guilty. But in any case, I ask you for mercy for my client." He paused and inclined his head toward India. "As a sworn jury you hold the power of life and death in your hands. You must decide whether to deprive this young woman of life or liberty or whether to set her free."

Philip braced his hands on the rail of the jury box and looked at each man in turn. "Shakespeare once wrote that mercy is an attribute of God Himself. And earthly power shows like God's when mercy seasons justice."

He nodded once and turned on his heel. The courtroom exploded into applause. The reporters scribbled in their notebooks.

The judge gaveled the room into silence. "This room will come to order. Any more of that and I'll clear this courtroom. Mr. McLendon, do you wish to address the jury?"

The prosecutor rose. "As compelling as Mr. Sinclair's oratory is, the fact is that there is no way to determine whether the lead ball found in the theater did in fact come from a wild shot fired from Miss Hartley's gun. Or whether it came from another gun, and had been there for weeks, months, or years. Mr. Sinclair has not offered up any other person with a reason to harm such a beloved local figure. This woman"—he turned and pointed to India—"came out of nowhere, came here to Savannah, and the next thing we know, our most talented thespian lies dead, our most beautiful theater is locked up tight, and our citizens are mourning a man who can never be replaced. I agree with my colleague that someone must pay for this death and grief and the disruption to our pleasant life here in Savannah, but that is where our agreement ends." He paused. "You should find her guilty."

Mr. McLendon sat down, and Philip resumed his seat beside India. Blinded by tears, she squeezed his hand. Whatever happened now, he had done his best. It was all she could ask.

Judge Bartlett spoke to the jury, but India was so terrified that his words might well have been spoken in Arabic. At length, they filed out, and she and Philip were escorted to the anteroom to wait.

He sprawled in the chair and raked a hand over his chin, too spent for words.

"You were brilliant," India said after half an hour had passed. She spoke quietly, out of the hearing of the officer stationed by the door. "Whatever happens, I want you to know I couldn't have expected a more thorough defense."

"I thought we'd get an acquittal based on the colonel's testimony. We would have, I'm sure, had Judge Russell heard the case. Bartlett is noted for deferring to the jury, but it was worth a try."

India watched a small flock of birds rise and fall along a distant rooftop. "I was surprised that Mr. McLendon seemed unprepared for the colonel's testimony about the two weapons."

"So was I." He ventured a weary smile. "The similarities between the two clearly caught him off guard."

"This morning you said we have a good chance. Do you still think so, Philip?"

"McLendon is trying to play upon the jury's fears by reminding them you are an outsider. And much of our case is circumstantial. We can't prove when that other bullet was fired or by whom."

"But the case against me is circumstantial too. They can't prove that I wanted to harm Mr. Sterling, or that I knew the gun was not the one Mr. Philbrick showed me. Surely they must give me the benefit of the doubt."

The door opened, and the clerk stuck his head in. "Mr. Sinclair, the jury's back."

ᘒᔧᔣ CHAPTER 20 ᔧᔣᘒ

DEEP OBLIVION PULLED AT HER, DRAGGED HER INTO blessed darkness. Something terrible had happened. She struggled to remember, but all she felt was an overwhelming sense of vertigo, of bumping up against the edges of the known world.

She was surrounded by silence and shadows. A sharp, medicinal smell permeated her cell, and she willed her eyes to open.

"You're awake." A rough, low whisper came from out of the darkness. A black-clad figure loomed over her. One hand covered her mouth, the other grasped her wrist. "Shhhhhh. Don't talk. Just listen."

She was fully awake now, every nerve taut. She tore at the hand covering her mouth.

"I'm here to get you out." The man tossed her a garment. "Put this on."

Now she realized this was not the jail, but a hospital. The man in the room was dressed as a priest, and the garment he'd given her was a nun's habit. Bits and pieces of yesterday's events came back to her. The spectators and reporters wedged into every nook of the courtroom—the circus-like atmosphere—as they waited for the verdict. The jurors' hard eyes as the decision was announced. Philip's muttered oath. A fear so intense her legs buckled. The loss of consciousness, the explosion of pain, and the gush of blood as she fell against the sharp edge of the table. She reached up to touch a thick bandage covering her head.

"We don't have much time," the priest said, his breath soft in her ear. "Can you walk?"

She nodded. "But I don't under—"

He grabbed the habit from her hands and pulled it over her head, threading her arms through the sleeves, tying the cord at her waist. He felt around in the darkness for her shoes and helped her put them on, then bundled her dress and hid it under his cassock.

Holding her back with one arm, he eased open the door, stepped into the darkened hallway, then motioned her to follow. "To your left and out the door. Be quick, but don't run. We don't want to attract attention or to wake the officer."

India noticed the policeman slumped over in his chair just outside her room. Obviously he'd been posted there to ensure that she didn't run.

"Chloroform," the priest whispered. "Go!"

Too confused to protest, India did as she was told, terror scraping at her insides. With the priest in the lead, they rounded the corner and nearly collided with a doctor just emerging from the indigents' ward.

"Father, I'm glad you're still here." The doctor shifted his medical bag to his other hand.

The priest grasped India's elbow, urging her on.

"A word with you, Father?" The doctor loomed in the dimly

lit corridor. His bulky form blocked their path and cast dark shadows on the walls.

"Yes, what is it?"

"It's Mrs. Ryan." The doctor nodded toward the ward he had just exited. "I doubt she'll last till morning, and there are nine fatherless children at home. Someone will have to take charge of them. If you could—"

"I'll see to it. Now if you'll excuse me, I must get Sister Luke here back to the—"

Rapid footsteps sounded behind them, and the police officer turned the corner. India froze, her heart jerking hard against her ribs.

"Good night, Doctor." The priest hurried India toward the door. As soon as they reached the outside, he grabbed her hand, and they ran between the buildings, crossing deserted yards, the policeman in pursuit. India slowed and pressed her hand to her side. At last the priest dragged her into an alley behind a boardinghouse, where a horse and rig waited. He boosted her inside, and they set off toward the river.

The night was cold. Gaslights formed a chain of stars along the quiet street. When the pain subsided and India caught her breath, she found her voice. "I don't understand what's happening, Father."

"Father. That's a good one."

Something in his voice seemed familiar. Her stomach dropped. "Mr. Lockwood?"

"In the flesh."

Huddled inside the jostling rig, her wounded head throbbing, India tried to make sense of the situation, but her thoughts were scattered like winter stars in wild disarray. Mr. Lockwood had no reason to harm her, but still . . . what did she really know about him? He was fond of drink. He needed money for his trip to Texas. Perhaps he intended to hold her for ransom. *Be careful who you trust.*

"Mr. Lockwood, what's the meaning of all this?"

"Sinclair is on the trail of another witness."

"But the trial is over. The jury has spoken." All of Philip's skilled arguments had not been enough to overcome the fact that she was an outsider and a woman engaged in a less-than-respectable profession. Mr. McLendon's assertions and Victoria Bryson's wrenching sobs had found their mark. "It's too late." Her voice cracked.

"Maybe not. The way it was explained to me, the judge wouldn't pronounce sentence because you were taken to the hospital with that head wound. Way I heard it, there was blood everywhere."

They passed a ragtag group of sailors hurrying toward the wharf, cloaks flying in the winter wind.

"I don't see what difference another witness could make now. And running away will make things worse."

"What's worse than a date with the gallows? Judge Bartlett has never had a decision reversed. He didn't want to sentence you in absentia and give Sinclair another reason to appeal. If Sinclair can find this other witness before the formal sentencing, he can ask the judge to reopen the case. And if the judge can't find you, he can't sentence you. Here we are. Now pipe down, and do as I tell you."

He halted the rig and helped her down. "We'll walk from here."

Keeping to the shadows, they hurried along the waterfront, down a flight of narrow steps, past a row of brigs and schooners anchored in the river, and made their way to a small skiff tied to the wooden pilings. Mr. Lockwood helped her enter the boat and pointed to a large blanket tucked into the bow. "Cover yourself until we clear the wharf."

The boat creaked as he untied the lines and cast off. On the wharf, the sailors laughed and whistled, their shouts and catcalls breaking the silence.

From beneath the blanket, India said, "Where are we going?"

"Isle of Hope. The Sinclairs have an old fishing camp there. It ain't much to look at, but it's secluded, and with any luck the police won't think to look for you there."

She felt the boat sway and settle on the river.

"Better not talk just now," Mr. Lockwood said, his voice low. "You never know when those sailors might get curious and take it upon themselves to investigate."

India lay motionless beneath the blanket. She had no choice now but to trust Mr. Lockwood. But who did Philip think would emerge as her savior? And anyway, who—

"Ahoy!" A shout carried across the river.

Through the fabric of the blanket, India saw a faint flicker of light. Another boat bumped theirs. A voice said, "Evenin', Father. You're out awfully late."

"That I am, Captain."

"Where you headed this time o' the night?"

India's legs had gone numb, but she dared not move. She breathed though her mouth, her ears straining to hear the conversation.

"Screven's Landing. Delivering some supplies to a couple o' hunters." Mr. Lockwood laughed. "They come up from the islands yesterday and got in a hurry and left all their belongings behind."

"And they prevailed on a priest to deliver them? In the middle of the night?"

"They wanted to get an early start in the mornin'. One of 'em is kin to me so I could hardly refuse his request. Besides, I extracted a promise of a donation to the poor box for my trouble. We must be forever vigilant for any source of help for those less fortunate."

"I reckon that's true enough. Well, you be careful, Father. Tide's coming in. Water's getting rough."

"Though waters roar, the Lord will shield me."

India heard the splash of oars as the boat moved away from theirs. Despite her terror she had to hand it to Mr. Lockwood. He had certainly played his part convincingly. She shifted beneath the blanket, her head throbbing. "Mr. Lockwood? How much longer?"

"A while yet. But you can come out now."

She threw off the blanket and gulped the chilly night air. The evening wore on. The boat bucked in the rising tide. Across the water a few faint lights gleamed and faded as dawn broke.

At last they reached the shore. Mr. Lockwood beached the boat and dragged it into the thick undergrowth. He took a large wooden box from the stern and in the gray light led India up a slight bluff and along an overgrown path. A faint light glimmered through the trees.

"That's Carsten Hall," he said, his voice low. "I'm not sure if anyone is at home just now. But the caretaker is probably around."

"It seems so lonely out here," India said. "I wouldn't want to live in the only house on the island."

"It isn't the only one. There are a few others the other side of the bluff. More are going up these days." He shifted his burden to his other arm. "Arthur Sterling was one of the first to build here after the war. Just down the road past Carsten Hall. The newspapers made quite a to-do over it at the time. I've never seen it myself, but they say it's twice the size of the Carstens' place."

A ten-minute walk brought them to a cabin nestled in a thick stand of old oaks. It loomed like a mirage in the pearlescent mist, its siding dark with age, its roof caving in. The porch sagged beneath their feet as Mr. Lockwood pushed open the door.

India brushed sticky cobwebs from her face and looked around. A thick layer of dust coated a scarred wooden table and three chairs. In the old brick fireplace, the ashes had hardened to a dull gray mass. The plank floor was littered with dead bugs and the desiccated skin of a snake. The stale air smelled faintly of rotten fish.

"Like I said, it isn't the Paris Plaza." Mr. Lockwood set the box down. "I'll pump you some water, but don't light a fire. You don't want to give that caretaker a reason to investigate."

He indicated the box. "There's another blanket in there. Enough food for a few days."

He fished a bucket from the box, and a few moments later India heard the groaning of the outdoor pump. She sank onto a dusty chair. Her head pounded. The knife wound on her arm burned. She didn't know whether to laugh or cry. How on earth had she wound up dressed as a nun and running from the law?

Mr. Lockwood returned and set the water bucket on the table. "This place is fairly deserted this time of year, but I'd advise you to stay inside as much as possible."

She nodded, too stunned for words.

"There's a privy out back. Just follow the path from the back door. Or, if you can't find the path, just follow your nose." He released a gusty breath. "With any luck, Sinclair will come to collect you in a few days."

He shook out her crumpled dress and draped it over the back of a chair. "I expect you'll want out of that religious garb."

"I would, yes. Where did you get it anyway? I can't imagine you found robes and a habit hanging on a clothesline somewhere."

"Borrowed 'em, you might say. From a friend of a friend." He scratched at his arms. "They're not all that comfortable are they? I must say wearin' this getup has given me a deeper appreciation for our men of the cloth."

Despite the circumstances, she laughed. "I have no idea why Mr. Sinclair thinks this scheme will work, but I'm in your debt, Mr. Lockwood. I'm not sure I can ever repay your kindness."

"Just put in a good word for me with Miss Amelia."

"I think you may find that she already holds you in high regard." The gravity of her situation came roaring back. "But I will press your case. If I ever see her again."

"You can't give up hope, miss. Once you do that, you're done for."

She blinked back the rush of tears behind her eyes.

"I'd better get going," he said. "It'll be full daylight soon, and I don't want anybody to see me leaving here."

He reached into the box again, and she noticed his palms were reddened and blistered from the long row across the river. "You're hurt."

He flexed his fingers. "It's been a while since I rowed eight miles. Should have worn gloves, I reckon."

"I'm sorry you must row all the way back."

"I've got a friend waiting with his fishing boat just down from Carsten Hall. I'll leave the rowboat there." He paused. "I brought you this. Just in case."

He pressed a revolver into her hands then disappeared into the woods.

India watched him go, the barrel of the weapon cold against her skin.

❧

As the first evening came down, the silence grew oppressive. India paced the small room, hummed every tune she knew, explored every nook and cranny of the small cabin. If only Mr. Lockwood had had the presence of mind to pack a book, a magazine, or writing paper. Anything to take her mind off her surroundings and away from the enormous risk Philip had taken to have her brought here.

The moon rose, luminous and full. Night creatures rustled the undergrowth. Beneath the window, a chorus of insects hummed. Moving in the darkness, India peered through the window and saw light flickering faintly in the caretaker's cottage.

She was too tense to eat, too uncomfortable to sleep. Too restless to simply sit and wait for Philip to ride to her rescue like a prince in a fairy tale. Suppose Arthur Sterling's house held the key to her freedom? Some clue as to who wanted to harm him and why. It was a long shot. She didn't even know what to look for. But she had to do something to help herself. To keep from going mad.

She changed out of the scratchy nun's garb, waited for full darkness, then set off along the path, the light in the cottage as her guide. A short walk brought her to a narrow dirt road leading upward toward the bluff. Nearing the caretaker's cottage, she could make out the dark outline of the main house beyond. Just as she passed the cottage, the door opened and lamplight spilled out, creating a yellow rectangle in the yard.

"Who's there?" A man's voice.

Her heart pounding, India crouched in the road and held her breath as he moved around the cottage, his lantern held high, passing so close that she caught a whiff of tobacco and spirits.

Her legs cramped. Something furry moved across her arm. She stifled a scream.

The caretaker went back inside. She got to her feet and quickened her steps.

The Sterling house was dark. Moonlight silvered a row of white-painted porch columns and illuminated manicured gardens on either side of a paved walkway. Twin chimneys pierced the night sky. India moved closer and rounded the porch to the side of the house. She jiggled the knob of the side door, but it held fast. She tried three windows before she found one unlocked. Hiking her skirts, she climbed inside. The room smelled of dust and mold. In the dark it was hard to know exactly where she was. She ran her fingers along the walls, her knees bumping into furniture. She touched a wall of books. A library, then.

A shard of moonlight fell across the room, revealing a small table upon which sat a lantern and a silver matchbox. India took this as a gift from Providence. Did she dare light the lamp? What if someone saw the flame and came to investigate? On the other hand, she had come this far.

She struck a match and lit the wick, turning down the flame as low as it would go. The faint light sent shadows dancing against the walls as she slid open the desk drawer. It contained nothing of interest—only a stack of receipts from the men's haberdashery, a pen with a broken tip, a folder containing old contracts, a deck of cards.

She closed the drawer and examined the rest of the room. On the shelves were bound copies of plays and poems, a few biographies. Last year's most popular novel. A couple of tintypes of Mr. Sterling in costume looking just as he had in life. Too handsome and too arrogant for his own good.

She tiptoed to the library door and opened it. A narrow hall hung with seascapes and a couple of portraits led to the front parlor. Lamplight played over the polished mahogany staircase opposite the marble-floored entry hall. India raised the lantern and took in the furnishings—two sofas flanking the fireplace, a leather chair positioned nearest the tall, heavily curtained windows. A hall tree draped with a man's woolen cloak and a battered felt hat.

India crossed the room to the hall tree and peered beneath the woolen cloak.

Behind her, the wooden stair creaked. India startled and gave an involuntary cry. Footsteps sounded on the bare floor.

India doused the light and whirled around, feeling her way down the corridor and back into the library. There, she dropped the lantern and climbed out the window.

She found the road and raced for the fishing cabin, not stopping until she reached safety. She flung herself onto her makeshift bed and gasped for breath, heedless of the army of brown, roach-like bugs marching across the floor just inches from her nose.

Later, she heard the shriek of a steamer coming up the river.

✦ CHAPTER 21 ✦

ON THE THIRD MORNING IN THE DESERTED CABIN, India woke from a dreamless sleep. She rose stiffly from her blankets on the floor, brushed at the dust on a chair, and dragged it closer to the window. The sun came up, staining the sky a rusty red and waking the sparrows that had taken shelter beneath the crumbling eaves. She pressed her fingers against the bandage on her head and winced when they found the deep gash. The dressing covering her knife wound was stiff with blood and dirt, but there was nothing she could do about that.

Her stomach rumbled, and she made a rudimentary breakfast from the contents of Mr. Lockwood's box: bread, a hunk of cheese, a few slices of cured ham, a jar of dried apples. She was desperate for tea, but there was none, and besides, she was too afraid of discovery to risk making a fire to boil water. She ate a few bites and carefully wrapped the rest, uncertain of how long these provisions would have to last.

As the morning wore on, she watched a squirrel darting among the tree branches, a lonely gull circling above the river. Would Philip come for her today? She couldn't wait to tell him what she had discovered at the Sterling house. He would admonish her for taking such a risk, but it had been worth the fright and the badly sprained wrist she'd gotten when she leapt from the library window.

When it became necessary, she found her way to the outhouse and returned quickly. She curled into a ball beneath the blankets and slept until the distant whistle of a steamboat wakened her. Then she amused herself by reciting every line of every play that she could remember, acting out the various parts in different voices. Every line reminded her of the best of her father. Even in this desolate place, her bright memories hovered like hummingbirds in the crisp winter air.

If only he had lived. If only her theater company had not been wrested from her. If only she had stood her ground with Mr. Philbrick and refused his order to change the play, her whole life would be different.

But during the long hours of another sleepless night, she realized that somehow she must resign herself to whatever fate had in store. A flash of color outside the cabin drew her attention. She stepped away from the window and into the shadows and took Mr. Lockwood's revolver from the bottom of the box. The undergrowth rustled, and she darted behind the door, holding the revolver close to her chest. Footsteps sounded on the porch. The door swung wide. She drew in a long choking breath, her face pressed to the rough wood. Her heart hammered in her chest.

"India?"

Her knees went weak. The gun clattered to the floor.

Philip held out his arm to steady her, and then she was in his arms. His lips pressed against her temple and moved to claim hers. She clung to him with all of the suppressed desire that had been building since their time together at Indigo Point. No matter what the future held, she would never forget this moment, this feeling of being protected. Safe.

He drew back to look at her. "Are you all right?"

"I think so." Now that the moment had passed, she felt awkward in his presence. Would he think her too bold to have pressed herself into his arms with such fervor? "I'm . . . glad to see you."

He seemed eager to put the conversation on a more neutral footing too. "I'm sorry that I had you kidnapped," he said. "But I couldn't think of any other plan."

"Mr. Lockwood said you were looking for another witness."

"Yes. During the colonel's testimony, I remembered something that made me believe you might have been right about my wife. And so I went looking. And I found her." He looked away.

"What?"

"When I first brought Laura to Indigo Point, she was terrified of alligators and snakes. She bought a revolver and insisted that I teach her how to shoot."

"But that doesn't have anything to do with me."

"Not in and of itself. But the notes you found prove that she was in love with someone else. And she knew how to fire a gun."

India nodded. "Listen, Philip, I have something to tell you. Night before last I searched Sterling's house here on the island, and I found—"

A shout echoed among the trees. Philip grabbed India, and they hid behind the cabin door, their bodies pressed into the dank, shadowed space. India could feel her heart pounding and Philip's warm breath on her ear.

The door creaked open. Footsteps sounded on the rotten planks.

"Somebody's campin' here." The voice was that of a young boy.

"They's food." Another voice. "They's some cheese and some—"

"Who cares? They's a gun. That oughta sell for some real money in town."

Through a crack in the door, India watched as one of the boys held up the nun's habit and shook it out, setting the wooden rosary beads to clattering. "Maybe we ought not to steal from a sister. God's liable to strike us dead in our tracks if we do."

"What's a nun doin' with a revolver?"

"Shootin' at snakes, I reckon."

"Well, I say we take it. Ain't nothin' else worth stealin'."

Philip released India and stepped from behind the door. Both boys yelped.

"Afternoon, fellows," Philip said. "What are you doing here?"

"Nothin'. We was just lookin' around. We didn't know you was stayin' here."

Philip held out his hand for the gun. "Well, now that you do, it's time to move on. Though you're welcome to the food if you want it."

"Nah, that's all right. We don't care much for cheese."

"Suit yourself."

The taller of the two frowned. "How come you got a nun's robes?"

"It's top secret," Philip said.

"You some kind of a spy! And that's your disguise."

India stifled a laugh at the mental picture of Philip dressed in holy garments.

He shooed them out the door.

"Let's get out of here."

"Where are we going?"

"Back to Savannah. We've got a date with Judge Bartlett."

India gaped at him, a dozen questions crowding her mind. But Philip was already moving about the cabin, folding her blankets and the discarded nun's habit and placing them in the wooden crate with the remnants of her food.

"I've a steamer waiting downriver to take us back to the city," he said. "Are you ready?"

"I suppose, but Philip, what's going to happen when we get there?"

"I spoke with the judge yesterday. He's agreed to hear Laura's testimony in chambers. With Mr. McLendon in attendance, of course." He paused in his preparations and studied her, his expression calm and wise. "Word of your absence has spread. You must be prepared for a large and noisy crowd, I'm afraid."

"It won't be the first time."

"No, but I hope it will be the last." He picked up the Remington, checked the chamber, and set it into the box.

CHAPTER 22

INDIA HURRIED TO KEEP UP AS PHILIP LED HER THROUGH the dense forest. A small steamer churned its way up the river and nudged the pier. Wordlessly, Philip helped her board, tossed the wooden box inside, and settled onto the seat beside her.

The captain, a young man with a neatly trimmed beard, turned the craft upriver just as the two boys emerged from the trees and raced onto the pier. If Philip noticed them, he didn't mention it. He sat with his head down, his hands clasped loosely between his knees, as if the effort of rescuing her had completely exhausted him.

India felt a rush of tenderness mixed with confusion and a simmering anger at the woman who had betrayed him. She was dying to tell him what she had discovered in Sterling's house, but he was in no shape just now to make sense of it. And she was exhausted, too, after three nights of hiding. The knife wound burned. The gash on her head throbbed painfully. She was covered in dust and sweat. And terrified at the prospect of facing the judge. He would not look kindly upon her disappearance, even if it hadn't been her idea.

The steamer quickly covered the eight miles to the city. India raked at her hair as the boat nudged the pier. The wharf was abuzz with the usual workday activity—workers loading cargo schooners, cotton factors rushing to and fro, passengers waiting to board steamers bound for Boston or New York.

Philip steadied her as they stepped off the steamer. "With any luck, we will pass unnoticed, but whatever happens, stay close to me. Keep moving, and keep your head up."

India was overcome with weariness and fear and with the effort of trying to staunch her tears. She felt her eyes welling up again as they climbed the stairs to the street, passed through the crowd, and entered a waiting carriage. "I must look like a derelict."

"You've been through an ordeal. But you'll have time to make yourself presentable before we meet the judge," Philip said. "Mrs. Mackay is expecting us."

"I'm grateful, but I don't want to get her into trouble for harboring a fugitive."

He managed a tired smile. "Leave me to worry about that. While you're getting cleaned up, I have business at the jail. I'll fetch you from the Mackays' at two then we'll go see the judge."

The carriage drew up at the terra cotta mansion on Madison Square.

"Philip, what's all this about? I don't understand how—"

"There isn't time to explain it just now." He cupped her cheek in his hand. "You have trusted me with your life. Trust me for just a bit longer."

He helped her out of the carriage and hurried up to the Mackays' door.

Mrs. Mackay herself answered the bell. "Oh, my dear. Please come in."

Philip touched the brim of his hat and returned to the carriage.

Mrs. Mackay ushered India inside. "Come on upstairs. I've had the maid draw a bath for you, and she's pressed the clothes Philip sent. There won't be much time to dress your hair, but perhaps a simple braid will do."

"Mrs. Mackay, I don't know how to thank you. I'm—"

"Call me Celia, please. Now come along."

Alone in the spacious bathing room, India shed her clothes and sank into the warm, fragrant water. She washed her hair and scrubbed the dirt from beneath her nails, acutely aware that this might be the last time she would be afforded such luxury, such freedom.

When the water cooled she rose from the tub, toweled off, dressed carefully, and braided her damp hair.

A knock sounded at the door, and Frannie Mackay stuck her head into the room. "Mama wants to know if you're hungry."

India finished fastening the buttons on her sleeves. "I am, actually."

The child bobbed her head, sending her curls dancing around her face. "I thought so. You look positively famished! Mama made sandwiches, and we have cake and milk. No tea, though, because Mrs. Whipple, she looks after us, forgot to get any last week."

"Milk sounds fine."

Frannie grabbed India's hand. "I'll show you to the parlor."

India let the enchanting child lead her into the gracious

room below, where her mother presided over a tray set before the fire.

"Mama, here's Miss India, and I was right. She's starving!"

"Well, we can remedy that." Mrs. Mackay's violet eyes glowed with love for her small daughter. "Would you excuse us now, Frannie? I'll be up later to read with you and hear your lessons."

"But I'll miss all the fun."

"Francesca Mackay—"

"Uh-oh." Frannie sighed and said to India, "When Mama calls me Francesca, I have to go."

She scampered across the room and up the curving staircase.

India watched her go, a longing for the kind of life and family Mrs. Mackay enjoyed building inside her. But it was not to be. Not now.

Mrs. Mackay filled a plate and passed it to India. "Philip told me he had you removed from the hospital while he looked for a witness."

India ate a bite of the sandwich and dabbed at her lips with a heavy damask napkin. "Yes, the experience was something straight from a dime novel." She briefly described Mr. Lockwood's rescue and her three days on Isle of Hope. "Then Philip showed up there early this morning and said he'd found the person he'd been seeking."

Mrs. Mackay gave a brief nod. "He told me he'd found Laura. After all this time. I've known Philip for years, and I must say I've never seen him so undone." Her violet eyes sought India's. "He loved her so. This discovery has cost him dearly."

"I'm sorry to have been the cause of it."

"Laura always was mercurial, hard to figure out. She was

quite beautiful, but she seemed not to trust herself." Mrs. Mackay stared into the dancing firelight. "Perhaps it comes from her upbringing. Her father was a baker, and they lived modestly here in town. But Laura planned to rise above her station in life. She met Philip during a Christmas celebration one year and set her cap for him. I think he was intrigued because she was so different from the others in our circle. She was happy enough when they lived in the city, but she was miserable at Indigo Point, and she made sure Philip knew it."

Recalling the notes she'd found, India nodded. Laura Sinclair had not been cut out to be a planter's wife. Especially when the war had decimated everything and all the planters struggled to hold onto their falling-down houses and worn-out fields. Clearly Laura's marriage to Philip had deteriorated.

But what about now? Did he still love her? How would he cope with such utter betrayal? Loss could bring a person down as surely as a fever, leaving permanent scars upon the heart.

A sudden pounding on the door startled them. Before Mrs. Whipple could reach the door, it opened, and two uniformed policemen barged in. The older one, a man with graying hair and a slight paunch, strode into the parlor. "Miss Hartley. I'm afraid you'll have to come with us."

Celia frowned. "Whatever for, Officer? Miss Hartley will appear in court whenever it's required. And I must say I do not appreciate your invading my home like this."

A loud chorus of angry voices filtered in from the street. India peered out the window. A crowd had gathered outside the front gate, brandishing signs that read Justice Is Blind, and No Favoritism in Savannah's Courts.

The younger officer jerked his thumb. "That's why, Miz Mackay. Word is out that Miss Hartley here is back in town. Judge Bartlett has been delayed and can't meet until tomorrow. He told us to fetch the prisoner. He can't afford to give the appearance of favoring one defendant over another."

"India?" Philip strode into the hallway. He had changed his clothes, and now he looked every inch the lawyer—competent, controlled, detached.

He took her hand. "I'm sorry about this, but it can't be helped. And it's best not to defy the judge's wishes." He turned to the officers. "I'll see that she reports to the jail."

The younger one looked uncertain. "We were told to fetch her, but if you say so, Mr. Sinclair."

Celia briefly embraced India, who followed Philip outside. With the officers riding right behind them, Philip handed India into his rig. "Can you bear another night in the county jail?"

"I suppose I have to."

"Fabienne will bring you a change of clothes. And Dr. Webb will be by to check on your head wound." His voice softened. "You gave me quite a scare when you fell. I was afraid you were seriously hurt. After all you've been through, I don't think I could stand to see anything else happen to you."

"The shock of a guilty verdict was too much to take. I was counting on Colonel Culpepper's testimony to win my case. Obviously they didn't believe him."

"Judge Bartlett believes in going strictly by the book. Which may work in our favor tomorrow." He flicked the reins. "Let's go."

India sat beside him, her hands clasped in her lap. She had allowed herself to hope that Philip Sinclair might one day become the love of her heart. The one she'd waited a lifetime to find. They'd known each other for such a short time, but already she loved his fine mind, his patience, and his quiet confidence. His humor and his faith in the law. But he was not hers. He could never be hers.

She thought of the day at Indigo Point when he'd saved her from the cottonmouth, the day they'd found a single rose blooming in Mrs. King's abandoned garden, the day he'd returned from Savannah bearing a plum pudding because she had expressed a fondness for it. She recalled the shock and concern in his eyes when Mrs. Catchpole had attacked her with the knife. She had hoped it meant something intimate and personal, but theirs was only a professional friendship, with Mrs. Mackay paying the bill.

India shifted on the hard seat as the rig jostled along the street. His concern for her was nothing more than that of a lawyer for his client. And now that he had found his wife alive after believing her dead . . . well, India could only imagine what he must be feeling. Confusion, most certainly, but surely profound relief too.

Another few moments brought them to the jail, and India saw with dismay that another crowd of reporters and townspeople had assembled to witness her return. Philip halted the rig.

"Are you ready?"

She felt vulnerable, as if her skin had been stripped away, leaving nothing but a mass of exposed nerves, but she stood and forced herself to breathe slowly and deeply—a trick she'd learned years ago to calm her stage fright. "I'm ready."

The crowd surged toward her as they exited the rig.

"Miss Hartley!" A reporter with a protruding belly and gin blossoms on his cheeks thrust his notebook into her face. "How did you escape from the hospital? Where have you been hiding?"

"India! Over here!" Another reporter pushed through the crowd. "How does it feel to be found guilty of murder?"

Philip shoved him aside. "Let us pass, please."

"Mr. Sinclair," the reporter persisted. "I assume you'll file an appeal. What are her chances of avoiding the gallows?"

"Much better than your chances of avoiding a collision with my fists if you don't get out of the way." Philip tightened his grip on her hand. They pushed through the crush of onlookers and he led her into the jail.

"I hate leaving you here," he said, "but it's only for one night. I'll be in my office all night, so send word there if you need me."

"I will."

"An officer will be there in the morning to escort you to the courthouse."

"All right."

He let out a gusty sigh. "I know this has been a nightmare. But it's almost over."

She wanted to believe him, but she was afraid now to hope. "How can you be so sure?"

An officer appeared, nodded to Philip, and snapped the manacles around her wrists. "Come along, miss."

With a backward glance at Philip, she followed the officer down the dank and smelly corridor. Back to the same cell where she'd been held during the trial.

The officer swung open the door and motioned her inside. He removed the shackles and indicated a tray sitting beside the cot. "Mr. Sinclair said he was bringing you in, so I had some food sent over. It's probably cold as a witch's . . . well, let's just say it's cold, but still edible, I expect."

She rubbed her wrists and pressed a hand to the bandage on her head. The last thing she wanted was more jailhouse food. But he had taken special pains to procure it. "Thank you, Officer."

"Sure." He stepped out, and the cell door clanged shut. "For what it's worth, miss, I sure am sorry for the way Savannah has treated you. Of course a man's romantic proclivities are rarely justification for murder, but it was no secret that Mr. Sterling collected female admirers the way some people collect coins. He had plenty of enemies in this town, but now that he's dead they're trying to make him into some kind of saint." He shook his head. "It ain't right."

"I appreciate your saying so."

"It's the truth." He regarded her thoughtfully. "All I can say is, I hope that new witness clears things up for you."

She sank onto the cot. "I hope so too."

"Well, you just rest now, and call for me if you need anything."

He turned away, his footfalls heavy on the wooden floor. India dropped onto the lumpy mattress and closed her eyes. After three nights of trying to sleep on the floor of the fish camp, she was grateful for the relative comfort of the rudimentary cot. Despite the noise of other occupants, the slamming of doors, the hollow echo of footsteps, India slept until Fabienne's voice woke her.

"*Mamselle.*"

India sat up, blinking in the dim light.

Fabienne regarded her with sorrowful eyes. The infectious

joy that usually animated her lovely features was gone. "I brought your things from Mrs. Mackay's." She indicated a policeman India hadn't seen before. "The officer has them."

"Thank you, Fabienne."

The young Frenchwoman stifled a sob. "Forgive me, *mamselle*. I did not wish to speak against you, but that lawyer gave me a paper and said that I—"

"It's all right. Mr. Sinclair explained it to me. I know you meant no harm."

Fabienne pulled an envelope from her pocket and slid it through the bars. "It's the money you left for me when you went away. I think you must need it more than I do."

India smiled. "I wish you'd keep it. You earned it. And besides, my bills are being paid by a friend. One I didn't even realize I had."

Fabienne sniffed. "You are certain?"

"Positive."

"*Merçi, mamselle.* Tomorrow I will—"

"Miss." The officer stepped forward. "This is a jail, and visiting hours are over. I expect you ought to go now."

"All right." Fabienne pressed both her palms against the bars. "Good-bye, *Mamselle.* You must not worry. *Le Bon Dieu* will protect you."

She hurried away. The officer unlocked the cell and handed India her clothes. "Doc Webb is on his way over. The judge is worried about that head of yours."

Just then the doctor arrived, accompanied by Officer Avery. The policeman barely nodded to India as he unlocked her cell and waved the doctor inside.

"Please be seated." The doctor indicated the cot, and India sat.

He began unwrapping the bandage, tugging gently to release the linen from the dried blood on her hair. He whistled softly. "That's quite a gash you've got there. But it seems to be doing all right."

He took a brown bottle of liquid from his medical bag and dabbed some onto a clean cloth. "This is apt to sting a little."

India sucked in a sharp breath as the antiseptic hit her wounded flesh. She clenched her teeth as tears sprang to her eyes.

"Sorry. But we don't want sepsis to set in."

He applied salve and covered the wound with a clean bandage. "That ought to do it. Be sure to keep that dry."

"I will."

The doctor called for the guard, and soon India was left alone again.

She pictured Philip in his office across town and was struck anew at the thought that his wife was still alive and that she might be India's last chance for freedom.

CHAPTER 23

JUDGE BARTLETT STRODE INTO HIS CHAMBERS, BLACK robes billowing. With a curt nod to those assembled he sat down behind his desk and folded his hands. "This had better be good, Mr. Sinclair, because I am very close to throwing the book at you for harboring a fugitive"—he broke off and glared at India— "and for thwarting the prerogatives of this court. You'll be lucky not to be disbarred."

"Begging your pardon, Judge." Philip rose and placed a hand on the back of India's chair. "Technically Miss Hartley is not a fugitive, and technically I was not the one who removed her to a place of safety in order to ensure that justice is done."

Philip glanced at Mr. McLendon before returning his attention to Judge Bartlett. "Before this day is done, you will thank me for this."

"Oh? What for?"

"For preserving your perfect record of never having been reversed on appeal."

"A jury declared her guilty."

"Because you refused to declare a mistrial despite the strong possibility there was a second shot in the theater that night."

The judge waved his hand. "All right. Now, is the new witness prepared to give a statement?"

"Yes, sir." Philip motioned to a police officer stationed inside the judge's door.

The officer disappeared and returned with a woman dressed in a simple blue day dress, her face half hidden by an enormous feathered hat anchored by two large pearl hat pins.

India gripped the arms of her chair and forced air into her lungs. Here was the very same woman India had seen loitering in the hallway at the theater wearing a distinctive purple cloak. The cloak India had discovered hanging on the hall tree in Arthur Sterling's house on Isle of Hope.

The officer showed her to a seat opposite the judge's gleaming wooden desk.

"State your name, please." The judge opened a ledger and took up his pen.

"Laura Sinclair."

The prosecutor came upright in his chair and grabbed his file.

"Now, Mrs. Sinclair," the judge began. "You are not on trial, but you are bound to tell the truth here just as you would be in court. Do you understand?"

The woman nodded, and India noted how her hands trembled.

"All right. Suppose you tell me what you know about the incident in the Southern Palace Theater last December."

"I went to the theater that night, but I wasn't intending to hurt anyone. Not when I first arrived. I only wanted to talk to

Arthur . . . Mr. Sterling . . . to ask him about . . . a personal matter."

"And were you able to do so?"

"No. He wouldn't speak to me. He told me he was too busy. But then I noticed he had plenty of time for Miss Bryson. She is . . . was . . . Miss Hartley's understudy. Something came over me then, and I knew I'd have to do something drastic to make him tell me why he no longer loved me."

Beside India, Philip made a small noise in his throat. But his face was a mask of professional objectivity as the judge motioned to Laura to continue.

"That night, before the show, I was waiting for Arthur in the hallway, and I heard Mr. Philbrick telling him he wanted Miss Hartley to pretend to shoot Arthur on stage, because he thought the play was too dull to impress an important critic."

"I see. Go on."

"Arthur spoke with Miss Hartley. He joked with her about wanting to do him harm because he had upstaged her on opening night. When he left, I followed him to his dressing room, where I saw him kissing that tart Miss Bryson. After giving him five years of my life!" Her voice broke, but she gathered herself. "I knew then that his affections were not true. I couldn't bear it. Not after everything I had done in order to be with him."

India thought of the red notebook filled with love notes. The burned chapel, the missing slave girl. The gold necklace she'd found amid the ashes. Did Philip believe her theory now? She stole a glance at him, but his expression was unreadable.

Laura Sinclair looked up at the judge. "May I have a glass of water?"

The officer poured from a pitcher sitting on a table behind the judge's desk and handed the cup to her. She sipped and went on.

"I knew Miss Hartley kept a gun in her trunk in the trap room."

"How did you know?"

"The day of the dress rehearsal, I came to speak to Arthur. I was standing near the trap room when Miss Hartley came in to get some more hairpins from her trunk. She had to take out several smaller boxes to find them, and that's when I saw the gun."

Laura set the water glass on the floor beside her chair and drew a handkerchief from her sleeve. "Everything went all wrong. I didn't intend to kill him. I thought if he were wounded he would realize how much he needed me, and he'd forget about Miss Bryson, and everything would go back to the way it was meant to be."

Outside the chambers, a man began shouting and pounding on the door. The policeman went out to quell the disturbance. Judge Bartlett leaned across his desk. "Mrs. Sinclair, are you confessing to the murder of Arthur Sterling?"

The door flew open, and a large red-faced man charged into the room.

Startled, India yelped, "Mr. Philbrick?"

"Order!" The judge slapped his desk and got to his feet. "What on earth is going on here?"

Cornelius Philbrick wrenched free and stood before the judge, panting heavily. "I admit I'm not the most upstanding citizen in Savannah, but I can't stand by and watch the woman I love go to the gallows for a crime she didn't commit."

India blinked. The woman he loved? What was he talking about? She and the theater manager barely tolerated each other. Especially after he'd threatened to replace her.

Philip got to his feet. "Maybe you ought to explain yourself, Mr. Philbrick."

The theater manager expelled a noisy breath. "Laura doesn't know how I feel about her. I never got up the nerve to tell her. But it made me angry to see the way Sterling treated her. Trampling on her tender feelings as if they didn't matter."

India stared at him. So it was Laura he loved, although she clearly cared for no one but Mr. Sterling. What a strange tale this was.

Mr. Philbrick turned to Laura Sinclair, who had gone pale as milk. "I saw you standing in the wings that night holding a gun, and I guessed what you had in mind. It's true I wanted to sensationalize the play to get people talking about it, but I never intended anyone to actually get hurt. So I took my own gun and followed you into the wings. I knew Miss Hartley's weapon was the fake and wouldn't fire. I had to stop you. I intended to shoot the gun from your hand. To save you from committing a crime."

Inexplicably, Laura laughed. "Oh, Cornelius. I'm afraid you wasted your gallantry unnecessarily."

"What do you mean?"

"The gun you saw in my hand was the fake one. After the prop manager placed it on the table on the stage, I took Miss Hartley's gun from her trunk and switched them." Laura's eyes went hard. "I admit I'm a coward. I wanted to hurt Arthur, but I wasn't brave enough to do it myself."

The judge pressed the heels of his hands to his temples and laced his fingers over his head as if to keep the facts from escaping. "Just a minute here, Mr. Philbrick. Are you asking me to believe that you actually expected to shoot a gun from her hand without harming her? And from the shadowed wings of a packed theater? It seems to me such a feat would have required an extraordinarily steady aim."

"I know it sounds unlikely. But in my younger days I was part of a troupe of traveling entertainers—magicians, acrobats, jugglers, and the like. My specialty was trick shooting." Mr. Philbrick shrugged. "In the war I was a sharpshooter. General Johnson once told me I was the best shot in the whole army. But that night at the theater, I missed my target and hit Mr. Sterling instead."

The judge shook his head. "And you let Miss Hartley take the blame."

"I never thought a jury would convict someone as famous as Miss Hartley. I thought she'd get off, and no one would be the wiser."

"Why confess now?" the judge asked.

Mr. Philbrick crossed the room and took Laura's hand. "I already told you why."

Philip looked ashen.

"Philip?" Laura looked up at him, her eyes brimming with tears. "There's something else you deserve to know."

He held up both hands, palms out. "I think I've had all the revelations I can take for one day."

She shook her head, and the feathers on her hat fluttered. "Judging from the extraordinary measures you took to defend Miss Hartley and keep her from sentencing, it's something you'll be glad to know."

He folded his arms across his chest. "All right. Let's have it."

"I'm not your wife." She dropped her gaze. "I never was."

Chapter 24

Judge Bartlett frowned. "Well, Mrs. Sinclair, that's quite a statement, but let's stick to the topic that brought us here." He swiveled in his chair to face the trembling theater manager. "Now, Mr. Philbrick, as I understand it, you are admitting to shooting Arthur Sterling."

"Not intentionally." Mr. Philbrick licked his lips. "But yes. The fault is wholly mine."

"You realize you will be brought before an inquest jury and most likely indicted."

"I expect so," Mr. Philbrick muttered.

"Very well." The judge pointed to Laura. "Don't you go anywhere until the prosecutor decides what to do with you."

Philip glanced at Mr. McLendon. "I promised her I'd put in a good word with you in exchange for her clearing Miss Hartley. After all, the only thing she's really guilty of is intent. And since Mr. Philbrick has confessed—"

"Mr. McLendon." Judge Bartlett motioned to the prosecutor, who had listened to the entire exchange without uttering a word. "You will withdraw all charges against Miss Hartley and expunge the record."

"Yes, Your Honor."

"The sooner the better." Philip gathered his papers and rose from his chair. "Thank you, Judge."

India slumped in her chair. Her ordeal was over, or nearly so. But her heart ached for Philip. And what on earth had Laura meant, that she was not really his wife?

"Miss Hartley." The judge scribbled on some papers as he spoke. "On behalf of all of us, I apologize for putting you through this. I wouldn't blame you if you never wanted to set foot in our city again."

He motioned for an officer to take charge of Mr. Philbrick. Laura Sinclair grabbed her cloak and reticule and fairly ran from the room, the faint scent of gardenias lingering in her wake. The others followed, leaving India and Philip alone.

India rummaged in her reticule for a handkerchief and blotted her eyes. She felt elated and dispirited at once. Now that she was free, she and Philip would go their separate ways. In time, she would recede into his memory as just another case. He would forget her. And she must try to forget him. Though at this moment, that seemed impossible.

Now Philip smiled down at her. "Thank God this nightmare is over."

"Yes."

"What will you do now?"

She had never let herself think too much about the future, but now that she had one, where would she go? What would she do with the rest of her life? Fate had handed her a second chance. It was up to her to make the most of it. To find some higher purpose to her days. "I'm not sure. For now, I'm simply grateful that I don't ever again have to set foot inside the Chatham County Jail. And it's all down to you. I can never repay you for all you've done."

"It was your suspicions about Laura that broke the case." He picked up his leather satchel and offered her his arm. "We caught a lucky break. Seeing you go free and the appropriate perpetrator apprehended is more than enough."

They left the judge's chambers and started down the hallway to the front entrance. Through the window, India saw that a crowd was already gathering on the front lawn. She recognized a couple of the reporters who had covered her trial, and she let out a disgusted sigh. Half the world made their living off the miseries of the other half, and there was nothing to be done about it.

"Mrs. Mackay's carriage is waiting," Philip said. "She and I agreed you'd be better off at her house than at the hotel." He gestured toward the street. "It seems the public's interest in your story hasn't yet waned. Just stick to me, and let me do the talking. Once they have a statement, they'll go away."

She clung more tightly to Philip's arm, not wanting to think about tomorrow, when he would no longer be her protector.

He pushed open the courthouse door, and the crowd surged toward them, shouting a barrage of questions.

"Miss Hartley, how does it feel to be free?"

"Are you going back on the stage?"

"Miss Hartley, is it true you were in love with Mr. Sterling?"

Philip tightened his grip on her arm. "Miss Hartley and I are both delighted with the outcome of today's proceedings. It has been a harrowing experience. Now she needs time to rest. We ask that you respect her privacy."

"Mr. Sinclair, is it true the woman who testified this morning is your wife?"

"We have nothing more to say. Now please let us pass."

Philip pushed through the onlookers and helped India into the waiting carriage. She tucked her skirts around her to make room for him, but he shook his head. "I have some things to do. Give my best to the Mackays."

He signaled the driver, and the carriage began to move. India watched him until he was lost in the crowd. She looked out the carriage window as they drove toward Madison Square. Palmettos rattled in the wind. A thin shaft of sunlight pierced the gray morning clouds and glinted off the windows of shops lining the street. Now that she had come so close to losing her freedom, every small detail of this ordinary morning took on new significance. Perhaps one day, this feeling would fade, but for now, she relished every sight and sound. Every breath felt like a gift.

The carriage drew to a stop. The driver helped her alight. Looking up, she saw movement at the window. The door opened before she had mounted the steps.

Celia Mackay, dressed in a simple forest-green day dress, clasped both of India's hands. "You're here, so I suppose that must mean Philip has won your freedom."

"Yes. Mr. Philbrick confessed."

Mrs. Mackay—India still had a hard time thinking of her as Celia—frowned. "The theater manager? Why on earth would he shoot Mr. Sterling?"

"It's complicated."

"So it seems. Oh, I am mightily relieved that our prayers

were answered. Please do come in. Frannie and I have finished breakfast, but I can use some tea. What about you?"

"It sounds heavenly."

Mrs. Mackay led the way to the now-familiar parlor and rang a little silver bell. Soon, a middle-aged woman in a crisp white apron appeared.

"Mrs. Whipple," Mrs. Mackay said. "We'd love some tea, and some shortbread if there is any left."

The woman shook her head. "I'm afraid Miss Frannie cleaned me out, Mrs. Mackay, after her riding lesson yesterday. But there's some scones left, and some of that strawberry jam you favor."

"That will be fine." Mrs. Mackay inclined her head, and Mrs. Whipple withdrew.

Mrs. Mackay motioned India to a seat before the fire. "I will admit I am extremely curious to know how Philip managed to solve the case, but if you'd rather not speak of it—"

India pulled off her gloves and laid them on the settee. "I barely understand it myself."

She related the events of the past days—Mr. Lockwood's taking her from the hospital to avoid sentencing while Philip searched for his star witness, Philip's appearance on Isle of Hope to bring her back, Mr. Philbrick's confession.

Mrs. Whipple came in with the tea things, and India paused while Mrs. Mackay poured, then passed her the plate of scones. The housekeeper stood hesitantly at the door, her hands clasped at her waist.

Mrs. Mackay looked up, brows raised. "Yes, Mrs. Whipple?"

"You remember I asked could I have the next three days off, on account of my sister's coming into town."

"I do remember, and you're free to go. I'm not altogether hopeless in the kitchen, and if we get too bored with my offerings, we can always have dinner at the hotel."

Mrs. Whipple beamed. "Thank you kindly, Mrs. Mackay."

When they were alone again Mrs. Mackay stirred her tea, a frown on her face. "The jury had already decided you were guilty. What made Mr. Philbrick come forward when he could have gotten away with it?"

"His great affection for the star witness." India struggled to speak the words that were like a knife to the heart. "Mr. Sinclair's . . . wife."

"I was stunned when he told me he had found her," Mrs. Mackay said. "A part of me still feels it's impossible. I was there when that poor woman was laid to rest in Laurel Grove. Philip brought her back here. He was nearly crazed with grief because he'd insisted on taking her to Indigo Point despite her distaste for it. He said he at least wanted her to rest in Savannah, a place she loved. I had understood she was very badly burned, so there was no viewing of the remains, but—"

India's heart lurched. There had been a burial, but clearly, the body wasn't Laura's. India's cup rattled in her saucer. She felt sick. "Hannah June."

"What?"

"There's no other explanation." India couldn't keep the urgency from her voice. "The body he buried had to belong to one of Mr. Sinclair's former slaves. A girl named Hannah June. Her sister Binah still helps look after things at Indigo Point."

"But why? How did—"

"Mama?" Frannie Mackay stuck her head into the room.

"My head hurts. And Miss Finlay said I should go straight back to bed and not do any more sums today."

"Oh? Come here, darling." Mrs. Mackay opened her arms and embraced her daughter.

"My head feels hot."

"Where is Miss Finlay now?"

"Up in the school room correcting my orthography test. But she's leaving soon. Because I feel sick."

Mrs. Mackay placed the back of her hand against Frannie's forehead. "You do feel warm. Go on upstairs, and I'll be right up with something to make you feel better."

Frannie obeyed, and a few moments later the tutor came downstairs, her hands full of books, her blue woolen cloak draped over her arm.

Mrs. Mackay went into the hallway and spoke briefly with the young woman before returning to the parlor.

India finished her tea. "Is everything all right?"

"I'm sure it's nothing serious. I'll sit with her a while. She'll be better tomorrow."

"I should get out of the way so you can see to her."

"Oh, you aren't in the way at all. This house is way too quiet when my husband is away. I'm grateful for your company. But you've had an eventful morning. Perhaps you would enjoy some time alone. Your room upstairs is just the way you left it. I've had Mrs. Whipple freshen the linens and lay a fire, but feel free to ring if you need anything."

Mrs. Mackay led the way up the staircase and headed for Frannie's room.

India turned the opposite direction and entered the room

that had been prepared for her. Something furry and warm pressed against her leg. She whirled around and let out a scream that brought Mrs. Mackay running.

"Heavens. What's the matter?"

"There's something alive in this room. It scared me."

Mrs. Mackay peered beneath the bed and emitted a piercing and most unladylike whistle. "Maxwell! You know very well you are not allowed up here. Come out this instant."

An old dog, mostly gray but once golden, judging from a few patches of hair on his chest, crawled from beneath the bed and turned his liquid brown eyes on India as if to apologize for her fright. He nuzzled her hand, and she bent to place a kiss on his grizzled head. "Oh, he's wonderful."

Mrs. Mackay laughed. "I think so. He was a present from Sutton the year we became engaged." She scratched beneath the old dog's chin. "Poor old boy is nearly thirteen now. Mostly he lies beside the fire in the kitchen and tries to avoid Frannie's cat, but I suppose his curiosity got the best of him whilst Mrs. Whipple was freshening up your room. He does so enjoy visitors." She smiled. "He's always keen for someone new to shower him with attention."

"Well, I'm glad of his company. If you don't mind his staying here, I certainly don't."

Mrs. Mackay knelt beside her beloved companion. "You seem to have made another friend, Maxwell. But don't make a nuisance of yourself, you hear?"

The dog thumped his tail against the floor. She rose. "If he gets to be too much trouble just let me know, and I'll send him back to the kitchen."

"We'll be fine. And thank you again for taking me in. I wasn't looking forward to returning to the hotel to face those reporters."

Mrs. Mackay's face clouded. "That lot never knows when to back away. Please excuse me. I must see to Frannie."

"Of course."

The door closed. India removed her hat, her shoes, and her stockings and dropped onto the woolen rug beside the old dog. He snuggled next to her as if he had known her forever, his breath warm on her cheek, and she felt the tensions of the day drain away. She draped one arm across his chest and closed her eyes. Someday, when she was settled, she would get a dog of her own. "Won't that be grand, Maxwell?"

He licked her hand as if to agree before they both fell asleep.

✒ CHAPTER 25 ✒

INDIA WOKE TO FRANNIE'S FRETFUL CRIES AND THE awful sound of retching. She sat up in bed and blinked, waiting for her head to clear. Sometime in the night, Maxwell had retired to a spot on the hearth, and she had climbed into bed without bothering to unpin her hair.

Now the fire was out, and a thin shaft of gray morning light fell across the counterpane.

"Mama!" Frannie's cries grew louder.

India pulled her dress over her head and hurried along the darkened hallway in her bare feet. Passing Mrs. Mackay's room, she saw her hostess huddled over the chamber pot, her dark hair hanging like a curtain across her face.

"I couldn't make it to the water closet." Celia's face was white as a winding sheet.

"What can I do to help?"

Celia wiped her mouth. "If you could see to Frannie for a moment—"

"Of course."

India pushed open the door to the child's room to find that

Frannie had soiled her sheets. Tears shimmered in the child's violet eyes. "I'm sorry."

"It's all right. Let me help you."

India stripped off the child's soiled nightdress and removed the dirty linens from the bed. "Let's get you cleaned up."

She followed Frannie into the bathing room. Frannie spun a handle and warm water gushed into the tub. India found soap and towels, and while Frannie bathed, she returned to the child's room to find a clean nightgown and made the bed with clean linens.

By the time she had settled Frannie into bed again, Celia was returning from emptying the chamber pot. She made it to the top of the stairs before her legs gave way, and she collapsed onto the floor.

India helped her to her feet. "Shall I run a bath for you?"

"Please. I am too weak to move."

While Celia bathed, India went downstairs and rummaged for tea and crackers. When the tea was ready, she took a tray upstairs. Celia was able to take a few sips, but Frannie pushed her cup away. "I don't want any."

"Would you like me to read to you?"

"No. I want my papa," Frannie said.

"I know just how you feel." India drew a chair closer to the bed. "Papas are the best at telling stories, aren't they?"

Frannie nodded. "My papa knows a million stories."

"A million? My goodness. I don't think I've ever met anyone who knows that many. What's your favorite?"

"The Black Pearl Pirate and the Ghost Ship of Spain."

"That does sound exciting. Maybe you could tell it to me when you feel better."

"I guess so." Frannie shivered. "It's cold in here."

"Tell me where the wood is kept, and I'll make a fire for you."

"In the shed behind the old carriage house. But watch out for spiders and mice and ghosts."

India checked on Celia, who seemed to be sleeping, and hurried out to the woodshed. Back inside, she laid fires in both the bedrooms. Soon the rooms glowed with warm light.

While Celia and Frannie slept, India tended to her own toilette and went downstairs. She made herself a pot of tea and ate a cold biscuit with strawberry jam. In the chilly library she opened the curtains to the gray February light and browsed the shelves for something to read.

But it was impossible to concentrate. She could think of nothing but Philip. She had become accustomed to his presence and his voice. At Indigo Point she had known when he was watching her, and she thought of him in the quiet hours before sleep when the old plantation house lay dark and still beside the sea. But she had seen the bruised look he'd given Laura in the judge's chambers. Whatever Laura might have done had not been enough to completely extinguish his feelings for her.

India thumbed through a stack of ladies' magazines and read at random from a poetry book until the afternoon had come and gone and the long shadows of another winter evening fell across the square. When the French mantel clock chimed the hour, she made her way back to the kitchen. Surely Celia and Frannie would wake soon, feeling better and hungry for something more substantial than tea and crackers.

Rummaging in the bins, she found potatoes, carrots, onions, and a few turnips and set about chopping them for soup. When that was done, it took several tries to get the cook stove going, but at last the pot began to bubble, sending the steamy fragrance of simmering vegetables into the room. In the bread bin she found half a loaf. She sliced it and fanned the slices onto a tray. She filled the teakettle and set it on to boil.

When everything was ready, she went upstairs to check on her charges. Frannie had soiled her bed again and was huddled in the corner clutching her porcelain doll, her little face streaked with tears.

"Stay put," India said softly. "I'll check on your mama, and then I'll be back to look after you."

She slipped into Celia's room across the hall and stopped short. Celia was lying atop the covers, her nightgown soaked with sweat. Her cheeks were mottled and red, her eyes were closed. Her chest rose and fell with her shallow, labored breaths.

"Celia?" India chafed Celia's hand, but her hostess didn't move.

It was time to get a doctor.

India returned to Frannie's room and rushed to change the bed and bathe the little girl. She returned her to her bed and tucked the doll in beside the sad-eyed child.

"Where's Mama?" Frannie whispered. "I'm scared."

"I won't lie to you, Frannie. I'm scared too. Your mama needs a doctor. Do you know his name? Where he lives?"

Frannie shook her head, her damp hair fanned out on the fresh linen pillowcase.

"What about Mrs. Whipple? Where can I find her?"

"I don't know." Frannie rubbed her eyes. "Uncle Philip prob'ly knows."

"That's a good idea. Where does he live?"

"In a big white house. On Abercorn Street. It's not far."

India remembered seeing Abercorn on her carriage rides to and from the Mackays', an easy walk from here. "Listen, Frannie. I'm going to have to leave you here for a moment while I find him. Can you stay right here with your doll until I get back?"

"Can Maxwell come in?"

"Sure. I bet he'd love to hear one of your stories while I'm gone."

"No he won't. He's too old. He falls asleep all the time. But I still want him."

India coaxed the old yellow dog into the child's room. "I'll be right back."

She grabbed her hat and cloak and hurried down the darkening street. A chill wind blew between the buildings, flickering the flames in the gaslights just coming on. A few rigs and carriages trundled along the streets. India found Abercorn and in the growing darkness, tried to figure out which of the big white houses might belong to Philip Sinclair. She was just about to knock on a door to ask when she saw a gaslight coming on down the block, illuminating a small neat sign announcing the Law Offices of Philip Sinclair.

She ran the rest of the way and lifted the heavy brass door knocker. She called his name and knocked again. She heard footsteps, the slow turn of the doorknob. And there he stood, looking so disheveled that at first she nearly didn't recognize him. His hair was uncombed, his face unshaven. His shirttail draped over a pair of rumpled trousers with a stain on one knee.

"India." His voice was slow and raspy. "You shouldn't have come here."

She frowned. "Are you inebriated?"

"What if I am? Who has a better right?"

His pain was palpable, and India knew its source. The wife returned from the grave. Her heart hurt for him. She longed to comfort him, but Celia was in trouble.

"I'm sorry to disturb you, but Mrs. Mackay is deathly ill with a fever, and Frannie is sick too. The housekeeper is away just now, and Frannie doesn't know the doctor's name. I didn't know anyone else to ask."

He seemed to sober up instantly. "Dr. Robbins looks after them. He lives just down the block." He pointed it out. "In the terra cotta house on the corner. I'd go for him myself but I'm hardly in a shape to appear in public."

"I can go." She turned away. "Take care of yourself, Philip."

"Wait." He drew her into his arms and pressed his lips to her hair. "I'm sorry you've found me in such a state."

"It's all right. After all of the risks you took for me, it's unlikely I'd question anything you do." She drew back to look up into his shadowed face. "Besides, you've had a great shock."

"Yes, and I want to tell you about it. But not tonight. Celia needs you."

He stood on the porch. "I'll watch from here to be sure you get there safely."

She could feel his eyes on her as she hurried down the street. When she reached the doctor's house, she rang the bell and turned just in time to see Philip closing the door.

CHAPTER 26

"MAMA, ANOTHER LADY HAS COME CALLING." KNEELING on the settee beneath the window, Frannie Mackay peered out at the gray winter afternoon, her nose pressed to the glass. "I think it's Mrs. Quarterman."

"Alicia's here?" A smile lit Celia's face. She was recovered but still pale after her weeklong illness. She had lost a bit of weight, too, but India could see that this morning's social calls had pleased her. "You may stay to say hello, Frannie, and then I want you to go upstairs and work on your lessons. You are frightfully behind, and you know Miss Finlay will be cross if you are unprepared for your recitations."

"I know. That's what Grandmama said too."

Celia's mother-in–law, Cornelia Mackay, had arrived first thing this morning and spent an hour chatting with them and playing a game with Frannie. The elder Mrs. Mackay had added her own apology for the trouble India had experienced in Savannah and expressed the hope that she and all of the theater patrons would one day have another chance to see an India Hartley play.

No sooner had Mrs. Mackay's carriage departed than another took its place, and a Mrs. Bennett came in, her cheeks pink from the February wind, her eyes bright with happy news. Her husband, Dr. Wade Bennett, had just been named head of the Philadelphia Medical College.

"Of course this means I have to live among the Yankees," she said, taking up her teacup. "But at least Wade and I will have our summers on Pawley's Island." She smiled at India. "Are you a beach fancier, Miss Hartley?"

"I am. Though I never get to spend much time there."

"Then perhaps you'll visit us at Osprey Cottage. It isn't in the best repair these days, but it's a dear old place. My husband proposed to me there."

Minutes later, she departed for a committee meeting at the circulating library.

Now, India rose from her chair once again as Mrs. Whipple announced Alicia Thayer Quarterman, who swooped Frannie into a bear hug and set her down again before crossing the room to embrace Celia.

"My dear. I am heartbroken that I was not in town last week when you needed me. Some friend I am! Are you quite recovered?"

Celia motioned to Frannie to go upstairs and smiled at Alicia. "I think so. India brought Dr. Robbins to the rescue and proved herself as adept at nursing as she is at acting."

Alicia beamed at India. "I read in the paper that your verdict is to be set aside. You must be terrifically relieved."

"I am." India resumed her seat.

Alicia took the seat opposite her and arranged her silk skirts just so. Mrs. Whipple came in to serve more tea, then withdrew, shutting the doors behind her. Alicia lifted her cup and sipped. "If there is anything more civilized than hot tea on a cold winter's day, I'm sure I don't know what it is." She leaned over to peer at the tray of sweets the housekeeper had left. "Celia, by any chance are those benne seed cookies?"

"They are. Mrs. Whipple makes them even when Sutton isn't here, because we enjoy them so. Our old housekeeper—rest her soul—gave Mrs. Whipple the recipe. But somehow they never taste quite the same as Mrs. Maguire's."

Alicia popped a cookie into her mouth, chewed, and swallowed. "They're still quite good, though." She took another sip of tea. "What news have you of that handsome husband of yours?"

"I had a letter yesterday, written upon his arrival in Jamaica. He seems pleased with the way the manager has taken care of things in his absence, but you know Sutton," Celia said with a fond smile. "He likes to be in the thick of things."

Alicia whooped. "That's an understatement." She turned to India. "Did Celia tell you Sutton became one of the most important blockade runners during the war?"

"No. We've had little time for conversation these past days. But during the war I read about the blockade runners in the Northern newspapers."

"Sutton Mackay nearly got his posterior shot off more than once, running medical supplies in here from Nassau," Mrs. Quarterman said. "Lots of people across Georgia would have died if not for Sutton's bravery and skill. The state of Georgia wanted to give him a medal. But he won't accept a word of praise for it."

"He saw it as his duty," Celia said to India. "On our honeymoon we went to Liverpool to have his boat built."

"I'm sure it was terribly romantic," Alicia said with a wry grin. "Keeping company with a bunch of rough men in a shipyard in the dead of winter."

Celia laughed. "It was, actually. Sutton has always made me feel a part of everything he does. I couldn't have married a man who expected to put me on a pedestal and leave me there, seen and not heard."

"Not likely, my dear. You are one of the most outspoken women I've ever met. But enough of that." Alicia turned to India. "Tell me, Miss Hartley, when will you resume your stage career?"

India set down her cup and smoothed her skirt. "I'm not sure that I can. Given my notoriety now, I would prove too great a distraction. It wouldn't be fair to the other players."

Celia Mackay studied her guest, her violet eyes intent upon India's face. "But my dear, the theater is your life."

"It was. But I suppose now I shall have to learn another trade. Or work in a shop. It isn't what I would choose, but it's respectable work."

Alicia Quarterman's brows rose. "I hardly think someone of your stature can be happy in a shop." She turned to face her friend. "Celia, we must think of something. If not for Miss Hartley's scandalous treatment here in Savannah, she wouldn't be in this fix. It's our duty to right the wrong that has been done."

"You're very kind," India said. "But I suppose in the same circumstances I would have been blamed regardless of where it happened."

Alicia waved one bejeweled hand. "You could write a book.

Not about the trial, of course, though I suppose certain people would certainly want to read about it. I'm talking about your life in the theater. Growing up on the stage in London must have been exciting and glamorous."

India smiled. "There were moments of excitement when Father and I performed together at the Prince of Wales Theater or at the Lyceum." She paused, remembering. "Lady Bancroft and I made our stage debuts at the Lyceum in the same season. Though of course she was Miss Wilton back then. But a life in the theater is much less glamorous than most people suppose. It's a frantic life really, running from rehearsals to performances, keeping late hours, and sleeping with one eye open so as not to be robbed of your hard-earned pay."

"You see?" Alicia said. "Fascinating. Such a book would surely prove very popular."

"Oh, I don't have the talent or the organizational skills to take on the writing of a book," India said. "My education was fairly haphazard after my aunt died. My father taught me all about running a theater company, thinking that one day the company he founded would be mine. But now I have no company to manage."

Celia came upright on her chair, her eyes glowing. "Of course. Why didn't I think of it sooner?"

She got up and began pacing back and forth in front of the black marble fireplace, her skirts whispering on the thick carpet. "It's the perfect solution, especially now that Mr. Philbrick will be going away."

"Celia Mackay, will you slow down?" Alicia said. "What on earth are you talking about?"

"India should take over management of the Southern Palace. Nobody in Savannah has her background or her experience in the theater. Why should the owners bring in someone else when we already have the perfect person to do it?" Celia stopped pacing and beamed at India. "Mr. Kennedy is the co-owner of the theater, and he sits right behind me every week in his pew at St. Johns. I shall introduce you to him this coming Sunday."

India felt a stirring of hope. She was capable of the job, if the people of Savannah were willing to give her a chance. She thought again of her ill-fated little acting troupe on St. Simons. Despite the resistance she had encountered there, she still believed that exposing children to the world of plays and stories was a good idea. Back in London, her father's friend Mrs. Cons had a dream to use the arts to improve the lives of the poor. Suppose India arranged entertainments at the Southern Palace to support such endeavors? That would be worth doing.

"Well, India?" Celia said. "Will you allow me to present you to Mr. Kennedy? He can seem awfully gruff at times, but that's mostly because he's preoccupied with all his business interests."

"You must say yes," Alicia Quarterman said, pulling on her kid gloves. "It's the only way we can repair the damage that was done." She pecked Celia's cheek. "I'm glad you are recovered, and I wish I could stay longer. But I must go. I'm terribly late to my appointment with the dressmaker."

Celia laughed. "Heaven forbid you should keep Mrs. Foyle waiting."

Alicia headed for the door. "No need to see me out, Celia. I know the way, and you must conserve your strength. You have a big job to do on Sunday, convincing Mr. Kennedy to hire Miss Hartley."

She reached the door just as the bell sounded. She called back to Celia, "I'll get it."

A moment later, Philip Sinclair entered the parlor.

India's heart lurched. He was impeccably dressed, his eyes clear, and his molasses-colored hair, still damp from his morning ablutions, curled about his starched collar.

"Mercy's sake, Philip," Celia said, crossing the room to greet him. "I wondered what had become of you. Frannie's been asking for you all week."

He kissed Celia's cheek. "I've been in court all week. I just came from Judge Bartlett's chambers and wanted to tell India the good news."

India stilled and looked up at him, her expression calm, hoping her acting skills would be enough to prevent his knowing how glad she was to see him. "My record has been expunged?"

"As of this morning. Mr. McLendon was as good as his word and filed the necessary papers with the court. Judge Bartlett has vacated your sentence. Your record is clear."

Though she had expected this news at some point, the reality of it brought the sting of tears to her eyes. Finally, in the eyes of the law at least, the entire episode was erased. The court of public opinion however was something altogether different.

"I can never repay you for everything you've done."

He smiled. "Defending people is what I do. It's always gratifying when a case breaks my way, but in this instance, particularly so."

"Would you care for tea, Philip?" Celia asked. "It's gone cold I'm afraid, but I can ask Mrs. Whipple to bring a fresh pot."

"Thank you, but I can't stay." Philip stood with his back to the fireplace, his hands clasped behind his back. "There's more news, India. Mr. Philbrick has decided to dispense with a jury trial."

"So I won't have to testify." Another wave of elation moved through her. She was free to leave town. She could be on the next boat to Boston. She could return to London. If Mr. Kennedy refused to hire her to manage the Southern Palace, perhaps her father's old friends would take her in, at least for a while.

Philip's eyes held hers, something new and intimate in his amber gaze. A longing that matched her own. But she would be a liability to him in a city where reputation and social position counted for everything. She might be desperately in love with him, but she couldn't jeopardize his future. Not after all it had cost him to save her own.

"You're free to leave Savannah any time you wish," he said, "but I hope you won't go away too soon. I have an enormous favor to ask."

"A favor?"

Celia got to her feet. "If you two will excuse me, I must speak to Mrs. Whipple about dinner." She winked at India and hurried from the room.

India took her seat and looked up at him, a question in her eyes. Philip settled into the chair across from hers. "You know about the plans for the resort Mr. Dodge and I want to build on St. Simons."

"Yes. It seems like an enormous undertaking."

"It is. And sadly, there are few men around here who can

afford to invest in it now. So we're looking to the North. Mr. Dodge has invited a half dozen potential investors and their wives to come to the island to see for themselves what we have in mind."

"I'm glad for you, Philip. It sounds very promising doesn't it?"

"Maybe." He shrugged. "I'm trying to keep my expectations in check."

But she could sense his excitement at the prospect of seeing his beloved island renewed and his workers employed at something better than scratching out a living on worn-out land.

"How can I help?"

"There really is no place on the island to entertain a dozen people except at Indigo Point, and Amelia is quite overwhelmed with planning dinners and amusements for such a large number of guests." He leaned forward in his chair. "I know it's an imposition after everything that happened to you there, but I was hoping you would come back to the Point with me and lend my sister a hand."

Back to the place of death and secrets? To the place where Mrs. Catchpole tried to kill her?

"Mrs. Catchpole is in a mental hospital near Atlanta," Philip said. "She can't harm you again."

India looked up at him, feeling surprised and relieved. And more than a little guilty. "Well, I'm sorry for the poor woman, and sorry for the grief I caused her."

"Neither Amelia nor I realized how her mind was failing, not until you came to the Point. Maybe we didn't want to admit it. We excused her moods and the things that went missing from time to time, blaming it on her advancing age. But I can see now that her grief for Laura, misplaced though it turned out to be, went much deeper than we knew." He paused. "Amelia found her down by the springhouse, half-dressed and nearly catatonic. There was nothing we could do for her. She'll be looked after now."

His eyes sought hers. "Indigo Point is undoubtedly the last place you want to be, but Almarene is too infirm to be of much help. There's only Binah to assist Amelia. I was hoping you might entertain the guests with some readings in the evenings. It would certainly give the ladies something to brag about once they return home."

India clasped her hands tightly. He was right. The last thing she wanted to do was to go back to Indigo Point with its water snakes and alligators, its shabbiness, and its dark secrets. Back to the place where Philip had loved Laura.

Nor was she ready to perform again, for anyone. Besides, she needed to meet Mr. Kennedy on Sunday.

But she owed Philip her very life. How could she refuse his request?

"Of course if you think it would help—"

"It will. I know it will." He paused, his eyes darkening with concern.

"This isn't only about Amelia's needing my help is it? Something is troubling you."

"I had a visitor late last night. A fellow who frequents the drinking establishments on the waterfront."

"I see. The men's library has not been a complete success, then."

"Don't joke about it."

"Forgive me. I'm too cynical."

"Not all the time." He leaned forward in his chair. "He claims that another man approached a friend of his, looking to hire someone to do you harm."

She went still. "Now there's a price on my head? What kind of a place is this?"

"It may be nothing more than a malicious rumor, or he may have been so far into his cups that he misunderstood the conversation entirely. But I won't take that chance. I must return to the Point, and I can't leave you here. I need to keep you safe, until I can figure out whether this threat is real."

She dropped her head and massaged her temples. Maybe she would be better off not even talking to Mr. Kennedy about managing the theater. Maybe she ought to leave Savannah on the next train. Or the next ship, no matter where it was bound.

"India." His reached for her hand. "There's a steamer departing for the Point at six this evening. I know it's short notice, but we have so little time before the investors arrive, and while it's true I need to protect you, it is also true that Amelia is overwhelmed."

"I can be ready."

He got to his feet. "I'll arrange for your ticket and call for you at five. In the meantime, stay right here with Celia. Don't leave the house until I come for you."

His warning sent a chill through her. Though he tried to discount it, this threat was real.

They crossed the room to the door. He removed his hat and coat from the hall tree and put them on. "I'll see you then."

"All right."

He lifted her chin and smiled into her eyes. "I will keep you safe. I promise."

He left and she returned to the parlor, only to hear the doorbell again. Another lady calling upon Celia, no doubt. Neither Celia nor Mrs. Whipple seemed to be about, so India opened the door.

Philip stood there holding a square white box tied with an enormous pink bow. "I nearly forgot. This is for you."

"But what—" She lifted the lid. "A plum pudding!"

"At Christmas I promised you another pudding when you were set free." His eyes sought hers and held. "And I always keep my promises."

❦ CHAPTER 27 ❧

INDIA PAUSED, FEATHER DUSTER IN HAND, AND PEERED through the window of the upstairs room she had been cleaning all morning. Another wagon laden with boxes and two fat mattresses rolled into the yard. When the driver set the brake and jumped down, India recognized Mrs. Wheeler, the woman she'd met at the steamer landing at Gascoigne Bluff the day she had driven there with Philip.

India called for Binah and then for Amelia, but neither responded. There was no telling where they were this morning. Everyone was working frantically to finish preparations before tomorrow's arrival of Mr. Dodge's investors. Since India's return to Indigo Point, she had risen early each day to clean and dust the long-vacant rooms that would house their guests for the weekend. She had washed windows, laundered and ironed curtains, beaten rugs, and polished mirrors until they shone. Yesterday she and Amelia, Binah, and Almarene had set up a kind of assembly line in the kitchen, turning out four pies, six loaves of bread, and dozens of cookies made from the boatload of supplies delivered by steamer at Philip's request.

The overseer at Fan Butler's place had sent three men to help tidy the yard and set up extra chairs, beds, and cots provided by other families for the dozen expected guests.

India's muscles ached from the unaccustomed labor, but it felt good to be doing something to help Philip. With a final flick of her duster, she left the room and ran lightly down the staircase to meet Mrs. Wheeler.

The older woman greeted her with a warm smile. "You're back."

"I am. Mr. Sinclair was shorthanded in getting ready for the weekend and asked for my help. It was the least I could do."

Mrs. Wheeler bobbed her head. "Newspaper said the real killer confessed."

"Yes. He says it was accidental, and I believe him. All the same, Philip says Mr. Philbrick will spend some time behind bars. If he's lucky enough to avoid the hangman's noose."

"Too bad, but better him than an innocent woman. You must feel like your whole life is starting over again."

"I do." India untied the bandanna she'd wrapped around her hair and shook her famous curls free. "It's a huge relief."

Mrs. Wheeler gestured toward her wagon. "I brought you a few things. I understand Philip's planning a fancy dinner for Saturday night. With entertainments following."

"Yes. As fancy as it can be under the circumstances." India indicated the piano in the corner of the parlor. "As far as entertainment goes, much depends upon whether the piano tuner Philip engaged actually shows up. We've been expecting him for three days."

One of the men from Butler's Island lumbered up the front

steps and snatched his cap from his head as he approached the door. "Mornin' Miz Wheeler. Mornin', miss."

"Good morning," India said.

"Me and Ben finished raking them empty flower beds and washin' all the winders. Reckon they ain't much more to be done with this place." He looked around with an air of satisfaction. "Indigo Point looks about as good as she's going to look, I 'spect."

"You've worked wonders," India said. "I know Mr. Sinclair is grateful for your efforts. I'm sure he will see that you are paid for your work."

"Before you go," Mrs. Wheeler said, "could you possibly bring those boxes and the mattresses inside?"

"Sure thing. Where you want 'em?"

Mrs. Wheeler supervised the moving of the boxes into the dining room, and India led the man up the stairs to the small bedroom she'd just finished cleaning. He deposited the mattresses side by side on the floor in front of the fireplace and dusted off his hands. He took in the sparkling windows, the crisp white curtains, the arrangement of glossy green leaves in a white vase sitting on the fireplace mantel.

"Looks right cozy in here."

India smiled. "It's too bad some of the ladies must sleep on the floor, but it can't be helped."

She followed him down the stairs and waved as he and Ben left the yard. In the dining room, Mrs. Wheeler was busy unpacking a set of delicate blue-and-gold china plates, cups, and saucers.

India lifted a cup. "It's beautiful."

"I think so. My mother got these on a trip to Paris back in

the forties. She traveled to the factory in Limoges and designed the pattern herself. When the Yankees came through here in '58, stirring up the Negroes, I buried every last piece of it under the floor in the barn. Left it there until the war was over. It came through without a single crack. Every time I use these pieces, I think of Mother."

"Perhaps they are too precious to be on loan," India said, carefully setting down the cup. "I would hate for anything to get broken."

"My mother always said there was no use in having beautiful things if you weren't planning to use them." Mrs. Wheeler's pale blue eyes shone. "I can't think of a better use than to help Philip impress those investors. If their money will build the resort he and Mr. Dodge are cooking up, then it's worth a broken cup or two."

"I'll try to see that they are all returned to you in perfect condition."

India helped the older woman finish the unpacking. Along with the china, Mrs. Wheeler had brought a pair of silver candlesticks and a large white vase.

"I remember Mrs. Catchpole saying once that there never were enough containers for flowers," Mrs. Wheeler said. "I brought these along even though not much is blooming in the dead of winter."

"Yesterday I saw some pretty mosses down by the old carriage house," India said. "And some of the trees are still green." She smiled. "It won't be as nice as having flowers, but everything looks better in candlelight."

Mrs. Wheeler laughed. "Including this old wrinkled face of

mine." She paused. "I was right sorry to hear about the way Mrs. Catchpole attacked you. The poor woman hasn't been herself since the night Mrs. Sinclair perished."

India froze. For a moment she was tempted to tell Mrs. Wheeler that Laura Sinclair was very much alive, and a possible murderer too. But even the most discreet of women could sometimes let secrets slip, and this was not the time to unleash more scandal on the island. "My wounds have healed. But I admit, I was terrified."

"Well of course! Anyone would be." Mrs. Wheeler clicked her tongue. "Such a shame. Well, my dear, I ought to be going. I'm sure you all have much more to do before tomorrow."

India followed her into the yard. "Thank you for everything."

"No trouble." Mrs. Wheeler climbed onto her wagon and released the brake. "I hope the piano tuner turns up."

Half an hour later he did. A small man with a thick mustache and a French accent to match, he introduced himself as Monsieur Bessette and with a wave of one hand demanded to be shown to the instrument.

India led him into the parlor, where Amelia was busy polishing the mahogany tables. When they came in, she looked up and tossed her dusting cloth onto the table.

"Thank goodness!" she said when the Frenchman introduced himself. "I was about to give up hope of your ever arriving."

He frowned. "Louis Bessette never breaks a promise, *mademoiselle*. Never."

He strode over to the piano, lifted the fallboard, and ran his fingers lightly over the keys. He shook his head and released a gusty sigh.

"I know," Amelia said. "It's almost impossible to keep it in tune here. The damp air, you know."

The Frenchman nodded. "And what is even more unfortunate, this instrument is not a Pleyel."

"My father thought it was important to support an American piano maker," Amelia said. "Though of course the Pleyel is a fine instrument."

"The finest!" the Frenchman said. "All others pale in comparison."

"Mr. Chickering's piano is more than adequate for me," Amelia said. "And he is very exacting. He accompanied the piano here from Boston himself to be sure it was not damaged on the trip." She ran a hand over the polished wood. "It was wasted effort, really. I have no affinity for it, nor much patience for practicing chords and scales. I'm afraid I was not a very good student."

"Regardless, every instrument deserves to be kept in tune." M. Bessette opened his toolbox. "If you ladies will excuse me, I shall see to this . . . Chickering, and do the best I can considering its inferior quality."

India and Amelia retreated to the kitchen, where Amelia flopped onto a chair and rolled her eyes. "Inferior quality. I'd have kicked his shins for that remark, except Philip is counting on having that thing in tune for Saturday night's soiree." She looked up at India. "I don't suppose I could persuade you to play in my stead?"

"I would spare you if I could, but I never learned how. Father and I were rarely in one place long enough to acquire a piano and for me to take lessons."

"Some people have all the luck." Amelia rose and poured tea. "Want some?"

"I should finish setting up the bathing room. Mrs. Garrison sent over some more linens yesterday. If we're lucky, each of the ladies will have her own clean towel. But the men might have to share."

"They won't care," Amelia said. "Men are thick as bricks. So long as there is plenty of food and their horses aren't lame and their rifles work, they're oblivious to anything else."

"Are you speaking of anyone in particular?"

"You know I mean Mr. Lockwood. He has been gone for weeks, and I've had not a single word, though he promised to write. He doesn't care that I am imagining all sorts of dire circumstances. He might be dead by now for all I know."

India was too exhausted and too upset by the appearance of Laura Sinclair to go into the details of Mr. Lockwood's daring rescue. But Amelia looked so anxious that India couldn't remain silent. "Mr. Lockwood helped Philip with my case. He was fine when I saw him in Savannah. He may still be on his way to Texas and hasn't had the chance to write to you. I wouldn't—"

India broke off as Binah stormed into the kitchen, her young face contorted with rage.

"Binah, what's the matter?"

"Just answer me one question," Binah said.

"Of course. If I can. What is it?"

Binah opened her fist to reveal the gold necklace that matched her own. "This is Hannah June's. Where did you get it?"

✦ CHAPTER 28 ✦

FEBRUARY 25

SEATED AT ONE END OF THE DINING TABLE WITH PHILIP at the other, India let her eyes roam over the candlelit table, the gleaming china and crystal, and the well-dressed guests. She released a sigh of quiet satisfaction. Mrs. Wheeler's Limoges china blended nicely with the Sinclairs' own pieces, and the candlelight illuminated the basket of mosses and ornamental leaves India had fashioned into a centerpiece.

This morning while the gentlemen toured the proposed resort site with Philip and Mr. Dodge, India and Amelia had taken the ladies on a walking tour of the property, ending with a luncheon on the beach. True, February was not the most salubrious time for an out-of-doors excursion, but the day dawned calm, the sun came out by noon, and the ladies, wrapped in their furs and gloves, had not seemed to mind the early morning chill. They asked dozens of questions about the house, the old gardens, the sea birds, and the rumors they'd heard about alligators stalking humans.

Surely some of them had read about India's trial, but they were too polite to say so. If they wondered about her presence at

Indigo Point, they kept those ruminations to themselves as well. In the late afternoon they returned to the house for tea, then retired for naps before dressing for dinner.

Now, as Binah and her young cousin Myrtilda served course after course, India determined not to dwell on Binah's discovery of Hannah June's necklace.

Even though India was annoyed that the girl had found it by pilfering her trunk, Binah deserved the truth—and soon, but not until India herself knew the whole story about what had happened in the chapel that fiery night. Judging from Philip's relaxed demeanor and Mr. Dodge's convivial dinner-table chatter, today's tour had gone well. India did not want to ask any question that would disturb their rising optimism, though one of these days she would have to. For now, she concentrated on the conversation taking place around the table.

One of the investors, a Mr. Terrell from New York, described the Atlantic City boardwalk that had been completed only last year. "We're entering a new era in America," he said. "People are recovering from the war and wanting to travel and have fun again. Forward-looking towns like Atlantic City will reap the benefits. I don't see why this little island ought not to get its share."

Mr. Dodge beamed. "I couldn't agree more, sir. And as you've seen from the plans Philip and I have devised, our resort will offer everything the discerning traveler could wish for."

"St. Simons is lovely. But what about those alligators?" Mrs. Fleming, who had been the one to ask Amelia about the creatures during their morning walk, looked worried. "I don't imagine mothers will be eager to expose their young children to such danger, regardless of the charm."

"We've thought of that," Philip assured her. "We'll build elevated walkways across the marshes and the tidal creeks. The known nesting areas will be protected. Signage will direct our guests to the safe areas. They will be able to glimpse the creatures in their natural habitat without endangering themselves or the wildlife."

He paused while Binah and Myrtilda removed the dinner plates and prepared to serve the pies and coffee. And when the conversation resumed, the talk turned to other matters. Mrs. Broomfield of Philadelphia recounted a recent meeting with a Mr. Burroughs who was writing a book on bird watching. Mrs. Tipton expressed her eagerness to see *Arrangement in Grey and Black*, a new painting by Mr. Whistler to be exhibited at the Pennsylvania Academy of Fine Arts.

"I am such a lover of all the arts, am I not, Hiram?" She looked down the table for confirmation from her husband, a thin bewhiskered man in a gray suit and a gaily colored paisley vest.

"Indeed you are, my dear. Indeed you are." He bobbed his head and tucked into his pie.

"I'm simply wild about the theater," Mrs. Tipton continued. "I can't wait for the new season this autumn." She turned her dark eyes on India. "Perhaps you can tell us, Miss Hartley, what plays are apt to be popular this year?"

India set down her glass. "I couldn't really say. The choice of material is usually left up to the individual theater managers. Most try to offer a balance of classics and modern drama along with lighter fare. And it depends, too, upon which performers are available at any given time."

Mrs. Broomfield finished her coffee and set down her cup.

"Well, if the theatrical offerings are not to one's liking, one can always count on Theodore Thomas and his traveling musical performances. We heard his orchestra perform in New York last season. I don't think I've ever heard Brahms and Liszt more exquisitely played."

"Speaking of which"—Mr. Zachary, the oldest member of the delegation, set down his fork and beamed at India—"I couldn't help noticing that lovely piano in the parlor. I do hope we are to be honored by hearing you play."

"Unfortunately I never mastered that skill, Mr. Zachary." India smiled, and he smiled back, clearly smitten by her attention.

"Amelia is the musician around here," Philip said. "Though I have been known to saw my way through the odd violin piece from time to time."

"Oh, Mr. Sinclair, you are too modest, I'm sure," Mrs. Tipton said. "But I, for one, would love to hear your sister play."

Amelia blanched, and India felt a stab of sympathy for her. Being expected to perform on cue was never a pleasant feeling, even when one felt in command of the material. And Amelia had freely admitted to being sadly out of practice.

Philip caught India's eye and gave a slight nod, her cue as his hostess to rise from the table. She stood, her professional smile in place, and the guests rose with her. They retired to the parlor, some of them bringing coffee with them, and arranged themselves on the chairs and settees. Some of the men perched on the deep windowsills while others leaned against the fireplace mantel.

Philip stoked the fire and turned up the lamps, bathing the room in soft golden light that picked up the shimmer of the ladies' jewels.

India squeezed Amelia's hand. "Just play something simple," she whispered. "We'll sing loudly, and if you miss a note, nobody will notice."

Amelia seated herself at the piano and rested her fingers on the keys. After a moment she began to play tentatively and to sing:

Twinkling stars are laughing love
Laughing at you and me.

India and Philip and several of the guests joined in.

While your bright eyes look in mine
Peeping stars they seem to be.

As Amelia gained confidence, she relaxed and the music soared, filling the shabby parlor.

Troubles come and go, love
Brightest scenes must leave our sight.
But the star of hope, love
Shines with radiant beams tonight.

The last notes faded, and the guests applauded.

"That was lovely, Miss Sinclair," Mr. Zachary said. "Do favor us with another song."

Amelia played one of Jenny Lind's songs, "By the Sad Sea Waves." Then she and India sang a duet, "What Are the Wild Waves Saying?"

When the applause faded, Amelia turned around, her smile triumphant. "I'm afraid that exhausts my repertoire, ladies and gentlemen."

"Then perhaps Miss Hartley will give us a dramatic reading," Mr. Tipton suggested.

India recited the passages she had practiced, after which the gentlemen retired to the front porch for cheroots and brandy while the ladies remained in the parlor. Mrs. Zachary discussed the latest fashions she'd seen on her trip to Paris. Mrs. Broomfield described her numerous charitable endeavors in excruciating detail before describing her upcoming trip to Saratoga.

When the mantel clock chimed, Mrs. Tipton stifled a yawn, then blushed. "Please excuse me, ladies. It isn't the conversation that has affected me this way." She smiled. "Just before we left on this trip I learned I'm to be a mother again."

"Why that's wonderful news," Mrs. Broomfield said. "Of course you need your rest. Shall I help you up to your bed?"

"No, I can manage, but thank you." Mrs. Tipton got to her feet. "Thank you for a lovely evening, Miss Sinclair. Miss Hartley. I don't know when I've had a more enjoyable time."

"Nor do I," Mrs. Zachary said. "But it's getting late, and we have a long trip home starting tomorrow. Perhaps we all ought to turn in."

One by one, the ladies clasped India's hands and then Amelia's, murmuring thanks before heading up the stairs. Soon, only Amelia and India remained in the parlor. Binah came in, her face sullen, to remove the last of the cups. She placed everything on a tray, then spun on her heel and marched out without so much as a single word or glance.

"You're going to have to give her an explanation, you know."

The edge in Amelia's voice brought India up short. "I know it. And I want to. But I must speak to Philip first, and there hasn't been time."

Amelia closed the piano and stacked her sheet music on the top. "In fact, I'd like to hear your explanation myself. Good night, India."

❧ CHAPTER 29 ❧

MARCH 1

INDIA WOKE UP THINKING ABOUT PHILIP. ABOUT THE intense way he looked into her eyes when they spoke, the way he leaned in to listen as if he didn't want to miss a single word. She thought of the endearing way he laughed and the slightly messy way his hair curled over his perfectly starched lawyer's collar, lending a certain boyishness to his appearance. Of the extraordinary measures he'd taken to keep her from harm.

His weekend at Indigo Point had been a great success. The guests had departed on Sunday following a brief prayer service in the parlor.

On this chilly Wednesday, the first of March, Indigo Point was returning to normal. Fan Butler's men had returned to retrieve the things Philip borrowed from Butler's Island. Yesterday Almarene had limped over to the house to bake bread and help Binah with pegging out the wash. Amelia had resumed her incessant letter writing, her papers and ink spread out over the dining room table every morning to take advantage of the pale sunlight coming through the tall windows.

India threw back her covers and poured water into her

washbasin. Today would be as good as any to talk to Philip about Laura. How he had found her and persuaded her to come to Judge Bartlett's chambers. Why she had asserted that she was not his wife. Whether he had learned anything about the threat on India's life.

Was Laura the one whose footsteps India had heard in Arthur Sterling's house on Isle of Hope? Certainly the distinctive purple cloak India had seen hanging on the hall tree was Laura's. But if the rumors were true and Mr. Sterling had begun a romance with Miss Bryson, perhaps the young understudy was the one who was in the house that night. Maybe it no longer mattered now that India was free. But the unanswered questions gnawed at her.

India dressed and went downstairs. It was still early. Perhaps she and Philip could walk on the beach after breakfast. Or go down to the boathouse. Someplace where they would not be overheard or disturbed.

Amelia glanced up and nodded as India came through to the kitchen to pour coffee and fill her plate from the skillet Binah had left on the stove. India slid into a chair opposite Amelia, who seemed disinclined to talk. The silence stretched out, broken only by the scratching of Amelia's pen.

India buttered a biscuit. "Have you seen Philip this morning?"

"No. He left before I got up. To catch the early steamer to the city, I expect."

"Oh. Any idea when he will return?"

"Philip comes and goes when he wants. He hardly ever consults me or apprises me of his plans."

India frowned at Amelia's tart reply. "Have I done something to offend you?"

Amelia tossed her pen onto the table. "I was perfectly capable of acting as hostess last week. I'm not sure why Philip thought it was necessary to install you in my place."

"I'm sure he didn't think of it that way. When he asked me to return, he said you needed help preparing for such a large number of guests, that's all. I was surprised when he asked me to sit at the foot of the table. I didn't ask for it, and I would have gladly changed places with you. I'm sorry to have caused you any unhappiness over it."

"My brother has grown to depend on you too much. What happens when you leave town? Where does that leave him then?"

"I may have a chance to remain in Savannah. I don't know for how long. But for as long as I am there, I hope he will always call upon me for help, as he would call upon any friend."

Amelia's dark brows rose. She retrieved her pen. "I must finish these letters so they can go out tomorrow."

"I won't keep you then." India rose. "Have Mrs. Wheeler's things been boxed up for return?"

"Binah finished packing the china yesterday. The boxes are on the porch."

"Maybe I'll return them this morning, if you can help me hitch the horse and rig."

Half an hour later, with the boxes packed closely beside her and Amelia's directions to Mrs. Wheeler's house jotted onto the back of a sheet of writing paper, India set off. Sunlight dappled the narrow road and illuminated a pair of cardinals flitting among the trees. The road twisted and turned, offering intermittent glimpses of the sea. Now and then a gust of sharp wind chilled her face. India laughed out loud as the horse trotted along. What a blessing freedom was. She still trembled when she thought of how close she had come to losing it.

Another few minutes brought India to Mrs. Wheeler's. The house, half hidden behind a thick growth of old trees, was a simple clapboard affair set above a tabby foundation. Twin chimneys rose from each end. In the side yard a horse stood cropping grass.

India halted the rig and set the brake. "Hello?"

The door opened, and Mrs. Wheeler emerged, drying her hands on the bottom of her faded blue apron. "Miss Hartley. What a lovely surprise."

India gestured toward the wagon. "I brought your dishes back. But the mattresses wouldn't fit."

"Oh, never mind those. I have no use for them. I am glad to have Mother's Limoges back though."

India helped her carry the boxes into the dining room. "We can unpack them if you like, to be sure nothing is broken."

"I'll do that later. I just finished breakfast. I slept later than usual this morning. Coffee's still hot if you want some."

"I would. Thank you."

Mrs. Wheeler poured two cups and handed India one. They crossed the hall to the parlor, where fine furnishings, paintings, sculptures, and gilt-framed portraits lent a museum-like quality to the spacious, high-ceilinged room.

"Don't be flummoxed by all this stuff." Mrs. Wheeler motioned India to a delicate chair upholstered in cranberry-and-green needlepoint. "It may remind some people of Versailles, but really it's only the remnants of an old life that is no more."

"Well, I think it's beautiful," India said.

Mrs. Wheeler dropped onto an overstuffed chair and set aside her cup. "Every time Mrs. Garrison visits here she tells me I ought to get rid of the clutter. She has no idea what these things mean to me."

India recalled Mrs. Wheeler's story of her mother's trip to France and the china she designed there. "It means a great deal to you."

"Yes, indeed. Every bit of it. Take that painting of the fox hunt there. My father brought that back from England in the '30s. It was a gift from his hosts for his skill on horseback. Duke somebody or other. Father was thrilled. He died not long after. Every time I look at that painting, I remember the pleasure it brought him, and it comforts me."

India sipped her coffee while Mrs. Wheeler recounted the provenance of a sculpture purchased on a tour of Europe when she was young. "It came from the smallest garret you can imagine. There was a sign on the street in Paris, directing me up the stairs to the gallery. Ha! Some gallery. There was hardly room to turn around. But that little piece caught my eye, and I had to have it. Now, that portrait there by the door, that's my mother. Painted when she was just eighteen. I can't imagine why Mrs. Garrison thinks I ought to part with it."

Mrs. Wheeler went on talking about the remnants of her life before the war stripped everything away, leaving her to live in genteel shabbiness. It wasn't the things themselves that mattered as much as the precious memories they held for her.

India listened. This house was more than four crumbling walls and a sagging roof. It was a refuge. Mrs. Wheeler knew who she was and where she belonged. And so did Philip. Indigo Point was as much a part of him as blood and bone.

She belonged to no one and to nothing.

"Anyway," Mrs. Wheeler went on. "I've rambled enough. I'm sure you have more important things to do than listen to an old woman's reminiscences."

"Actually, I enjoyed it."

"Did you? Well then, you must come again. I have a whole box of tintypes upstairs. We'll go through them together. I've got stories that will curl your hair. More than it already is."

The older woman followed India out into the yard. "Now that you know where I am, don't be a stranger."

India waved and turned the rig for home.

It was nearly noon when India rounded the last bend in the road and Indigo Point came into view. She left the horse tethered in the yard and went inside. Apparently Almarene and Binah had finished their chores and left for the day. The kitchen was tidy, the skillets and pans washed and dried and hanging on their hooks. The iron was still warm, and the faint smell of starch lingered in the air.

In the dining room a scribbled note from Amelia announced that she had driven with Mrs. Garrison to visit the Couper cousins, who were ailing again. India went upstairs and removed her hat. She opened her trunk and began folding some of her things inside. Now that she was no longer needed at Indigo Point, she was eager to return to Savannah, as soon as Philip thought it was safe, to meet with Mr. Kennedy. She hoped he hadn't already hired someone else to manage his theater. She had expected a letter from Celia Mackay this week, but so far, nothing.

Wheels crunched on the road and India peered out the

window. An unfamiliar rig was coming along the drive. India went downstairs as the rig rolled to a stop.

A woman wearing an enormous plumed hat stepped out, placing one delicately booted foot and then the other onto the dusty ground. She started up the front steps.

"Hello again." The voice was low and melodious. And unmistakable.

Laura Sinclair had returned to Indigo Point.

❦ CHAPTER 30 ❧

INDIA FOUND HER VOICE. "WHAT ARE YOU DOING HERE?"

"I could ask you the same thing."

"I was invited."

"I'm sure." Laura shifted a large tapestry satchel onto her other arm and glanced up at the house.

"The Sinclairs are not at home," India said. "You've made a fruitless trip, I'm afraid."

"Not at all." Laura swept past India and pushed her way into the entry hall. She released a loud sigh. "Just as shabby and unappealing as it ever was. I swan, I do not know why anyone would choose to live here."

Laura started up the stairs.

"Just a minute," India said. "I'm not sure I ought to let you go up there."

Laura laughed, a light tinkling sound. "Why ever not? It was my home, however briefly, once upon a time. I've come to collect what's mine."

Laura removed a key from her pocket and unlocked the room at the top of the stairs. India followed her inside. The room smelled faintly of disuse and candle wax. A thin shaft of light lay across the satin gown covering the bed. The forest of little glass candle holders still lay scattered across the floor where they had fallen during India's confrontation with Mrs. Catchpole.

Laura opened her satchel and began rifling through the drawers of the mahogany chest. She opened the wardrobe and began stuffing shoes and shawls and a small leather jewel case inside. "You can keep the dresses," she said. "They are hopelessly out of fashion. But there ought to be something here that I can sell. Apart from my portrait I mean. I don't think I can part with it. It's quite a nice likeness, don't you think?"

"Why did you do it?" India stood in the open doorway, arms crossed against her chest.

"Do what?"

"Why did you burn the chapel? With an innocent girl inside?"

"Philip told you?"

India waited.

"When he found me in Savannah, he told me he suspected I had conspired with Mr. Sterling to set fire to the chapel. But it's nothing more than wild conjecture."

"But you were concerned enough to agree to meet with Judge Bartlett. To explain to him how you switched guns so I would shoot Mr. Sterling for you."

"Well, yes. I'm sure you know by now Philip can be quite charming and persuasive when he wants to be. He convinced me it would be best to admit my part in the whole thing."

"You were willing to commit murder to leave Indigo Point. In order to be with Mr. Sterling."

"You can't prove it."

"'Fire is bright. Let temple burn, or flax; an equal light leaps in the flame from cedar plank or weed. And love is fire.' I'm the one who found your letter book in an abandoned boat near King's Retreat."

"And clever one that you are, you pieced together the details of my duplicity." Laura paled and released a mirthless laugh. "I never did have any kind of luck."

India swept one hand around the dimly lit room. "Poor Mrs. Catchpole mourned you every day. She kept this room as a shrine to your memory. She wouldn't let anyone come in here. She tried to kill me when I did."

"Poor Mrs. Catchpole? Is that what you think? That shrewd old crone was in on the whole thing."

"What?"

"She needed money for a sick relation back in England. So we made a trade. I gave her a handsome check, and she helped me stage my death. The night of the fire, she helped me sneak away to King's Retreat where the boat was waiting. But the fire caused such a commotion that everyone on this end of the island rushed over here. Just as I was about to shove off, we saw two men coming toward the landing. I jumped out, and Mrs. Catchpole and I ran through the woods to meet up with Arthur near Butler's Island." Laura sighed. "The next day I realized the letter book was missing, but I hoped it had fallen into the water."

So. It wasn't grief that had unhinged the housekeeper. It was guilt. And perhaps the fear that her secret would one day come to light. "Then you and Mr. Sterling lived together on Isle of Hope."

"Not for the first year. Arthur thought it would be best if I went abroad for a time, until the furor died down. He engaged a companion for me, and I spent a year in Europe, traveling under an assumed name. It appealed to his sense of the dramatic."

India trembled with rage. "How could you do that to Philip?"

"You have no idea what it was like for me here. I felt trapped on this island. Like I couldn't get my breath. I had to get away."

"You could have told Philip the truth. People do get divorced these days. Leaving him would have been so much kinder than letting him think you were dead."

"It wasn't that simple."

"In the judge's chambers you told Philip you never were his wife. Is that true?"

Laura seemed not to hear the question. She went on, as if trying to convince herself. "When I finally left this forsaken place, I thought I would be free. But I had to be so careful not to be recognized that I lived like a hermit. It's true that I went to extremes to escape Indigo Point, but I ended up in another kind of prison. Even so, it was worth it, because I had Arthur. And then Victoria Bryson came along and turned his head—after everything I had risked for him—and well, something simply had to be done."

India stood in the doorway, momentarily stunned into silence. How could this woman be so cavalier about murder? "So. Not only did you hope I'd shoot Mr. Sterling for you, you lured that poor girl to the chapel. You must have locked her inside somehow. Then you struck a match to the benzene and left her there to die."

"I didn't want to kill anyone, but I had to have a body to be discovered. I left my reliquary necklace behind so Philip would think it was I who perished. Who would have thought a former slave would possess a gold necklace that would survive the fire?

And that it would turn up in the ashes after so long a time? When Philip told me, I didn't believe him." Laura shrugged. "More bad luck."

India frowned. "If Mrs. Catchpole knew you were still alive, why keep a shrine?"

"The poor misguided creature still hoped I'd come back to Philip one day. She doted on him you know. She always did. It became annoying after a while." Laura snapped her satchel shut and left the room.

"But that makes no sense." India followed her into the hall-way. "How could you ever explain coming back from the dead?"

Laura shrugged. "A long illness in a foreign land. A loss of memory suddenly restored. An escape from a clever kidnapper. We talked about it once. Or rather, Mrs. Catchpole did. I knew that once I escaped this horrid place I would never return."

"And yet here you are."

"I never expected to be spurned and left destitute. You, of all people, ought to know how quickly one's fortunes can change."

Laura advanced on India, her ice-blue eyes glittering with malice. "If you hadn't nosed around and pilfered that letter book, and blabbed to Philip about it, he never would have found me. With Arthur dead, I could have remained comfortable and anonymous on Isle of Hope. Because of you, I'm forced to flee before the authorities lock me up and throw away the key."

The hard glint in Laura's eyes nearly stole India's breath. "It's you. You are the one who wanted me dead."

"Can you blame me?" Laura laughed. "You're smarter than I gave you credit for. Though not smart enough to avoid walking into a trap."

"What are you talking about?" India inched her way along the hallway toward the staircase, watching for a chance to put more distance between them.

"Oh come now. It's simple enough. I knew if Philip had the slightest inkling someone wanted to harm you he would bring you here, to his beloved old ruin, where he could keep an eye on you." Laura shoved India hard against the stair railing. "And here you are. Dear Philip has brought you back to me."

It took all of India's stage training to remain calm, to appear fearless. "Harming me won't help you. Even if it can't be proved that you burned Hannah to death, Judge Bartlett and Mr. McLendon know about your role in Mr. Sterling's death. I'm surprised you aren't locked up already."

Laura grinned. "They have to find me first. But they won't. I've become quite adept at disguise. The one useful thing Arthur taught me."

Laura moved closer. India could see beads of perspiration forming on Laura's brow.

"Now I want you to move to the top of the stairs," Laura said. "They're steep enough to cause a broken neck when you fall. I'm sure it won't be pleasant, but probably not as unpleasant as death by fire."

India shook her head. "I'm not moving one inch. And if you know what's good for you, you'll get out now. Before—"

"India!"

Philip sprinted up the stairs, two uniformed officers at his heels. Laura clutched her satchel so tightly her knuckles turned white. "How did you know I was here?"

"You were spotted boarding the steamer last night." After assuring himself that India was unharmed, he turned his gaze on Laura, his fury barely contained. "How dare you come here, after everything you've done?"

"I came to get my things."

"Paid for with my money. When I thought you were my wife."

"You can be angry with me about that too. I guess I deserve it. But I'm broke, Philip. I'm all alone in the world." A single tear rolled down her face. "I don't suppose you'd give me a loan. You loved me once, after all."

"I loved the woman you pretended to be. But the qualities I admired in you were all an act. Besides, you won't be needing money for a long time." He turned to India. "She is the one behind the plot to do you harm."

"You always were a good detective, Philip." Laura looked at the officers as if seeing them for the first time. As if the crimes she had just described—bribery, arson, murder—had been committed by someone else. "But I'm not going anywhere. Except to any place as far away from here as I can get."

The older, heavier officer stepped forward. "Laura Sinclair, you are under arrest for the murder of Hannah June Washington. And for malicious intent in the murder of Arthur Sterling."

Laura's eyes went wide. "Murder? That's ridiculous. I'm not the one who pulled the trigger. And Hannah June was only a—"

"Only a what?" Philip said. "Only a former slave whose life didn't matter? Just an unimportant bit of humanity who could be sacrificed for your own selfish reasons? Binah and Almarene deserve justice for Hannah. I intend to see that they get it."

"You're on their side?"

Philip handed a paper to the officer. "She is no longer a Sinclair. Legally she never was. This document clears that up."

"Come along now," the officer said to Laura, tucking the paper inside his jacket. "We don't want to miss the steamer." He reached out to place manacles on her wrists.

"I can't." Laura shook him off, her eyes glassy and wild with terror. "I'll go crazy in a cell."

"Maybe you shoulda thought of that before you burned that chapel to the ground. I don't want to hurt you, but I will if you won't come quietly."

Laura began to sob. "All right. But may I at least get my handkerchief?"

"Be quick then."

Laura opened her satchel and whipped out a revolver. "Get back, all of you."

The younger officer calmly planted his feet and cocked his head. "Laura. You don't want to do anything foolish. It'll only make matters worse for you." He held out his hand. "Why don't you give me that weapon, and we can talk about things."

"I don't want to talk. I only want out of here. So please. Step aside and let me go."

"Now you know we can't do that," he said, his voice low and reasonable. "We have to take you in."

"Then you leave me no choice." Her hands shaking, Laura leveled the weapon at the officers.

"Laura." Philip's voice was strained, urgent. "I forgive you for everything. Let me help in your defense. We'll plead mental impairment or—"

"Mental impairment?" Laura slowly shook her head. "I'd be locked up like old Catchpole. The same as if I were in prison." She waved the weapon. "Get out of my way."

India's mouth went dry. Laura had killed Hannah and plotted Mr. Sterling's murder and hers too. She had nothing to lose by shooting someone else. "Anyone can see you are in distress," India said softly. "Why don't you do as Philip suggests? Perhaps one day, when you are better, you can be released. And think of Mr. Philbrick's tender feelings for you. The sacrifice he's made on your behalf."

A burst of sardonic laughter escaped Laura's lips. "Cornelius Philbrick feels nothing for me and never did."

India frowned. "Then why would he confess to shooting Mr. Sterling?"

"He had his reasons. If you can't figure it out, you are not as smart as I thought you were."

Laura's gaze hardened. She cocked the revolver.

"No!" Philip yelled.

He and the older officer lunged for it, but Laura stepped back, pressed the barrel to her temple, and fired.

✒ CHAPTER 31 ✒

MARCH 3

THE MOST INSIDIOUS THING ABOUT EVIL, INDIA MUSED, is that it lulls and seduces. It ensnares before a person realizes it's even there. Evil lived at Indigo Point and had overtaken them all when it was least expected.

Laura's reappearance and her dramatic death galvanized the entire island. Once again, Indigo Point became a beehive of activity. Neighbors came to stare at the burned-out chapel, to assert that they had always known something bad had happened there.

The papers in Savannah were quick to pick up on the story, naming Laura "The Wife Who Died Twice." India found the stories and the neighbors' gossip distasteful and distressing, not only for Philip but for Binah and Almarene.

Late in the afternoon, she accompanied Philip down the narrow footpath to the small cabin where the two women had taken refuge against the tidal wave of sensationalism and gossip.

At Philip's knock, Binah peered through the drawn curtain, then slowly opened the door.

"Binah," Philip said softly. "May we come in?"

Binah, her eyes swollen from crying, stood aside. India and Philip went in.

The two-room cabin was neat and clean and sparsely furnished. Two arm chairs, the velvet upholstery shiny with wear, flanked a fireplace. A small wooden table and two chairs were tucked beneath the window. On the other side of the room were two cots covered with pink-and-white quilts. In one of them Almarene slept, her gnarled hands folded across her chest.

"Mama's nearly wore out from grief," Binah said quietly. "I fixed her favorite, hog jowl and cabbage, but she won't touch it. Hasn't eat a thing all day."

"Binah, I'm so sorry about all of this," India said. "I know it's a terrible shock."

"Where did you get my sister's necklace? People say you found it in the chapel."

"That's right. When I first saw it, I knew it must belong to Hannah because it matched yours. I was afraid something terrible had happened to her, but I wasn't sure until I found some other clues."

"Binah," Philip said. "Miss Laura is the one responsible for Hannah's death."

"I heard from Miz Garrison. But I don't know why Miss Laura hated Hannah June. Hannah June never done nothin' to her."

Almarene stirred and sat up, blinking against the late-afternoon sunlight. "What you doing down here, Mr. Philip?"

"We wanted to say how sorry we are for this grave injustice."

"What's done is done. If it's true Miss Laura burned up my girl, and Miss Laura is dead now, too, then I'm satisfied. I don't keep no hatred in my heart. 'Vengeance is mine,' says the Lord. I reckon He'll deal with Miss Laura in His own way."

"At least Hannah's necklace is back where it belongs," India said. "It's worth a tidy sum, if you ever want to sell it. To pay for school or a new start somewhere else."

Binah frowned. "Somewhere else? I don't reckon I know where I would go. Long as Mama and Mr. Philip is at Indigo Point, I don't have no hankering to go runnin' off. But I might take me a trip sometime, wear that fancy hat of mine." She clasped Almarene's hand. "Me and Mama might just take a notion to see Niagara Falls one of these days. People say it's a sight to behold."

India clasped Binah's hand. "I'm going back to the city in a couple of days. But I won't ever forget you. Or Almarene."

"I'm sorry I pilfered your trunk. I never should have gone through your things. I was just curious."

"It's all right. So long as you don't make a habit of it."

Philip held the door for India, and they went out into the early evening. It was nearly twilight. Long shadows fell across the footpath as they retraced their steps.

"Let's walk awhile," Philip said.

They skirted the ravaged chapel and continued past the carriage house, the tool shed, the remains of the old slave hospital. What had once seemed so foreign now felt comforting and familiar. India slipped her hand into his.

They reached the beach and followed the curving shoreline to the boat shed. Philip propped open the door and they went in.

"I didn't know you were working on a boat."

"I started on it last fall. But then I got busy."

"Because of me."

"Actually it's because of you that it's nearly finished. I came down here to work on it at night when I was thinking about your case and couldn't sleep." He inspected his handiwork. The varnish had dried, leaving behind only a faint smell.

"Good as new," he said, running his hands over the satiny wood. "Soon as I get some new rigging, she'll be seaworthy again. I might decide to head out for a while. Clear my head. Once my current cases are finished. I . . ." He paused, blushing, and shrugged. "I'm babbling like a schoolboy, aren't I?"

India smiled. "You've had a lot on your mind lately."

He leaned against the boat and crossed his arms and ankles. "I've been trying to figure out the best way to explain to you about Laura."

"You don't have to explain, if you'd rather not. It couldn't have been easy for you, finding out she was still alive." India paused. "She's beautiful. I can see why men would be smitten with her."

"*Smitten* is too mild a word to explain the effect she had on people. Not just me. She had a way of drawing you in, making you believe nothing else mattered. When I first met her, she told me she was a widow who had lost her husband during the war. I was taken by her beauty, of course. But I felt sorry for her too. So young and pretty and so recently out of mourning. When I proposed, she accepted immediately."

India could hardly blame Laura for her eagerness. Who wouldn't want to marry Philip Sinclair? "But she said she was not your wife."

"After our session in the judge's chambers, Laura left a note for me at my office. Her story was that she found out her husband was alive and had been released from a prisoner of war camp just before our wedding, and she didn't know how to tell me. Or how to stop the elaborate plans she'd made. So she went through with the wedding and hoped neither he nor I would find out."

He stared out at the gently rolling surf. "She hated everything about Indigo Point. She didn't know how to work with the blacks. She hated the heat and the tedium of daily life here. She was terrified of water snakes and alligators. That was when she learned to use a gun. She couldn't make friends with the other women on the island. I thought all she needed was time to adjust. I thought that because she cared for me, she would learn to love Indigo Point. But she never did."

"I'm sorry. I know that must have hurt you."

He shrugged. "She thought the other planters were vapid and cruel and ignorant. Some were, of course. But she never appreciated the beauty of this island. Or the courage some people showed during the war when the chips were down.

"The irony is that I was the one who first invited Arthur Sterling to visit the Point. Laura enjoyed the theater, and I thought having him here might make her feel less isolated. She saw him as an escape from her life."

India thought of the final entry in the lost letter book. The PS didn't stand for "post script." It stood for Philip Sinclair. *PS: I think he knows*. But he hadn't.

She reached for his hand as he continued. "After the fire, I thought my life was over and that nothing would ever be right again. For months after the funeral I didn't leave the plantation. I handed off my court cases to another lawyer and holed up with my grief. I hardly slept. I barely ate."

"But you survived."

"Yes. I finally made peace with what she had done, and with myself. I had my law practice, my plans for the Point. My workers were depending on me. So I went on with life. Then you found the necklace and the letter book. I should have given more credence to your theory earlier than I did, but I didn't want to believe Laura felt nothing for me. That she was capable of such terrible things."

India saw that his words, so harsh and unsparing, cut straight to his own heart. Truth was the sharpest knife for such a procedure.

"People believe what they need to believe," she said quietly, "in order to keep going."

He tipped his head so that it rested against hers. They sat in silence listening to the calls of the seabirds and the gentle whoosh of the outgoing tide.

"Anyway," Philip said finally, "I'm sorry I didn't believe you."

He took her face in his hands and kissed her. She went into his arms, and they clung together like survivors in an open sea, two people who had been torn from all they knew and loved.

Something alive and gossamer as a moth's wing hovered in the air between them. She felt the warmth of his breath on her cheek, the faint pulsing of his heart through the fabric of his shirt. She thought this might be the beginning of their future. Certainly he was capable of living alone, but he needed someone. He needed her. And she longed to make whole again what Laura's shameful treatment of him had broken.

The moment passed and he released her. "We ought to go. Amelia will wonder what became of us."

He closed the boat shed, and they retraced their steps along the beach.

"I hope I haven't burdened you with my sad tale," Philip said as they reached the house.

"Not at all. I'm glad you trusted me with it. But it's in the past now. Over and done."

"Almost," he said as Amelia stepped onto the porch to greet them. "There's one more thing I have to do."

CHAPTER 32

MARCH 12

INDIA SMOOTHED THE SKIRT OF HER BEST DRESS AND watched from the corner of her eye as Celia Mackay settled into her family's pew and opened her prayer book. The stillness of St. John's settled around them, bringing a rare moment of perfect peace. How long had it been since she sat in absolute quiet, her mind emptied of its myriad worries? She could not remember.

Like India's schooling, her religious training had fallen by the wayside after her aunt's death, and now she was uncertain of the order of the service and of the responses. She could only follow Celia's lead and hope not to embarrass herself by speaking or kneeling at the wrong time.

The service began with the ringing of a bell that echoed throughout the opulent space. During the general confession, she heard a booming voice just behind her left shoulder. She turned around and saw a bear of a man with a red beard and a shiny bald pate looking right back at her, his bright blue eyes friendly and curious.

India quickly faced the front again. Surely this was Mr. Kennedy, the co-owner of the theater. Celia had looked for him when she and India and Frannie entered the church, but the pew was half empty. Now that the introductions were forthcoming, India worried that despite everything, Mr. Kennedy might blame her for the tragedy that had taken Mr. Sterling's life. He might think her too young for the responsibility of managing such an important theater. He might not think any woman capable of the task. And his partner in the enterprise would no doubt have ideas of his own.

"Psst!"

India looked to her right to see that Celia was kneeling and Frannie was motioning India to follow. India hastily knelt and winked at the little girl, who clapped one hand over her mouth to smother a giggle.

At last the rector pronounced the benediction in a sonorous voice that seemed to beam straight from heaven itself. People filed from the pews and headed for the doors. Celia wasted no time in making the introductions. She tapped Mr. Kennedy's sleeve.

"Good morning."

"Mrs. Mackay. Good to see you."

"You, too, sir. It has been too long. How is Mrs. Kennedy?"

"About the same, I'm afraid. She misses coming to church. She will be pleased to know you asked after her."

"Tell her I hope to call on her when she feels up to receiving visitors."

"I will." He turned his blue eyes on India. "This, of course is the fair Miss Hartley."

India inclined her head. "Mr. Kennedy."

"I saw you on the stage once in Boston. It must be nigh on to five years or more. A memorable performance it was, alongside your father. I was most grieved to hear of his death last spring."

"Thank you."

A couple of people stopped to chat with Celia. She made quick introductions and sent Frannie out to play in the church-yard, then turned her most dazzling smile on Mr. Kennedy.

"I'm glad you've seen Miss Hartley's work. I don't have to tell you what an asset she would be to the Southern Palace."

"As a player, absolutely." He frowned. "But managing a theater calls for a boatload of skills besides acting. As I'm sure you know."

India could feel her heart kicking inside her chest. "Mr. Kennedy, my father owned a touring company that he hoped one day to leave to me. For years I assisted him in every aspect of managing it. Of course it isn't precisely the same thing, but I'm certain I can manage the Southern Palace and make it profitable."

The church had emptied. Mr. Kennedy offered an arm to Celia and the other to India. "Shall we?"

They went out into the pale March sunshine. Rigs and car-riages lined up along the street as the worshippers headed home. Frannie played with a small group of children on the gray stone steps, her thick dark braid hanging loose over one shoulder.

"Miss Hartley has much more in mind than merely making a profit," Celia said, taking up the conversation again. "Tell him, India."

The wind gusted up. India clamped her hand to her hat to keep it in place and briefly explained her wish to use the theater for education as well as for entertainment. "Besides bringing culture and knowledge to the young people, such a program encourages the next generation to become theatergoers. It ensures that the Southern Palace can stay profitable into the future."

"I think India's idea is wonderful," Celia said. "And a useful complement to the men's library you helped us open last fall. The library is already helping to keep the working-class men of Savannah away from the grog houses and . . . other undesirable pursuits. Just think of how much more we could elevate the culture of the city if we had India's program in place at the theater."

Mr. Kennedy said, "I'm all for helping the city move forward, but I'm not sure it can work."

"One thing I've learned in life is that nothing is assured," India said. "Everything we do, from crossing a street to visiting the dentist, is a calculated risk. But the possibility of catastrophe doesn't prevent us from going ahead, does it?"

"No, I suppose not," Mr. Kennedy mused.

"All I'm asking is a chance to try it," India went on. "If it proves unsuccessful or unworkable, then—"

"Mr. Kennedy! There you are." India's understudy, the blond Miss Bryson, came tripping across the churchyard, an obviously new and expensive reticule dangling from one arm. If she regretted her testimony at the trial, she didn't show it. She barely glanced at India. "Mr. Kennedy, I've heard the theater is about to reopen, and I wanted to offer my services in whatever production is—"

"That news is a bit premature, Miss Bryson. There is much to be done before we're underway again. When the time comes, you're welcome to audition for any suitable role."

"Audition? But—"

Celia stepped closer. "Please excuse us, Miss Bryson. We

were just in the middle of an important discussion. I'm sure you understand."

The girl looked flustered. "Oh. Of course."

She turned on her heel and entered a waiting carriage.

India pressed a hand to her forehead. Miss Bryson aspired to be a great actress, but she lacked the skill to conceal her unbridled ambition. If India did become manager of the Southern Palace, she would have to find some way to deal with the budding actress. The world of the theater was a small one. Word got around—good or bad—and the last thing any manager needed was a player with an inflated opinion of her own worth.

Mr. Kennedy turned back to India. "I must be getting home. My wife is expecting me. I will give some thought to your proposal and discuss it with Mr. Shakleford when he returns from Charleston. I couldn't make a decision without consulting my partner."

"Of course not. I wouldn't expect you to."

"He's the one who put up most of the money to build the theater. I'm just the idea man. If he's interested, he will want to speak to you himself."

"I'll look forward to it."

He bobbed his head. "Good day, ladies."

Celia called to Frannie, who joined them as they headed for Madison Square.

"Well," Celia said to India, "All in all, I think that went very well."

"What went well, Mama?" Frannie caught her mother's hand and skipped along the street.

"Nothing of interest to you, my sweet. Just a discussion

about the theater. Grown-up stuff. Very boring." Celia tugged on her daughter's messy braid. "What happened to your hair?"

"Charlie Stiles pulled out my ribbons, and then the pins fell, and I couldn't find them. I told him he was being mean, but then Bessie Frost told me when a boy pulls your hair that means he likes you. Is that true?"

Celia laughed. "In my experience, yes, it's true. But you are too young for boys. Your papa would have a fit if he thought you were interested in Charlie Stiles."

"I'm trying to get older," Frannie said. "And anyway, Papa fell in love with you when you were twelve. I'll be twelve in four more years."

They reached the Mackays' house and went inside. Mrs. Whipple served lunch. Frannie went to her room for a nap, and Celia and India settled into the parlor.

"Don't worry about what Mr. Kennedy's partner will say," Celia said. "Mr. Shakleford is not the type to question Mr. Kennedy's decisions. If Mr. Kennedy decides in your favor, Mr. Shakleford won't stand in the way. I only hope he returns from Charleston soon."

"Oh, I hope so too. And I can't thank you enough for the introduction. And for your hospitality. But it's high time I found somewhere else to hang my hat. I've depended upon your good graces far too long."

"Nonsense. I've enjoyed your company. But I wouldn't blame you if you wanted to find someplace quieter." Celia laughed, crinkling the corners of her violet eyes. "Frannie and Maxwell and the cat can be too much at times. You might find the hotel a more tranquil place."

"Until I find a position of some kind, I can't afford it. And I won't take another penny from you. So don't even suggest it. There must be less expensive lodgings somewhere around here. A boardinghouse, perhaps, or a ladies' hotel."

Celia frowned. "Boardinghouses. Yes, but not at all suitable for someone like you."

"I don't need anything fancy. I'm quite accustomed to less than luxurious accommodations. After all, I spent three nights alone in a fish camp on a practically deserted island."

Celia inclined her head. "I still don't understand how Philip managed that. Or how he found Laura. Not that it's any of my business. I'm only glad you are free."

"I don't know how he found her either. But I'm awfully glad he did. I finally feel as if my life has begun again. Or it will, as soon as I'm settled somewhere."

"Mr. Philbrick occupied the manager's apartment adjacent to the theater. Perhaps Mr. Kennedy will offer you those rooms if you are hired to manage the Southern Palace."

"That would be a godsend. I can't imagine he will offer very much in the way of salary, and whatever I earn will go further if I don't have to hire a carriage every day."

Celia smiled. "Something tells me Philip Sinclair will be more than happy to drive you anywhere you need to go."

"He has been wonderful."

"But you aren't certain how he feels about you."

"Not at all."

Celia's brows rose. "Do you have feelings for him?"

India released a pent-up sigh. "Deeper affection than is good for me, I fear."

"Then you must give him time, my dear. He has suffered a tremendous shock, finding Laura alive, learning of her duplicity, and then watching her take her own life."

"It was horrible for all of us."

"I'm sure it was. But especially so for Philip, who must wonder whether anything apart from the law is real or true. If you care for him, you must give him the chance to see that you are not one bit like Laura. I've known him most of my life. He can be slow to trust, but once he does, he doesn't do anything by halves. He's worth the wait."

Carriage wheels sounded on the street. Celia peered out the window. "Here he comes now." She got to her feet and planted a swift kiss on India's cheek. "I need a nap, and you two need some time alone. Give Philip my regards and remind him he is expected for dinner on Tuesday night. I've promised the Sons of Temperance a meeting with Philip. Some legal thing they want sorted out."

Celia hurried up the stairs. Mrs. Whipple answered the door, then hurried away. Philip came in. His eyes lit up when he saw India. "Sorry I missed you at church. Mr. Quarterman asked me to look into a property claim one of his former bondsmen is filing, and by the time he wound down you and Celia were deep into conversation with Mr. Kennedy. It looked serious so I figured I ought not to interrupt."

India led him into the parlor. "Celia and I are trying to convince him to let me manage the theater and to mount some educational programs along with plays and readings."

Mrs. Whipple returned with a tray, her brows raised in question. Philip politely declined the tea and leaned against the door frame. "What do you think of your chances?"

"I don't know. He seemed mildly interested but he has to confer with his business partner."

"Shakleford won't say no, if Kennedy agrees."

"So Celia says."

Philip glanced around. "Where is she anyway? Not feeling poorly again, I hope."

"No, she's quite well. She thought we needed some time to talk."

He smiled, and India noticed the weariness in his eyes. "Wise woman. Actually I was hoping you might come with me to the cemetery."

"Sure. But why?"

"Something I need to take care of. Would you mind if we headed over there now?"

India retrieved her wrap. Philip handed her into his waiting rig, and they set off for Laurel Grove Cemetery. They entered the gates and drove along a lane lined with stands of magnolia, dogwood, live oaks, and pine trees. He pointed out the graves of mayors and Confederate generals. Moments later he stopped the rig before an impressive tombstone with an elaborate carved base. "Celia's father is buried there. Mr. Browning was a leading citizen of Savannah before the war. He passed just before it started."

Philip flicked the reins, and the rig lurched forward. A few yards down, he stopped before a grave surrounded by a black wrought-iron fence and marked by a simple granite stone. They got out of the rig. India leaned forward to read the inscription:

Laura Sinclair
Beloved Wife
1839–1866

A wagon appeared on the road in front of them, a tall man in a gray woolen coat and wide-brimmed hat at the reins. He drew up alongside Philip's rig and halted the wagon. Philip got out of the rig. The man jumped down, and the two men embraced.

He was shorter than Philip and dark-skinned, with high prominent cheekbones and straight black hair worn a bit longer than was fashionable. Ice-blue eyes appraised her as Philip made the introductions.

"So, Miss Hartley, we meet at last," the man said, smiling into her eyes. "Lucius Fall."

"Mr. Fall is an old friend of mine," Philip said. "And the best detective between here and Boston. He gets the credit for finding Laura for me."

The detective shrugged, but India saw how pleased he was by the compliment. "You'd be surprised how often missing people are found hiding in plain sight. In Miss Laura's case, knowing how she felt about Arthur Sterling, I figured if she had faked her disappearance, she wouldn't have gone too far afield. She had me stumped for a while, but once I discovered he had a place on Isle of Hope, it wasn't hard to track her down."

India shivered at the memory of her clandestine visit to the actor's house.

"She lived in seclusion most of the time," Mr. Fall said. "I suppose she was afraid of being recognized if she spent too much time in public."

"She had access to Sterling's stage makeup, to all kinds of costumes and wigs," Philip said. "And of course no one would have expected to see her on the street. In a busy town like Savannah, she could move about undetected if she was careful."

Mr. Fall placed a hand on Philip's shoulder. "I'm sorry as I can be for the shock to you, my friend. There were times I almost wished I wouldn't find her. But I couldn't let Miss Hartley here take the blame for something she didn't do."

"No." Philip squeezed India's hand. "I admit I was taken aback, and embarrassed, too, to have been so thoroughly deceived. But it was worth it to see Miss Hartley proved innocent."

"It's too bad this thing ended up the way it did," Mr. Fall went on. "When I heard that she had shot herself, I figured she couldn't come to terms with what she'd done to that poor slave girl. Not to mention that she was facing the prospect of a long prison sentence. It must have proved unbearable for her in the end."

"Yes." Philip cleared his throat. "Did you bring the stone?"

"Got it right here." Mr. Fall removed a canvas cover from a tombstone carved in white marble and adorned with angels. "The stone carver balked when I asked him to finish this right away, but a greasing of the palm improved his attitude considerably." He smiled at India. "As it so often does."

He took a shovel from the wagon, and he and Philip entered the enclosure. They removed Laura's tombstone and replaced it with the new one.

Here lies Hannah June Washington.
1843–1866
Safe in the arms of the angels.

When Hannah's marker was set into place, Philip and Mr. Fall hoisted Laura's stone onto the wagon and drove it to the new grave beneath a magnolia tree, where Laura rested. They wrestled the heavy marker into place and stood back to make sure it was level.

"Looks good," Mr. Fall said. "Soon as the grass grows up around it a bit, it will look as if it has always been there. Though of course the date of death is wrong now." He frowned. "Maybe the stonecutter could somehow change the—"

"Leave it." Philip reached for India's hand and held on. "Let her be. It doesn't matter now."

Despite everything Laura had done, India couldn't help feeling sorry for her. The woman was a sad example of what became of those who chose darkness over light. India shaded her eyes and looked around. "At least she's at rest in a place of great beauty."

"Laurel Grove is as fine a place as there is." Mr. Fall pointed south, to another field of graves some distance away. "Over there is where the black folks are buried. Slaves and freedmen alike. I reckon Hannah June may be the only black woman buried in the white folks' side." He looked at Philip. "But my lips are sealed, my friend."

"Appreciate your help, Lucius."

"Any time." Mr. Fall tipped his hat to India, climbed onto the wagon, and drove away.

"What an interesting man." India accepted Philip's arm as they returned to his rig.

"That he is." He brushed at a thread of Spanish moss that drifted onto his sleeve. "I met Lucius at school, but after we graduated we lost touch until the war began."

"You fought together?"

The wind picked up. India drew her wrap about her shoulders.

"In a manner of speaking. I spent some time with the Confederate Secret Service. Lucius served as a courier out of

Richmond. He was captured once—in Maryland—but managed to escape. He never lost that taste for danger. After the war he joined Pinkerton's detective agency to track down train robbers and embezzlers and such."

They reached the rig. Philip boosted India inside and picked up the reins.

She tucked in her skirts and folded her hands in her lap. "How did Mr. Fall wind up in Savannah tracking down missing persons?"

"Mr. Pinkerton had a strict code that forbade his operatives from taking on scandalous cases. Lucius took one anyway, to help a friend he believed was in grave danger. When Pinkerton found out, Lucius was dismissed."

"That hardly seems fair. Of course rules must be respected, but things are not always black and white, are they?"

Philip smiled. "In the lawyering game things are rarely black and white. But Lucius has done all right for himself. I hired him for a complicated case I was working on back then. He came to town then and never left. He stays busy assisting several lawyers in town. And the odd private client. Last year he helped one of Mrs. Garrison's cousins track down a lost inheritance. He could have retired on his fee from that case, but he loves the thrill of the chase."

They drove out of the cemetery and headed for Madison Square.

India turned toward Philip. "Well, I admire Mr. Fall for doing what he thought was right." She paused. "He's so unusual-looking I wonder how he is able to blend into the background when he's working. I know I would remember those eyes. So intense. He gives the impression he can see right through to your soul."

"He comes from a wild mixture of a family. His grandmother was Swedish, which may account for his eyes. His mother was Seminole and his father was African—quite a successful Boston merchant back in our boyhood days. We've never discussed his appearance, but I imagine he might use it to his advantage. Sometimes it's useful for a suspect to know he's being sought. That makes him skittish and prone to mistakes."

They neared Madison Square, busy in the spring afternoon. Couples strolled beneath the sun-washed sky, carriages and rigs plied the crowded street. Gentlemen tipped their hats before hurrying to their own pursuits. Under the watchful eyes of their mothers and nurses, children played in the leafy square.

India reveled in the simple pleasure of a Sunday drive without being accosted by reporters and curiosity seekers. Mr. Philbrick's startling confession and impending sentence seemed to have satisfied the public's need for justice. And other events taking place in Savannah had captured everyone's attention. A series of fires on Commerce Row had everyone speculating about the identity of an arsonist. The ladies in charge of fund-raising for the circulating library had recently announced that the author of a new book about Kate Warne, America's first female detective, had agreed to give a lecture in May. India Hartley and her troubles were swiftly becoming yesterday's news.

Philip drew up at the Mackays' house on Madison Square. He turned to her and took both her hands in his. "Thank you for coming with me. It made the whole thing easier to bear."

"I'm glad to do whatever I can for you, Philip. I am forever in your debt."

"I don't want you to feel indebted to me. I want you to feel—"

"Philip! There you are."

Amelia Sinclair, her cheeks as pink as her new dress, hurried over and peered into the rig. Philip and India got out, and Philip embraced his sister. "This is a surprise. What are you doing in town? If you'd let me know you were coming, I'd have arranged to meet you at the landing."

Amelia laughed. "I didn't know I was coming until last evening's mail arrived."

She fished a tattered letter from her pocket and held it out to him. "It's from Mr. Lockwood. He made it to Texas and found work at a ranch called the Rocking C. It's owned by a Mr. Jake Caldwell and his son, Wyatt. Only it seems Wyatt is running his lumber mill in Tennessee right now, and looking after his aunt Lillian. Mr. Caldwell told Mr. Lockwood that one day his son will come home to the ranch, but right now, he is terribly shorthanded and he hired Cuyler—I mean, Mr. Lockwood—to help with the cattle and such."

Amelia paused for breath. "Mr. Lockwood intends to save up his money so that when Wyatt Caldwell comes home, he will have enough put away to start a ranch of his own. And the best news of all is that Mr. Lockwood wants to marry me."

"I see." Philip scanned the letter.

"I know you think he isn't nearly good enough for me, but it isn't as if the world is full of eligible gentlemen anymore. And Mr. Lockwood is kind, and steady, and obviously not afraid of hard work."

India saw the hesitation in Philip's eyes. Cuyler Lockwood had proved his mettle in helping her to escape to the Isle of Hope. And clearly, Amelia was smitten with him. But it was not her place to interfere in the Sinclairs' personal affairs. She touched Philip's sleeve. "Perhaps I should go inside and leave you to your discussion."

"Oh, no, India," Amelia said. "Please stay and help me convince my brother I know what's best for myself."

Philip handed his sister the letter. "Lockwood is not the worst choice you could have made. And if your mind is made up—"

"It is," Amelia said. "I've already written to him to accept. I only wanted your blessing before sending it."

Philip heaved a resigned sigh. "In that case, I suppose we've a wedding to plan. When did you have in mind?"

"I'm going to Texas and marrying him there."

Philip frowned. "That's hardly proper, Amelia."

"Oh, who cares what's proper? Those days are long gone. And besides, Cuyler needs to save his money for our future. He can't afford to pay for a train ticket to come here, plus two tickets for us to return."

"I'll pay for the tickets," Philip said. "Consider them a wedding present."

"I do appreciate the offer, but honestly, who would I invite? There is only you and a few friends on St. Simons. And India, of course. The church at Fredericka is a wreck. We'd have to marry at Indigo Point, and considering everything that's happened there, it would cast a pall over what is supposed to be a happy day."

India could see the hurt in Philip's eyes. Clearly he wanted to be a part of Amelia's wedding, but she seemed just as determined to do things her way. "Perhaps you and Mr. Lockwood could plan to come home for Christmas. We could arrange a reception at the hotel. Maybe an evening affair, with greenery and candlelight. It could be quite lovely."

Amelia beamed. "That's a perfect solution. What do you think, Philip?"

"I think," he said slowly, "that I have no say in any of this. If you ladies will excuse me, I must see to the horse."

He climbed into the rig and drove away.

⚜ CHAPTER 33 ⚜

MARCH 22

THE OFFICES OF SHAKLEFORD AND KENNEDY OCCUPIED a handsome pink stucco building nestled between a jewelry store and a men's haberdashery. Tall windows with dark green shutters overlooked a small courtyard enclosed behind a wrought-iron fence. A discreet brass plaque affixed to the right side of the door bore the names of the two gentlemen who had summoned India to a meeting at ten o'clock sharp.

Celia's carriage driver delivered India to the front door and settled down to wait for her.

She climbed the steps and rang the bell. Presently a small, round woman with gentle features, her dark hair threaded with gray, opened the door and ushered India into a spacious, high-ceilinged room. Brown leather chairs, glass-fronted bookcases, and wooden tables piled with ledgers, magazines, maps, and yellowed telegrams filled the space.

"Forgive the mess," the woman said. "I try to keep things tidy, but Mr. Kennedy has his own way of organizing things, and he gets upset if I put his papers and such where he can't find them. May I bring you some tea?"

"If it isn't too much trouble." All morning India had battled a bad case of nerves. So much depended upon this interview with Mr. Shakleford. A nice cup of tea might help calm her trembling hands and slow her racing heart.

"No trouble. I won't be but a few minutes. Mr. Shakleford is running late, as usual. Just make yourself at home."

She left, and India perched on the leather chair nearest the window. Outside on the street a gray cat was inspecting Celia's carriage, and a group of small boys played with a ball. Rigs and carriages traversed the busy street. Two women carrying enormous dress boxes climbed into a rig and drove away.

A distant train whistle broke the silence. India thought of Amelia, who had left yesterday for Texas, accompanied by Binah, who had decided to see something of the wider world after all. Almarene had gone to stay with Mrs. Garrison's sister. India pictured Indigo Point completely deserted now, so burdened by the war's destruction, the elements, and its own sad history.

She hadn't seen Philip since last Sunday, when Amelia had arrived to announce her intention to wed Mr. Lockwood. India hoped he wasn't blaming her for encouraging Amelia in her plans. As if she, India, held sway over anyone. But she couldn't shake the feeling that she had displeased or hurt him somehow. The thought worried her. Because something profound happened when she was with Philip, a sense that she was where she belonged.

Perhaps he was only busy. Yesterday's *Morning Herald* had carried another story about Mr. Philbrick's impending sentencing. Though she was grateful he had admitted his role in

Mr. Sterling's death, something about his story didn't ring true. His assertion that he had done it all for the love of Laura had stunned everyone, including Laura herself. Of course there were cases of secret admirers. India had encountered a few of her own over the years—men enamored with the exotic glamour of the theater. But Mr. Philbrick didn't seem the kind of man to be swayed by sentiment. Money seemed to be the thing uppermost in his mind. Or it had been the night he ordered the change in the script.

The door opened, and the woman returned with a tea tray. She set it down on the small side table next to India's chair. "Here you are, miss. It won't be long now. Mr. Shakleford has just arrived."

India poured a cup and had just taken her first sip when Mr. Kennedy blustered in, followed by a stocky, barrel-chested, wide-shouldered man. His brown hair was thin, receding a bit. His features were robust, his manner expansive.

"Miss Hartley." Mr. Kennedy bowed over her hand. "Lovely to see you. May I present Mr. Shakleford."

Mr. Shakleford offered a brisk nod. "Miss Hartley. Mrs. Warren has brought you tea, I see." He rubbed his hands together. "Shall we get down to business?"

The two men took their seats.

"I've described your plans to my partner," Mr. Kennedy began. "But he has a few questions."

"All right." India released a shaky breath. Her profession was to inhabit another's skin, to assume a different demeanor and different emotions. To mask her own feelings. But this meeting was more crucial than any stage performance. She had no other prospects for her future. When her meager savings ran out, she would be at the mercy of her creditors.

Mr. Shakleford leaned forward in his chair. "You managed a touring theater company with your father."

"For several years, yes. I kept the accounts, paid the bills, kept track of the schedule. My father and I also wrote several plays, which were produced in smaller theaters in the East."

"Mr. Kennedy tells me you have big plans for the Southern Palace."

India described her hope that the theater might be used for education as well as for entertainment. "It's a beautiful theater, Mr. Shakleford. It would mean so much to people who have never before had the chance to attend a play. And as I've expressed to Mr. Kennedy, I hope we might improve the lives of the less fortunate. In an indirect way at least."

"How do you mean?"

"In the same way that the Sons of Temperance are improving the lives of many families by offering the menfolk an alternative to drinking and brawling."

"You mean the men's library."

"Yes. I believe that deep down, most people want to do the right thing. Sometimes they have never been taught what the right thing is. My plan is to offer classes at the theater, to teach people to make better choices, just as many men now are choosing books over the bottle."

India paused, afraid that she had said too much. Surely she sounded like some overbearing, wild-eyed do-gooder.

Mr. Shakleford chewed his lip. "It's an ambitious plan. And far be it from me to stand in the way of social progress. But I have to keep an eye on the bottom line. And I'll be frank. I haven't quite understood why our profits last season were so meager, when the theater was full almost every night."

India carefully considered her next words. "I wasn't at the Southern Palace very long before the tragedy happened. But one thing I noticed was that Mr. Philbrick seemed to have hired a number of people to perform very small jobs."

"What do you mean?"

"Well, for example, there were people who only moved scenery. Others whose only job was to repair costumes or build props. In my father's touring company, of necessity everyone was able to handle the many tasks required to mount a production. I don't see why we can't train a few talented people to do more than one job. Or assign certain responsibilities to the bit players, as my father did. It would not only better organize rehearsals, it would also save money."

Mr. Kennedy spoke for the first time. "Well, Hiram? Has this young lady satisfied your questions as to her abilities?"

Mr. Shakleford stood and crossed to India's chair. He stuck out his hand. "Congratulations, Miss Hartley. You're the new manager of the Southern Palace."

Mr. Kennedy cleared his throat. "Now, Miss Hartley, there is the matter of your salary, which we can discuss later. Mrs. Mackay tells me you are in need of accommodations."

"I am. I've been her guest far too long, and now that I will be spending more time at the theater—"

Mr. Shakleford raised one hand, palm out. "You can have the manager's apartment across from the theater. I can't guarantee what kind of shape it's in. Mr. Philbrick is a bachelor, you know, and speaking as a bachelor myself, we are not the tidiest of men."

"I'll see to it that Philbrick's things are removed and the rooms are cleaned this afternoon," Mr. Kennedy said. "Poor devil won't need any of it now."

Mr. Shakleford accompanied India to the door. She climbed into Celia's carriage for the short ride to the Mackays' feeling almost giddy. Her name was cleared, her future settled. She watched the scenery rolling past, her mind busy with new ideas and new plans for her theater.

If only Philip wasn't angry with her. But perhaps her good news would put him in a better frame of mind.

As the carriage rolled toward Madison Square, India mentally replayed her conversation with the two investors. Mr. Shakleford was right. It didn't make sense that the theater showed such a slim profit despite strong ticket sales.

India couldn't put her finger on it, but she was certain that something was terribly wrong.

⁂

MARCH 24

The rooms so recently occupied by Mr. Philbrick had been cleared and thoroughly cleaned, and now the air smelled like soap and lemon wax. India set down her valise and looked around, scarcely believing that she was home at last. The rooms were modest—only a small parlor, a bedroom, and a tiny bathing room—but the compact space suited her needs perfectly.

In the front parlor a silk rug in muted tones of gold and

celadon lay across a gleaming wood floor. Two cozy chairs upholstered in deep green velvet sat before the fireplace. On the opposite wall a pair of handsome glass-fronted bookcases waited to be filled.

India removed her hat and gloves and carried her valise into the bedroom. Here, a high narrow bed made up with fresh white linens and a pale blue coverlet was positioned at an angle beneath a single window that afforded a glimpse of a distant church steeple. The only other furnishings were a wardrobe and a small side table that held a plain white ewer and basin.

She unpacked and hung her dresses and shawl in the wardrobe, placing her spare pair of shoes beneath.

A rig drew up outside, and a man in a gray coat knocked at her door.

"Mr. Quinn! What a surprise."

The young stagehand snatched off his cap and ducked his head. "Miss Hartley. It is purely a pleasure to see you again. And I sure am glad everything turned out all right for you."

"Thank you. So am I."

"Mr. Kennedy asked me to bring your trunk over from the theater." He jerked his thumb. "Got it there in the rig. Where do you want it?"

"The parlor will be fine."

He turned away just as a familiar horse and rig drew up at the gate. Philip climbed out and started up the steps carrying an enormous bouquet of yellow and white freesias.

He handed her the bouquet. "I wasn't as gracious as I should have been upon hearing Amelia's news. Brought you a peace offering."

"Come in." She led him into the parlor before burying her nose in the fragrant blooms. "Such an extravagance. Where ever did you find these so early in the season?"

Riley Quinn returned, staggering beneath the weight of the trunk. He set it down near the fireplace and dusted off his hands. "Them's some flowers you got there, miss."

"Aren't they though?"

India made the introductions. The young man stuck out his hand and looked up at Philip with an expression akin to hero worship. "Everybody in Savannah is talkin' about what a fine piece of lawyerin' you did to clear Miss Hartley. I sure am pleased to make your acquaintance, Mr. Sinclair."

"Likewise, Mr. Quinn. India tells me you were quite a help to her last fall."

Mr. Quinn blushed. "It isn't every day we get someone at the Palace as famous as Miss Hartley. Everybody is itching to get back to work." He turned to India. "When do you reckon we can reopen?"

"Soon, I hope. I was hired only two days ago. But I think we can mount one production before people start leaving the city for the summer. And next fall we'll plan on a full theater season."

"Oh, I get it. Sorta like whetting the appetite and getting people to looking forward to what's next."

"Something like that."

"Well, you just let me know what I can do to help, miss."

"I will, Mr. Quinn. Thank you again for bringing over the trunk."

"No trouble." Mr. Quinn nodded to Philip. "Good to meet you, sir."

He hurried down the steps and drove off.

India filled the ewer with water from the pump in the bathing room and arranged the freesias. She set them on the parlor table and took another whiff of the light, sweet scent.

"These are lovely, Philip. But a peace offering was hardly necessary. I overstepped my bounds when I suggested Amelia hold a reception in Savannah. I could see that you were unhappy about her wedding plans, and I tried to effect a compromise. But I should have left that to you and your sister. I don't blame you for being angry with me."

He leaned against the fireplace. "I wasn't as angry with you as I was with myself. I should have made more of an effort to find a suitable husband for Amelia. But I was busy with my law practice, and with trying to woo Mr. Dodge to Indigo Point. And then with your defense."

"Mr. Lockwood seems steady enough these days. And he was courageous and inventive when it came to getting me out of Savannah." She paused. "He told me you arranged everything."

"It was risky, but not entirely without precedent. Some years back a woman convicted of murder in Missouri was taken from jail and spirited out of town while her verdict was on appeal. But her case didn't end as happily as ours."

He looked around the room, and India saw it through his eyes. "It's rather barren at the moment," she said, "but I intend to make it a real home."

"Then I ought to get going and leave you to your nest building." He smiled then, and she felt a rush of warmth stronger than the heat of any fire. If only he felt the same heat when he looked at her. But she couldn't blame him for keeping his distance. Four months was hardly enough time to develop the kind of trust he needed in order to open his heart again.

"Philip?" She started to tell him of her suspicions about Mr. Philbrick, but he was already moving toward the door, his mind clearly on other things.

He turned back, one brow raised in question.

"Never mind," she said. "Thank you for the flowers."

"You're welcome." He studied her for a moment. "I'm leaving this evening for Indigo Point."

"Oh?" She schooled her expression, but inside she felt a stab of panic. Was this good-bye?

"Surveyors are on the way to lay out the resort."

"It's going to happen, then."

"Yes. We got word a few days ago. But I wanted to be sure you were settled before I left."

"That was kind of you. Will you be away long?"

"Hard to say. It depends on the weather and on how efficient the surveyors are. But you can always send a message with the steamer captain if you need me."

"I'm sure I'll be all right." She swept a hand around the room. "I'm almost settled here, but I haven't been to the theater yet. No doubt there will be plenty to sort out."

When his rig disappeared from view, she opened the trunk. She took out her father's few personal effects: a scrapbook of her theater notices, several bound copies of plays, a half-finished sketch he had begun before illness overtook him. A carte de visite taken at Mr. Sarony's New York studio. A packet of letters tied with a faded blue ribbon. That the essence of his life could be contained in so few things filled her with sadness. With a start, she realized that today was the first anniversary of his death. How could she have forgotten?

Bittersweet memories of their strange and magical life rushed in. Her father's barely contained anticipation as the curtain rose on a new production, his childlike delight in the camaraderie of their fellow players. His deep belly laugh, and the hint of mischief in his eyes. The backstage smells of greasepaint and damp wool, the sharp crack of applause after a well-delivered line.

She set the book of clippings on the table next to the freesias and ran her fingers over the cracked leather cover. Some people thought of the theater as a tacky underworld of fantasy, but her father had regarded it as a portal to a wider world of thoughts and ideas. Perhaps through her work at the Southern Palace she could pay tribute to that vision.

India rose and propped his carte de visite on the mantel. And for a moment his presence in the room felt so strong she expected to hear him speak. Having these few reminders of her father made the nearly empty apartment seem more like home. She clutched the packet of letters to her chest, overcome with longing for a place of permanence. A place that was more than four walls and a roof. A place that would anchor her to her past and give her hope for the future.

A refuge that no theater on earth could ever provide.

✍ CHAPTER 34 ✍

In contrast to the barren cleanliness of her private rooms, the manager's office at the Southern Palace was a dusty, disorganized mess strewn with old scripts, stacks of bills, receipts, ledgers, books, and advertising posters. Cobwebs clung to the heavy curtains and to the worn wool rug covering the wide plank floor.

On her first day India spent hours cleaning and boxing up the last of Mr. Philbrick's personal effects—a framed photograph of himself as Hamlet, his personal copies of Shakespeare's plays, and the last of his props and costumes, which had taken up every inch of space in the dressing room that adjoined the office.

Now, these tasks were completed. The gleaming window let in the bright April sunlight that fell in golden bars across the tidy desk where India sat, going over the profit-and-loss ledgers from last season. The more she read, the more convinced she became that Mr. Shakleford's concerns were indeed well founded. For one thing, in many instances the receipts for a specific performance didn't match the number of tickets sold. On evenings when the house was full, and every seat accounted for, the take would have been close to six hundred dollars. But often the amount deposited to the bank was considerably less. Some of the discrepancy could be accounted for by the complimentary tickets sometimes awarded to special theater patrons and out-of-town guests. She herself had provided tickets for her young carriage driver and his sister the night of the accident. Other cast members no doubt did so, too, from time to time. And it was possible that Mr. Philbrick retained a small amount of the nightly profits to cover unexpected incidentals that always cropped up during a play's run. But if he had, there was no record of it.

She found a folder stuffed with contracts of the players hired for the season. Those contracts matched the amounts recorded in the ledgers' accounts payable columns, but there were lists of expenses with no amounts attached to them. Unless they were recorded elsewhere.

For a man who had ruled the theater with an iron fist and supreme self-confidence, Cornelius Philbrick had proven himself a sloppy, incompetent businessman.

Voices in the hallway interrupted her work. She pressed her fingers to her eyes and went to the door to find Riley Quinn and his new assistant, Alexander Hatcher, wrestling with an unwieldy flat still reeking of fresh paint.

Mr. Quinn rested his end of the burden on the toe of his boot and wiped his forehead with his shirt sleeve. "Just picked this up from the painters," he told her. "It came out real good. What do you think?"

India stood back to study the elaborately detailed scene of the city of Ephesus. For her only production of the spring, she had chosen *The Comedy of Errors*, not only because it was lighthearted and required fewer scenes and fewer actors than any other of the Bard's plays, but because she could make do with only a few large pieces of scenery to suggest the setting. This one, in vibrant colors of red, gold, and green, would do nicely for the opening.

"It's wonderful, Mr. Quinn. Exactly the effect I wanted. Can you put it into place on the stage so I can see how it will look from the back of the theater?"

"Sure thing, Miss Hartley."

Mr. Hatcher, a thin boy with a thatch of dark hair and black eyes that snapped with impatience, sighed. "Can we get on with it then, Riley? This thing is gettin' awfully heavy."

"Hold your horses." Mr. Quinn grinned at India. "We'll have it set up for you in half an hour, tops."

"Thank you."

The two men lifted the flat and carried it down the hall.

The seamstress India had hired to sew costumes for the two sets of twins featured in the play hurried to meet her. "Miss Hartley, I've finished basting one of the Dromio costumes, but you oughta look at it before I go any further. In case you want it different."

"I'll come and take a look now."

India inspected the costume, which featured a row of gold-colored buttons over an icy gray satin tunic paired with tight breeches in a darker shade. She held the tunic up to the light and frowned.

The seamstress stood silently, her hands tightly clasped. "If you don't like it, I can—"

"It isn't your fault, Miss Sawyer. You've done exactly as I

asked. But now that I see it, I'm not sure this color is right. I don't want something so bright it upstages the other actors, but this seems a bit drab."

"Yes, ma'am, I think so too. I can start over if you want to pick another color, but—"

"I'm afraid we haven't the time or the money for that," India said. "Perhaps some kind of scarf would work. Or—"

The seamstress held up a hand. "I've got just the thing." From her commodious supplies basket she brought out a length of red braid shot through with silver threads. "What if I sew this to the neckline and along the outer sleeve?" She picked up the costume and laid the braid across the fabric. "Smartens it up a good bit, eh?"

India smiled, relieved. "Much better. Thank you, Miss Sawyer. When do you think the other costumes will be finished?"

"Another week should give me plenty of time. Almost everything is done except for the merchant's costume and Dr. Pinch's." She removed a blue dress from a hook on the wall and held it up for India's inspection. "This is what I made for the character of Nell. You said you wanted something as unflattering as possible."

"It's what the play calls for," India said. "Nell is described as spherical, like a globe. This dress ought to make her seem positively rotund."

Miss Sawyer laughed. "I sure have enjoyed working here since Mr. Shakleford and Mr. Kennedy put you in charge. You are a caution, if you don't mind me sayin' so."

India turned to go, her mind already returning to the problem of finances. The budget for her first production was so modest that some of the players would wear their own costumes, and Riley Quinn would have to handle the limelighting contraption on his own. At least there were few sound effects he couldn't handle. She didn't blame the theater owners for the small budget. She hadn't yet proved herself as manager, and there still was the problem of the disorganized bookkeeping to figure out.

She stepped inside her office and gave a startled yelp.

Victoria Bryson whirled around, a small blue book in her hand. "Miss Hartley. You frightened me."

"Same here," India said. "What are you doing?"

"I . . . I wanted to ask you a question. About . . . my character." The young understudy licked her lips and patted her hat, a blue-and-white concoction India had admired in a shop window downtown only last Saturday. She had been tempted to buy it for the theater reopening, but it was frightfully expensive and in the end she had passed it by. Obviously the cost had not deterred the younger woman.

"All right. What is it you wish to know?" India perched on the corner of her desk. Against her better judgment, she had cast Miss Bryson as Luciana, and the girl had been walking on air ever since.

"Well," the girl began. "I was wondering. Luciana is Adriana's sister, but I'm not sure how close the sisters are supposed to be. Does Luciana love Adriana, or is she jealous of her, because, you know, Adriana is married to a rich man?"

"What does the play tell you?"

"Ma'am?"

"*The Comedy of Errors* is just that," India said. "It's a farce.

Hence the wordplay and the puns and the slapstick. It isn't meant to delve too deeply into the human psyche."

She swallowed her impatience. She had too much work to do to teach this ambitious but empty-headed young woman the finer points of characterization. "The task of the players is always to interpret the playwright's intent. I'm sure if you carefully consider Luciana's lines, you will figure out how best to fulfill Mr. Shakespeare's vision."

"Oh." Miss Bryson edged toward the door. "I will think about it. And thank you, Miss Hartley. You have been most helpful I am sure."

In her haste, she caught a toe on the edge of the rug and went sprawling onto the floor, her skirts flying up around her.

India rushed to her side. "Are you all right?"

"I . . . I think so." Miss Bryson got to her feet and straightened her hat. "Please excuse me. I'm late!"

India watched her through the window, then returned to her desk to find that the bottom drawer was slightly ajar. India frowned. She hadn't looked in that drawer in several days. She was certain she hadn't left it open.

Obviously, Victoria Bryson had been looking for something other than acting advice.

APRIL 14

The Chatham County Jail was the last place on earth India wanted to see again, but another thorough look at Mr. Philbrick's bookkeeping had at last suggested a theory as to why the theater had earned so little last season. Unfortunately, the only one who could confirm it was the jailed manager himself.

Following his confession in Judge Bartlett's chambers and his waiving of a jury trial, India had supposed his sentencing would take place right away. But according to the latest newspaper reports, Mr. Philbrick had decided to hire a lawyer after all, and now the sentencing was delayed while the lawyer, a Mr. Thurmond who kept offices in Reynolds Square, reviewed the case.

"Here we are, miss. The jailhouse." The driver of the hired carriage opened the door and offered India his hand. "You want me to wait on you?"

"Yes, please. I'll try not to be too long."

He shrugged and tugged on his ear. "It's your money."

India paused for a moment, gathering her courage. Just the sight of this foreboding building set her heart to racing and jangled her nerves. The thought of stepping inside made her want to turn and run. But Mr. Shakleford and Mr. Kennedy were depending on her. She couldn't let them down.

She crossed the street to the door and stepped into the noise and smells of the busy jailhouse, which on this day was crowded with the usual pickpockets, drunks, and other miscreants. India made her way to the desk at the end of the hallway, where a young officer sat writing out a report.

"Good morning, Officer." India raised her voice to be heard above the noise of shouts and clanging metal. "I'm here to see one of your prisoners."

"Visiting hour is five to six," he said without looking up from his writing.

"But this is important." She clutched her reticule to keep

her hands from shaking. Unfortunately even her stage training couldn't quell the nervous quaver in her voice.

He looked up at last and blinked. "Miss Hartley? Saints in a sock. I sure never expected to see you darken our door again."

"Nor did I. But I have business with Mr. Philbrick concerning the theater."

He frowned. "I'm not sure it's legal for you to talk to him, seeing as how you are a part of his case." He glanced past her shoulder. "You shoulda brought that lawyer of yours."

"I would have, but he's on St. Simons, looking after his business interests there. I'm not sure when he can return, and my business with Mr. Philbrick can't wait."

"Why the hurry? I hear he ain't going anywhere till his fancy lawyer figures out a way for him to beat the charges."

"This won't take long," India said. "Can't you give me ten minutes?"

He blew out a long breath. "I'll take you up to his cell, but if anybody asks me how you got up there, I am going to plead ignorance. You understand?"

"Perfectly."

He glanced around. "Come on then."

He led her up the stairs and down the long corridor to a cell identical to the one where she had been held. She suppressed another shudder.

The officer banged the metal bars with his nightstick. "Visitor for you, Philbrick."

Cornelius Philbrick looked up from the book he was reading, his brow furrowed. "It isn't time for visitors, and besides, I have nothing to say."

"Suit yourself." The officer shot India a hard look. "Ten minutes, and I'll be back to escort you out of here. Sooner, if the officer in charge finds out you're breakin' the rules."

When the officer was out of earshot, India stepped closer to the cell. The smells of urine, onions, mold, and cooked cabbage wafted up. "Mr. Philbrick. As you just heard, I don't have much time. I've been going through the records at the theater and preparing for our spring play, and I have a few questions for you."

"I don't have to answer any questions. You ought to be grateful I saved your hide and leave it at that."

"I am grateful. Deeply so. But I'm managing the theater now, and in going through the books I find—"

"That the numbers don't add up."

"Correct. But I'm sure you can explain."

He laughed. "Don't try that ploy with me, Miss Hartley. You're a good actress, but not that good."

She stared at him through the cold metal bars. "I don't know what you mean."

"Listen. I know you heard me arguing with Arthur Sterling at the opening-night party last December."

India had forgotten about that row until now. Mr. Philbrick was the excitable type, unaccustomed to compromise and unafraid to browbeat anyone who opposed him. His argument with Mr. Sterling that night had been unusually loud but not all that rare. "Everyone heard. It would have been hard not to. Both of you were shouting." She paused. "Each of you must have cared deeply for Laura Sinclair. At least in that moment."

A piercing yell from another prisoner filled the air, and two uniformed officers pounded up the stairs.

Cornelius Philbrick shook his head. "I never had you pegged for such a hopeless romantic. You think Sterling and I were arguing over a woman?"

"Weren't you?"

He rolled his eyes. "Good gravy. How naïve can you be?"

"Miss?" One of the officers approached and crooked his finger. "You don't belong up here. You'll have to come with me. You can come back this afternoon at five."

"That won't be necessary, Officer," Mr. Philbrick said. "I have nothing more to say to this woman." He retreated to the back of his cell and turned his back to her. Dismissed.

India left the jail and waved to her carriage driver.

"Where to, Miss Hartley?"

"Back to the theater, please."

Back to the beginning.

❦ Chapter 35 ❧

"Miss Bryson, would you please come in for a moment?" India waved the actress into her office. In the days since her visit to Mr. Philbrick, India had turned his words over and over in her mind. If he and Mr. Sterling had not been arguing over Laura's affections and Mr. Sterling's callous treatment of her, then the only other possibility was money. According to the ledgers, Mr. Sterling had been paid handsomely for his services to the Southern Palace. But India had the strong feeling that she still didn't know the whole story, and now that Laura was gone, the truth would prove even more elusive.

Victoria Bryson entered the office, a frown creasing her pale brow. "What is it, Miss Hartley? Not a problem with the play, I hope."

"No."

"If it's about last Saturday's rehearsal, I know I missed a cue, but I promise it won't happen again." Miss Bryson fluffed the feathers on her pale yellow hat. "I want to give a wonderful performance, and I just know I can. I need more practice, that's all."

"Sit down, Miss Bryson." India closed her office door and leaned against it.

349

The young actress perched on the edge of her chair. "What is it?"

"I want to know why you were pilfering my office last week. What were you looking for?"

"I . . . I wasn't. I don't know what you mean."

"When I came in, you were standing beside my desk with a small blue book in your hand. After you left, tripping on your own feet in your haste, I might add, I found a desk drawer standing open."

"I'm sorry. The book was a gift from Mr. Philbrick. When he was taken to jail, I realized I had left it here. I wanted it back. I admit I looked in the desk, but it wasn't there. I finally found it behind the bookcase."

"You could have asked me about it."

Miss Bryson shook her head. "It's private."

India folded her arms. "Don't tell me that you and Mr. Philbrick were—"

"No. Nothing like that. I was in love with Mr. Sterling." The girl's blue eyes filled. "I guess a part of me always will be. Oh, I know he was faithless, and a liar to boot, but still—"

"And Mr. Philbrick?"

Miss Bryson went still. "Am I in trouble, Miss Hartley?"

"I don't know. Are you?"

The girl burst into tears. "Oh, more trouble than you can ever imagine."

India crossed the room and sat behind her desk, waiting for Miss Bryson to compose herself. At last she said, "Maybe you should begin at the beginning."

Miss Bryson sniffed and wiped her eyes. "I didn't mean to do anything wrong. Right after I started working at the theater, I was assigned to the odd jobs, helping with the scenery and keeping up with costumes and such. Hoping for my big chance to actually be in a play. Finally, last spring, Mr. Sterling noticed me and asked Mr. Philbrick to give me a small part in *King Lear.* You know that play?"

India smiled. "I do. Go on."

"Well, I took sick, and Mr. Philbrick replaced me. I know he had to. The show must go on and all that. But I was heartbroken at missing my chance. I couldn't stay away from the Southern Palace. It's like a home to me, you know? I feel dead inside when I'm not here. So I started helping Mr. Philbrick in the office. Just to be a part of it." Miss Bryson hiccupped. "Then one day I heard Mr. Philbrick and Mr. Sterling arguing. I was in the hallway, so I could hear most of what was said. Mr. Sterling was angry because Mr. Philbrick had charged some expensive dinners against the house receipts, and Mr. Sterling denied ever having attended them. He was afraid the theater owners would fire him for being too expensive, and he threatened to tell the owners what he knew."

"That Mr. Philbrick was falsifying the expense reports and keeping the money for himself."

Miss Bryson bobbed her head. "And then the door flew open unexpectedly, and Mr. Philbrick caught me with my ear pressed to the wall."

"I see. Then what?" India had a good idea of what had transpired next, but she wanted to hear it from the girl herself.

"Mr. Philbrick threw me out. He told me never to set foot inside the theater again. But I couldn't do that. The theater is everything to me. So we made a deal."

India recalled the girl's expensive reticule, her outrageous hats. The money for such fine things had to come from somewhere. "Mr. Philbrick agreed to pay you for your silence."

"Yes. I know it was wrong, but he gave me no choice."

"We always have choices, Miss Bryson. We might not like them, but there they are, all the same."

The young woman drew the small blue book from her reticule. "It's all here. The amounts he paid to me and the dates. When he went to jail, I got scared. That's why I came here to find it. Mr. Philbrick might seem like a good man, at least some of the time. But he will stop anyone who gets in his way." She paused. "What happens to me now, Miss Hartley? Will I go to jail?"

"I don't know. But I do know you are going to need a good lawyer."

"Will Mr. Sinclair help me? I suppose he's just about the best there is."

"I'll send word to Indigo Point. We'll see what he says."

"All right."

"In the meantime, we will carry on."

"You're not firing me?"

"I don't approve of blackmail. But you are young, and I can see how this happened. For now it's best if you don't say anything to anyone. Not until we hear from Mr. Sinclair."

Miss Bryson rose unsteadily and released a shuddering sigh. "Thank you, Miss Hartley. And I'm sorry for the things I said at the trial. And for what I said to you, about being old, and such."

India saw her out, then returned to her desk and collapsed into her chair. She needed to inform Mr. Shakleford about Mr. Philbrick's embezzlement, and she needed to compose a letter to Philip. It was still early enough that the letter could leave on this evening's steamer. If he received it tomorrow morning, she might possibly receive a reply by Wednesday. The whole thing was worrisome, but not as disturbing as the new, darker suspicions rising to the surface of her mind.

At the opening-night party, Cornelius Philbrick had quarreled with Mr. Sterling. Had Arthur Sterling threatened to expose Mr. Philbrick's deception? If so, the theater manager would have wanted to stop him. And what better way to do so than to hatch a plan to kill the man in the middle of a performance?

India shuddered at the cold-blooded nature of it all. But with Miss Bryson's confession, the final piece of the puzzle fell into place. Now India saw how everything had come together in a real-life scenario as intricate as any playwright could devise.

Laura Sinclair, already a murderess, discovered that Arthur Sterling had transferred his affections to Victoria Bryson. When Cornelius Philbrick changed the play, Laura seized her chance for revenge and switched the weapons, hoping that India would shoot Laura's faithless lover. At the same time, Mr. Philbrick, fearing that Mr. Sterling might at any moment expose his crime, decided to shoot the actor himself. In her last moments,

Laura contended that there was nothing between them. But he must have had some reason for showing up when he did, professing his devotion to her.

A knock sounded at her office door, and Riley Quinn stuck his head inside. "Ready for dress rehearsal, Miss Hartley. And everything looks spectacular, even if I do say so myself."

"Thank you, Mr. Quinn. I'll be right up."

India collected her script and pencils, her notes and her keys, and climbed the stairs to the stage. She had worked hard for weeks to get to this point, but the sense of happy anticipation she usually felt when a play was about to open was buried beneath a shroud of worry. If only Philip would come home.

The cast broke into applause as she made her way to her seat in the third row, center. She acknowledged them with a smile, then clapped her hands to signal silence. "All right, everybody. Act one, scene one. Please begin."

⁓

APRIL 20

India returned from an early dinner with Fabienne to find Philip waiting on her doorstep. Wordlessly, he folded her into an embrace. She leaned against him, breathing in the scents of soap and fresh starch. In his arms was a safety far greater than any walls could afford.

"Thank goodness you're home." She drew back to look up at him. "You got my letter about Miss Bryson?"

"I did. What a royal mess."

She fished her key from her reticule and opened her door.

"I'm sorry I wasn't here when you arrived. Fabienne just returned from a month of travel and wanted to assure me she intends to help out at the opening on Saturday night."

They went inside. She motioned him to a chair. "I'd offer you some tea, but sadly, this apartment has no kitchen."

"I don't need anything." He eased into the overstuffed chair. "This feels good after a day on the steamer."

She perched on the edge of the chair opposite and leaned forward until their knees were almost touching. "Miss Bryson has broken the law, but she's young and without anyone to guide her. I didn't know what else to do but write to you."

"I'd have been disappointed if you didn't. I hope you know you can always count on me." He leaned forward in his chair, hands on his knees, and smiled into her eyes.

"I do know that." Her voice was barely a whisper. From their first meeting, Philip had the power to take her breath away. She forced herself to think of the problem at hand. "I hope this doesn't turn into another scandal. I am sorry Miss Bryson has placed herself into such a troublesome position, but I couldn't ignore it."

"Of course not."

"Mr. Shakleford and Mr. Kennedy have put their trust in me. Fabienne, Mr. Quinn and his new assistant, and Miss Sawyer, to say nothing of the players themselves, are depending upon me to make the theater a success." She paused. "Maybe I'm wrong to suspect Mr. Philbrick of plotting to murder Arthur Sterling. Maybe I ought to have kept my suspicions to myself, but why would he have brought his gun to the theater that night, if he didn't have plans to use it? And why would he have confessed to the judge when no one suspected him? Unless he feared he might go to jail longer for embezzlement than for an accidental shooting. He must have felt something for Laura, despite her assertions to the contrary. It—"

"India. Wait a minute. Whether he did or not, it isn't your burden to bear. Tomorrow I'll speak to the prosecutor and lay out the facts. The embezzled money, the blackmail, the arguments between Sterling and Philbrick. Then it will be up to Mr. McLendon to investigate, to decide what charges are warranted, and to prove those charges in court. Let it go. The way I've let go of Laura and the things she did."

India realized that she was crying. Relief, regret, and hope warred inside her. What a joy it would be to wake up without the prospect of another disaster crowding her thoughts.

"What's this?" His voice was gentle. "No need for tears." Philip took out his handkerchief and dabbed her cheeks. "Deceit may prosper a person in the beginning, but sooner or later the truth comes out, and then there is nothing but misery and shame. Perhaps Philbrick is guilty of more than we realize. But it has nothing to do with us."

Darkness had fallen. India rose to light the lamp and regarded him through tear-spiked lashes, her heart full of hope, afraid to ask what he meant. Afraid not to, lest the moment slip away.

But he took both her hands in his, a solemn expression in his eyes. "Perhaps this isn't the best time to declare my intentions, but—"

"Intentions?" Joy flooded her heart as she searched his face. "By all means, Mr. Sinclair, if you have intentions, do tell."

He laughed softly and tucked away his sodden handkerchief. "All the time I was at Indigo Point, I couldn't stop thinking about you. Missing your presence in that old wreck of a house. Hearing your laugh at the dinner table. I realized that I didn't want to face the prospect of a future without you."

She thought of the day he had saved her from the water snake. She pictured him as he'd looked kneeling in the dirt at the deserted plantation trying to nurture a single, straggling rose. The heat and intensity of their first kiss. His boyish delight in bringing her those plum puddings. The extraordinary risks he'd taken to win her freedom. She swallowed. "Oh, I—"

"I realize I haven't been the kind of attentive suitor most ladies dream of. I've been removed at times and slow to declare my feelings. But I had to be certain that my past was truly in the past. That I had let it all go. It wouldn't have been fair to you otherwise."

She found that her heart was so full she couldn't speak. So she merely nodded.

"Ah. Does that mean, 'Yes, Mr. Sinclair, you may court me' or 'Leave me in peace, you quailing, boil-brained fool'?"

She laughed. "Somebody has been reading Mr. Shakespeare again."

"Brushing up before opening night."

He drew her closer, and she leaned into his embrace. This was where she belonged. Of course there would be obstacles ahead. For both of them. To some in Savannah, there was no such thing as a respectable actress. Certain doors would remain closed to her. But Celia Mackay was a powerful ally. As were Mr. Kennedy and Mr. Shakleford. She wouldn't think of any of it right now. For now there was only a rush of wordless joy and the sense of having come home at last. Philip was right.

From the ruin of her old life had come this love, this priceless treasure.

Philip released her and smiled into her eyes. "Did you save me a seat?"

She stood on tiptoe to kiss him. "What do you think?"

❧ CHAPTER 36 ❧

Ten minutes to curtain, and the theater vibrated with the nervous energy of cast and crew. Mr. Quinn's assistant, Alexander Hatcher, had fallen ill, and India had had to press one of the minor players into service to help Mr. Quinn move the scenery and take charge of the limelight. The actor playing the part of Dromio of Ephesus was late, and the girl playing the spherical Nell was crying quietly into her handkerchief, apparently devastated by the way her costume accentuated her shape. Fabienne was standing with an arm around the unhappy player, murmuring soothing words in her own unique mix of English and French. Victoria Bryson had arrived at the theater two hours early, in costume, and had spent the time pacing the hallway, muttering her lines to herself.

Miss Sawyer, the seamstress, was acting as prompter this evening. She stood at the ready, her spectacles perched on the end of her nose, an open script in her hands.

Riley Quinn found India in the wings. "Everything's ready, Miss Hartley. Lime's heating up real good, the mirrors are all in place, and the first flat is safe and secure, center stage, just like you wanted."

"Good."

"Me and Alexander did a fine job painting the Duke's palace. Not that I've ever been inside such a place, but I reckon it looks like the real thing. At least from a distance."

"Thank you, Mr. Quinn."

"No, ma'am. I figure it's us ought to be thanking you." He grinned. "I took a peek out front just now. The place is packed."

"Then perhaps we'll make some money tonight."

"I sure hope so," said a booming voice behind her.

She turned. "Mr. Shakleford. I wasn't expecting to see you until after the show."

"I wanted to wish you good luck, Miss Hartley. And to thank you for uncovering the embezzlement scheme. I should have kept closer watch on the books, but I was away most of the season, and I trusted Philbrick. Misplaced, as it turns out."

"I'm sure to make mistakes along the way, but I can promise you they will be honest ones."

"I have no doubt of that." Mr. Shakleford craned his neck to take a look at the stage where the players were assembling. "It looks to be a handsome production. Well done."

India felt her nerves unwinding, replaced by the old anticipation she always felt on opening night. "I hope you still feel that way after the final curtain."

He took off his spectacles and polished them on his sleeve. "I ought to find my seat. Don't want to miss anything."

He left and India quickly counted heads, making sure all of

the players were in their proper places for the opening scene: the duke, the merchant of Syracuse, the jailer, and the attendants.

A church bell down the street tolled the hour. The crowd settled. Murmured conversations, the rustling of silks, and the tread of boots gave way to hushed anticipation. India briefly closed her eyes and blew out a long breath. At her signal, the curtain rose, and the theater reverberated with the sound of applause.

"Proceed, Solinus, to procure my fall . . ." the first player began.

From her place in the wings, India whispered the opening lines to herself. The actor delivered them flawlessly, but India, too nervous to stand in one place through the play's five acts, made her way down the spiral stair and along the dimly lit corridor to her office. She turned up the gas lamp and sat behind her desk, feeling grateful and more than a little stunned at how her life had changed, how it had come full circle since that strange and awful night last December.

Yesterday she had been so busy with final rehearsals and last-minute details that there hadn't been time to ask Philip what had happened at his meeting with the prosecutor. Perhaps Mr. McLendon would give credence to her suspicions, or perhaps he would decide that Mr. Philbrick's punishment for the death of Arthur Sterling—however it had happened—added on to the embezzlement charge would be enough. She worried about what would happen to Victoria Bryson and hoped the girl would be shown mercy, but Philip was right. The entire situation was out of her hands.

A burst of applause and the rumble of scenery being moved

signaled the end of the first act, and then later, the theater exploded in laughter as the cases of mistaken identity and the outrageous dialog that formed the backbone of the story reached a fever pitch.

India relaxed at last. She had been right to choose *The Comedy of Errors*. After the events of the past months, everyone associated with the Southern Palace needed a reason to laugh.

Sometime later, Riley Quinn stuck his head into her office. "Final curtain in five minutes, miss. Everybody's askin' for you."

"Thank you, Mr. Quinn." India rose and followed him up the stairs to the wings.

The last lines were spoken, and the players exited the stage. A moment of silence ensued as the audience emerged from the world of fantasy and returned to the present. The applause and cheers were enthusiastic and prolonged, swelling anew as each of the players returned to the stage for a final bow.

When Victoria Bryson's turn came, she dropped a quick curtsy, then ran to the wings and grabbed India's hand.

"Come on!" Her eyes luminous with triumph, the girl tugged India onto the stage, then led another round of applause. Moving as one, the players took a step back, leaving India alone in the dazzling limelight.

She looked out at the packed house. Philip sat in the front row to the left of center, flanked by Mr. Shakleford and Mr. Kennedy. Philip blew her a kiss, and she briefly bowed her head, both hands clasped to her chest.

Across the aisle sat Celia Mackay with Frannie and an attractive man India realized must be Celia's husband, Sutton, returned from his travels at last. From their places in the wings,

Riley Quinn, Miss Sawyer, and Fabienne were clapping wildly, tears running down their faces.

India's eyes welled up as the applause washed over her, a wave of affection that filled her heart to bursting. Life was lived on an ever-turning wheel that sooner or later brought a person back to her truest self. She thought of everything she had lost and gained. Everything she had been through that had led her here.

Someone tossed a bouquet of jonquils onto the stage. She retrieved it and pressed the blossoms to her nose. She thought of her father, that dear, flawed man whose faith in her had never wavered. She could almost feel his presence on the stage beside her, his favorite line from *King Lear* a whisper in her ear.

The wheel is come full circle. I am here.

THE END

Author's Note

Dear Readers,

This novel, like all of my others, is inspired by the life of a real nineteenth-century woman. *A Respectable Actress* owes its beginnings to Frances "Fanny" Anne Kemble, one of the most famous and beloved actresses of her day and the inspiration for my fictional actress India Hartley.

Born into an English family of actors that included her aunt Sarah Siddons, Fanny made her London stage debut as Juliet at age nineteen and was an immediate sensation. She often acted with her father, Charles, a Shakespearean actor who managed the Covent Garden theater. As her fame grew and his popularity waned, she found herself the family's major breadwinner.

In 1832, after three dazzling seasons in London, Fanny traveled to America with her father, in part to help pay for her father's increasing debts. Accustomed to acclaim everywhere they went, the Kembles were surprised to find the American aristocracy suspicious of theater people. The majority of native-born actors and actresses were from the lower social classes. But Fanny's opening-night performance and many that followed enchanted the critics and soon made her a celebrity. University students cut classes to attend her matinee performances. Women copied her hairstyle, and garden clubs named flowers in her honor.

During a tour in Philadelphia, Fanny met Pierce Butler, scion of a wealthy Georgia plantation owner. Though he was engaged to another woman, Butler began courting Fanny. They married in June of 1834, and two years later Pierce Butler inherited the second largest slaveholding empire in Georgia.

Fanny was horrified. She began keeping a journal during her time at Butler's Island, which is part of St. Simons Island, where my fictional hero Philip Sinclair has his plantation, Indigo Point. Fanny's journal details her discomfort and unhappiness among the slaves, snakes, and plantation families of the island, but more importantly her journal is a commentary on slavery, race, and the rights of women. It was published in 1863 as *Journal of a Residence on a Georgian Plantation*, and it became a popular argument against slavery. Some historians have speculated that some of the details she supplied in her journal may have been exaggerated, though there is no doubt the slaves were subjected to inhumane treatment before Butler sold them in one of the largest auctions of human beings ever recorded. I used Fanny's journal in creating my character Laura Sinclair, whose distaste for plantation life at Indigo Point leads to dire consequences.

Fanny and Pierce Butler had two daughters, born on the same day three years apart. When the Butlers divorced in 1849, Sarah Butler sided with her mother and eventually married Owen Jones Wister, a wealthy physician. Their son, also named Owen Wister, was the celebrated author of *The Virginian*, widely acknowledged as the first cowboy novel. The Butlers' other daughter, named Frances but called "Fan," supported her father and after the war attempted to salvage his plantations on Butler's Island. It is this daughter who has an offstage role in *A Respectable Actress* as friend to my fictional Amelia Sinclair.

Indigo Point is entirely fictional, but it's modeled after King's Retreat, a large plantation on the southern tip of St. Simons Island. In the 1870s and 1880s, Anson Dodge and his business partner at King's Retreat operated a lumber mill that grew to be the third largest in the country. In creating Indigo Point, I relied upon the collected letters of Anna Matilda Page King, who inherited King's Retreat from her father and reared her ten children there, managing it during her husband's long absences.

Modern readers may wonder how India's murder trial could have lasted for only a few days. And they may wonder about India's escape to the Isle of Hope. Both of these events are taken from the pages of history. In creating India's trial, I read the handwritten records of murder trials of the mid-to late nineteenth century, many of which lasted only two to three days. One record describes the trial of a Missouri slave woman accused in the death of her master. Known only as "Molly," she was convicted in two days' time on the testimony of a handful of witnesses and swiftly sentenced to death by hanging. While she was in jail awaiting the results of her appeal, someone who was never identified spirited Molly out of the jail and hid her in a place of safety until her appeal was processed. Of course it was denied, and Molly was subsequently hanged.

The interested-party rule that Philip Sinclair mentions was indeed a rule that prevented the accused from testifying on their own behalf.

Readers of *The Bracelet* will recognize the main character

from that story, Celia Browning Mackay. I loved Celia so much I couldn't leave her behind, and since St. Simons Island is so close to Savannah, it was easy to bring her back into this story as India's champion and benefactor. I hope fans of Celia's story will enjoy catching up with her ten years after she set sail for Liverpool with her new husband.

The Southern Palace Theater and all other characters in the novel are fictional.

A Respectable Actress is a story of love and betrayal, of courage and hope, and a window into the world of the nineteenth-century theater and the history and beauty of St. Simons, one of the loveliest places I know. It is surely deserving of its nickname as a "golden isle."

San Antonio, March 2015

DISCUSSION QUESTIONS

1. How does the notion of "respectability" affect the way in which India sees herself? How does it color her perception of her relationship with Philip?

2. India's nomadic lifestyle causes her to long for a real home—a refuge no theater can provide. What is your definition of home?

3. India suffers the effects of being thought of as an outsider. Have you ever felt that way about yourself? How did it influence your choices?

4. What do you think acting means to India? How do her skills influence the outcome of the story?

5. Were you surprised by the outcome of India's trial? Why or why not?

6. What did you think of Philip's decision not to tell India about his past until he was forced to do so? How would his revelations have altered the story and their relationship?

7. If you have read *The Bracelet*, what did you enjoy most about this glimpse into Celia Mackay's life ten years later? Were you surprised that she took up India's cause?

8. What role do the two islands—St Simons and Isle of Hope—play in the story? What do they mean to Philip? To India? To Amelia?

9. Toward the end of the story, Philip tells India to let go of her worries about Mr. Philbrick and his crimes. What do you think will happen to Mr. Philbrick?

10. Imagine India's and Philip's lives ten years later. What are they doing? Where do they live? How have their triumphs and tragedies shaped their lives?

ACKNOWLEDGMENTS

BEGINNING WITH THE WONDERFUL PUBLISHING TEAM at Thomas Nelson who takes such great care of me and my work, thank you to my publisher, Daisy Hutton, and to my editors, Becky Philpott and Erin Healy. Your careful reading and insightful comments make my work better. Kristin Ingebretson, thank you for another stunning book cover. I appreciate your talent more than words can say. To my copy editors and marketing and sales teams and all who work behind the scenes to bring a book to completion, thank you so much.

Natasha Kern, thank you for your wisdom and kindness. Working with you is a joy.

I'm indebted to the authors of several books I consulted regularly as I worked on this novel including *Fanny Kemble's Civil Wars* by Catherine Clinton; *Anna, The Letters of a St. Simons Island Plantation Mistress* by Anna Matilda Page King (edited by Melanie Pavich-Lindsay); *Journal of a Residence on a Georgian Plantation in 1838–1839* by Frances Anne (Fanny) Kemble, and *Within the Plantation Household: Black and White Women of the Old South* by Elizabeth Fox-Genovese.

To family and friends near and far, your love and encouragement are a daily blessing to me, and I thank you all.

THE MYSTERY SURROUNDING CELIA'S
home in Savannah threatens her family
reputation . . . and her very life.

THE
BRACELET

A NOVEL

DOROTHY LOVE

DURING THE MOST TURBULENT DECADE OF OUR NATION'S history, four Southern women—their destinies forged by birth and heritage—face nearly impossible choices on their journeys in life . . . and in love.

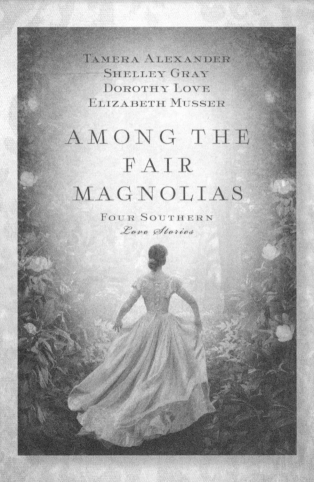

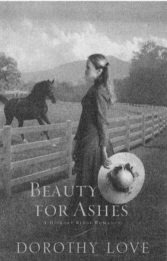

About the Author

A NATIVE OF WEST TENNESSEE, DOROTHY Love makes her home in the Texas hill country with her husband and their golden retriever. An award-winning author of numerous young adult novels, Dorothy made her adult debut with the Hickory Ridge novels.